I0602320

Parlatheas Press Titles:

<u>The Cayn Trilogy:</u>

Son of Cayn
City of Cayn
Blood of Cayn

<u>Chronicles of Damage Inc.:</u>

Phantoms of Ruthaer
Mask of the Vampire

Phantoms of Ruthaer

Chronicles of Damage, Inc.

Jason McDonald
Stormy McDonald

Parlatheas Press, LLC
Hollywood, SC

DEDICATION

To our third musketeer and great friend, Alan. Without the all-night gaming sessions of our youth and general world building discussions that followed, none of this would have been possible. Although time and space conspire to keep us apart geographically, you are always in our thoughts and prayers.

Jason and Stormy

"In addition to the seven Heavens and the infinite depths of
the Abyss, numerous worlds besides our own exist in the ebb
and flow of the Aether, moving and shifting in a dance as
complicated as that of the stars in the night sky. Only a rare
few are accessible at any given time, but once every
millennium all the worlds drift together. The ancient
Korellan scholars of Val Magus called this *the Convergence*.
Tread carefully during this time. If you dare open a portal to
these other realms, you will find both the extraordinary and
the terrifying await you. There are even some where magic
has faded to mere myth, and to tarry would leave you
stranded with no way home."

– Angus McHeath, Archmagus
from his lecture, *Introduction to Interplanar Travel*
Academia de Artes Magicae, Tydway
4231_{K.E.}

"Their will was resolute and remorseless, and as it proved,
unconquerable. It fell to me to express it."

– Winston Churchill

CHAPTER 1
ORLEANS

June 28, 4237 K.E.

4:30am

A longhaired, swarthy-skinned rider in russet leather pants and a stiff-collared jerkin emerged from the moist, swirling veil of fog that rolled along the empty cobblestoned street. Loose sleeves of creamy homespun cotton flowed from his shoulders and ended at tight cuffs. Slender hands with long tapering fingers like those of an artist — or a thief — loosely held the reins of a lean, buckskin-colored horse. The clip-clop of its iron-shod hooves echoed off multi-story buildings, each with their shutters drawn against the moonless night.

Hazy candlelight from street lanterns illuminated wooden signs indicating a bakery, a draper, and other merchants along the thoroughfare. The light glinted off the rider's platinum signet ring. Subconsciously, his thumb twisted the metal around his finger and pressed against the dagger-pierced globe inscribed on its surface. The tracking spell embedded within stirred to life, giving him a general direction of five matching rings. The strength of the magic's pull indicated distance, growing stronger by proximity. Only two were in Orleans — one across town, and the other in his belt pouch. The other three were scattered several weeks' ride to the northeast with the rest of his team.

Between one lamppost and the next, a shadow darted out of a narrow alley, barking and growling. Instead of bucking, the Akhal-teke lunged at the mongrel and bit it on the scruff of the neck. Squalling, the dog ducked its head and fled back into the alley, tail between its legs.

"*Caballo*, did you have to do that?" the rider asked his mount. Without missing a step, the horse bobbed its head up and down.

Silence settled over the night-bound shops, and the rider couldn't help but wonder at the uniformity, despite the different trades. Rectangular planters hung from wrought iron balcony rails, trailing the proper amount of white and green ivy to be pleasing to the eye. With a distinct lack of refuse on the street and its spotless facades, the neighborhood seemed prepped and ready for inspection.

Ahead, the diffused light of two lamps marked the corner entrance to the gaol. The three-story jail was strong and... the rider thought for a moment... forbidding. With its austere lines of red brick and grey mortar, evenly spaced arrow-loop windows, and leering grotesques along the eaves to channel rainwater, it practically screamed government, especially when compared to the surrounding buildings.

An elaborate plaque emblazoned with a gold-leaf fleur-de-lis, the emblem of King Edmond Bourbon d'Orlèans, hung beside the recessed ironwood door. Polished brass fittings gleamed in the lamplight. On the other side of the door, a second plaque, written in Francescan, read, "Ward #5, City of Orleans, Capital of the Province of Amienes and the Kingdom of Francesca."

Using only pressure from his knees, the rider directed his horse to the nearby hitching post and eased out of the saddle. Although he seemed relaxed, his gaze never stopped moving, scanning the shadows for danger. He adjusted his sword belt, making sure his weapons were within easy reach, before running his hands through his jet-black hair and tying it in a queue at his nape with a leather thong.

He draped the reins over the hitching post but didn't tie them. "Watch the door. If this doesn't go well, I'll need you to stop him."

Caballo shook his dark mane and snorted, giving his human a dubious look as he retreated, one hesitant step at a time, in preparation to bolt. The rider snatched the reins, forcing the horse to meet his glare.

"You. Watch that door. Don't let him escape."

Not waiting for an answer, the man let go of the reins and pounded on the door with his fist. A wicket panel behind a square, steel grate slid open and two suspicious eyes peered out. The rider turned his face to the light and recognition dawned in the gendarme's expression.

"Monsieur de los Santos, I'm glad you are here." The man spoke Glaxon with a heavy Francescan accent.

"Enfin, remerciez Dieu," someone inside muttered as the panel closed, followed by the scrape of a heavy bar being lifted from the other side. Light streamed out, and Hector waited for his eyes to adjust before entering.

The soldier holding the door wore chainmail under blue and white striped livery. Dark yellow fleurs-de-lis marched down each blue stripe, and gold chevrons adorned his collar. At his waist hung a broadsword with a fleur-de-lis emblazoned on the pommel. Behind him, a round oak table sat in the center of the guardroom, darkened by years of use, the remnants of an unfinished card game scattered over its surface.

Hector stepped across the threshold and paused. Two muscular gendarmes, also in blue and white livery but lacking any rank insignia, stood in the far-right corners, holding loaded crossbows. Between them, an iron-bound door concealed stairs leading up to the prison cells. Directly ahead, another door guarded the barracks, offices, storage rooms, and the kitchen.

Hand-sketched portraits covered the upper half of the left-hand wall, each with a name, crime, and bounty listed below. He noted several new posters had been added to the bottom row.

The younger of the two gendarmes glowered at the leather clad Espian strolling across the room like he was in the local tavern. His eyes narrowed at the sight of Hector's scimitar, its guard wrapped in a bright silken kerchief, suspended from a wide weapon belt adorned with various sized pouches. A bone-handled knife and a dagger with a leather-wrapped hilt hung opposite the hunter's sword, and he carried knives in the tops of his boots.

"Sergeant, shouldn't we take the bounty hunter's weapons?" the crossbowman asked in a low voice.

"Non ça va," the commander replied.

Studying the posters, Hector asked, "Sergeant D'Arnoit, how long has he been here?"

"King Edmond's personal guard brought him two days ago. He tried to break into Le Chateau d'Orleans in the middle of the night. When the guards refused to let him see the king, he started a fight." Stepping closer so as not to be overheard he said, "You should hear the things he says in his sleep. It frightens the other prisoners. Monsieur, we have our orders, but..." The sergeant's voice died under the bounty hunter's piercing gaze.

Hector took a deep breath. "Where is he?"

The sergeant jerked a thumb toward the prison door with its barred window. "In a cage."

Hector rubbed his jaw and nodded. All things considered, it was probably the best place for him, especially when he fell into one of his dark moods. "Good work, Sergeant. Let's get him out of here."

"Yes, sir." Sergeant D'Arnoit banged on the door leading to the prisoners and yelled, "Open up!"

A bearded guard appeared behind the grated wicket.

"Prisoner release," the sergeant said.

At the landing on the third floor, a different guard inserted a thick iron key into the ornate lock of another ironbound door. With a sharp click, the door swung wide, revealing a hallway and a series of barred cells on the left-hand side. On the right, narrow windows cut into the thick exterior wall let in the night air.

Even with the ventilation, the place smelled damp with a miasma of vomit and urine. A motley crew of humans, elves, and a pair of small, gangly gnomes occupied the first few cells. At this hour, most of them were sleeping off their drunken overindulgences on wood benches or the cold stone floor. The few still awake perked up, their curiosity assailing Hector as he stepped inside.

The sergeant made to escort him, but the hunter put a hand on his arm.

"It's best if I do this alone."

Relief flooded the sergeant's countenance before he caught himself. "Oui. Très bon. Let me know if you need anything."

"Just the key, señor."

The guard at the door unhooked a ring of skeleton keys from his belt and sorted through until he found the correct one. He handed it to Hector and said, "It's the last cell."

Hector started down the hall, then turned back. "Is he armed?"

The sergeant nodded. "Only his bow. The rest of his personal effects are locked up downstairs."

"Then I'll need to borrow a truncheon, too."

"Prends le mien, monsieur," the sergeant said, sliding out a short, thick club.

Truncheon in hand, Hector strode toward the cage at the far end of the hall, glancing through each barred door as he passed. He recognized a few of the petty thieves, but most of the prisoners were strangers.

The acrid smell of alcohol-laden vomit grew stronger the closer he got to the end. Hector stopped at the last cell. The man he'd come to retrieve — one of the few people on any of Gaia's four continents he considered a friend — lay curled up on the straw-covered floor with his cheek resting against the yew limb of a hand-carved longbow. He wore stained leather pants and boots, but his tattooed torso and arms were bare. Elven tribal markings and a Gaelic knot-work dragon hid savage scars on his neck, shoulders, and upper arms from the casual observer, but not from Hector. Dark, unruly hair hung in greasy clumps and obscured the sleeping man's face. A seal-grey cloak lay huddled in the corner.

"Dave," Hector whispered. Other than the gentle rise and fall of his chest, the body on the floor neither moved nor made a sound.

"Dave," he repeated, louder.

Not getting a response, Hector looked around. The last thing he wanted to do was make a scene. Hefting the ring of keys, he unlocked the cell. Dave still didn't move. Leaving the key in the door, Hector opened it wide. His eyes never left the figure on the floor as he entered in a half-crouch, the truncheon gripped tight.

The stench was overpowering, and Hector fought the bile rising in his throat. Just as he put the back of his hand up to cover his mouth, Dave struck him with his bow, slapping it against Hector's side.

"Dave!"

Hector spun when Dave rolled to his knees and lashed out again. The tip of the yew limb hit nothing but air. Continuing his spin until he was behind his off-balance friend, Hector used both hands to press the truncheon hard against Dave's throat just above his windpipe.

"It's me," Hector hissed.

Dave emitted an animalistic snarl as he struggled, his torpid senses fighting to understand what was happening. Hector pressed harder. A guard appeared at the door, ready to slam and lock it should things go wrong for the Espian.

"Dave! It's Hector."

Red-rimmed eyes peered around the dim cell. "Where are we?"

"King Edmond's gendarmes locked you up. They caught you breaking into the palace." Hector relaxed and Dave stood, his tall, lanky form towering over the Espian.

Still glassy-eyed, Dave turned around, rubbing his neck. A fading red line marked where the truncheon had rested. "What was I doing there?"

Hector tucked the truncheon in his belt and shrugged. "You tell me. Be glad King Edmond likes you."

"I need a drink."

"You need a bath."

The tall man scowled. The effect was ruined when he lost his balance and gripped Hector's shoulder to steady himself.

"Still having nightmares?"

Dave gave a curt nod. "Ymara..." His mouth compressed into a thin line before he grumbled, "That vampire's still inside my head. She's trying to make me do things." His hand fumbled at his belt, and he cursed when he realized the short square holster was empty.

"Dave, she's dead. I killed her."

The tall man let out a doubtful grunt and asked, "What about the sorceress? Any leads? "

Hector's expression darkened, and he shook his head. "The trail's gone cold. All I found were old rumors. Just things Consuelo and her demon, Magali, did before the fiasco in Santander. Qué espectáculo de mierda. No one's seen or heard from them since they escaped."

Glaring at Hector, Dave made a sign against evil. "Bad luck to speak a demon's name. It's just a matter of time before they ambush us."

Hector nodded in agreement. "We'll be ready." Changing the subject, he said, "We have another job."

"This one isn't done yet."

"That's why I turned it down, at first — that, and it's charity work." The shocked expression on Dave's face was almost comical.

"You only have two rules about bounties. Who the hell convinced you to break them both in one go?"

"Aislinn."

Dave swallowed hard at the mention of her name. His eyes darted around, searching the shadows.

"Relax. I left Aislinn and Hummingbird at Bayeux Cathedral."

"So, what's this job she's bent on taking?" Dave asked.

Hector shook his head. "Aislinn's the client. Brand sent her a message from an old Sea Ranger friend of hers named Tallinn. Apparently, a few people have disappeared from a village on the Carolingian coast, possibly murdered. Some place called Ruthaer. She's hiring us herself."

Dave stooped to collect his cloak. When he straightened, furrows had formed on his forehead. "Ruthaer? Are you sure?"

"Why?"

"You don't remember, do you?" When Hector shrugged, he said, "It's where Aislinn's family lived when she was a little girl. Where her father died." Dave's scowl deepened. "Is that dragon here?"

"No." Hector raised a hand to his scalp, as if scratching an itch, and surreptitiously tapped his temple to indicate Aislinn's conversation with Brand was mental rather than verbal. As far as the bounty hunter knew, her connection with the bronze dragon was unique. "Brand'll be holed up in that cave of his in Ozera for the next month or two. Oonveytik Ssifruen," he added as explanation.

"Already?" Dave asked. "Hell, he's over fifty feet long as it is."

"All I know is Aislinn says he's sleeping through his growing pains. We're supposed to catch up with him in Ozera after we finish this job in Ruthaer." Hector paused, his lips pursed, as he replayed the conversation with Aislinn in his head. "It was weird, though. She seemed... distracted. Like there was more to it, but I didn't push."

The archer rolled his head to the back and side, resulting in a series of pops from his vertebrae. "Fan-fucking-tastic," he grumbled. "I keep telling you she's trouble. We should have left her in that mine."

Hector had known Dave for the better part of a decade, and the only person the surly bowman ever admitted to liking in any way, shape, or form was his cousin, Robert. The three of them, along with the Glaxon mage, Jasper Thredd, had met and freed Aislinn from an unsanctioned slave mine while working one of Hector's earliest bounty jobs for the seaport of Rowanoake. However, that was a long time ago, before the city council decided to put a price on their heads, even though they had returned the councilman's son alive — mostly. Five years later, they still felt safer outside the country of Gallowen, and far away from the coastal city of Rowanoake.

Hector grinned at Dave. "You like her, and we both know it. Besides, we need Aislinn, and not just for her tracking skills."

Dave glared at Hector, the look on his face clearly questioning the Espian's sanity. "You think she's hiding something about the dragon or the job?"

"Could be either, but it doesn't really matter."

Dave sniffed the air and groused, "You smell that? It's the shit we're about to step into."

"Cheer up! Damage, Inc. rides again," Hector said, slapping Dave on the back. "That reminds me. You forgot this." He reached into one of the small pouches on his belt and held out a platinum signet ring inscribed with a dagger-pierced globe.

Dave took the ring with an exasperated huff and held it in the flat of his palm for several long seconds.

"We talked about this, Dave. Our old hematite rings wouldn't hold Jasper's tracking spell more than a few days. If you'd had this on, it wouldn't have taken me all night to find you." Hector stared at the archer until he slipped the ring onto his right hand.

The guard at the cell door stepped aside, one hand tight on his weapon, giving the two a clear path out of the prison.

"You know no one in this world understands what Damage, Inc. means," Dave said. "Hell, they don't even have corporations here."

With a mischievous glint in his eye, Hector said, "I know. That's half the fun."

Back in the guardroom, the card game had been cleared from the table, replaced by Dave's weapons and personal effects. Turning to the sergeant, Hector returned the club and asked, "Is there any paperwork I need to fill out?"

"Non, monsieur," he replied. "He is free to go."

Once outside, Dave stretched his long limbs but stopped short.

"Hector?"

"¿Sí?" the bounty hunter replied as he mounted Caballo.

"There's only one horse here."

"I know. You get to walk and sober up."

"Fucker." Dave pulled a silver flask from his belt and unscrewed the cap.

Caballo turned and ambled back the way they had come.

"What was that?" Hector asked over his shoulder, one eyebrow raised in a subtle dare.

"Nothing," Dave muttered as he stomped after the bounty hunter.

CHAPTER 2
SHELTER ME

August 1, 4237 K.E.

5:12pm

Frothy water splashed over the bow of the single-masted skiff, threatening to capsize it. Riding the turbulent waves, Dave gripped the tiller with both hands as he fought to maintain their distance from the tall, grey cliffs marking the barrier islands. Seawater pooled around his bare feet.

Over his shoulder to the east, a roiling bank of greenish-black clouds loomed ever closer. *'Run, damn it! Run,'* he silently urged the small craft. The unnatural storm had appeared on the horizon less than half an hour ago and raced toward shore as if steered by some unseen hand. The waves grew taller by the second, driving their tiny vessel toward the unforgiving rocks.

In the bow, Aislinn stared northward, searching the waters ahead. Her long, autumn-gold hair swirled around her like campfire flames and briefly exposed her pointed ears. She'd been acting odd since they left Orleans. Aislinn's moods were volatile at the best of times, but not once in the time they'd known her had she ever been frigging *giddy*. Yet, for the three and a half weeks they spent crossing Francesca and Peninsular Espia, she'd been running the gamut from overly cheerful to downright morose.

When they'd reached the border town of Santa Casilda in Malaga, Aislinn insisted on leaving their horses and sailing up the coast because it would be faster. Hector had argued with her — he was loathe to leave Caballo with an unknown stableman — but Aislinn won, of course. Luck was on her side. They acquired a smuggler's skiff and found a shop with current navigation charts. Now, here they were five days later, about to die in a damned storm.

"We're not going to make it to Ruthaer!" Dave shouted over the wind.

Aislinn turned, but her hair obscured her face. "The lighthouse can't be too much farther."

A wave broke against the starboard side of the craft, spraying all those inside. "The sea's pushing us too hard," said Dave. "Find us a safe harbor or we're going to smash against those rocks!"

The wind stole Aislinn's response.

"What?!"

"I said, there's a cave!" she called out between cupped hands. "Not far. I just need to find the right inlet."

"How are we supposed to get into a cave in this rough water?" Hector demanded.

Buffeting wind tore away most of her response, leaving Dave with only the words "traversable" and "shelter."

A powerful gust plowed into the mainsail and the line securing it snapped. The boom shifted, and wind filled the canvas. Creaking under the strain, the mast held, but the boat listed precariously.

"Grab that line!" Dave yelled.

Already in motion, a small, spikey-haired waif of an elf with red whorls and white dots on her forehead and cheeks snatched the frayed mainsheet trailing from the boom. Hector grabbed the coil of braided rope attached to the mooring ring with one hand and reached toward the girl with the other.

"Hummingbird, give me your end!"

She stretched toward him. Her drenched sleeve rode up, exposing a black lotus tattooed on the back of her left wrist. The boom swung back as the wind shifted, knocking her into Hector. They both crashed to the deck.

Holding onto the boom with both arms, Hector wrestled it steady while Hummingbird reran the line through the clew and joined the snapped ends with a Carrick bend, her thin arms and deft fingers working quickly.

As soon as Hummingbird finished, Dave grabbed the mainsheet and gave it a sharp tug. The boom angled out and the boat straightened. Dave yelled more instructions over the din of the storm, adjusting the mainsail to gain more speed out of the small craft.

With a lurch, everything seemed to slow; the boat rose and topped the crest of a wave. There was a moment of perfect stillness before they plummeted into the trough.

Neon purple lightning clawed its way over the churning sea. The storm swallowed the sun, shrouding them in dusky gloom, and rain the size of a person's thumbnail pelted the deck.

"¡Madre de Dios! Storms are not supposed to look like this," Hector shouted, his Espian accent growing thicker. "Where's this shelter of yours, Aislinn?"

Aislinn leaned out over the bow like a figurehead, peering through the rain and gloom at the line of cliffs. Rain-soaked hair clung to her angular features in matted clumps and partially masked her furrowed brow. She didn't respond to Hector. Instead, her almond-shaped eyes narrowed as she studied the inlets and channels between the rising walls of the barrier islands.

Dave watched Aislinn, waiting for her signal, but thinking about the past month. One night, he'd woken and caught her sitting by their campfire when she was supposed to be on watch, staring at him with the same intensity she wore now. The only thing he could figure was something was wrong. If she didn't tell them what it was by the time they reached Ozera, he'd get that dragon-brother of hers to talk, one way or another. Dave risked a glance back at the towering thunderheads bearing down on them — *if* they made it to Ozera.

The beacon from a distant lighthouse atop the cliffs cut through the swirls of rain. The roiling waves worsened, and the light vanished.

"Aislinn!" Hector yelled. "Was that your lighthouse?"

She started as Hector's voice broke through whatever thoughts occupied her mind. Pointing toward a small gap within the cliffs, she shouted, "There!"

Dave looked where she indicated. "You're crazy!"

"You shoot smaller targets all the time!"

"Yeah, with arrows, not a *fucking boat*!"

"Just do it!"

Dave heaved on the tiller, urging the craft closer to the cliffs. Under his feet, he felt the small boat shiver with fear.

"Drop the mainsail! Grab the oars!"

Hector unstrapped the oars from the portside ribs while Hummingbird loosened lines and furled the mainsail. With only the jib to propel it, the boat slowed, and a wave crashed broadside of the hull. The boat heeled over, and the gunwale kissed the water.

"Who's steering this thing?" Hector asked through clenched teeth.

"You want to do it?" Dave shouted. His eyes focused on the narrow gap as he gauged distances. He looped the line controlling the jib around his wrist and pulled. The boat instantly responded, righting itself.

"No," Hector said, the oar in his hand, ready. Opposite him, Hummingbird sat with hers, waiting for Dave to give the word.

"What do you want me to do?" Aislinn asked, facing him.

"Keep pointing!"

Dave leaned into the tiller as another wave caught the boat's stern, tossing it forward.

Towering cliffs loomed closer by the second. Waves smashed against jagged rocks jutting up from the sea like hideous fangs, sending up geysers of white spray and foam.

Blood drained from Hector's face, leaving it a sickly olivine color. "That's a death trap!"

Dave silently agreed. However, going back out to deeper waters or even trying for the elusive lighthouse was not an option. The storm surge had them in its grasp and propelled them toward the rocks.

Aislinn didn't need to point anymore. Everyone could see the craggy fissure in the salt-rimed cliff. She hunkered down and prayed.

Spear-points of lightning plunged into the waves around them. A hissing acthnici shimmered into existence atop the mast, growing and spreading its eerie phosphorescent glow over the entire vessel.

Hector rapidly crossed himself, and his lips moved in a silent prayer. Dave wished he had a hand free to make a sign against evil. Hummingbird turned huge, fear-filled eyes toward the archer as the azure light spread down the rigging and over the deck, but he had neither the words nor the time to reassure her.

A plunging breaker buffeted the boat, causing it to list heavily. Dave braced himself against the hull and adjusted the jib. Wind filled the sail once more. The skiff knifed through the crest of a colossal swell into open air before landing in the trough beyond with a bone-jarring splash.

"Put your oars in the water!" he shouted. "Try to slow us down!"

The rocky fissure became a narrow channel.

"Hummingbird! When I tell you, lift your oar! Everyone else hold on!"

Wiry muscles bulged as Dave wrestled the sea for control of the tiller and kept the bow aimed at his target. As they slowed, the raging sea seized the skiff as if it were nothing more than errant flotsam. The wave behind them peaked and began to curl, forming a lip overhead. With a grimace, he adjusted their course. The bow came out of the water, level with the aft rail. Surfing just above the trough, Dave began to count to himself. The concave wall of whitecapped water grew larger and larger, threatening to collapse at any moment.

"NOW!" he shouted and released the jib sheet. The thin sail billowed out, the cloth brushing the top of Aislinn's head. The sudden loss of resistance on one side spun the boat about its keel.

The boat shot into the crevice aft first, a split second before the mammoth wave crashed against the cliff, filling the boat halfway to the gunwales. Hummingbird and Hector shoved their oars against the rapidly approaching wall. Between the two of them, the boat slowed enough not to smash itself to kindling.

The sky above became a thin strip of grey, and silvery curtains of rain fell across their path, lending the channel a dream-like quality. The skiff sloshed through choppy waters that were only a dim reflection of the raging storm outside. Another large wave crashed against the mouth of the crevice, spraying them.

Her eyes wide, Aislinn shoved her drenched hair back so she could see. She looked out toward the mountainous swells and then back at Dave. His disheveled face lit with a rare smile, only partially hidden by his saturated beard and mustache.

Together, Hector and Hummingbird dipped their oars into the water and rowed them farther from the towering sea, while Dave started bailing. Slick granite walls speckled with feldspar and smoky quartz glided by as if they were travelling through a tunnel.

Aislinn unhooked and furled the jib before starting her way aft. Something jarred the hull, and she grabbed the mast to steady herself. Hector stuck his oar into the water and hit solid rock.

"I thought you said this was atravesable?" Hector asked, staring into the murky waters.

"It is passable — at high tide."

"That's comforting." He offered her a hand. "Step back by Dave. Let's see if shifting our weight helps."

Standing on either side of the mast, Hector and Hummingbird waited on a swell to roll into the passage. The moment the bow lifted, they used their oars to push the boat off the rock pinnacle. It scraped the bottom, bowing the hull in the process.

Dave grimaced, thinking about the time and cost of repairs. Beside him, Aislinn tensed, holding her breath. With a final shove from the oars, the boat grated free.

"How far is this cave?" Dave asked as he dumped another bucketful of seawater over the side.

A fierce gust of wind scoured the rock walls, peppering the boat with sand and debris. Outside the crevice, the storm's intensity grew.

"There's the entrance," Aislinn replied, pointing at a bend in the channel and the dark edge of a water-filled tunnel on the right-hand side.

CRSO

6:36pm

"This sucks," Dave muttered. He stood on a submerged ledge, one shoulder propped against the tunnel wall a few feet inside the cave mouth. Howling wind drove sheets of rain over the water, obscuring the sheer rock forming the other side of the channel less than a dozen yards away. Nobody was leaving this cave until the storm vented its fury. To make matters worse, swells rolled past at mid-calf and broke against the far wall. The water had only been ankle deep twenty minutes earlier, when he trekked out to check on the storm.

He turned and retraced his steps along the slimy ledge. Round and smooth, the sewer-like tunnel made a sharp turn and sloped up into a broad cavern with a damp sandy beach. A knot of concern formed in his stomach when he realized water stains marked the walls within inches of the ceiling.

Dave took a pull from his metal flask and watched his companions. Aislinn and Hummingbird huddled over a tiny fire at the far end of the beach, trying to get dry. Hector crouched in the boat, digging through the food locker. The unstepped mast lay along the midline of the craft, above furled sails and coiled rigging. Dave frowned. Wet lines were going to be a bitch to re-rig.

Condensation fell from the cave ceiling in fat drops, and one splattered on Dave's shoulder. He hurried onto the sandy shore, following the water's edge. Blue-legged crabs with green bodies scuttled through the shallows, chasing small fish. The reek of briny air mixed with rotting seaweed rankled his nose. He kept his mouth closed tight, taking only shallow breaths. It wouldn't be long before the stench saturated everything they owned.

Twisted shadows slithered away from the fire, over the sand and stone. A shiver coursed down Dave's spine, and he made a sign against evil. In response, thunder exploded in the tunnel mouth. He dropped to a knee, hands over his ears as a shower of condensation mixed with grit rained down upon him.

When the rumbling finally subsided, Hector climbed out of the boat and dragged it higher on shore. Another loud crash shook the rocky island above their heads and the foursome cast doubtful glances at one another. Small waves lapped onto the cave floor, eating away a few more inches.

"Did you find anything?" Hector shouted as Dave prowled past. Dave shook his head. They had wasted the better part of the last hour searching for a way to get above the high tide mark on the wall. Aislinn's supposed shelter — this cave — really was a death trap.

⊂ℛℰ⊃

6:41pm

Aislinn felt Hummingbird's attention but kept her gaze on the orange and yellow flame, noticing how it smoked and sizzled when a drop of water from above fell into it. The smoke drifted away, as insubstantial as a memory of happier times long past.

In her peripheral vision, she saw Hummingbird sign, "What's wrong?"

The plains elf was mute, but whether from trauma or by choice, Aislinn didn't know. She was uncomfortably aware of how easy it was for the girl to read her emotions. Hummingbird's people were empaths by nature, but there were times when her abilities bordered on the preternatural. Aislinn shook her head in an attempt to forestall the inevitable. Deep inside she knew what she had to do, but it felt like a betrayal of both her father's memory and Brand's trust.

Dave and Hector came to a stop on the opposite side of the fire. The archer glanced up at the water stains near the ceiling before turning an accusatory glare on Aislinn. "Why did you bring us here?" he demanded.

Fear-fueled anger ignited in Aislinn's heart. She surged up from her crouch. A short step and she stood close enough to Dave to jab a finger against his chest. "You said you couldn't make it to the lighthouse, so here we are!"

"We never would have made it!" Dave bellowed. "We're just lucky to be alive right now. If I hadn't caught that wave just right and steered us through that butt crack *inlet*, we'd all be dead!"

"I had faith you would hit your target," she replied through clenched teeth.

Hector pushed his way between Aislinn and Dave. "Look you two, fighting's not going to stop the water rising! What are our options?"

Aislinn swore under her breath. She knew what she had to do, but, dammit, she really wished there was another way. Finally, she said, "I know a place we can go to get above the water."

Another roll of thunder shook the cavern. Dave stared at the skiff and back out at the cave exit, calculating their chances of surviving the storm. He took a long pull from his flask.

"We have to swim!" Aislinn said.

"You're crazy!" Dave yelled over the din.

Aislinn shook her head and pointed at the dark water climbing ominously toward them. "There's a submerged tunnel that passes under this beach. We have to swim through it to another cave behind this one."

Hector, Dave, and Hummingbird cast doubt-filled glances at the rippling water. "Are you sure?" Hector asked.

"Of course I'm sure!"

"Fine! Take only what you can carry!" Hector yelled, unstrapping his sword belt. "Put everything else in the boat and let it float!"

Dave's face went pale.

"You have to leave your bow!" Hector shouted. "The seawater will ruin it, if it hasn't already!"

Dave crossed his arms and remained rooted in place.

"Dave! Look at the high-water mark. How much higher will it be with the storm surge?" Hector gestured with his hand and yelled, "This entire cavern will be flooded in an hour, two at the most!"

Grumbling, Dave followed Hector to the skiff where he unbuckled his sword belt and opened the boat's aft storage locker. Dave checked his gear, shifting things to suit an organization only he understood before turning his attention to the oilcloth wrapped around his most prized possessions. With all the care of a mother tending a newborn babe, he rewrapped the bow and arrows, laid them inside, and closed the lid tight. Made to look like part of the skiff, the locker and lid disappeared seamlessly into the bulkhead when he locked it.

Returning to the beach, Hector pulled the cap off a small bone tube, releasing a narrow beam of white light that flared and refracted off the dripping water. He pocketed the cap and handed the flameless torch to Aislinn. "You'll need this, amiga."

She took it and trudged into the shallows. From the corner of her eye, she saw Hector and Dave exchange a worried look.

Aislinn waited for the two men to join her in the waist deep water. Hummingbird waited with her, trying and failing to keep her fear from showing. "Deep breaths," Aislinn instructed. "We're going straight down and under this beach. It's not a short swim, but you can make it. I know where I'm going. All you have to do is follow the light."

After receiving nods from everyone, Aislinn dove into the murky water. Below, an enormous cavern spread in every direction. She led them down through scintillating clouds of silvery fish into a broad, dark tunnel. The four swam abreast without touching, and the smooth, glassy sides slid past, reflecting their passage.

Aislinn counted the seconds as they swam. Although she told Hummingbird they could make the swim, she worried. None of her friends had the advantage of a soul-bond with a dragon for the past twenty-five years, or of having been trained by one of the Iron Tower's legendary rangers, Edge Garrett. At ninety seconds, she caught Hummingbird's hand and swam harder. The tunnel angled upward and the four broke the surface as Aislinn's count reached one hundred eighteen seconds. She treaded water while her companions gasped for air. When their breathing quieted, she tucked away Hector's light and let the darkness envelope them. Sounds of the storm outside were nothing more than a dull rumble.

"What are you doing?" Dave griped. "We need that light."

"Shush," she whispered. "Wait for it." The darkness gradually faded, replaced by a soft green glow from bioluminescent fungi on the cavern walls and ceiling. Water lapped against a broad stone ledge littered with boulders and debris of varying sizes and shapes. Compared to the late summer heat outside, the cavern air was frigid.

Dave and Hector led the way ashore. Aislinn knew the exact moment when the pair recognized what occupied the stone floor. The two heaved themselves onto the ledge and, at the sight of it, froze on their hands and knees, as if they might lunge back into the relative safety of the water.

Aislinn laid a hand on each of their shoulders in passing, seawater running down her face like tears. The gigantic skeletal remains of an adult dragon covered more than half the floor. Dried bits of flesh hung off the bones and bronze scutes lay scattered about. An idle air current caressed the fragile tatters of skin clinging to the verdigris shaft of a harpoon trapped in a shattered rib. Its barbed tip hung where the dragon's heart once beat. Even in death, the dark hollows of the dragon's skull watched them above teeth that gleamed in a leering grin.

"Hänen nimensä oli Aleuria," Aislinn said, slipping into Elven. Her voice echoed softly. "I was twenty-four, almost twenty-five, summers when my father met her." She glanced at Hector's and Dave's confused expressions. Aislinn could almost hear their mental gears grinding as they tried to figure out the age equivalent to a human child. "About eight summers old, in human terms," she explained. "One night, when they thought I was sleeping, I overheard Isä and Emä — that's what I called my parents. Isä said he met a dragon while he was fishing. Aleuria had asked him to keep her egg — Brand's egg — safe."

Aislinn turned away from the bones and crossed to a ring of knee-high stones. She climbed inside and knelt in a bed of dark sand amid seashells and pieces of cream-colored eggshell striated with veins of dark bronze. She ran a finger along one of the metallic lines, remembering how they shimmered twenty-five years ago, almost as bright as new copper, exactly the color of Brand's scales the day he hatched.

"Isä was careful about what he said and did, so it was weeks before I found my way here. I was determined to meet a dragon and help protect her egg, but I was too late. Aleuria was already dead." She looked up at Hector and Dave, allowing them a glimpse of her sadness. Neither moved nor spoke, but it didn't matter. Their mere presence was comforting. "There used to be a narrow passage from the island-top, so I didn't have to make the swim back then. After I found it, I came back here every day. I couldn't help myself." She gave them a rueful smile. "Isä eventually caught me, of course.

"I'd been visiting the egg for months. One day, three or four months before it hatched, I don't know why, but I curled up beside it and fell asleep. Somehow, something in Brand and me connected. When Isä woke me, I could feel Brand, here," she said, placing a hand over her heart. "He's been my brother ever since."

"Who attacked the mother dragon?" Hector asked.

Aislinn looked up at the harpoon. "We never found out. Pirates? Dragon hunters? Maybe someone who was just scared of Aleuria."

Hector left her side and studied the skeleton closely. "I don't know much about dragons, but isn't it strange this one sought out your father?"

Taking a deep breath, Aislinn said, "It was random chance."

"I don't think so," Hector said, more to himself. "It's too odd a choice."

Aislinn climbed out of the nest and followed him. "What makes you say that?"

Not seeing Aislinn's hurt expression, Hector replied, "Well, look how it turned out. Brand hatched and you two share an amazing bond. Aleuria needed someone who could raise her child. She didn't choose another dragon; she chose your father. Of course, her injury may have limited her search. But still..."

"What was so special about Isä?"

Hector faced her with a smile in his eyes. "You."

Aislinn blushed as she returned his smile.

"Or at least your bloodline," Dave said, shattering the moment. They both turned to him. "We've travelled all over the world and never seen another pair like you and Brand. I wouldn't be surprised if Brand's mother somehow knew you were the one."

Aislinn blinked in surprise at the lanky archer's insight, and a wave of sadness washed over her heart. "It doesn't really matter, I suppose. It's all history now," she said with a tone of finality in her voice. "Let's set up camp in the nest. It'll be better than sleeping on cold rock."

CB80

6:53pm

Hummingbird stood at the water's edge; her eyes fixed on the sprawling skeleton. Though cloaked under layers of dust, sea, and salt, the scent of death assailed her. Sighs and moans emanated from a jumble of rocks and sand beyond the dragon's skull. Near the floor, the corner of a roughhewn stair tread jutted out. For a moment, she expected ghosts to appear, but then she realized the sounds were errant draughts that slithered through cracks and gaps in the cave-in, coming in time with distant rumbles of thunder.

The storm, and now the prospect of spending the night in a tomb, seemed the worst kind of omens. She wished she was a shaman like her grandmother and could understand the portents.

The ancient elf's smiling face appeared in Hummingbird's memory, sunlight shimmering on her snowy braids and laughter in her deep turquoise-colored eyes. A pair of telgid, portable homes built with woven grass mats, framed a view of the sun setting over the rolling plains around their summer campsite. Sadness seeped into the memory, and Hummingbird snapped back to the present. For a moment, she allowed her pain and loss to mingle with the cavern's lingering aura, then slowly pushed it away. As far as Hummingbird knew, she was the last of her tribe, and no amount of tears or self-pity could change that fact. When she once again had her emotions locked down tight, she squared her thin shoulders and joined her companions.

CHAPTER 3
OYSTER RAKES

August 2, 4237 K.E.

5:46am

*D*espite the four of them having lain huddled together to sleep, Hector woke stiff and achy from the chill cavern air. A faint *plop-plop-plop* sound echoed from the cavern ceiling. His brow furrowed as he tried to identify what he heard. Stone scraped on stone, and a flicker of movement preceded a repetition of the plopping noise. A lean shadow outside the ring of nest stones resolved itself into Dave, his back to his companions, zipping pebbles across the still water's surface.

Hector eased away from Aislinn and stretched, uncomfortably aware of sand in his hair and clothes as he climbed to his feet and joined the archer. "¿Qué pasa, amigo?"

Dave shrugged and took a long drink from his flask. He cast another flat stone across the water before offering his friend a drink.

Hector waved away the flask. "No, thanks. It's a long swim out of here."

The archer's shoulder twitched. "Warms the blood."

"That's what fire is for." Hector tilted his head, listening. "Sounds quiet. I'm going to wake the girls."

In a matter of minutes, he had collected a few rocks into a pyramid and doused them liberally with lamp oil. Returning the -small copper vial to one of his many belt pouches, he produced flint and steel.

"Do you have any breakfast in there?" Aislinn asked as Hector lit the oil-soaked rocks.

"I wish. Everything's in the boat."

"Not everything," Dave said. He crossed the shallow beach to stand by the fire before taking a swig from his flask. The harsh, burning scent of grain alcohol mingled with the salt air.

"You're starting early," Aislinn said.

Dave gave her a quizzical look. "Starting? I never finished."

After they warmed themselves and worked out the worst of the aches, they swam back through the underwater passage to the outer cave. Compared to the rage and fury of yesterday's storm, the world seemed eerily silent. Pale light slid over glassy water from the entrance tunnel to the sandy beach.

Their boat straddled the waterline, its anchor buried in the sand. Once Dave was satisfied it remained seaworthy, albeit battered and scraped, he turned his attention to the aft locker and its contents. Following suit, Hector and the girls unpacked the other lockers and checked their gear.

Aislinn watched Hummingbird dip seawater from their food locker and sighed.

"Sorry, amiga," Hector said, "looks like we're going without breakfast today."

"At least our spare clothes are dry," Aislinn replied. "We can pick up breakfast in Ruthaer."

Dave and Hector shot each other a glance.

"What about the Sea Ranger who sent you the message? Shouldn't we go see what he wants?" Hector asked.

"No, I want to find out who's in charge and get a feel for the situation. The last thing we want is to upset the local authorities," Aislinn said, giving Dave a pointed look.

Dave opened his mouth to protest but Hector cut in front of him. "Ruthaer?" he asked Aislinn. "That's where you grew up, right?"

"Yeah, before my mother and I moved to Ozera. The lighthouse we saw yesterday is at the mouth of the Emmassa River. Ruthaer lies upriver, roughly two miles inland as the dragon flies, above the brackish line. It's a little over an hour's walk from here, if we don't dally."

Dave and Hector both looked at the boat. "Walk?" Hector asked.

Aislinn gauged the water level with a practiced eye. "It's nearly low tide. We can cross the marsh from here to the mainland on foot. It shouldn't be any trouble, if we stick to the game trails and creek beds. Besides, I think we've had enough boating for a while."

"Wet boots will make for a miserable hike," Hector argued.

"They'll dry fast enough once we reach shore. Trust me, it's going to be hot today, just like yesterday," Aislinn retorted.

"Give up, Hector. You aren't going to win this one either," Dave said. After donning his boots, the archer untied the oilskin protecting his longbow. Bending the yew limbs, he looped the bowstring over the notches at each end. Next, he uncapped his quiver and checked each arrow — from the razor-sharp tip, acid-etched to resemble a hawk's head, to the custom fletching. Two-thirds of the shafts bore rounded red feathers and the rest carried pitch black vulture feathers ending in sharp points half a finger-width from the arrow's nock. Once satisfied they were dry, he repacked them and buckled on his sabre. Beside him, Hector rummaged through his gear, his scimitar strapped to his side and boots on his feet.

"You boys done yet?"

Hector gave Aislinn a sheepish grin. "Almost."

After Hector tucked his unselected gear back in the skiff, Dave locked everything down. Quiver belted on his hip opposite his sword, Dave hefted his longbow. He and Hector followed the girls to the cave entrance, where they found the outside world wrapped in a thick blanket of morning fog.

CƷ℘

7:07am

Aislinn led them single file along the channel's edge. Hummingbird kept her right hand on the cliff and her eyes fixed on the narrow ledge beneath her feet. Knee-high water sucked at their legs and tried to pull them out to sea. It seemed the water was warning them away from their chosen path.

The air echoed with peculiar clicking and popping, as if someone was throwing stones at the cliffs. However, her three companions gave no hint of concern over the sounds. Instead, it was the sudden appearance of a long, pale grey fish with coal-black eyes and a shovel nose that sent a jolt of fear through them. The creature glided past, riding the current in the center of the channel, its dorsal fin slicing the water's surface. Aislinn, Dave, and Hector pressed their backs to the granite cliff as they groped for their weapons.

"Welcome to Shark Hole Creek," Aislinn said through a fierce grin. Her eyes followed the swift predator. It turned around with a splash and headed back toward them.

Hector shot her a quick look. "You're enjoying this, aren't you?"

Panic coursed through Hummingbird. She'd never seen such a beast.

"Stand still," Dave murmured to the wide-eyed elf. "Sharks are attracted to splashing. One that size can bite half your leg off before it realizes you aren't a fish."

Hummingbird said a quick prayer to her ancestors, bottling her fear. The shark darted through the channel, not giving them a second glance. Only after it had moved off to open water did Aislinn motion them forward.

Heart still in her throat, Hummingbird borrowed a little courage from Dave and steadied her breathing before following.

At the end of the crevice, the ledge met a shallow, rock and shell covered streambed fringed by a wall of sharp-bladed grass. There was no picturesque beach, no sea oats or snow-white dunes like she saw along the Espian shores. Only grey mud and lots of it. To the north, the stair-stepped cliffs vanished into the dull grey mist, and Hummingbird wondered how far they stretched.

Aislinn led them south along the stream to a narrow break in the grass. She took this trail, and the ground sloped upward. At the top of the hill, she paused in the waist-high spartina grass and drew in a deep breath. "I've missed this smell."

"You're joking, right?" Hector asked.

Aislinn laughed. "Nope. Sometimes the marsh smells to high heaven, but, right now, it's all fresh and briny to me. Like sunshine and freedom."

"I don't know if you noticed, but it's foggy as hell right now," said Dave.

Aislinn stuck her tongue out at the archer, then her smile returned. "You three stick close. This place is a meandering maze of grass, creeks, and pluff mud. I'd hate to lose you."

Turning west, she crossed the hillock and descended into another creek. Hummingbird studied the glistening mud topped by spongey masses of brown roots and grass who's top six inches were several shades lighter than the rest of the stalk. She came to the sudden realization the entire saltmarsh flooded at high tide.

Her eyes grew wide again when she discovered the strange popping noise she kept hearing came from clusters of grey shells embedded in the brown-grey creek banks. Each time one snapped open, the sound echoed over the receding water, and a drop of spit shot into the air.

Hummingbird marveled at a long-legged bird with deep blue feathers and bright orange eyes wading in the shallows while clusters of small brown birds raced the banks, spearing the mud with their sharp beaks. Tiny crabs skittered in front of them, occasionally raising their claws and blowing bubbles in warning. It was amazing to see how quickly nature recovered after the previous day's fierce storm.

After crossing the muddy streambed, Aislinn turned northwest and led them up a path that was more brown than grey. While firm enough, the ground still oozed up around their feet and sucked at their boots with each step.

"Son of a bitch!" Dave yelled.

Hummingbird whipped around, her hands reaching for the daggers on her belt. Dave stood with one foot on the path and the other mired up to his knee in the gooey morass of pluff mud. Behind her, she could feel Aislinn and Hector struggling to contain their mirth. The girl glanced back at them.

Aislinn had one hand on the hatchet at her hip, and the other covering her mouth. Her shoulders shook with silent laughter. Hector resheathed his scimitar and grinned.

Dave tried to pull his leg free, but the mud held fast. He heaved again, lost his balance, and ended up sinking another few inches. A glob of mud oozed over the top of his boot and inside.

A bubble of laughter escaped Aislinn.

Hummingbird offered the archer a hand, but he was too tall, and she wasn't strong enough to pull him free.

"I can't wait to tell Robert about this when we see him," Hector snickered.

"Oh, go and help him," Aislinn smiled.

The bounty hunter grabbed the taller man by the wrist, giving Dave the leverage he needed. The mud emitted a sickening, sucking slurp, and his leg came free — without his boot.

Wide-eyed surprise turned to embarrassed frustration as Dave lost his balance and stepped into the ooze once again before he made it onto solid ground. A fresh bout of laughter burst from Aislinn. Each time Hummingbird thought the older girl was done, a new fit of giggles overtook her, until tears dampened her cheeks.

Dave scowled at the pluff mud. Muttering more curses, he wrenched his boot free and scrubbed at his leg with a handful of marsh grass. "Damned stuff doesn't come off."

"Yeah, and it smells," Aislinn gasped, trying to catch her breath. She moved up the path, still trying to compose herself.

Dave stuffed his foot back into his boot and stomped down. The mud inside squelched.

"Damn it all to Hell!"

"Stop complaining," Aislinn's voice floated back. "You should know better than to step off the oyster shells and sand." Both she and Hector were hidden by the grass.

"Hummingbird," Dave said. When she glanced back, he held out his closed fist. "Here. Cup your hands."

She followed his instruction, and he dropped a tiny brown crab onto her palm. Its dark legs ended in sharp points that prickled her skin, but she gazed in wonder at the creature's perfect symmetry. A pair of black stalks rose from shallow depressions along the edge of its shell, and a cloud of iridescent bubbles formed at its mouth. Hummingbird glanced up at the bowman, her aquamarine eyes wide. A shy smile crept onto her face.

"It's a fiddler crab," Dave said. "Parlatheas is the only continent that has them, and only along the southeastern coast. This one's a girl."

"¡Oye! Come on, you two!" Hector called.

Hummingbird started, and her head jerked up to see Hector and Aislinn descending a bank of shells into the next creek. In a flash, the crab scurried over her fingers, dropped to the ground, and hid in a pluff mud hole. She heaved a disappointed sigh.

"You can catch another one," Dave said. "I'll show you how later."

They climbed up the far bank. At its top, tall stalks of grey-green cordgrass carpeted the saltmarsh. Overhead, the sun was a solid white disk shrouded behind cotton gauze.

Aislinn led them westward, away from the cliffs and sea, wading through more waist-high grass, following twisting creeks and rivulets until she found solid crossing points. All the while, the temperature rose, and the fog continued to diminish.   A dense cluster of short pines and cedars appeared to the northwest, and Aislinn adjusted their course toward it.

Crossing another creek due south of the island of trees, flashes of white and grey caught Hummingbird's eye, and she stopped. Beside her, Dave paused and followed her gaze. Letting out a sharp whistle to get Hector and Aislinn's attention, he pointed with his bow.

A dense flock of gulls fought over something trapped in a shallow pool at a bend in the tidal creek. The gentle tug of water made the object sway, but it was stuck fast on a shell bed. Stepping gingerly, they drew closer and saw a cast of crabs at war with the gulls, each tearing at their prey, then dashing away.

Dave and Hector raced forward, clearing away the scavengers. The wind shifted and the smell of death enveloped them.

Hummingbird stood frozen in wide-eyed horror, staring at the body of a young girl. Shells trapped the child's tattered dress and flaxen hair, keeping her from floating away with the tide. Her ravaged arms and legs lay at odd angles, and her hands were little more than a jumble of fractured bones jutting out of ripped flesh.

Dave and Hector knelt beside the mangled corpse. Though they wore stony masks, their revulsion coated Hummingbird's skin like slime, causing her stomach to churn and twist. She wanted to look away from the grisly scene but found she couldn't. Death's mysteries both frightened and fascinated her.

"Do you think she drowned?" Aislinn asked in a hoarse whisper.

"No sé. There's too much animal damage to know anything for sure," Hector replied.

Dave shooed away a crab and gently brushed aside the veil of hair over the child's face, revealing bloodstained bones and shreds of pallid skin. He recoiled and was about to stand when his eyes narrowed, and he reached for something tangled in her hair. Taking shallow breaths, Dave leaned closer to work the item loose. When it came free, he rinsed his find in the creek and held it up, revealing a copper rectangle on a matching chain. From her vantage point,

Hummingbird could see something stamped on the metal, but she couldn't make out any details.

"What is it?" Aislinn asked.

"Parece una insignia d'esclava," Hector answered.

"A what?" She leaned over Dave's shoulder and captured the copper pendant against her fingers.

"A tag for a slave," Hector said, and spat in the creek. "It's common in some of the Rhodinan countries. Dave and I witnessed an auction when we were up north in Vologda a few years ago. If I remember correctly, those symbols represent her household along with some type of identifying information like her name or a number and her job."

"Can you read it?" Dave asked.

"Sorry, no."

"How long do you think she's been here?" Aislinn asked.

"Not long," Dave said, eyeing the crabs.

Hummingbird retreated up the oyster rake into the tall grass, trying to escape the odor, but it clung to her like a second skin. Death was a recent acquaintance for her. Until she lost her family, along with most of her tribe, in a single night of horror, it had existed only in rumors and myths told by the shaman. Nightmarish visions of the raid and the days after swam before her. The ones who had survived, she and the other children who had been captured along with her, had all prayed for death until, one by one, only Hummingbird remained.

She would have succumbed, too, if Dave and Hector hadn't bought and freed her from the slave market. Death, it seemed, took pleasure in its constant reminders.

"What do we do with her?" Hector asked.

"Leave it here," the archer said with a shrug.

"We can't do that," Aislinn said.

"You wanna carry the body?" asked Dave. "We don't have anything to wrap it up in."

"She's a child."

"Not anymore."

Aislinn glared at him. Even from a distance, Hummingbird could sense Aislinn's frustration, but there was no malice in Dave's voice — just harsh practicality.

"Move aside," Aislinn said. Placing her hands on the corpse, she said a short prayer. Dark tendrils rose from the body, coalescing into a heavy shadow. Cracks and sparks slowly grew, transforming it into a pale azure nimbus like the acthnici fire on their mast during the storm. As it faded, a sense of peace rippled through the air.

Suddenly, the body twitched and moved of its own volition. Its stomach bulged and a slimy, black eel erupted from a tear in the child's dress.

"Fuck me!" Dave exclaimed as he and Hector jumped backward. The water boiled underneath the body and clouds of mud obscured the passage of tiny creatures. When the water stilled, the smell of decomposition dissipated.

"Alright, gentlemen, she's purged," Aislinn said. "Let's take her with us to Ruthaer. She deserves a proper burial."

Dave nudged Hector toward the body. Hector in turn pulled at Dave. Both kept their distance from the corpse.

"Oh, for crying out loud. I'll do it," Aislinn said, scooping up the stiff body.

Hector stepped in front of her. "I'll take her," he offered.

"No. I've got her," Aislinn said. She marched up the embankment and started down another trail only she could see. Hummingbird gave her plenty of room to pass. Behind her, Dave and Hector hurried to catch up.

They marched on in silence, everyone lost in their own thoughts. A line of loblolly pines and oaks became visible in the fading fog, marking the shore.

In the upper branches of a sprawling live oak, an indistinct, hunched shape stood sentinel over the grass-laden waterways. An ice-cold hand gripped Hummingbird's heart, and she felt certain something watched them. Even with the growing sunlight, she couldn't make out what it was. The creature seemed to be made entirely of shadows. Hugging herself, Hummingbird shivered despite the rising temperature.

Dave stopped beside her, trying to see what she saw.

Hummingbird scanned the tree line and shook her head. Her hands and fingers made a few quick gestures. "I think it's a bird," she signed.

Dave squinted at the dark forest. "Damned elf vision," he muttered. "I can't see a thing."

Just before they turned away, the shadow creature unfurled broad wings, revealing alternating bands of dusky grey and white. A crown of ragged feathers adorned its head, giving it the appearance of an outcast prince. The raptor dove from the tree, circled to gain altitude, and drifted inland over the forest.

CHAPTER 4
SHIPWRECK

August 2, 4237 K.E.

7:32am

They topped another rise in the undulating marsh grass, and Aislinn continued down the other side. Before Dave could follow, Hummingbird grabbed his arm.

Dave peered northward in the direction Hummingbird pointed. Off in the distance, the last vestiges of fog rolled and shifted. For a moment, sunlight shimmered on the surface of a wide river channel, silhouetting a triple-mast, multi-decked galleon propped against a grassy bank. Even from where they stood, Dave could see the ship's ragged, rectangular sails fluttering weakly over empty decks.

"There's a ship!" Dave shouted. "It looks abandoned."

"What!" Hector exclaimed and rushed back up the bank. "I thought those charts we bought said the river wasn't deep enough for a galleon."

"It's not," Aislinn replied. She started up the steep bank with her burden and made it about half-way before sliding back down. She heaved an exasperated sounding sigh. "A little help would be nice, you know."

Hector clambered back to her side and gripped her elbow, providing the extra balance Aislinn needed. "Where does the river come out?" he asked. "We should have come that way yesterday."

"It comes out at the lighthouse," Aislinn said with a glare aimed at Dave.

"We never would have made it," Dave growled.

"Do you think el galeón was a victim of yesterday's storm?" Hector asked, cutting off the previous day's argument before it could escalate again. He nodded toward the broken body Aislinn carried. "Maybe la niña came from it. We should check it out."

Aislinn shook her head slowly. "Fishermen would have been out before dawn to catch the outgoing tide. Even if that ship is a victim of yesterday's storm, someone from Ruthaer would have already discovered it. I'm sure the local authorities have this under control."

Dave flinched at the word 'authorities.'

"We should still check it out," Hector said, his eyes never leaving the ship. "Is there a way to get to her?"

Aislinn's head drooped. "Yes. Over there."

CLIO

7:39am

The two men headed in the direction Aislinn indicated.

"Since when do we ever just let the locals handle it?" Aislinn muttered to herself. From the corner of her eye, she saw Hummingbird's brow furrow and her head tilt. She offered the elven girl a half-smile. "Hector suffers from an incurable compulsion to stick his nose in places where it doesn't belong. If he didn't have nine lives like a cat..." Her voice trailed off and she shrugged. "Let's just say he tends to find trouble."

Aislinn stepped on the cordgrass, mashing it flat, and laid down her burden. "This should keep you safe until I return," she whispered to the corpse.

By the time they made it to the ship's prow, the late summer sun shone bright overhead. The air was hot and sticky despite an occasional hint of breeze. Aislinn eyed the water warily. Dead low tide could come at any minute, and then it would be a race to make it out of the marsh ahead of the inflow.

Resting at an angle against the river's southern bank, the galleon listed heavily on her port side. The ship's prow bit deep into the grass and mud, a testament to the force with which she ran aground. From the looks of it, Aislinn guessed it couldn't have been there longer than a week.

Frothy grey water swirled about the stern of the ship, forming little eddies that traveled along her exposed starboard side, where broken oyster shells stuck out like jagged teeth. More shells dotted the hull below the waterline. Amidships, wooden planks splintered outward and revealed a large portion of the hold.

"The captain must have been completely out of his mind. The channel's tricky on a good day; if you don't know how to navigate it, the oyster rakes will rip your bottom out," Aislinn told her friends. She pointed to the broken bits of shell embedded in the hull. "They must have struck an oyster rake on the far side of the channel. The helmsman panicked, overcompensated, and then ran them aground."

"Yeah, that explains the shells, but what about that?" Dave said, gesturing at the gaping hole in the hull.

Hector studied the warped and shattered boards jutting outward. "Looks like something exploded, but I don't see any scorch marks."

"The cargo could have broken loose and burst the hull," reasoned Aislinn. "Sometimes, things just happen."

The bounty hunter nodded. "Maybe. Then again, could be someone or something wanted out muy pronto."

"Let's explore," Dave said as he slung his bow across his back and waded through the shallow water along the starboard side. His tattooed shoulder muscles bunched as he hoisted himself up a section of ribbed hull and disappeared inside the hold.

"Dave!" Aislinn yelled. The lapping waves were the only response.

She was about to step into the water when, "Hey! This is a nice ship," echoed back at her.

"Great." Aislinn turned and found Hector near the prow, tugging on a rope.

"The crew didn't escape through that hole. They came down this line," Hector said before shinnying up the rope. Once he was close to the bowsprit, he grabbed the rail and boarded the ship. Directly under where he crossed the rail, a bronze plaque riveted to the hull bore the Cyrillic inscription, ИНКВИЗИТОР.

"Look!" he called down. "She's Rhodinan." He turned away from the rail, then added, "Are you two coming up, or what?"

Aislinn rolled her eyes. "Terrans."

Confusion clouded Hummingbird's features. She raised her hands to sign then stopped, as if struggling with the unfamiliar word.

"Terrans," Aislinn repeated. Seeing Hummingbird was still confused, she said, "I thought you knew. It's just like them to leave it to me to explain.

"There are other worlds besides ours, Terra being one of them. Gateways link Gaia to these other realms. From what our friend, Jasper Thredd, was able to learn, some realms are easier to access than others, but a mage needs specific knowledge of the destination they want. I don't know if it was an accident or fate that brought those two," Aislinn said, waving a hand at the men on the ship, "along with Dave's cousin Robert, through one of those gates six years ago."

"Didn't they want to return home?"

"Absolutely, at first, but they couldn't find a way. Apparently, it's almost impossible to open a gate to Terra. The portal that brought them to Rowanoake was an ordinary door after they came through it. After a while, the three of them stopped searching," Aislinn replied. She smiled wistfully at the plains-elf. "It's a good thing, too. Neither you nor I would be here if it weren't for them." Shaking her head to dispel the memories, she said, "Come on, we'd better catch up with Hector and Dave before they get into trouble. They're worse than magpies after a shiny coin."

Belaying pins lay strewn about the deck amid tangled mounds of line and other debris. The broken foremast hung precariously above them, trapped in a web of ratlines and rigging. The yards of the mainmast and mizzenmast creaked with every breeze and groaned with each wave. Bereft of the power to escape the pluff mud, the tattered sails rippled forlornly in the breeze and seemed to whisper, *Hope is dead.*

Hector stood over a line of deep, dark reddish-brown gouges in the wood planking. "They almost look like claw marks... or maybe from a small pickaxe," he said to himself. He bent down and scraped at the wood with his knife, releasing the aroma of pine tar. Cutting a small piece loose, he held it against the blade with his thumb and showed it to the girls. "Blood."

"It has to be old, or it would have washed away in the rain," Aislinn replied.

The bounty hunter shrugged. "Can't be too old; no older than these gouges, anyway. We still need to check for survivors and bodies."

"I didn't find any bodies," Dave said from the head of the companionway leading down to the ship's lower decks. Sweat poured down his tattooed chest. "I searched the galley, lower decks, and the hold — but most everything below is flooded. Looks like the ship's been stripped clean."

Aislinn put her fists on her hips. "I told you the fishermen would have salvaged everything by now."

"Or it was sailing empty," Hector said.

"Doubt it," Dave replied. He strode across the deck to see what his friends found. "What made those tracks?"

Hector shrugged and the two men followed the gouges to the rail. They leaned over the side, trying to determine if the tracks led up or continued down the side of the ship. "Whatever it was, it was big," Hector commented. "Aislinn, do you know of anything in this part of the world that could make tracks like these?"

"Nothing I can think of right off-hand," she replied and nudged Hummingbird with her elbow. "But that doesn't mean some mad mage hasn't created a giant tree crab to use for nefarious purposes."

Hector and Dave whipped around from the rail, their eyes wide with shock.

Aislinn burst out laughing.

"That's not funny, woman," Dave grumbled.

"No, not funny." She giggled. "The looks on your faces were hilarious!" Somewhere within the ship's stern, a door slammed. Aislinn's mirth abandoned her.

Moving aft on silent feet, Aislinn strained to catch more sounds. Grand port and starboard side ladders with ornate balusters climbed to the quarterdeck where the spoked ship's wheel and mizzenmast were located. Midways between the stairs on the main deck, a louvered door led to the aft cabins. The stern shifted, and the door creaked open. Beyond, shadows shrouded the narrow passageway.

"Stay behind me," Aislinn whispered. Before she took her first step, Hummingbird grabbed her arm with both hands. The elf shook her head and urged Aislinn to back away from the threshold.

CRSO

8:44am

"¿Qué pasa?" Hector asked quietly.

Hummingbird's fingers flew from sign to sign. Unable to keep up, Aislinn and Hector watched Dave expectantly.

"She says something's in there," replied Dave. He crept toward the doorway and strained to pierce the gloom with his gaze. Hector and Aislinn joined him, their weapons ready.

Using the tip of his sabre, Dave pushed the door open farther and peered inside. On his right, the closest door lay in splintered pieces, and one to the left sported a hole in place of its latch. "What the hell? Somebody busted in the doors." He glanced back at Aislinn. "Salvage crew?" When she shrugged, he gripped the hatch's upper edge and leaned inside. "Passageway doglegs to the left. Looks like there's five cabins: two right here and three more farther down," he described, then stepped inside, stooping to clear the low overhead formed by rough-hewn timbers and the quarterdeck above. Except for the door at the far end of the passageway, the others hung awkwardly from their hinges.

Hector followed close behind, the cramped quarters making it difficult to maneuver. Dave stepped into the room on the right while Hector ducked into the cabin on the left. Behind them, Aislinn and Hummingbird stood guard.

More a closet than a cabin, Dave took in the small space with a glance. Other than a small nest of soiled blankets piled on the floor, it was empty. Back in the passageway, Hector confirmed the cabin on his side lay empty as well.

Moving down, Dave slipped inside the next room to the right. Large and stately by comparison, this cabin dwarfed the previous one. Dark velvet drapes concealed what he suspected to be a porthole. A deep framed bed with masterfully carved eagle heads adorning the bedposts took up most of the floor space. To his left, a teak dresser supported a wood frame, crowned by three twisting spires. Razor-like slivers of mirror rimmed the frame, reflecting skewed versions of the archer. A triangular shard the length of Dave's forearm lay on the dresser top, its edge coated in dried blood. The remaining fragments covered the floor.

His boots crunched on the scattered bits as he moved between the two pieces of furniture to open the drapes. Avoiding the bloodstained glass, he checked the dresser drawers and found them empty. He stooped down and checked under the bed. A round, silver brooch inlaid with a balas ruby roughly the size of a grape winked back at him.

"Hector!" the archer called out.

The hunter stuck his head through the doorway. "Amigo, you got the interesting room."

"Look here."

Hector knelt beside him and reached under the bed.

"Don't touch it!" Dave warned. "It may be cursed."

Instantly the hand halted. Dave watched various emotions war across Hector's face until caution finally won out. Using only the blade of his dagger, Hector nudged the brooch out from under the bed. An unusual array of arcane symbols circled the silver edge. In the center, a red spinel caught the sunlight and each facet sparkled with an inner fire, but a black hairline fracture deep within marred its splendor.

"That jewel is enchanted," Aislinn said from the doorway.

"Is it cursed?" Hector asked.

Aislinn crossed the room and crouched between the two men before whispering a few words. When finished, she shook her head. "No, but do you see that crack? Damage like that will affect its function — if it even works at all."

"I wonder what it's supposed to do," Hector mused. He bent down and picked it up. More engraved symbols covered the back. "Do you recognize any of these markings?" he asked, handing it to Aislinn.

She studied the brooch for a few minutes. "Sorry," she replied, handing it back. Her eyes took in the expensive furnishings. "This doesn't look like a ship officer's cabin, merchant or otherwise. I wonder where this ship was heading, and what happened to its passengers and crew."

Dave watched Hector drop the damaged jewel into his pocket and promptly forgot about it. Hummingbird stood in the passageway, her gaze fixed on the intact door at the end.

The archer studied the door's brass fittings. There seemed to be a thin sheen of fresh oil on the hinges. "Last room. If anyone's aboard, that's where they're hiding."

"Be careful," the girl signed. "There's something terrible on the other side of that door."

"Who wants this one?" Hector asked, drawing his scimitar.

Dave nodded his head toward Hector and then toward the door. Taking a step back, he gave their leader plenty of room.

"Thanks," Hector muttered. He gripped the door handle and shoved. The door glided open on silent hinges then banged against the bulkhead.

The captain's cabin took up the width of the stern. A hulking wooden desk squatted in the room's center atop feet the shape of eagle's claws, each clutching a smooth ball. Behind it, a series of lead-paned windows lit the room.

Along the starboard side, tongue-in-groove paneling covered the ship's ribs, carved with a chart of the southeastern Parlathean coastline.   Starting where the desert known as the Sea of Glass met the cerulean expanse of the Karukera Sea, it ran past Francesca, wound around peninsular Espia, up the eastern seaboard of Carolingias, and stopped at the Gael territories north of Gallowen. Aislinn traced her finger along the Carolingian coastline until she came to a small symbol in the shape of a lighthouse near where Ruthaer should be.   Beside it, Cyrillic writing identified the town.

A narrow bunk clung to the portside hull. Beside it, an empty footlocker lay open.

"There's no one here," Dave said to Hummingbird. The small elf stepped inside, her wide eyes darting from one corner to the next.

Hector went through the desk, opening and closing the drawers. "Nada. Looks like it's been cleaned out, too."

Dave turned to Hummingbird and asked, "Do you see anything?" His eyes bore into hers, not accusatory but searching. She shivered involuntarily and wrapped her arms about herself.   Goosebumps covered the skin on her forearms.

Aislinn crossed her heart and said, "There's someone walking across my grave."

"Mine too," Hector said.

Everyone jumped when the door slammed shut. Behind them, the cabin's heavy curtains dropped over the windows, throwing a black cloak over the room.

An ice-cold hand shoved Dave aside, and Hummingbird exhaled a hoarse gasp.

Pale light lanced out from the bone tube in Hector's hand. A gaunt man wearing a dark blue wool jacket with tarnished gold epaulettes, distinguishing him as the ship's captain, held Hummingbird by the throat. Her breath puffed out in tiny frozen clouds, and a blue tinge crept into her cheeks and lips.

The man yanked Hummingbird around, using her to shield him from the light. Milky eyes glared at Hector as the captain struggled to stay in the darkness.

"Revenant!" Aislinn shouted. "Don't let him bite her!"

The creature's lips parted, revealing broken, yellow teeth, and the stench of his graveyard breath filled the cabin. Before he could bite Hummingbird, Aislinn jabbed him with her longsword. Her silvered-steel blade ripped open his side, sliding all the way up to the hilt. Thick, oily blood oozed from his wound.

Throwing Hummingbird toward Hector, the creature rounded on Aislinn and backhanded her hard enough to send her flying against the door.

The wraithlike man disappeared.

"Where the hell did it go?" Dave demanded.

"He's still here," Aislinn said. She held her sword in one hand and an oak wheel-cross embossed with a leaf and knot pattern in the other.

Hector knelt beside Hummingbird, checking for a pulse. An unseen blow struck the bone tube in his other hand. It sailed across the room and struck the map wall before skittering out of sight. Darkness swallowed them.

"Son of a bitch!" Dave boomed. He struggled to move against the chill air cramping his muscles. "Somebody, open a curtain or something!"

An azure nimbus emanated from Aislinn's wheel-cross. She held it out in front of her, lips moving in prayer. Every muscle tense with determination, she stalked toward the undead captain, now crouched by his former bunk.

The thing spat at her and raised its arms to shield itself from the light.

"Cineres cineribus, pulverem pulveri," Aislinn repeated. Each time she stepped forward, her voice grew louder. The revenant lashed out, flailing at the pale blue light, but everywhere the light touched, its skin peeled away and crumbled. Its face a mask of impotent fury, the undead captain writhed and groaned but could not escape.

"Ty umresh," it hissed between clenched teeth. "Dama ub'yet vas. Dama budet ubit' vas vsekh." The blue light seared into its skin and chunks fell away, revealing charred bone and sinew.

Touching her wheel-cross to the revenant's forehead, Aislinn said, "Requiescite in pace, *fellator*."

The light winked out and silence settled over the cabin.

Dave tore down the curtain. Sunlight streamed into the room, burning the unnatural chill from the air. Only a mound of dust in the corner remained of the undead captain.

"Did either of you understand what it said?" asked Aislinn.

"I did," Dave answered. "He said 'The Lady' will kill us all."

CHAPTER 5
RUTHAER

August 2, 4237 K.E.

9:05am

"You missed a spot."

Crouched at the edge of the creek where they first spotted the ship, Hummingbird wiped the oily smear off her cheek. She swished her small piece of sailcloth in the water and scrubbed at another spot on her shirt. Dave looked her over, helping her find more speckles of black blood.

She caught him staring at the red handprint on her throat and signed, "I'm alright."

Dave gave her a skeptical look, but remained silent, debating the wisdom of taking her into town in her battered and bruised state. It would be their luck the local authorities would think he or Hector was abusing the elf.

The girl's shoulders drooped. "May I have a few minutes to myself?" she signed.

"Don't be long," he replied and nodded down at the water. "Tide's turned. The creeks between us and the mainland are going to fill up quick. We'll have to hurry if we don't want to swim."

At the top of the hill, Hector and Aislinn worked together to wrap the dead girl's body in a length of sailcloth from the ship. Nobody wanted to enter town with the corpse exposed to every pair of eyes they passed. When Dave approached, they both looked up.

"How's Hummingbird coming along?" asked Hector.

Dave shrugged.

Aislinn stood, leaving Hector to secure their improvised shroud. With a questioning tilt to her head she asked, "Is something wrong? Besides the obvious, I mean."

"Says she's fine, but I don't know."

Hector searched his friend's face. "Amigo, she's survived worse than this."

"She doesn't need a reminder," Dave said with a frown. He waved a hand toward the bruise blooming on Aislinn's cheek from the revenant's backhanded blow. "We should skip going to town for a few days."

Aislinn laid a hand on his wrist. "It could just as easily be you and Hector wearing these bruises."

Dave shook his head and opened his mouth to reply, but Hector interrupted. "I did get kicked in the hand, you know. It hurt."

"I'm sure it did," Dave said. "The rest of us aren't infected with troll blood."

"I don't have troll blood!" Hector snapped.

"The *point*," Aislinn said, drawing the archer's attention back to her, "is Hummingbird's a fighter, and you're a good teacher."

"I don't know what she could possibly learn from me. Except ways to get killed."

Aislinn punched his chest. He rocked back and scowled at her. Her eyes narrowed. "You stop that kind of talk."

With a huff, Dave stomped off toward the mainland.

"I guess we're leaving," Hector said, lifting the bundled body. "Come on, Hummingbird! We have to catch up with Dave before he gets stuck again."

CRSO

9:15am

The ground rose steadily, and the wet mud turned to a firm sandy clay. Thick tufts of cordgrass lined each side of a well-used path, turning the hillocks into a series of grassy tunnels. Each creek they traversed was deeper than the one before. In the last, the water was inches from the spongey mass of grass roots, and froth covered wavelets swept past.

Hector shifted the cloth-wrapped body to his right shoulder and offered his free hand to Aislinn. She locked wrists with him and reached for Hummingbird.

"We need to go with the water at an angle," Aislinn advised. "Let it push us across."

Together, they eased into the rising tidewater. Oyster shells shifted and scraped under their feet with each step. All too soon, water flooded into their boots and climbed their legs. By the time the bottom leveled out beneath them, the water was over Hector and Aislinn's waists, and chest deep on Hummingbird.

When they emerged on the far bank, Hector lowered the sodden bundle from his shoulder and sat in the grass to drain the water from his boots. "Do you see Dave?"

Aislinn nodded. "He's at the edge of the marsh... and now he's in the trees. Where does he think he's going without us?"

The bounty hunter tugged his boots back on, climbed to his feet, and lifted the sailcloth bundle over his shoulder. He didn't try to guess at an answer to Aislinn's question.

At the base of the tree line marking the mainland, a weather-beaten bank spilled a gnarled mass of roots into the marsh. The sun-bleached trunk of a fallen pine served as a bridge into the forest. Above their heads, branches covered with bearded moss blocked out the sun. Limbs from some of the older oaks sprawled over the ground, forming a series of obstacles and arches along the forest floor. Off in the distance, the constant drumming of a woodpecker echoed in the maritime forest.

Aislinn led the way, her attention split between the leaf litter, underbrush, and the surrounding trees. She kept a brisk pace, pushing to catch up with their surly archer. A few minutes later, she raised a fist in the air, signaling Hector and Hummingbird to stop. Hector lowered the sailcloth bundle and crept up beside her. Fifty yards ahead, Dave stood stock-still beside a tall pine. He had his longbow out and an arrow with red fletching nocked.

Motioning for the girls to stay back, Hector slunk forward. Like a morning shadow, he moved from tree to tree without a sound. Up ahead, the path seemed clear, with no signs of danger. He eased up behind Dave and peered around the opposite side of the tree, searching for the archer's target.

A small, white shape bobbed its head up and then back down.

Hector sighed and shook his head. "Don't shoot the chicken."

"Why not?" Dave responded.

Another white shape appeared. It jumped up on a low branch, stretched, and crowed. Dave shifted targets.

"Those chickens probably belong to a local farmer. The last thing we want to do is get in trouble for killing them."

Dave's bow dropped, but Hector noticed the arrow was still ready.

"You sure?" Dave asked, the disappointment plain in his voice.

Seeing Dave and Hector relax, Aislinn and Hummingbird quickly joined them. Their noise sent the chickens running; the birds' clucking faded into the distance.

Hector leaned against the pine bole and took a long drink from his waterskin. "Aislinn, where does this path lead?"

"The path is actually that way a bit," she pointed southwest. "We aren't too far off, though. It used to come out at the Knowles farm but that was over twenty years ago."

"Well, if they're still there, I hope they don't mind four desperados showing up in their backyard," Hector said.

"With a dead body," Aislinn added.

Hector turned to Dave and said, "Aislinn and I will take lead."

Dave returned his arrow to its quiver and slung his bow over his back. "Suit yourself."

"That means it your turn to carry the corpse."

Dave's eyes narrowed, then relaxed as he gave Hector an accepting grunt.

Hector shared a surprised look with Aislinn. He had the sinking feeling he had just stepped in a trap.

Dave gently scooped up the cloth bundle. "Let's go," he said when he rejoined them.

The trees thinned as they walked, and golden swaths of light illuminated thick patches of underbrush. Aislinn adjusted their course onto a vague track, twisting around brambles and between vines. Hector wondered if it was an animal trail, until he saw Aislinn brush her hand over a vertical slash-mark on a broad pine trunk. Thirty yards past that tree, another slash leaned south, and she adjusted their course to match. The path wound past muscadine vines laden with fruit, and before long, Aislinn had gathered a handful.

"What happens if we get attacked?" Hector asked. "Are you going to throw grapes at them?"

"Hell, no. I'm going to sit back and spit seeds at them."

"I think you've been hanging around Dave too long," Hector said with a smile.

"I heard that," Dave said. "Pass some back here."

Handing her stash to Hummingbird, Aislinn found another grapevine and replenished her stock.

"So why did your family leave Ruthaer?" Hector asked as they walked.

Aislinn popped another grape in her mouth and looked around at the pines and oaks. Memories clouded her eyes.

"I visited Brand's egg every day. Weeks turned into months, and my connection to him grew stronger. Looking back, I can't tell you exactly when we started to share thoughts and dreams. It got to the point where I couldn't tell where I stopped and he started, as if we were a single soul in two bodies.

"One morning, he called out to me and said he was hungry. I remember being so excited. I snuck out with a bag of smoked fish and ran to the cave. By the time I got there, Brand had already made a few small holes with his egg tooth. I watched for most of the day while he broke out of his shell." Aislinn gave a short laugh. "His first steps were so clumsy, but eventually he got the hang of walking." She paused and shook her head. "You wouldn't think a creature with wings could swim, but he took to the water as if he belonged there. When we left the cave, it was late in the afternoon and the tide was only just starting to go out."

Aislinn stopped and turned, and her companions stopped with her. Although she seemed to study their back-trail, Hector could tell she wasn't really seeing it. Her expression darkened. "Brand and I took the same route across the marsh we followed this morning, but he and I wasted time, splashing in creeks and chasing crabs. The day seemed so perfect. I thought nothing could spoil it, but then the wind shifted, and a huge cloud of black smoke drifted across the top of the trees." She shivered and drew her clenched fists up across her heart.

Hector laid a hand on her back. "Madre de Dios..."

"A small ship appeared in the channel as if it was following the smoke out to sea," she said. "It had flax colored sails. I didn't understand what that meant until I saw their damned black flag with a pale skull clutched in a blood-colored tentacle. It was the first time I ever saw a pirate ship.

"I didn't know what to do. Brand was scared — I was scared. The sun was sinking, and I didn't dare take him into town, not knowing what we'd find. I made him go back to the cave while I went home.

"It was a nightmare. I found my mother crying over Isä's body. He... He had rallied the townsfolk after the constable was killed, and they drove off the pirates. Nobody knew Isä was wounded until he fell, and then it was too late."

Weeping openly, Aislinn leaned heavily against Hector. He wrapped his arms around her and pulled her against his chest. "Lo siento, Aislinn. Yo no sabía," he said, stroking her hair. "In your mother's place, I'd have taken you and Brand to Ozera as well."

Over her shoulder, he could see Dave staring down the path toward the marsh and river. He imagined the archer saw it in a new light, too. Off to one side, Hummingbird was on her knees, an arm wrapped around her stomach and one hand over her mouth. Silent tears streamed down her cheeks.

"Why did you want to take this job?" Hector asked.

Aislinn blinked away her tears and gently stepped from Hector's embrace. She shrugged. "The lighthouse keeper was Isä's friend, and this was my home before Ozera. Tallinn's message mentioned disappearances and odd weather. I don't know what kind of trouble they have here, but I want to help, if we can."

"Aislinn, that was what — twenty, twenty-five years ago?" When she nodded, he brushed a stray tear from her cheek. "That's a long time in human terms. These people don't know you anymore. Besides, I don't know how much help we're going to be if their problem is supernatural storms."

A distant look came over Aislinn and her voice grew soft. "Maybe I was just trying to recapture a bit of the past. Perhaps find the pieces of my soul I lost when Isä died and life got so... complicated."

"I can understand that," Hector said. He turned toward the body in Dave's arms. "Unfortunately, we can never go back."

CR&SO

9:51am

The trail broke out of the trees at the edge of a cornfield. Silky gold tassels sprouted from ears nearly ready for harvest. A multicolored brood of chickens strutted around the base of the stalks, scratching at the ground and chasing bugs. One bold hen covered in black and white stripes raced over and pecked the top of Dave's boot. He scowled and aimed a half-hearted kick at the bird, which missed, but sent her flapping and squawking back into the corn.

Aislinn skirted the field and brought them to a stop at the verge of a sandy road. In one direction, the road followed a field of short, leafy canes with dense, russet colored seed-heads before disappearing back into the forest. In the other direction, it curved around the corn field to a rail fence draped in rambling rose, jasmine, and red trumpet-flower vines. Beyond stood a single-story farmhouse, painted sunshine yellow, with a broad porch sporting a swing on one end and several rocking chairs on the other. The ring of a hammer striking metal carried from the barn on the other side of the house.

Aislinn eyed the wood-shingled house with its open shutters and empty yard. At her back, she could feel her friends watching, wondering why she hesitated.

The moment she stepped onto the road, barking erupted from the farmyard, and a pack of dogs clambered out from under the porch. No two were the same size or color. Most were hounds, but several sported the block-shaped head common to bulldog mixed-breeds.

Dave's burden hit the ground with a dull thump, and she didn't need to look to know he had his bow in hand and an arrow nocked. Aislinn waved him off.

"Put it away," she murmured. She heard him huff an exasperated sigh.

A middle-aged, heavy-set woman in a flowery dress stormed out of the house, carrying an old crossbow. The banging from the barn had stopped. Four boys — ranging in age from ten to sixteen summers — met her in the yard and charged after the dogs. Each carried a different tool as a weapon.

Passing through the gate in the rail fence, the woman yelled, "Get out of my cornfield!"

Aislinn raised her open hands and took two steps toward the family. The dogs rushed her, sniffing her pants-legs and boots, wagging their tails. The largest of the group, an exuberant brown dog with drooping red eyes, jumped up and licked the tip of Aislinn's nose. Aislinn staggered back and planted her feet wide when the same dog reared up and put its front paws on her chest.

"Rosie!" the woman called. "Get over here!"

"She's very friendly," Aislinn said as she gently pushed the dog away and bent to give it a good scratch behind both ears.

The woman and her sons crept closer. "She likes you," the woman said.

The other dogs clustered around Hummingbird, alternately barking and growling at Hector and Dave, who had recovered the sailcloth wrapped corpse. The woman pointed with her crossbow and said, "But they're not sure about those two."

Aislinn smiled back at them and said, "Yeah, me neither."

"Who are you, and what do you want?" the woman asked.

Aislinn straightened, eliciting a disappointed woof from Rosie. The dog pawed at her new friend's leg and jumped up again.

The youngest of the four boys darted forward and grabbed the dog's collar. "Come on, you goober," he said, dragging the dog away. "Nobody's got time for you."

"Thank you," Aislinn said, catching her breath. "I apologize. We didn't mean to trespass. We were just following the old marsh path."

"Are you new in town? I haven't seen you before," the tallest of the four boys said.

"Yes and no. We camped near Shark Hole Creek last night and found a body in the marsh this morning. We were taking it to the constable."

The matron eyed the sailcloth in Dave's arms. News of a death should have elicited shock or disbelief. Instead, the woman gave no reaction beyond a tightening of the lips.

"There's nowhere to camp at Shark Hole Creek," the oldest boy said softly to his mother.

Fear filled the farmer's eyes and she raised her crossbow. "Who are you people?" she asked.

Aislinn splayed her fingers wide and raised her hands. "My name is Aislinn Yves. My family lived in Ruthaer when I was little. These —"

"Yves?" the woman interrupted.

"Yes, ma'am. My father is... was Alaric Yves."

The woman's eyes went wide. She aimed her crossbow directly at Aislinn's forehead. "Alaric Yves died more than twenty years ago. You don't look to be a day over eighteen. His daughter is my age or older."

"Yes, ma'am, I am. His wife, Shayla, *my mother*, is an elf."

"You better not be lying to me," the woman said. Her sons gripped their impromptu weapons tighter. "Let me see your ears," she demanded.

Aislinn tucked her reddish-blonde hair behind one ear, exposing a delicate tip. Though less pronounced than the points of Hummingbird's ears, the shape proved her elven heritage.

The youngest boy gasped. "Wait'l I tell Ricky!"

"Hush, Billy," the next youngest hissed.

The woman handed her crossbow to her nearest son. "Here, Luke. You, Pete, and Billy take the dogs and get back to your chores," she instructed. After the three younger boys were gone, she stepped closer to Aislinn and her friends. "My name is Anne Farigest, and this is my oldest, Frankie. You've been gone a long time. Those who remember your pa talk like he was a great man."

"I like to think so," Aislinn said with a smile. "Mrs. Farigest, these are my friends, Hector, Dave, and Hummingbird."

Anne nodded to each of them in turn, but her eyes lingered on the small bundle in Dave's arms. "Poor lamb," she murmured. "I've delayed you long enough. Frankie will see you to town."

Frankie was a tall and broad-shouldered young man with deep-tanned skin and hair bleached cottony white by the sun. He stooped and gave his mother a quick peck on the cheek before motioning for the four to follow him. Hummingbird eyed him cautiously, using Dave as partial cover.

Young and full of energy, Frankie moved like a deer. Aislinn's lips twitched into a smile. He bounced down the road, barely allowing them time to say their goodbyes to his mother.

"How long have you and your family lived here?" Aislinn asked Frankie when she caught up to him.

"My whole life," he replied with a shrug. "Mum inherited the farm from Aunt Harmony."

"Ms. Harmony Knowles was your aunt?" Aislinn asked. "I'm sorry to hear she's gone. She made the best sweet rolls and sticky buns for church picnics."

"What about your father?" Hector asked.

Frankie waved a hand to the east. "Chasing pirates, last we heard. He's a captain, based out of Port Remley."

"Do you get to see him much?" Aislinn asked.

"He stops in from time to time," Frankie said. "What about you? What brings you to Ruthaer?"

Aislinn and Hector exchanged a look behind the boy's back, silently agreeing to keep their purpose to themselves for the time being. "Believe it or not," he said to Frankie, "we're on vacation."

"Must be nice to have time for travel. You want my advice?" the young man asked. "Go somewhere else."

Aislinn glanced over at Hector, one eyebrow raised. He shrugged in return. "Why?" she asked their guide.

Frankie stopped and turned. He was silent as he studied the four strangers.

Aislinn knew what the teen saw. Each of them carried multiple weapons, and only Dave was without leather armor — but then again, the man wasn't even wearing a shirt.

Frankie shook his head slowly. "Nights are dangerous, Miss Yves. It's best to be inside four solid walls when the sun sets." The young farmer took in their stoic expressions. "Can't say I didn't warn you," he said, and headed down the road again.

They rounded a bend, and the narrow lane intersected a wide road. Frankie turned north. At the top of a low hill, they found the town spread before them. One and two-story buildings of all shapes and sizes filled a careful grid of perfectly straight streets. The main road bisected the town on its way to the Emmassa River, with narrow lanes running east and west. On the far side of the black water, sunlight sparkled on a broad plutonic dome filling the northern skyline. Rising one-hundred feet above the river, it loomed over the town.

"Ruthaer is a lot bigger than I remember," Aislinn said.

Frankie beamed and said, "Yeah, I bet. Come on, I want to show you something." The youth picked up speed as he strode into town.

Aislinn studied the buildings they passed, searching for any she recognized. Almost every single building looked new, with oyster shell tabby coating the lower levels, and fresh whitewash on the clapboard siding above. Down the narrow lanes, she glimpsed small wood-framed homes and workshops.

Frankie led them into a square where two long pole sheds sheltered an open-air market. Shoppers haggled with farmers and traveling merchants. Packs of children ran around the tables dodging their parents. Aislinn took it all in with bemused wonder. This town, with its quaint shops, carefully planned streets, and expanded population, bore little resemblance to the tiny village she remembered.

"Hey, Frankie!" a voice called. "Who's that you've got in tow?"

"Ms. Yves and her friends, come to visit! I'm taking her to Fisherman's Wharf!"

Heads turned and the buzzing tone of the crowd grew more excited as people exchanged shopping for gossip about the young woman, the painted elf, and the men following her.

Aislinn grew worried. She had yet to see anyone she recognized, but these strangers somehow knew of her family. She reached out and tapped their guide on his shoulder. "Frankie, we need to see the constable then pick up some supplies so we can get back to our camp. We really shouldn't sightsee."

"This is on the way, I promise," the boy replied.

"Amiga, we have company," Hector said, drawing her attention to the people behind them.

"Um, Frankie? Why are people following us?"

The boy looked back and grinned. "I imagine they want to see what you think about our park."

In place of the fenced central pasture Aislinn remembered, the road split and circled around a grassy sward. Frankie followed the right-hand course, past a low stone fence topped with wrought iron spikes and backed by a rank of cedar trees. A wide iron gate hung inside a stone archway revealing the graveyard beyond. That, too, had grown in the past twenty years, along with the granite-veneered church beside it.

More than a score of people milled along behind them. Faint snatches of conversation reached Aislinn. Some spoke of her father as if they knew him, but most whispered about her, her friends, and the weapons they carried with an awe that seemed to border on reverence. She thought about Frankie's warning and the fear in Anne Farigest's eyes and wondered what it all meant.

Whitewashed buildings gave way to older structures of bare wood in dull browns and weather-aged greys. They leaned against each other like old friends sharing a dark secret. All except for the proud, three-story, stone tower located at the northwest part of town. Topped by a blue and white checkered flag fluttering in the breeze, it gave Aislinn the impression of a stern parent watching over unruly children.

Frankie led them to a small park overlooking the riverfront pier. Surrounded by a low wall, a finely detailed statue of a man stood on a pedestal facing empty docks. They walked around to the front. Cut and chiseled from a single block of granite, there were no joints at the arms, body, or legs. His hands held a net made from twisted strands of tarnished silver wire, positioned as if it were about to be cast out into the river. At the base of the statue a plaque read:

IN MEMORY OF ALARIC YVES
JUNE 10, 4212
THE MAN WHO SAVED OUR TOWN THROUGH
COURAGE, BRAVERY, AND SACRIFICE
THOUGH HE IS NO LONGER WITH US,
HIS PRESENCE IS FELT BY ALL

Aislinn gasped when she saw it, raising her hand to cover her mouth. The crowd of followers pressed close, eager faces trying to see and hear her reaction.

Her eyes darted from person to person. Life had taught her danger often lurked in unexpected places, and the sudden press of strangers set off warning bells in her mind. The urge to find a defensible position was strong, despite the general lack of hostility in the sea of people around her. Seeing Frankie's jovial grin, she drew a deep breath and managed a slight smile.

Out of the crowd, a tall, seasoned soldier wearing a blue and white surcoat with three golden stag heads emblazoned on the front strode up to them. Framed by thinning silver hair streaked black at the temples, his rugged, clean-shaven face carried the weight of his years. A sheathed longsword clanked at his side.

"Welcome to..." His eyes bulged. "Aislinn?"

Before she knew what was happening, he wrapped her in a bear hug that lifted her off her feet and crushed her against the breastplate concealed beneath his surcoat. A bolt of fear stabbed her chest, and she struggled in his arms.

There was sudden shuffling, followed by a gasp from the crowd, and Dave was there, his hand wrapped around the soldier's upper arm. "Let her go," the archer demanded.

The soldier's eyebrows disappeared into his hairline. Putting Aislinn down, he took a step back and raised his hands in a sign of peace. "Aislinn, don't you recognize me?" His shoulders slumped in disappointment when she shook her head and retreated. Collecting himself, he offered a polite nod to Aislinn and each of her friends. "My apologies. Let me introduce myself.   I'm Sir Francis Courtenay, the constable."

"Francis!" Aislinn exclaimed. "Is it really you?" She rushed forward and reached out to clasp wrists with him. "You look so different, so... distinguished."

The constable grinned. "Are you calling me old?"

She laughed in return. "Absolutely, but the grey hair suits you." Aislinn waved a hand at the shrievalty and the village. "When did Ruthaer get so *big*?"

Francis shook his head ruefully. "Places change, just like people. Let me break up this crowd, and we'll get out of the sun and talk."

CHAPTER 6
TOO MANY QUESTIONS

August 2, 4237 K.E.

10:36am

Sir Francis raised his arms to get the crowd's attention and said, "All right everyone. Let's give Miss Yves and her friends some room to breathe."

The townsfolk continued talking amongst themselves. Despite not knowing her personally, it seemed Aislinn's surname made her a celebrity in their eyes, and their sense of awe extended to her companions. Some of them came up and shook Hector's hand. A few tried do the same with Dave, or to reach Aislinn, but Dave fended them off with a well-aimed scowl. Holding the dead girl's body over his shoulder, Hector overheard one young lad telling his mother the tall man had growled at him.

"Let's try this again," Sir Francis muttered under his breath. He stepped closer to the knot of people and bellowed, "Everyone go about your business! I'm sure Miss Yves and her friends didn't travel here to be gawked at by the likes of us. Perhaps our visitors will agree to stay on for a while and give each of you opportunity to pay your respects."

Before Frankie could leave, Sir Francis caught him by the elbow and said, "Run and fetch Father Blackwood. Ask him to come to the Meeting House."

"Yes, sir," Frankie replied. With a quick turn, he shot off across town.

"Aislinn, you and your friends, please follow me," Sir Francis said.

The Meeting House was a large, rectangular building with lapped siding and high eaves. Two rows of six equally spaced windows bracketed by wooden shutters lined each of the long sidewalls, one directly above the other. An off-centered cupola squatted on the roof ridge like a fat toad and housed the warning bell. At the cupola's peak, a metal weathervane swung gently on a faint breath of air. Fronted by a wide porch, the building faced east toward the granite church across the grass covered commons. One represented the heart and the other the soul of the town, Hector mused, which left the watchtower as the brains. He eyed Sir Francis speculatively, hoping for the best.

Inside the Meeting House, two rows of thick timber posts supported a narrow balcony running along each of the long sidewalls. Centered on the west wall was an ornate wooden table atop a rostrum. A variety of spindle-backed chairs were pushed in underneath, facing the room.

"You can place the body on the table," Sir Francis said as he closed the door.

"You knew?" Aislinn said.

"It's a bit obvious. Plus, news travels fast in our town," Sir Francis answered.

Hector gently laid his bundle down and backed away.

"Where did you find it?" Sir Francis asked as he began to unwrap the sailcloth.

"Down at the oyster rakes," Aislinn replied. "It was trapped in one of the tide pools. We think she came from the ship."

Sir Francis looked down at the body and frowned. "The ship? Are you sure?"

"Why? When did it arrive?" Aislinn asked.

"Four days ago, after a freak squall — even worse than the one yesterday. We figure the ship's captain was trying to find a place to weather the storm. Do you remember Tallinn, the lighthouse keeper? He and his apprentice discovered it."

"What's a Rhodinan ship doing in these parts?" Hector asked.

"Did you go aboard?" Sir Francis countered.

"Sí, señor. It was empty," Hector replied, "like someone went in and took everything not bolted down."

Sir Francis looked up from the girl on the table. "Other than food stores, the *Inquisitor* didn't carry any cargo," he replied.

"Don't you find the lack of cargo a bit odd, señor? What about the crew? Or passengers, perhaps?"

"It isn't odd for a diplomat's ship," the constable said. He studied Hector, then Dave. His eyebrows drew together. "You two look familiar. What are your names?"

Before Hector could answer, the door opened, revealing an elderly man wearing brown robes. Sunlight glistened in the sweat beading his tonsured scalp. He shooed away Frankie before coming inside and closing the door behind him.

"Cecil." Sir Francis stepped off the rostrum and shook the priest's hand. "How are you today?"

"Doing well, doing well," Father Blackwood replied as the two men walked back to the table. "Who do we have here?"

"Father Cecil Blackwood, may I introduce to you Aislinn Yves," Sir Francis said, "and..."

Hector bowed low and said, "I'm Hector de los Santos." With a sweep of his hand, he introduced their other two companions. "This is Dave Blood and his protégé, Hummingbird."

The priest nodded in greeting to Aislinn and Hector, but he froze as he took in the sight of Dave's tattoo-covered body. Then he saw the elf-girl lurking in the bowman's shadow, and his mouth dropped open in an "O" of surprise.

"Hummingbird is from a distant continent called Altaira, Father Blackwood," Aislinn said.

The priest nodded but continued to stare at the plains-elf. His eyes darted from the girl to Aislinn and back, seeming to compare the peaches and cream tone of Aislinn's skin to the rich amber of Hummingbird's, with her tribal markings and wild nimbus of spikey crimson hair.

"Father, we were just talking about the wreck of the *Inquisitor*," Sir Francis said.

Father Blackwood pried his attention from the newcomers. "Yes. Such an unfortunate incident." Despite the sunlight streaming in through the windows, the priest opened a cabinet, produced a pair of candles, and used their light to examine the corpse. He was slow and methodical, occasionally shifting the body on the sailcloth to get a better view.

While the priest worked, Aislinn studied the constable's grey hair and frown lines. "So, *Sir* Francis," she teased, "how and when did a boatwright's son turned soldier become a nobleman?"

He rubbed the back of his neck and gave her a rueful smile. "Not a nobleman, a knight, if you can believe it. Order of the Golden Stag. It's one of those landless titles Queen Ambrose bestows on common soldiers who show enough leadership skills to take command of a shrievalty." He glanced out the window at the town and passersby. "For the past sixteen years, I've been responsible for the safety of these people. From the river south and from the coast west, roughly forty miles in each direction. It's more than I ever could have imagined when you and I were kids playing in the woods and the marsh."

"The Queen of Carolingias wouldn't have given it to you if she or her advisors thought you couldn't handle it," Aislinn replied. An impish grin spread across her face. "Besides, you were always bossy."

Sir Francis gently turned Aislinn's head with a fingertip on her chin. "Where'd you get this bruise?"

"Rough trip."

"And the handprint on Hummingbird's throat?"

"A dead man."

"Huh," said Father Blackwood as if in response to Aislinn's comment. Leaning down close to the corpse, he drew in a deep breath through his bulbous nose before holding his hands out over the body with his fingers splayed.

Dave stepped forward. "Creepy bastard," he muttered as his hand reached for his sabre. Hector grabbed the taller man's wrist and shook his head.

"That's odd," the priest remarked, oblivious to the exchange between Hector and Dave. "There's no smell of decay." His brow furrowed in thought.

Aislinn cleared her throat and said, "Father Blackwood, I cast a preservation spell."

"Really? I didn't know you were a member of the cloth." The priest straightened and looked Aislinn up and down, his expression skeptical as he took in her worn leather and the weapons on her belt.

"I'm not, at least not officially. I trained with Phaedrus in Ozera."

"Phaedrus, the half-elf?"

"Yes, sir."

Father Blackwood glanced at Sir Francis. "Miss Yves has interesting friends."

"Mmhm," Sir Francis responded distractedly. He studied Hector and Dave as if trying to place where he'd seen them.

Father Blackwood stretched his back and said, "It's hard to say what happened. There's too much damage, but, if I had to guess, I'd say she was struck on the neck. That's where the oldest damage appears to be focused."

"Struck, Padre, or do you mean bitten?" Hector asked.

Father Blackwood cast a quick glance at Sir Francis before answering. "I don't know." The priest lifted the corners of the sailcloth and carefully rewrapped the corpse. "Who was she?"

Hector dug in his pocket and handed him the small metallic badge. "She wore this."

The priest looked at it and shook his head sadly. "A slave?" He handed the small object to Sir Francis, who held it up next to a candle, trying to decipher the Cyrillic writing.

"Señor, you never answered my question about the crew and passengers," said Hector.

Handing the slave badge back to the Espian, Sir Francis replied, "You sure ask a lot of questions."

"Occupational habit, señor."

Sir Francis rubbed his chin as he mulled over Hector's response, dissatisfaction plain in his expression.

The priest cleared his throat. "If they have ties to Phaedrus, they can be trusted, Francis."

The constable stared deep into the candle's flame and said, "As soon as Tallinn sent us word about the ship, I assembled my men, along with some of the local fishermen, and we sailed out to the *Inquisitor*. We hoped to rescue survivors and salvage anything important. There was nothing there. Not a single sailor. Just some fancy clothes, charts, and other odds and ends. Nothing worth salvaging."

"Bodies?" Aislinn asked.

"No. I had people scour the creeks, looking for anyone washed overboard." He gave the small corpse a sad look. "She was probably out there, hurt and terrified, but no one saw her."

"Not all was lost," Father Blackwood said gently. "You did find one survivor aboard the ship."

"¿Qué? ¿De verdad?" Hector asked. "Who is he? Where is he?"

Sir Francis turned grim. "Count Dodz. You can find him at the Griffon Inn across the street from the market."

Laying a hand on the constable's, Aislinn asked, "Francis, is something *else* going on here? When we met Mrs. Farigest, she seemed suspicious. More than that... she seemed truly frightened."

With a deep sigh, Sir Francis said, "That blasted ship has everyone on edge. Things will settle down soon."

Aislinn stepped closer to the constable and said, "Are you sure that's all it is? We can help you."

Sir Francis smiled at Aislinn and said, "It does my heart good to see you again after all these years. Thank you for bringing us the girl, but I'll take it from here."

Aislinn gave the constable a quick hug and said, "If you change your mind, we're anchored in one of the sea caves near Shark Hole Creek for tonight, but we plan to go up and visit with Tallinn tomorrow. Probably stay at the lighthouse for a few days before we move on."

Turning to her friends, Sir Francis said, "Enjoy your stay in Ruthaer. We have everything under control."

"I'd best be off, too," Father Blackwood stated. "I need to see about gravediggers and ask the carpenter for a coffin. If I can arrange it, we'll bury the child's body tomorrow under the oak in the graveyard." He offered a farewell nod to Hector and the others. "You are more than welcome to come join the service."

Aislinn nodded to the priest and headed for the door. Behind her, Hector gave a short bow to the constable and priest and rushed to catch up with her, Dave, and Hummingbird.

When she opened the door, Aislinn surprised a young man wearing a blue and white checked surcoat over chain armor. Behind him, a brown and white paint horse quivered from exertion. The soldier pushed past Aislinn and Hector, and almost ran headlong into Dave.

"Timothy," Sir Francis said, "why aren't you on patrol?"

Dave moved aside. The soldier stumbled to his commander. "The monastery!" he gasped. "It's been attacked, sir!"

Sir Francis grabbed Timothy by his upper arms to steady him. "What? When?"

"We found the monks a little over two hours ago, sir. They're all dead. By the looks of it, it happened earlier this morning."

"Where's your patrol now?"

"I left them at the monastery."

"Good. Go to the shrievalty and find Big Mike. Tell him to gather the men."

"Yes, sir."

Aislinn and Hector watched Timothy race away and stepped back inside to confront the constable. "Francis, you need us," she said, holding up a hand to forestall any argument. "Let me introduce you to Damage, Inc."

"The *bounty hunters*?" the constable spluttered.

She nodded and gestured to each person as she reintroduced them. "Hector de los Santos, team leader."

The Espian gave the constable and the priest another sweeping bow. "At your service, señores."

"Dave Blood, archer and swordsman. Hummingbird of Altaira, empath." Aislinn indicated herself last. "I serve as the team's tracker and healer. We received a message via Ozera, asking us to come here. Let us help you."

"This is Tallinn's doing, isn't it? I told that old seadog we didn't need outside help," Sir Francis said, pacing the floor. When he returned, he assessed Aislinn and each of her companions. His gaze came to rest on Dave's longbow. Finally, he said, "Alright, but don't get in the way."

The constable turned to Father Blackwood.

"I know, my son," the priest said. "Go. Find out what happened. I'll gather tools and volunteers."

The five flew out of the Meeting House, drawing alarmed gasps from the citizenry as they rushed past. The shrievalty, a walled estate dominated by a square-shaped stone tower on the northwest side of town, held a commanding view of both the river road and the waterway. The bailey already swarmed with activity when they arrived. One team of guards prepared a dozen horses to travel while another, smaller group readied a wagon and checked weapons.

"Corporal Ponds!" Sir Francis shouted.

"Yes, sir," replied a young man with the beginnings of a mustache.

"Saddle four more horses."

"Three more," Aislinn corrected.

Sir Francis nodded and said, "Three more horses."

"Yes, sir," he said and ran off.

"Wait here," Sir Francis said, before retreating inside the tower.

Aislinn followed Corporal Ponds to the stable yard to help with the horses, leaving Hector, Dave, and Hummingbird near the gate.

Hector's eyes roved over the walls, buildings, and tower, assessing their strengths and weaknesses. Thick steel bars covered the windows on the tower's lowest floor, but the arched windows on the upper floors were glass, flanked by heavy storm shutters. High above, a single guard kept watch behind the crenelated parapet. In the courtyard, the smith and armorer worked their trades under an open-air pole building situated against the left-hand estate wall. Along the right, a long, wooden building with a tiled shed roof served as the barracks.

Laughter drew Hector's attention to a knot of guards in blue and white surcoats. They were mostly boys, and he suspected they lacked any actual fighting experience. Hearing their excited talk, he wondered how many had ever travelled more than a day's journey from their front door. They were probably excellent game hunters, but it was hard to tell if they would perform well as a group. Scattered amongst the boys, veterans remained quiet, grim with worry.

Hector watched one of the older patrolmen size them up before he approached.

"You aren't new recruits," he said.

"No, señor, not recruits. Able-handed volunteers."

"More like volun-*told*," Dave muttered.

The soldier gave Dave a sharp-eyed look. "That bow looks longer than you are tall. Can you actually draw that thing?"

In answer, Dave slid the bow from his back and drew a red-fletched arrow by feel. He held the thick arrow against the right side of the bow with the first and second fingers of his right hand but didn't pull back. Instead, he seemed to push the bow forward with his left, letting the thick arrow shaft slide over his hand until the arrowhead touched his knuckles, and the tip of his right middle finger brushed his cheek. At the far back of the yard, beyond the shrievalty tower, several practice dummies leaned against the wall. In the space between one breath and the next, Dave released the bowstring.

The soldier turned, following the arrow's path. It lodged itself deep into a manikin's straw filled chest before the twang of the bowstring faded. The man let out an appreciative whistle. "What kind of range does that thing have?"

Dave shrugged and went to retrieve his arrow.

"I've seen him bring down a buck at over two hundred yards," Hector replied and nodded toward the shrievalty door, where Sir Francis had just emerged. The sun gleamed on the polished steel armor now covering his arms and legs.

Aislinn and Corporal Ponds returned with three sorrel quarter horses, saddled and ready to go. The excitement from the younger soldiers spread, and the horses pawed anxiously at the ground. Hector eyed them warily, wishing he had Caballo.

"Men!" Sir Francis stood on the stone steps outside the tower with an open-faced bascinet in his hand. "The western patrol has reported an attack on the monastery. Make no mistake; this is going to be rough. We are all likely to see things we wish we hadn't. I do not know if there are any survivors or if the culprits are still in the vicinity, so stay sharp. Stay with your partners. If you see something, do not go running off. This is no time to be a hero."

Turning to the four companions, he said, "I have asked Miss Yves and her friends to help us. Don't mistake them for enemies later."

A stable boy brought around a large, golden brown horse with black socks and mane. Sir Francis strapped on his helmet and mounted, signaling the troops to do the same. Aislinn swung into her saddle, then reached down, grabbed Hummingbird by the forearm, and pulled her up in back. Nearby, Hector and Dave sat on their horses, checking their weapons and gear one last time.

"Let's go!" Sir Francis commanded.

Outside the shrievalty, a crowd stood by the roadside. Some looked curious, others frightened by the rumors already spreading through town. Sir Francis paused to speak to the crowd, offering what assurances he could. A giant of a man with wheat straw hair took his place and led the soldiers through town at a fast clip only slightly slower than a trot. As they passed beyond the last building, he urged his mount into an easy lope.

Oaks and cypress flew by; moss-covered branches crisscrossed overhead and threw dapples of shadow across their path. The ground along either side of the road grew mushy in spots as they paralleled the river. Tall cypress knees lined the water's edge like rows of pointed teeth. A loud splash attracted Hector's attention, and he watched an alligator swim away.

"How familiar are you with this area?" Hector asked Aislinn, his eyes more on the river than on the road.

"I was born in Ruthaer," Aislinn answered with a smile, then she chuckled. "I learned to swim in that river."

She rode beside him, pointing out different trees and animals to Hummingbird. Hector marveled at the number of things she picked out of the dense foliage. Movement overhead drew both girls' gazes. He looked up in time to catch a glimpse of a broad-winged bird through a break in the canopy, sailing west as if it was also going to the monastery.

A few minutes later, Sir Francis rejoined the group and drew up his mount alongside Hector's. The constable glanced at Aislinn then motioned for Dave and the bounty hunter to slow their horses. When they fell behind the wagon, he reached into a pouch and pulled out two pieces of parchment rolled up together.

"Take it," Sir Francis said, handing the papers to Hector. "I knew I'd seen you before."

Hector unrolled the pages, glanced at each, then passed them to Dave, who flipped through them. One had a good sketch of Hector, the other a not-so-good sketch of Dave. At the top in big bold letters, it read, 'WANTED.' The fine print at the bottom said, "Fugitive Wanted for Escaping Prison, Considered Dangerous," signed by Lord Mitchell Rockwood, Mayor of the Free City of Rowanoake.

Dave handed it back, saying, "They misspelled your name."

Hector rolled the posters together without looking. "Yeah, I know. They spelled it L-A-S, not L-O-S. How many times did I tell them?"

"Some bounty hunter you are. Five years on the run, and you can't even catch yourself," Dave quipped.

Hector offered the posters back to Sir Francis, who only shook his head. "Keep them. We'll discuss it when we get back."

"Sir Francis, that was a long time ago," Hector said, but the constable was already moving to the front of the line.

"Isn't there a statute of limitations on that sort of thing?" Hector asked.

"You'd think," Dave replied.

Aislinn and Hummingbird were waiting when they rode up. "What was that all about?" Aislinn asked.

"Nothing," Hector and Dave replied in unison.

"Uh-huh," she said. "Fess up. What did Francis want?"

Instead of answering, Hector showed her the sheets of paper. After scanning them, she said, "Rowanoake has no authority here in Carolingias. You don't think..."

Hector shrugged as he put away the Wanted posters. "Gallowen and Carolingias are founding members of the Confederation of Nations, and, technically, Rowanoake is in Gallowen. Those posters are old, so I don't know what to think. I guess Dave can burn that bridge when we get there."

The forest grew thicker, and the humidity mixed with the heat of the afternoon sun broiled them. With only the rhythmic clip-clop of the horses' hooves breaking the silence, the troop followed the road southwest as it pulled away from the river and sought firmer ground.

They travelled six miles before seeing a small wooden sign marking the northerly turnoff for the monastery. Pecan trees with clusters of fall webworm nests in their branches lined each side of a gravel drive. At the end, a tall, brick wall with a black iron gate blocked their way. Set into the masonry above the gate, the remains of what had once been a bronze wheel-cross stood twisted into a single spike. Impaled on top was a young man's decapitated head.

Timothy sat atop his horse staring up at his patrol-mate's head, horror etched into his features. Sir Francis eased his horse beside the young soldier and said, "Son, you did the right thing coming back for help."

"But, sir," Timothy's voice cracked, and he struggled against the tears in his eyes. "When I left my patrol, the gate was open."

CHAPTER 7
MURDER AT THE MONASTERY

August 2, 4237 K.E.

12:19pm

Cries of outrage and fear filled the air. Aislinn tossed her reigns to Hector and slid from her horse. Eyes on the ground, she darted around the patrol to the monastery's gate.

"Francis, keep the men back!" she called. "Before anyone tramples over the tracks, let me figure out what happened here."

The constable gave her a curt nod and gathered his men around him.

"What gives her the right to order you around, sir?" Big Mike muttered. Several others nodded their agreement. "We have men in there."

"Do as she says," Sir Francis replied.

"She's one of the best trackers I've ever met," Hector said. "I'll take her over an hombre with a bloodhound every time. If this is a trap, she'll uncover it before we step in it." Although he spoke to the men, his eyes roved over the wall and watched the grounds beyond the gate. Dave stood in his stirrups, bow held horizontal and an arrow nocked, watching the forest around them and the road behind.

The air was utterly still. No birds sang in the trees. The ever-present drone of insects was missing. Even the squirrels, who should have been busy in the pecan trees, were nowhere to be seen.

Hector waited for Aislinn to turn her attention to the wall and the grisly ornament above the gate arch before he dismounted and joined her. Sir Francis followed him.

"Four men on horses went in; one came out and headed back toward town. I'll assume, for now, the tracks belong to Timothy and his patrol." She nodded at the young man, now sitting on the ground, head in his hands. "I also found a partial footprint over there," she pointed to one side of the gate. "Small, like a woman's, but that isn't the strange part." Aislinn stepped closer to the wall and pointed out a series of chips and scratches in the brickwork. Motioning Hector and Sir Francis to follow, she measured off five paces, and pointed out another set of chips and scratches.

"What are you showing me?" Sir Francis asked. "All I see are scratches in the brick."

Aislinn fingered one of the chip marks and showed him the brick dust. "These marks are new. Something climbed this wall, Francis. Something big. We found similar marks down the side of the shipwreck." She scanned the ground around them, then pointed to several gouges leading west into the trees. "Do you want me to track it?"

"No, my missing men and the monastery take priority. Keep quiet about this for now. We don't need a panic on top of everything else," Sir Francis said. He turned back to his waiting troops.

"Henry! Open the gate! Hoyt, find a way up there and get poor Ray's head down!"

"Sir, the gate's fused shut. What do you want us to do?" Henry asked, making every attempt not to look at Timothy.

"Tear it down," Sir Francis commanded.

Soldiers looped ropes through the bars of the gate and tied them to several of the horses. At a shout from the men, the horses lunged forward. The gate fell with a screeching crash.

A deep-throated, raucous call erupted from the treetops at the commotion.

"What was that?!" One of the younger men jerked around in his saddle and groped for his weapon. His horse turned, following the tug on its reigns.

"Don't piss yourself, Alfie," a soldier with frizzy red hair laughed. "It's just a bird." Nervous laughter spread through the small group.

The heron spread its cloud-like wings and sprang into the air. Aislinn watched it turn away from the monastery and disappear beyond the tree line. Heavy silence settled over the group. "Alright, we're burning daylight," she announced. Searching the grounds as she went, she led Sir Francis and his troops past the ruined gate and inside the monastery.

Bordered by stone-covered paths, the lawn spread out before them like verdant carpet. Directly in the center of the compound, a gleaming white church exemplified Clesiastic architecture with its classic cross shape, west-facing entrance, and majestic approaches. A steep pitched roof rose up to the heavens, adorned with alternating columns of convex and concave barrel tiles. At its peak, a gold wheel-cross glinted in the sunlight.

To the right and adjacent to the church, four smaller, flat-roofed buildings connected back to the main building via a series of ornate colonnades. To the left, a meticulously pruned hedge surrounded a ten-foot-tall marble wheel-cross. A turkey vulture perched atop the statue, eyeing something on the ground.

"Sir!" Aislinn called. "You might want to look at this!" She knelt in the grass midway between the outer wall and the hedge, studying divots torn from the lawn. "See this? Horses fled northwest around the church while someone or some*thing* chased your men east toward the outbuildings." She looked up at the constable and asked, "What do you want us to do?"

His gaze drifted across the empty grounds, and he appeared to age before her eyes. "Despite your reputation, there's nothing a team of bounty hunters can do for us. Take your friends and get out of here."

"No, sir. You know me better than that," Aislinn replied. She stood and rested her fists on her hips. "I've never run away from trouble in my life."

Sir Francis shook his head. "No, you never did," he replied. "But, as I recall, it was usually you who started it, and then needed me to get you out of it."

"If I help you out of this, how about we call it even?" Aislinn replied. Nearby, Hector and Dave observed silently. She hoped Francis would extend the bargain to them as well.

"Sure," he said finally. "Have you been to the monastery before?"

"My parents used to bring me here every Yuletide, but that was a lifetime ago."

Sir Francis pointed as he said, "Those two small buildings farther out house the winter stores. The one closest to us with the large chimney is the kitchen, and that one next to it is the dining hall. The monk's cells are in the north and south wings of the church. The library is in the basement below the southern wing. Take a look around and see what you can find."

Aislinn grabbed Dave and Hector by the arm and pulled them away before the constable changed his mind. Sir Francis left them to join his men, who still waited near the gate. "There are three of our men and ten monks in this compound," he said. "Find them!"

Hummingbird stopped in front of Dave. She wrinkled her nose and pointed at the ground. Her hands flashed through a series of signs.

"What is it?" Hector asked.

"She says something's wrong with the ground," Dave said, giving the grass under his feet a suspicious glare.

"I feel it too," Aislinn said. "The ground feels tainted."

Dave cut a divot and flipped it over with the toe of his boot. "Looks like dirt. What's wrong with it?"

"The grounds are no longer holy. They've been desecrated," she replied softly.

Dave's eyes went wide as he took in the expanse of the monastery grounds. He made a sign against evil. "The church too?"

"Probably."

"What could do that?" Hector asked.

Aislinn shook her head and turned in a slow circle. Three soldiers stood near the hedge while a fourth lost the contents of his stomach. She could only suppose they had found a body at the foot of the wheel-cross. Sir Francis led a second group toward the main doors of the church while a third group aimed for the outbuildings.

"Hummingbird!" she said suddenly.

The young elf flinched, and her eyes flew wide.

"Is anyone still here?" Aislinn asked.

The elf closed her eyes and concentrated. After a moment, she opened them. Extending her arm, she pointed to the wing of the church closest to them and then beneath it.

"Someone's in the basement?" Hector asked.

Hummingbird nodded and made a quick sign.

"He's hurt?" Hector said.

Hummingbird shrugged and signed, "I can't tell."

Fist clenched around his scimitar and sword knot draped around his wrist, Hector headed for the small portico sheltering the southern entrance to the church. Behind him, Dave, Aislinn, and Hummingbird fanned out, intentionally trying not to form a line.

Standing in front of a six-paneled, oaken door with an arched header, Hector glanced over his shoulder to make sure the others were in position before gripping the brass handle. With a twist, the latch released. Hector jerked the door all the way open to let Dave have room to shoot. Light from a cross-shaped stained-glass window illuminated the empty hall. Dust motes danced in pastel patches of yellow, blue, and green.

A putrid stench of decay oozed from the building's interior, accompanied by the drone of flies. Dark red footprints crisscrossed the flagstone floor, leading in and out of shadow-filled cells along both sides of the corridor. At the far end, another six-paneled door with an arched header guarded the way into the main chapel.

Dave poked his head into the first room on the left and slammed to a stop on the threshold. His hand clenched the doorjamb until his knuckles turned white and the wood creaked.

Aislinn moved to join Dave, but the tall man closed the door, barring the way.

Across the hall, Hector slammed his door shut. He leaned back against the wall and wiped cold sweat from his brow.

"Dave?" Aislinn said.

"You don't need to go in there," Dave said hoarsely.

"Move out of my way," said Aislinn, her eyes boring into his.

"Have it your way," Dave said, "but Hummingbird stays out here."

Aislinn braced herself and went inside. At first, her mind couldn't make sense of what she saw. Then, with a sudden, sickening twist, the scene resolved itself. A monk lay on his cot, his body ripped open from throat to groin. Broken ribs jutted out of the empty chest cavity. Blood drenched his tattered robes and the sheets beneath him, forming a drip line on the floor. Sprays of blood spattered the ceiling and walls, intermingled with various pieces of organs and entrails. Only his head, arms, and legs were undamaged.

Nausea churned in her gut, and she retreated to the hall, trembling. "What could have done that... in a church?" she whispered.

Dave offered her his flask and said, "A demon."

"But this is a church," she protested. "Holy ground."

"Not anymore," Hector murmured. "This is Santander all

over again. Consuelo, the sorceress we were hunting, summoned a demon to do her bidding. Its handiwork looked a lot like these monks."

"I told you before we left Orleans that they'd find us," said Dave.

CR&SO

12:34pm

Hummingbird surveyed the corridor, tears glistening in her haunted eyes. Evil, redolent with fear and lust, clung to the walls like a festering wound. She closed her eyes but couldn't shut it out. Raw emotions bombarded her from every side, more powerful than the revulsion and disgust she felt coming from her companions, triggering violent memories of her own tragic past. Bile rising in the back of her throat, she sprinted out into the sunlight.

The others found her on her knees with her hands flat on the ground, taking in great lungsful of air to clear the stench from her sinuses. Hector reached her first and laid a hand on her back. Although she knew he meant no harm, instinct made her shy away as if he had tried to strike her.

Aislinn gently pulled him away and knelt beside her. "Are you alright?" she asked.

"I feel the emotions," Hummingbird signed, then with a heave she retched into the shrubbery. Aislinn stroked the young elf's spikey crimson hair. When Hummingbird finally collected herself, she signed, "I'm sorry," stealing a glance at Dave and Hector.

"No need to apologize," Aislinn said. "The smell alone is enough to make anyone sick."

Hummingbird shrugged and signed, "Sometimes, I wish I was numb inside and couldn't feel anything. Like now." She gripped Aislinn's arm and shakily climbed to her feet. "The one who did this, whatever it was, enjoyed killing those men. I feel the evil it left behind, like the thing in Santander, only stronger."

"We need to go back inside in case there's a survivor or, worse, a revenant like on the galleon," Hector said. "Do you want to stay out here?"

With false bravado apparent to all, Hummingbird signed, "No, I'm ready."

CR&SO

12:47pm

The four moved down the hall, giving each room a cursory glance to check for survivors, only to discover more bodies, six in all, each one lying flat on his back and gutted.

Sir Francis' voice echoed from the sanctuary. It sounded as though he and his men had found more bodies in the chapel.

Toward the end of the corridor, a pair of bloody footprints led out of one of the rooms and under the last door on the right, petite toes and a bare heel clearly distinguishable.

Scanning his companion's faces, Hector held up two fingers near his eyes, then pointed to the tracks. Moving toward the door, he listened. Dave put his back to the wall beside the door and waited, sabre ready. The bounty hunter yanked the door open and jumped aside.

When there was no response, Dave and Hector peeked around the doorjamb into darkness. Light from the dormitory entrance barely reached the threshold. Pulling out his bone tube, Hector shined the pale light around. The bloody tracks continued down stone steps to the basement.

With a wary glower, Dave tightened his grip on his sword.

"I don't like it either," said Hector.

Hummingbird signed, "It's down there."

"Alive or dead?" Hector asked. Hummingbird shrugged and slid out her two daggers. Beside her, Aislinn held a longsword in one hand and her wheel-cross in the other.

As they slowly moved down the stairs, the air chilled and humidity dropped, as if by magic. The smell of parchment and leather replaced the stench of death. With each step the bloody footprints faded, until all that remained was an occasional scarlet droplet.

Hector stopped on the bottom tread and panned his light across the quarter-landing from left to right. A red stain in the shape of a boot heel lay in the center of the next step. "Someone else came down here," he whispered.

"It could have been one of the patrolmen," Aislinn replied. She stepped past Hector into the room and gasped. Six rows of waist-high mahogany bookshelves topped with an odd assortment of clay fragments and broken carvings filled the room's center. A pair of scriveners' desks alongside a large worktable bearing sheets of leather, a variety of hand tools, and a partially bound book in a wooden sewing frame occupied the wall to their immediate right.

Straight ahead, leather bound tomes lay in small piles atop a writing desk, their covers and exposed pages smeared in blood. Darkening red stains trailed across a fresco covering the wall beside the desk, blotting out the painting's upper third.

Movement caught Hector's attention, and he swung his light toward it. A tonsured man wearing brown robes stood in the far corner behind the last row of shelves. Fresh blood covered his mouth and chin and matted his hair.

"Thank the Eternal Father you are here," he said. "My prayers have been answered." His robes rustled as he shambled toward the bounty hunter's team.

"Padre, what are you doing down here?" Hector asked. "It's dangerous."

"Look at his eyes," Aislinn hissed. "They're like the captain's."

Milky-white orbs like two cold moons fixed on Aislinn. "I've been so hungry, but nothing seems to satisfy me." Hummingbird backed toward the stairs, and the monk's predatory gaze followed her. He stalked toward the young woman, but Dave and Hector blocked his way.

"Who did this to you?" Aislinn asked.

The monk blinked and replied, "An angel."

"An *angel*?"

"She came to me during the night and blessed me."

"What about the others?" Hector asked.

"The others?" the monk said. "They're upstairs. Have you not seen them? The angel revealed herself to them as well."

"They're dead," Dave said, flatly.

The monk smiled at him and said, "But they are not. They shall rise, blessed and reborn."

"Not from what I saw," Dave said. "There's not that much left."

Uncertain, the monk glanced back at the corner from which he had risen. He turned to them and said, "I am so *hungry*."

"Can you describe this angel?" Hector asked. "How did you meet it?"

"How can one describe the perfection of the Eternal Father's work with mortal words? She called to me and said I was the chosen one. She said I would bring new life to this land."

"New life?" Aislinn challenged. "You've brought death to your brothers."

"No! They are alive. You will see."

Aislinn raised her wheel-cross. It glowed a pale azure, and the monk raised his arms to shield himself, steam wafting up from his robes.

"Why do you do this? I have answered your questions!"

"You have betrayed the Eternal Father," Aislinn said, stepping between Dave and Hector. "You have betrayed your brethren." She held her cross out in front of her, forcing the monk back against the wall.

Out of the corner of her eye, she saw the body of one of Francis' guards lying on the floor. His sightless eyes stared toward the ceiling. Ghastly wounds covered his upper body and neck where the fallen monk had gnawed upon him. She shook her head, trying to clear the image from her mind. In that moment, her light faltered.

With a snarl, the monk lunged at Aislinn, his mouth wide in anticipation.

A silver sabre streaked over her shoulder and plunged into the monk's mouth. At the same time, Aislinn's wheel-cross flared even brighter. The blade exploded out the back of the monk's head, and black ooze spattered the wall.

Dave pushed his sword all the way up to its D-shaped guard, forcing the creature away from Aislinn. Ignoring the revenant's flailing arms, he shoved the monk to his knees and kicked him hard in the chest, dislodging his weapon. As soon as the monk slipped free of the sabre, Hector swung his scimitar and decapitated him.

All four found themselves staring at the body and head as they tried to make sense of what had just happened. Hector was the first to move. He knelt to examine the soldier, while Dave wiped his blade on the monk's robe.

"Is it bad luck to kill a monk?" Dave asked, breaking the silence.

"Probably not, but I wouldn't make a habit of it," Hector answered. He waited expectantly, and when Dave failed to react, he repeated. "Make a *habit* of it?"

When Dave still did not react, he said, "Do you not speak Glaxon? That was funny."

Aislinn rolled her eyes and turned away from the men. She joined Hummingbird, who found an oil lamp on the writing desk and lit it. A warm glow illuminated the basement library.

Atop one of several stacks covering the desk, a book lay open with most of its pages ripped out. Delicate red fingerprints stained the margins, and the uppermost page was partially torn. Aislinn flipped through the remaining pages noting the date in the upper left-hand or right-hand corner. Flowing script, while elegant, made the entries difficult to read.

"I found a diary," Aislinn said. "Most of the pages are torn out, but I have one entry from this month one year ago."

"What does it say?" Hector said, still examining the soldier's wounds.

Aislinn bent closer. "This entry reads August 5, 4236. *Margaret Potter, wife of Hew Potter died today. Survived by her husband and their son, Conrad. She was 49. Whippoorwills in the fog. There must be a way to stop him.*" She turned the book for Hector to see. "The last two lines are in the margin, like it was written later, and fog's underlined... twice."

"Who do they need to stop, her husband or her son?" Hector asked. "Do you think one of them killed her?"

"That seems like something the writer would have mentioned, Hector."

"Whose diary is it?"

Aislinn flipped to the first page of the book and read, "Brother Powell — 4236."

Hector joined her and said, "Seems odd for one of the monks to have written her necrology, don't you think? Father Blackwood sure, but why a monk?"

"Maybe. What about this fog?"

"Let's see if he mentions it anywhere else." Hector searched around the desk while Aislinn flipped through the other entries. Moving on, he pulled book after book off the shelves.

After he had skimmed through several tomes, Aislinn asked, "Find anything?"

"These are all books belonging to Brother Powell: one for each year," said Hector. Holding one open, he handed it to Aislinn. She laid it beside the book on the table and traced a passage with her finger, reading, "August 5, 4235. *Daniel Tanner, age 36. Found dead beside his boat. Survived by his niece Arianna Tanner Miser.*" Scribbled in the margin a single line said, "*The fog has returned.*"

Aislinn rechecked the date, looking back from one book to the other. "It's the same date, a year earlier than Margaret Potter, and it mentions the fog."

"Strange, don't you think? Even stranger, I can't find this year's diary or the one for 4234."

"Speaking of weird, take a look at this." Dave gestured at the mural on the wall. "It's a coastal map, but it's drawn wrong. If I follow this river, it passes near Ruthaer here." He pointed to a circle with the name partially obscured by a bloody thumbprint. Just to the right and above the circle, a jumble of dark red handprints and thick smears completely covered the fresco, destroying whatever information had been there. "If you look down this way, you can see where the south end of the barrier islands should be. But they're drawn as a single landmass."

"Who drew this?" Aislinn said, standing beside him.

"I'd guess one of the monks," Dave answered. "Do you think it's possible the barrier islands were once connected?"

"Maybe," replied Aislinn, "but that would've been ages ago."

"What about this area?" Dave said, indicating the hidden portion of the mural.

"They've always been a maze of islands and channels. I don't remember anyone ever saying otherwise. Isä and I went fishing up there once, but when the tide goes out, the water gets shallow really quick. Easy to get stuck or bust out your hull on the rocks."

Dave studied the smeared mural. "Damn it to hell. Whoever bloodied this map wanted to keep something a secret."

"Find anything?" Sir Francis surveyed the library from the bottom of the stairs. Two of his men were in the stairwell behind him.

"Yes, señor," Hector said. "One of the monks must have invited something in he shouldn't have."

Spying the body on the floor, Sir Francis rushed into the room. Before he could make it across, Hector grabbed him by the arm and said, "Señor, it's not pretty. One of your men lies in the corner."

"I know that monk," Sir Francis said. "That was Brother Powell, the monastery's historian."

Pushing past Hector, the knight knelt beside the cleric, then moved to the dead soldier. "What have I done?" he whispered.

Aislinn opened her mouth to ask Sir Francis the myriad questions forming in her mind, but Hummingbird shook her head, surreptitiously pointing toward the guards on the stairs.

Sir Francis turned from the body at his feet. "Corporal Ponds! You and Jared find Big Mike," he ordered. "Tell him to take four men and bring Father Blackwood back here. I don't want any civilians — I just want him. Got that? And tell him to bring enough digging tools for everyone. If we hurry, we can bury the monks before sundown."

CHAPTER 8
BLOODY BATHS

August 2, 4237 K.E.

6:06pm

Weary soldiers formed ranks in front of the Meeting House. Lagging behind them, a single mule pulled a wooden cart into town. Three corpses wrapped in linens lay in the back among the shovels. Aislinn, Hummingbird, Dave, and Hector rode beside the cart in silence. They had spent the better part of the afternoon collecting bodies and prepping them for burial.

Aislinn helped Father Blackwood administer last rites, but Hector wondered if it was a wasted effort. The nature of the monks' deaths combined with the monastery's desecration led him to believe the men's spirits had been gone long before Timothy and his patrol stumbled onto the scene.

The smell of cook-fires drifted across the square, and Dave's stomach rumbled. "Is there a good place to eat?" he asked.

"How can you think of food?" Aislinn asked. She raised a hand as if to cover her mouth, looked at it, and groaned. "I would go jump in the river to wash this off, but the gators might mistake me for their supper."

"I'm hungry," Dave shrugged and followed his nose. It led him to a two-story building with a wooden sign hanging from a yardarm over the front door. The sign read 'Griffon Inn' in bold blue letters. Under the name was the image of a creature with the body and tail of a lion, but the head, wings, and claws of an eagle. Beneath it, a smaller sign hanging from a pair of hooks read, "Rooms for Rent."

Two rusty horseshoes hung above the door, one facing up like a cup and the other pointed down. Lead paned windows, with their sashes raised and shutters thrown open to invite a breeze, emitted the warm, inviting glow of lanterns hanging from the rafters. Aislinn pointed to the iron boot scrapers shaped like fish with raised dorsal fins positioned on either side of the porch steps. While she and Hector showed Hummingbird how to use the devices, Dave strode into the inn.

"Hey!" shouted a portly woman in her early fifties. "I run a respectable establishment here." She charged across the dining room, arms spread wide as if to corral him.

Dave backpedaled, rejoining the others on the porch.

The woman glared from the doorway. "You can just turn around and go back to where you came from."

Hector took in their bedraggled appearance and could only guess what the innkeeper was thinking. Thankfully, the dining room was empty.

"Señora, forgive our appearance. We just came from assisting Sir Francis," Hector said. "We're tired and would like a room and baths, if you have any available."

The innkeeper eyed each of them. "Two rooms: one for the men and one for the women, unless you're married. It's a half-shil per day for each room, and two-pence apiece for the baths."

"Agreed," Hector said, handing her two silver coins.

She slipped the money into her apron and said, "Welcome to the Griffon Inn. I'm Jenna Griffon and my husband's Sidney. I'll show you to your rooms."

She walked them to the back of the inn where spiral stairs led to the second floor. Oil paintings lined the wall, each of them sunrises over the marsh and islands.

"This is your room," Mrs. Griffon said to Aislinn and Hummingbird. "Come to the kitchen after your baths, and I'll give you a tincture for those bruises." She gave Hector and Dave a narrow-eyed look. "You men will be across the hall."

"Gracias, señora," Hector replied.

"Baths are out back. I'll have Rhonda make sure the water is fresh and ask her to do something with your clothes." Eyeing Dave's tattooed chest and arms warily, she added, "Shirts are required at the dinner table."

"I don't have a shirt," Dave growled.

"Then you don't eat."

Aislinn stepped between them and said, "We'll clean up before we come to the dining room. However, we only have what we're wearing right now. Do you have a shirt he can have? We'll pay for it."

"What?!" Dave exclaimed.

"Shut up," Aislinn said out of the corner of her mouth.

"I'll see what I can do," Mrs. Griffon replied.

As she left, Dave said, "I don't know why I have to wear a shirt or have a bloody bath."

Aislinn gave him a pointed sniff. She made a gagging sound and shuddered at the mixture of sweat, saltwater, mud, and everything else he had been through that day. "Stop complaining," she said, backing away. "At least you get to eat."

ଔଶୀ

7:58pm

"Milady, you're up early," a sultry voice said from the bathtub.

Shadows crossed the bedroom floor as the sun dipped below the horizon. A tall, lean woman with long black hair stood stiffly in the doorway. She wore a long-sleeved, low-cut black dress that revealed tawny skin. A bone mask hid her face — a mask that moved as though it was something alive. Strange sigils etched into its surface glowed eerily in the half-light. She looked down at the woman in the tub and said, "You went back to the monastery."

As the room grew darker, the bone mask morphed into high cheekbones, arched eyebrows, and a narrow face that would have been beautiful if not for its coldness.

While the lady was winter, the woman in the tub was summer. A long, elegant leg stretched luxuriously from the soapy bath water. Lustrous brown hair framed an angelic face with luminous blue eyes and full lips. She exuded sexuality like an expensive perfume. It touched and caressed the senses, with only the barest tease of things to come. Leathery wings like those of a bat lay nestled behind her.

"Of course I went back!" exclaimed the creature in the tub. "You ordered me to cover the map and retrieve the monk's journals. I just did it my way."

The shadows behind the masked woman coalesced into a ghostly knight. His form flickered in and out of existence even as his sepulchral voice filled the room. "You destroyed the monks. They were my children."

"I couldn't resist." The woman dipped underneath the water and came back up with a splash. "Don't worry. I left you one."

"Magali, you will do as I say."

Melodic laugher filled the room. "I do as you say as long as it suits me. You have no power over me. Not like Mistress Consuelo."

The woman at the doorway stepped forward, and the spectral shape gripping her shoulders grew larger. His voice took on an ominous rumble. "You do as I say, demon, or I will send you back to the Abyss."

Magali sat up straight and said, "You can't do that."

"Try me."

She eyed the spectre and the masked woman in his grasp. Giving the dark shape a coy smile, the demoness said, "Punish me if you can, ghost, but I am not yours to command."

The dark form continued to flicker like an image on a zoetrope, but its voice spoke clearly. "The daughter of Alaric Yves has returned, and she has power."

"Perhaps when compared to that pathetic priest, Cecil Blackwood," Magali scoffed, "but she will be just as helpless against Mistress Consuelo."

"She destroyed the sea captain on his own ship. Helplessness is not one of her attributes."

The demoness smirked at the ghost. "Surely you don't fear a lone woman."

"Aislinn isn't alone. She escaped my storm with an Espian bounty hunter, an archer, and an elven empath."

Concentration creased Magali's features. "Finally."

The ghost surged into the room and loomed over the tub. "Forget why you came here!"

"You still need to get rid of them," she said, petulantly. Staring at the entity above her, she continued, "It will be easiest if we catch them by surprise."

"They are of no matter."

Splashing the dark form with water, Magali said, "Of course they matter. If anyone is going to interfere with your plans, it will be Damage, Inc. They know who I am, and they know Mistress Consuelo."

The spectral shape backed away and said, "Very well. I will take care of the Yves woman tonight. You can have the others."

"I can't go out like this. Not tonight. I don't have anything to wear." Magali smirked. "Besides, I want to prepare something special for them, something deserving of Damage, Inc."

"If they are as dangerous as you say, do not dally with them, demon."

The demoness smiled and slid underwater. When she came up, she motioned toward a corner of the bedroom. "Come to me, girl." A tall, teenage girl with freckled cheeks approached with her eyes fixed on those of the demoness.

"No, don't!" another voice begged from the same corner. It was the girl's father.

Staring straight ahead, the young woman knelt at the side of the tub. She held out her arms over the water, wrists up. In her hand, she gripped a silver dagger. The demoness sat up in the water, her legs tucked underneath her. The spade-shaped tip of her tail flicked from side to side in the air.

"Do it," the demoness said. Excitement sparkled in her eyes.

"No!" the father's voice croaked.

The girl slid the tip of the dagger up her wrist, finding the artery nested amongst the tendons and cartilage. At first, it did not appear she had cut deep enough, but then a thin red line of blood welled up. Magali grasped the girl's hand and bent it back. The wound gaped. The girl's lifeblood squirted out with each heartbeat, leaving a warm trail down the demon's breast. It dripped into the water, forming red clouds.

The demoness peered into the girl's eyes, feeding on her innocence. Taking the dagger from her victim, Magali slid it along the girl's other wrist. A small gasp escaped the girl's lips. Skin opened and blood ran freely, turning the water pink, then a deeper red.

"Consuelo, come join me," Magali said, holding the girl's hands.

The tall, icy woman eyed the blood hungrily, and she took a half-step forward. Just as quickly, her expression went blank, and she stood immobile. The man's voice said, "Consuelo is mine."

"She will kill you once she's free."

Discordant masculine laughter erupted from the spectre-ridden woman. At odds with the rage flashing in her eyes, the phantom's voice issuing from Consuelo's lips was amused. "She will never be free. Even now, the mask she wears devours her. In another cycle of the moon, the vampire will be all that remains." She backed out of the room, a marionette rather than the sorceress who bound a demon to her service or the vampire whose power the bone mask was meant to give her. Seconds later, the sound of a closing door echoed through the house.

The demoness returned its attention to the girl, whose eyes had begun to close. Strength flowed from the young body, and Magali let her slump over the side of the tub, dropping her hands in the water. Holding the girl's face, Magali watched intently as she drew in ragged breaths. The demoness leaned forward and pressed her mouth over the girl's, drawing her victim's final breath into herself.

Magali released her victim, allowing the dead girl's head to thump against the side of the tub as the corpse slid to the floor. The demoness sank under the cloudy water with barely a ripple. Shadows stretched across the room, punctuated by an old man's sobbing.

Lighting a candle, the demoness gazed into the dresser mirror. The freckled face and nubile body reflected back at her was an exact match of the dead girl sprawled on the floor by the bloodstained tub.

"Hello, Allyrian Carmichael, teamster's daughter," she greeted her new form just to hear the timber and pitch of her stolen voice. "Let's see what mischief we can get into."

Turning around, she spied the dead girl's father in the corner.

CHAPTER 9
COUNT DODZ

August 2, 4237 K.E.

8:17pm

His hair still damp from his bath, Dave tugged on his boots. In a feat that bordered on miraculous, the innkeepers' wench, Rhonda, had cleaned the mud and gore from his clothes without leaving them wet. He glared at the soft, white cotton shirt draped across his bed. The laces up the front and billowy sleeves weren't what he would have chosen, but that was an argument he lost an hour ago. Snatching the shirt from the bed, he pulled it over his head and rolled the sleeves up to his elbows. In a final act of defiance, he left the laces undone and stomped down the stairs.

At a round table in the corner of the common room, his companions waited with an empty chair already pushed out for him. Rhonda came by with a metal bucket filled with red potatoes, small ears of white corn, onions, sausage, blue crab, and shrimp. She wore a low-cut dress that exposed an ample amount of cleavage. When Dave sat down, she leaned over the table and asked, "Is there anything else I can get you?"

Dave tried to look anywhere but at Rhonda. Aislinn stifled a laugh and replied, "We'll need another bucket for the shells."

"Be right back."

The spicy aroma from the seafood boil wafted over them. Dave popped a sausage into his mouth and set about picking meat from a crab. Beside him, Hummingbird nibbled on an ear of corn. He offered her a lump of claw meat. "Here, try this."

She looked at the broken, spider-like body on the table and shook her head.

"Why not?" he demanded.

She wrinkled her nose. "It's a scavenger, and it was in the creek this morning," she signed.

Dave frowned and glanced over at Hector and Aislinn, who were too busy peeling shrimp to notice Hummingbird's answer. He stuffed the crabmeat in his mouth. "More for me."

All too soon, they emptied the first bucket and ordered another.

A small group of soldiers took a table near the four friends. Behind them, Corporal Aaron Ponds entered carrying a quart jar filled with an opaque liquid. Two peaches swirled around its bottom. Mrs. Griffon frowned. "Go easy on that stuff," she warned.

"Yes, ma'am," he said.

Dave spotted the jar and asked, "What's that?"

"Peach homebrew," Aaron replied.

Dragging his chair over to their table, Dave asked, "Mind if I try some?"

"Dave?" Hector said.

"I just want a taste."

Aaron cast a furtive glance at Aislinn before handing his jar to the tall archer. Dave took a swig and felt the fiery liquid burn all the way down. He closed his eyes, and, for a brief moment, the vampire's voice in his head quieted.

Dave gave the jar back to Aaron and slapped the palm of his hand on the table. "Good stuff. Did you make that?"

"My uncle did," Aaron answered as he took a swallow then passed the jar around the table. On the third round, the young soldier asked the question on all their minds. "Who do you think killed the monks?"

Dave wiped his mouth with the back of his hand and growled, "Demons." A wave of shock and fear washed over the soldiers.

Overhearing his reply, Hector said, "Dave, you've had enough."

"Are you sure?" one of the soldiers asked.

"Yeah. We've seen it before."

Another soldier looked as if he might throw up.

Hector pulled the jar from Dave's hands. "Amigo, leave it. You're scaring them."

"Hector, they need to know the truth."

"Demons? What do you know of *demons*, sluga?" a man seated alone on the far side of the room asked in a thick Rhodinan accent. He wore a high-collared white shirt made of the finest silk, and draped over the chair behind him was a small, fanciful cape trimmed in silky, black mink fur.

Dave jumped to his feet, knocking over his chair. He placed a hand on the hilt of his sabre and said, "I'm no one's servant."

"You speak Rhodinan. Good," the man said as he rose, brandishing a politician's smile. With a flourish, he bowed, and said, "I am Count Dodz."

Hector walked around the soldier's table and stepped in front of Dave. With Aislinn and Hummingbird behind him, the bounty hunter returned the bow and replied, "Milord, I am Hector de los Santos, and my companions are Aislinn Yves, Hummingbird, and the tall gentleman there is Dave Blood."

"Rad znakomstvu s vami," Count Dodz said, gesturing to the empty chairs at his table. "Please." The four sat down and watched as he cut a delicate bite of rare steak, dipped it in the au jus on his plate, and chewed it.

"Señor, you were on the *Inquisitor.* What happened?"

"A catastrophe, no? The storm came upon us sudden during the night, and the kapitan sought shelter. He picked the wrong channel."

"What about the crew?" Hector asked.

"Washed overboard. Lady Fortune smiled on me. When the ship ran aground, I was only knocked insensible. I woke in my kabina and everyone was gone." The count studied the four friends and said, "You saw something today, no? You mentioned demons?"

Hector waved a hand as if to brush away the idea. "There was an attack on the monastery, and all the monks were killed."

"Is nasty business, demons," the count said, then swallowed another bite of steak.

"Count, there was a rather large hole in the side of your ship. Do you know how it got there? Perhaps something you were carrying in the hold?"

"Nothing, mes'ye. The ship's hold was empty. She carried myself, my betrothed, and her two servants."

Pulling the necklace with the copper rectangle from his pouch, Hector dropped it on the table beside the count's plate. "Then you will recognize this."

The count picked up the slave badge and rubbed his thumb over the Cyrillic writing. "Her name was Klara. Did you find her?"

"Yes. Her body got caught in a tidal pool, and we brought her here to the Meeting House. Father Blackwood plans to bury her tomorrow."

"Did you find anyone else?" asked the count coolly.

"I'm sorry, Milord. We only found the girl."

"Prayhaps there is still hope, no?"

"Klara was a slave, wasn't she?" Dave asked. The distaste in his voice permeated the air. The other diners in the room fell silent, watching to see what would happen.

The count's eyes narrowed, and he replied, "Da. She was slave, but she had good life."

"She died a slave," Dave said, his voice growing louder as his anger built, "wearing a sarding bill of sale!"

Count Dodz nodded toward Hummingbird, and she shrank down in her chair, unwilling to meet his gaze. "I recognize the slave flower on her wrist. Ask the pornai if she has good life. She is yours, da?"

"No, she belongs to herself," Dave replied through gritted teeth. "She is free."

"Free? Once a slave, always a slave. That is the way life works. Maybe you sell her to me?"

Dave exploded to his feet in rage, pushing over the table. The plate and silverware clattered to the floor. He grabbed the Rhodinan by his shirt and threw him against the wall. Count Dodz held up his hands to block the archer's fist, which reared back like a coiled snake.

Two small hands wrapped around Dave's fist and eased it down. While Hummingbird tugged the archer back toward their table, the count fluffed his shirt, shaking out the wrinkles.

"Count Dodz, are you alright?" asked Mr. Griffon. Mrs. Griffon and Rhonda busied themselves with righting the table and clearing the mess from the floor.

"Da, just the drink talking," the count replied calmly, but his frost-blue eyes betrayed his ire as they shot daggers at Dave. Count Dodz grabbed his cape from the floor and clasped it around his neck. He bowed to the innkeeper and stalked outside.

"That is an evil man," Hummingbird signed.

"Did you see his arm?" Hector whispered as he watched the count leave.

"I wasn't looking at the bastard's arms," Dave said.

"The one I saw was covered in half-healed scratches and at least one bite. It looked like the count tangled with a vampire."

Aaron walked up beside the archer and handed him the half-full jar of homebrew. "Come on. Why don't y'all join us?"

 C3ED

8:56pm

Aaron's companions had four chairs added to their table. The corporal smiled and courteously offered Aislinn the seat beside his own. Hummingbird sat on Aislinn's other side, leaving Dave and Hector to fill the remaining spots. Dave sipped from the jar in his hand and passed it to Hummingbird. She sniffed the jar's contents, scrunched her nose, and handed it to Aislinn.

Aislinn took a tentative sip. The syrupy sweet concoction coated her tongue and throat, followed by a warm burn in her belly. "Wow," she breathed. "That is some good stuff." She took a second sip before passing it on to her left. "Corporal Ponds, how long has your family lived in Ruthaer?"

"Just call me Aaron."

"Aaron," she repeated.

"Been here most of my life," he replied. "My dad and uncle are carpenters, and my older brother carves." He gestured to the inn's fireplace. "That's his handiwork there." A griffon head and forelimbs supported either end of the heavy mantle, each feather carved in such detail, Aislinn half expected them to be soft to the touch.

"It's beautiful," she replied. "Do you do woodwork, too?"

"Nah, I don't have the patience for it." He grinned. "I got banned from the shop after I made practice swords for myself and my friends out of Espian spicewood Pa had set aside for a fancy hope chest."

The jar came around again, and Aislinn took another sip. "The town has changed a lot since my mother and I left. Sir Francis is the only person I've recognized so far. He mentioned Tallinn is still manning the lighthouse. Is there anyone else here from the old days?"

Aaron shrugged. "There's a few of the founding families left. Let's see... Other than Sir Francis and Tallinn, there's the Brooks widow and Carradoc — he carved the statue of your father at Fisherman's Wharf."

"Eryl Morris runs the farrier barn with his old man," another soldier supplied.

"Don't forget Hew Potter and his family, and the Tidewells own most of the fishing fleet," said a third.

Aaron nodded. "I think that's about it. Wait, the Weavers have been here forever, too."

Aislinn leaned back in her chair, mulling over whom she may know, but all she had were vague childhood impressions. If Dave was right and there was a demon in town, things were going to go from bad to worse. The bigger questions, in her mind, were whether the revenants and the demon were connected, and why Francis hadn't sought help from either the Queen or the Church.

It was too much to hope they had destroyed all the revenants. If anything, there would be more. Damage, Inc. had that kind of luck.

"What can you tell us about Count Dodz?" Hector asked.

"Not much. He keeps to himself mostly," Aaron said.

"Or hangs out at the shrievalty with Sir Francis," added one of the soldiers.

"Did any of you know Margaret Potter?" Aislinn asked.

The patrolmen shook their heads.

"I remember her," said Rhonda. "Margaret died last year, didn't she? Fell off her horse." The barmaid leaned between Dave and Hummingbird to collect empty plates. The archer shifted toward Hector to give the server more room. Even so, she brushed against his shoulder and gave him a sly wink.

"That's not what I heard," Mrs. Griffon said softly, wiping down a table. "She was attacked by ghosts."

"Ghosts?" Hector asked.

"Mark my words. You'll see 'em too."

The inn fell silent. Aislinn looked around and realized they were the last patrons in the dining room.

A log cracked and shifted in the fireplace, causing everyone to jump.

Mrs. Griffon finished wiping her table and moved closer, as if afraid someone might overhear their conversation. "The fog's got everyone on edge. It comes every night, now."

"The fog?" Aislinn asked. "What about the Rhodinan ship?"

"Forget the ship," Mrs. Griffon answered. "The fog's been here longer. There are *things* in the fog. Evil lurks just out of sight, and it's growing. Not on the surface, mind you, but deep down, rotting everything. It wasn't noticeable before..." Her lips pressed together in a thin, white line, and she trembled as she cast a glance at the darkness beyond the windows.

"And now?" Hector prompted.

"We've had a number of disappearances the past few months," Aaron answered. "Animals, mostly, but people too. Old Man Cunningham just up and vanished into the fog. I watched him walk right into it. No one's seen or heard from him since. Ms. Garfield, too, and now this business at the monastery. Best not go anywhere at night, not even the privy, if you want to see the dawn."

CHAPTER 10
NIGHT CHILLS

August 2, 4237 K.E.

11:00pm

Scattered streetlamps twinkled along Ruthaer's main street, valiantly fighting against the blackness of the night. Locals had long since hurried home and locked their doors.

From the treetops, tiny birds chanted, *"Whip-poor-will...whip-poor-will...whip-poor-will."*

Thick coils of mist rose from the river and slithered through the streets. From the sea, a fog tsunami rolled over the barrier islands and marsh, overwhelming the forest in its obscuring mass. Still it came, swallowing farms, sucking up the tendrils from the river, drowning the town and its inhabitants. Only when it passed the desecrated monastery did the wall halt its relentless advance.

Ghostly shapes with tortured faces floated past sunken buildings, plucking at shuttered windows, staring longingly at the sleeping forms inside. Above the doorways of true believers and the truly superstitious, the cold iron of double horseshoes emitted a pale glow.

The barking of a lone dog abruptly ended in a cry of pain. The protest of hinges preceded a man's voice. "Buster! Where are you, boy?" Boards creaked, followed by a gasp, a thud, then silence.

Whip-poor-will...whip-poor-will...whip-poor-will.

A small girl with empty eyes wearing a ragged dress stepped out of the fog. Klara moved with a purpose toward the Griffon Inn.

⚜

11:25pm

Aislinn pulled the blanket tighter. A chill had seeped into her room and held her prisoner in that realm between sleeping and waking. Her eyes slid open. Light from the lamp in the hallway filtered through a small gap at the bottom of her door. She cast a groggy glance toward Hummingbird, who slept soundly in her bed on the opposite side. Sighing, she curled onto her side and pulled the blanket up so only her eyes and nose remained exposed.

The door creaked. Aislinn opened her eyes again. The room looked the same, but something felt *wrong*.

Her eyelids were so heavy. They slid closed, and she fought them open once more. A small silhouette at the foot of the bed resolved into the dead girl from the marsh. The apparition drifted closer. Dark blood oozed from her shredded skin and dripped on the floor. Klara's eyes glowed milky white.

Aislinn jolted awake but couldn't move. Her voice refused to obey her need to call out. Aethereal hands from below grabbed her wrists and ankles; others reached across her body. Bitter cold seeped into her soul.

The room turned to grey mist and her ghostly captors dragged her down through the bed and floor. Aislinn fell to the kitchen below. Grey men with hollow eyes surrounded her. Rolling to her feet, she darted under a pair of grasping hands toward the door, only to feel something snag the back of her borrowed nightgown. The collar tightened around her throat. One of the grey men snatched back on the fistful of soft fabric, and she felt it rip, allowing icy air to slide down her bare back.

Aislinn spun and punched the shadowy being. More grey men swarmed into the kitchen, cutting off the exits. Those closest pushed in from all sides, grasping at her hair and clothes. The nightgown shredded in their rough hands as they grabbed her and dragged her outside. Aislinn tried to scream, to shout a prayer, anything, but no sound came. Panic-stricken, she thrashed wildly. Oblivious to her struggles, the grey men picked her up and carried her down the street. Other grey shapes approached and tried to reach her, but the ones who held her pushed them away.

A waist-high wall of pale stone blocks topped with wrought iron spikes appeared out of the mists ahead. Aislinn renewed her struggles when she realized they were taking her to the graveyard. She managed to get an arm free, but too many held her captive. They walked through the open archway, past carved monuments and simple markers, to the churchyard's far corner, where workmen had demolished a section of wall to accommodate the growing burial ground. Only then did the world become more solid.

The grey men faded away, and Aislinn found herself at the foot of a freshly dug grave. A mound of dirt lay to one side. Klara suddenly materialized behind Aislinn and shoved her into the six-foot deep hole. She landed face-down, stiff and aching from the cold. Gnashing her teeth, Aislinn tried to push up onto her hands and knees, but a heavy blanket of icy air pinned her in place.

Fog seeped up from below and trickled through the walls of the grave. It condensed above her and fell like rain. Under her hands, the saturated earth turned to mud. The bottom of the grave grew deeper and stickier, like quicksand, sucking her downward. She clawed at the grave walls, but they crumbled under her hands. Her voice remained frozen in the confines of her throat; there would be no cries for help. Panic railed against rational thought to the galloping rhythm of her heartbeat.

For a moment, her upper torso cleared the mud, then the wall gave way and she plunged down again. It was all she could do to keep her head above the sludge. Her breathing grew more and more labored in the water-laden air. Mud slithered up her neck and licked the edge of her earlobes.

A sonorous thump echoed in the night. Eerie green faerie-fire blossomed overhead, consuming the fog. The chill faded, leaving the night hot and humid. No longer drowning in mud, Aislinn lay half-buried in loose soil. She rolled over, gasping for air.

Before she could sit up, a short, gangly-bodied gnome sailed over the edge of the pit and landed at her feet with a sickening thud. Mouth agape, his saucer-sized eyes and swollen tongue bulged out like some horrible caricature of a living being.

At the top of the grave, an elf covered head to toe in black rags gazed down at Aislinn. His almond-shaped eyes shimmered silver in the pearly moonlight and, to her, he seemed surprised, though it was difficult to tell with most of him hidden.

Aislinn amended her first impression. Not an elf: a dærganfae.

He jumped down, planting his feet on either side of her hips. Dærganfae were merciless killers, yet this one had just saved her from being buried alive. She reached up, daring to hope he would help her out of the hole. Instead, he knelt and grasped her head with claw-like fingers. His thumbs pressed against her temples and his fingertips dug into the base of her skull. His eyes captured hers. It was like staring at the full moon from a mountaintop.

Too late, she struggled against his grip. Pain seared through her as he forced his way into her mind. For a brief moment, she held him at bay, then they shared a consciousness. Memories raced past her mind's eye. The dærganfae's power bored deeper and deeper.

Sweat streamed from her body as she struggled to break free. Even though he still clutched her head, it felt as if the dærganfae grasped her soul.

Her captor raised a hand. Twined around his pale fingers, bronze tendrils of her spirit stretched out from her body. Lightning sparked along the tendrils' lengths. When the dærganfae turned his hand, webs of consciousness tugged and pulled, and she arched her back in pain. His almond shaped eyes narrowed as he studied the flickering energy.

Aislinn realized she was going to die. "Eternal Father," she silently prayed, "please help Hector, Dave, and Hummingbird save Ruthaer. Be with them when I'm gone. Please comfort Emä and Brand." At the thought of Brand, energy pulsed through her, in time with her heartbeat. The dærganfae jerked back, releasing her. She felt the second heartbeat again, stronger this time.

A cool mountain breeze blew through her, giving her strength, and for a moment, she was with Brand. The bronze dragon lay curled in sleep amidst his hoard, his young body transitioning to that of a juvenile. Steam trailed from his nostrils, and he pawed at the ground.

Aislinn sat up with a gasp. The sweat-stained sheet fell away. She was in her room at the inn. She drew up her knees and hugged them. It was just a nightmare.

Her heart throbbed in her chest, as though it had grown too big for her body. For a moment, she feared it would burst, until Brand's warm, muzzy thoughts blanketed her.

"*Sleep.*" The dragon's deep voice in her mind was comforting and soporific.

She lay back down, oblivious to the damp bedding. Instead, she felt Brand's warm scales. His heart beat strong and in harmony with hers.

CHAPTER 11
TALLINN

August 3, 4237 K.E.

7:04am

With tattered remnants of a nightmare drifting at the edges of her memory, Aislinn cracked one bleary eye. Sunlight slipped through the window shutter to reveal Hummingbird's empty bed. More exhausted than when she'd fallen asleep, Aislinn swung her feet to the floor and realized she had lost her nightgown. She put her head in her hands and looked down at her toes.

They were black with dirt.

She was filthy, naked, and her muscles ached. It felt as if she had been fighting the entire night — or been in a grave. The vestiges of her nightmare coalesced into solid memory, sending a shiver coursing through her body.

The ghosts and graveyard had been real.

Trying to distract herself, she moved through a series of stretches to loosen cramped muscles. A sharp pain stabbed behind her left ear when she rolled her head from one side to the other. Aislinn ran her fingers into her hair, dislodging a shower of dirt, and grimaced at the mess. Probing with just her fingertips, she found scabs at the base of her hairline. Aislinn pulled back her tangled hair and leaned toward the mirror on the chifforobe door.

An angry bruise surrounded two blood crusted lesions. The wounds were almost identical to the scars Dave bore from his encounter with the vampire Hector dubbed 'Lady D.' Unbidden, the memory of Dave under the vampire's control burst into her mind. Aislinn stumbled back from the mirror and sat down hard on the end of her bed.

She searched her memories, but the space between her encounter in the graveyard and falling asleep with Brand's comforting presence remained frighteningly blank. She could only assume it was the dærganfae who bit her.

Her hands shook as she thought about the savage killer Dave had become under Lady D's influence, unable to recognize his friends. No, they were more than friends — they were family — and Lady D had made Dave see them as his prey. Cold dread swept through Aislinn. Would she eventually become a vicious monster? Aislinn thought of Brand and her mother and wrestled her emotions under control. If necessary, Hector and Damage, Inc. would stop her.

She snatched the stained sheet from the bed and wrapped it around herself. Clothes in hand, she listened long and hard at the door before opening it. Fearful of meeting someone along the way, she raced down the back stairs to the bathhouse.

C3&80

7:38am

At a table beside a bay window in the Griffon Inn's common room, Hector, Dave, and Hummingbird ate breakfast. On the porch, Mr. Griffon stood on a chair, hammer in one hand, nailing a pair of horseshoes above the doorframe. When finished, he jumped off the chair and carried it back inside, muttering to himself about hooligans stealing his horseshoes.

Mrs. Griffon sat down beside Hummingbird and said, "We had two deaths last night."

Hector put his fork down and said, "Really? What happened?"

"Father Blackwood and the gravediggers found the bodies in the graveyard this morning: a pair of gnomes from the quarry. I overheard one of the soldiers say they didn't have a mark on them."

"Quarry?"

The matron pointed out the window toward the granite mass filling the skyline. "Yeah, across the river, on the north side of the dome. I can't imagine what they were doing over here at night. Normally, they keep to themselves. And you know what else?"

"What?" Hector asked. He could see the woman was torn between her desire to gossip and her worry for the town.

"That girl you brought in yesterday." The woman leaned forward, a glimmer of fear in her eyes.

"¿Sí?"

"They found her body in the graveyard, too. *Decapitated*," she whispered.

Hector glanced at Dave. He didn't need Hummingbird's empathic ability to know the archer shared his unease.

Aislinn slipped in the back door. Her damp hair hung in loose waves, and he could see a troubled look in her eyes as she crossed the room.

"¡Buenos días, amiga!" called Hector. "We wondered if you planned to sleep all day. Mrs. Griffon was just telling us there was more trouble last night."

Mrs. Griffon jumped up and said, "Here, dear, I'll get you something from the kitchen."

"No thanks, Mrs. Griffon. I'm not hungry," Aislinn replied.

Hummingbird threw Aislinn a quizzical look but Aislinn ignored her. She walked to the door. The fog had burned off and sunlight flooded the streets. A crowd milled about near the churchyard wall, old and young alike craning to see what was happening within.

Hector joined her and followed her gaze. Sir Francis appeared to be trying to reassure and disperse the crowd of onlookers. "You want to go check it out?"

Aislinn jumped at the sound of his voice. She crossed her arms and gripped her biceps. "No. I need some fresh air. Let's get our boat and go out to the lighthouse."

"You sure, cariña?"

"Yeah. It's past time we go see Tallinn."

The trip back to the cave was quiet. Aislinn's somber mood infected everyone. Hector and Dave busied themselves stepping the boat's mast and tying off the lines while Aislinn and Hummingbird dug through the lockers to find a change of clothes.

The sails were of no use until they were clear of the cliffs, so Hector and Hummingbird took up the craft's oars and rowed them out of the crevice. As the smooth stone walls glided by, Hector found himself thinking about the strange mural at the monastery and imagining what it would have been like if the barrier islands were joined.

Once past the rocks, Hummingbird and Hector stowed their oars and clambered to different ends of the boat. With Dave pointing to this line or that, they pulled hand over hand, raising the mainsail and jib. As soon as the canvas was up, it snapped tight and filled with wind.

The current pulled them southeast. Dave manned the tiller and brought them about in a wide loop. "Where to?"

Aislinn pointed north. "Fangpoint Lighthouse, please."

"Yeah, I know that, but it's on top of a big-ass cliff. Where are we supposed to go ashore?"

"About three hundred yards upriver, there's a cove with a dock and stairs to the top," Aislinn replied.

"It's a real cove, right? Not some pissant crack and a waterlogged cave like that *inlet* we just left?"

Aislinn turned her back on the archer.

Grumbling to himself, Dave pulled on the tiller while Hummingbird adjusted the rigging. The boat instantly responded, slicing through the water like a knife.

Aislinn huddled at the front of the boat, staring out to sea. A wave broke on the hull and sprayed her. She didn't seem to notice.

"Are you alright?" Hector asked, taking a nearby seat.

"I'm fine," Aislinn said.

"Aislinn, you're a million miles away. What's wrong?"

"Do you ever wonder why the blind can't see us? Or why the deaf don't hear us?"

Hector was quiet for a moment. He watched three pelicans fly in formation, low over the water, and said, "They can't see the light or feel the vibrations we call sound."

"Right. It's not that the light doesn't exist. They just can't see it."

"Alright..."

"What if the dead are the same way?"

"What do you mean?"

"Well, we can't see them, we can't hear them, but they're all around us. To the dead, wouldn't we appear deaf, dumb, and blind?"

"Maybe, but don't the dead move on? Go to Heaven or Hell?"

"Some do, but what about the ones stuck here? Remember how the ship captain disappeared and reappeared? What if he simply moved where we couldn't see him?"

"¿El reino de los muertos?"

"Yes."

Her gaze drifted across the rolling swells. Another wave splashed over the gunwale and Hector wondered if she had any more to say.

"¿Qué pasa con el reino de los muertos?" Hector asked gently.

"I went out in the fog last night," Aislinn said.

"What! Aaron warned us not to go out alone." Alarm made Hector's voice sharper than he meant, and he struggled to soften his tone. "Aislinn, you know we never split the party; bad things happen."

"I wasn't given a choice," she replied with a shiver.

Hector wanted to know how someone forced Aislinn out of the inn without raising a ruckus, but he could see from her expression that she wasn't ready to talk about it. Instead, he reached over and cupped her hand. "So, what did you find out?" His gentle words masked the worry he felt in the pit of his stomach.

"It's not really fog," Aislinn answered. "I remember a discussion I had with Phaedrus years ago. He called it Luminiferous Aether, the universal medium. It's funny. I don't remember how the subject came up, but Jasper and I talked about it one night over the campfire. He said mages call it the 'Misty Road' — the land of the hollow men. I think it may be purgatory."

"What are you talking about?"

"Hector, I saw ghosts everywhere in the fog."

"Ghosts? What were they doing?"

"What would you do if you were trapped and suddenly found a way out?"

"Try to escape," Hector said, his voice quiet. "So, you think someone opened a gateway to this aethereal realm?"

"The veil between the realms of the living and the dead couldn't thin this much naturally. So yeah, someone with serious magic has to be behind this. Someone who can control the weather."

"Maybe it *is* a demon like Dave said yesterday."

"We've fought demons before. Ghosts and revenants aren't their bailiwick. Even with their eternity of experience, they're still just personifications of the nine vices: gluttony, lust, avarice, indolence, pride, despair, wrath, envy, and cruelty. There may be a demon, but I believe something else is here as well. What I don't understand is how, or even if, the disappearances Aaron mentioned and the murders at the monastery are related."

Lost in thought, Hector turned northward, letting the sea breeze wash over him, and the lighthouse came into view.

Perched atop a seventy-five-foot cliff forming the north bank of the Emmassa River mouth, Fangpoint Lighthouse stood vigil over the sea. Glowing whitewash covered the round tower, except for a black zigzag pattern near the top that gave the impression of a mouthful of fangs. Above that, a narrow gallery surrounded the copper framed lantern.

A wide channel cut behind the pinnacle into a rounded cove with a rocky beach and a small wooden dock. Dave aimed straight for it. As they drew closer, Hector and Hummingbird furled the sails, and Aislinn grabbed the forward mooring line. She looped it around a timber piling while Dave tied up the stern. With the craft secure, the four leapt onto the dock.

A rush of wings drew their eyes toward the sun, where they glimpsed a white horse with a pink nose and golden wings diving toward them. Momentarily blinded, they each dropped into a crouch and reached for their weapons. The hippoætós' shadow passed overhead as it banked and landed on the beach. It turned toward them, pawing at the ground, and dipped its head to reveal two magnificent, ringed horns that arched backwards several feet and ended at sharp points. Behind it, steep steps carved into the cliff led up to the lighthouse. High above them at the head of the stairs, dark shapes ambled along the precipice.

"Is it safe?" Dave asked.

Aislinn shrugged with a sly smile. She walked slowly toward the hippoætós with her hand out, palm-up. "It's good to see you again, Tasunke," Aislinn said. The winged horse stamped and snorted.

As they approached, Hector noticed the steed's sagging skin, and its sway back. Even though it looked old, there was no mistaking the fierceness in its eyes.

"We've come to see Tallinn," Aislinn said. The horse tossed its head and nickered. "It's alright, old man. We're friends." She rested her hand on his muzzle and rubbed his wrinkled nose. "Guys, meet Tasunke."

"You know him?" Hector asked. He kept a cautious distance. Hummingbird rushed past the men and wrapped her thin arms around the horse's neck. Tasunke rested his head over her shoulder and rubbed his cheek and chin along her back.

"You don't see that every day," Dave said.

"What? A winged horse?" Hector asked.

"No. Hummingbird hugging something."

"Are we that jaded, my friend?"

Dave grunted his assent. "Jaded and suspicious."

The horse moved aside, and Aislinn motioned the others toward the steps. As they climbed, the wind buffeted them and threatened to blow them away, forcing them to hug the rock wall.

Tasunke watched them from the base of the stairs. Once they passed the midway mark, the hippoœtós spread his wings and jumped into the air. He flew by and disappeared back into the sun.

At the top of the stairs, knee-high grass and wildflowers clung to the rocky terrain. A half-dozen yards away, two fat-bellied brown bears guarded the lighthouse path. Each one easily weighed over a thousand pounds. As the strangers approached, they reared up on their hind legs and gave warning growls.

Aislinn briefly held up a clenched fist and waited.

Behind her, Hector glanced at Dave and whispered, "Finally, something that speaks your language."

"Asshole," Dave grumbled.

Neither man dared to reach for his weapons. If the bears decided the visitors were a threat, things would quickly get out of hand.

Hummingbird signed, "Do bears eat people?"

"They eat anything," Dave signed back.

"And everything," Hector added. The small elf ducked behind Dave and watched, her eyes wide.

"Who's there?" a gravelly voice asked from behind the bears.

"Tallinn, it's me, Aislinn."

A short, stocky man with white hair shuffled forward. He wore a white sash over a night-blue shirt. Embroidered on the sash in silver thread were two diagonal tridents over a black tower, the symbol of the Sea Ranger Corps. Holding a long rod in his left hand, he waved it over the ground in front of him as he walked. The bears dropped down on all fours and wandered off, eliciting a sigh of relief from Hummingbird.

"It's good to hear your voice again," Tallinn said, throwing his arms around Aislinn. "About time you showed up. What took so long?"

"We were in Orleans when your message reached Brand. We came as quickly as we could."

"How is the dragonling these days?"

"Getting bigger," Aislinn replied. "He's curled up in that cave he calls a nest, sleeping off his growing pains."

"Cari and Nettaru tell me you've brought friends."

"Did the bears give themselves those names?"

"Don't be ridiculous," the old man scoffed. "I couldn't say their real names, so I gave them something I could pronounce. Means the same thing, though," he added. "Enough about that. Introduce me to this bounty hunting team I've heard so much about from your mother." The old man moved around Aislinn and found Hector. Cataracts clouded his eyes, and Hector noticed that even though the old ranger knew where he stood, he didn't look directly at him.

"Espian?"

"Hector de los Santos, at your service, señor." Tallinn shifted slightly and clasped wrists with Hector. "The others are Dave Blood and Hummingbird of Altaira. Please forgive them if they don't shake hands."

"Just the four of you?" Tallinn asked. "What happened to the rest of your team — the mage and the swordsman?"

"Jasper's teaching at the Academia in Tydway, and we haven't seen Robert since we returned from Altaira six months ago," Aislinn replied, her voice ending on a sad note. "Why don't we go inside? You can tell us why you sent for us."

Tallinn nodded and headed toward a single-story house with a steeply pitched roof. The lighthouse jutted up from the middle of the ridge like one of the fabled beanstalks. Matching its tower, the whitewashed house glowed as if freshly polished. Red clay tiles covered the roof, each piece meticulously overlapped. Beyond lay a forest of short, stubby trees, some with their tops shorn off.

"Don't get visitors much," Tallinn said, mounting the front steps.

"Who's manning the tower?" Aislinn asked.

"Hank, but you wouldn't know him. He signed on a few years ago."

Directly inside the front door, circular stairs wound up into the lighthouse proper. However, Tallinn motioned for them to turn right toward a common room. The keeper's house smelled of brine and beeswax. Its wood floors gleamed like new, and various nautical instruments made of brass hung on the walls. All the windows were propped open, letting the constant sea breeze cool the interior. A heavy oak table and chairs dominated the center of the room.

On the back wall, a narrow doorway and a pass-through fireplace gave glimpses of the kitchen. A curl of smoke drifted up from banked coals. Above the hearth, small knick-knacks adorned a polished mantle.

Tallinn closed the door behind them and said, "Make yourselves comfortable. I'll put on a pot of tea."

"When did you start making tea?" Aislinn asked, following him into the kitchen. "It isn't made with seaweed, is it?"

The blind ranger took an iron kettle with a wooden handle from the shelf and filled it with water from a trough. "Smart-aleck. Make yourself useful and put this on the fire," he said.

Aislinn returned to the common room with the kettle and stirred the coals to life, while Tallinn found tealeaves, tin cups, and a pot.

"We sure could use you and Brand. I have a spare room set up and everything," Tallinn said when he reentered the room. He placed the pot down at the edge of the table and carefully arranged five cups beside it. Once everything was to his satisfaction, he moved to tend the fire.

Aislinn rolled her eyes heavenward and replied, "You're still trying to recruit me for the Sea Rangers?"

"Always," said Tallinn. He stoked the fire and continued, "Liked the mountains more than the sea, I guess."

"That's not true."

"What's this?" Hector asked, feeling like he had stepped into the middle of an argument.

"Sorry, it's a long story," Aislinn said.

"You chose Edge over me," the sea ranger said.

Aislinn's eyes narrowed and her jaw clenched at the mention of her former mentor. Recognizing the signs of her rising temper, Hector searched the room for cover.

"Tallinn, we talked about this. I didn't have a choice."

"Of course you had a choice! You *always* have a choice."

Aislinn's fists clenched, and Hector could see her limbs quivering with suppressed emotions. "You didn't understand then, and you don't understand now!"

"What's to understand? You're Alaric's daughter. The sea's in your blood, girl! You and Brand belong here, training with me, like your father wanted."

"I'm also my mother's daughter, and Edge needed help — for all the good Brand and I did him," she replied bitterly. "The dærganfae killed him anyway."

The kettle whistled. Both rangers jerked toward the sound. For a moment, neither moved, then they each seemed to relax, the momentum of their quarrel lost.

"Aislinn, I'm sorry," Tallinn said. "I didn't summon you here to rehash old arguments." He poured hot water into the teapot. The scent of black tea underlain by an almost imperceptible hint of bee balm filled the room.

"Never mind," Aislinn replied. "It's water down the coast."

After the tea steeped for a few minutes, Tallinn poured it into the tin cups.

"Be careful, it's hot," he announced to everyone. "Honey's on the table, if you want it."

A tall, husky-built youth with a shock of sandy-brown hair appeared in the doorway. "Tallinn, is everything alright? I heard voices."

"Hank, great timing." The old man waved the youth into the room. "Get yourself a cup. You can sit and have some tea."

After introductions were made, Aislinn took a steaming cup and gently blew on it. Hector and Hummingbird followed suit, picking up their cups and taking a seat at the large table. Dave slouched at the table's far end with his flask in hand. Hector shook his head and nodded toward the tea. Dave raised his flask and took a drink. The hunter shook his head a little more vigorously this time.

"I don't drink tea," Dave mouthed.

Aislinn glared at him. She picked up the last cup and carried it to him.

"Put your flask away. I need you sober," Hector heard her whisper.

Dave raised his flask as he stared into her eyes. Whatever the archer saw must have shaken him. His defiance melted. He tucked his flask into its pouch and reached for the tea.

Tallinn took a seat and poured a generous dollop of honey into his cup.

Sitting next to the ranger, Aislinn said, "What's going on around here? An unnatural-looking storm popped up out of nowhere and nearly sank us the day before yesterday. We went into town, and the locals are scared of their own shadows. There's talk about disappearances, evil fog, and ghosts — it's as if the world has turned upside down."

Hector watched the play of anger and sadness across her face as she spoke. Coming home was never easy, he thought.

"Nothing odd about fog on the coast. Least ways, not normally," said Hank, leaning forward, his elbows on the table, "but this fog is different. Here lately, it's every night, and its growing stronger, thicker. Not only that, but it doesn't act like fog should. Last week, I was up in the tower, checking the light at dusk, and watched the fog form. It rose straight out of the sea for miles, like a wall around all the barrier islands. The shore-side grew, rolling in along the waterways. A flock of gulls took to the air, trying to get away, but I swear the fog reached up and snatched them out of the sky. Then... *then,* a herd of deer — there must have been a dozen of them — burst from a thicket on one of the southern islands. They raced toward the cliffs like the Dark One's hounds were on their heels. Each one jumped to their deaths just to avoid the fog's touch."

"The storms began last year," Tallinn said, taking up the tale. "A few more than normal for the summer season, but they didn't stop once winter rolled around. About four months ago, things got worse. That's when the storms took on weird colors, and acthnici started plaguing the lighthouse." The old man rubbed his jaw. "The Corps sent people to investigate, as if they could track and predict the weather. You know what happened while they were nosing around? Not one blasted thing. They decided the storms were isolated and redirected the shipping lanes.

"With animals behaving strange and people disappearing into the fog with no sign of a predator, I thought of you and your Damage, Inc. Francis has put up a brave front, but the boy's out of his depth. That's why I sent for you. He needs help. He's just too stubborn to ask for it. I figured he might trust you, considering you were once friends and all."

"Do you know what's causing the fog or the storms?" Hector asked.

"Evil," Tallinn answered.

"Seems like the Dark One's priests would have better things to do than fiddle with the weather," the bounty hunter countered.

"Natural weather isn't green and purple, young man, and I didn't say it was one of the Sha'iry. I said evil is to blame."

"Disculpe, señor, but does this evil have a name? We aren't going to be any help against weather. Especially... What did you call the fog, Aislinn?"

"Luminiferous Aether."

"Luminiferous Aether," he repeated. "I take it you've seen the ghosts in the fog?"

Tallinn gave him a wistful smile and said, "No, young man, I haven't seen them. Fortunately, being up here at the lighthouse, we're usually above it."

"I have," Hank said softly. "Early in the morning, when the light's rising but the sun hasn't cracked the horizon, these islands are swarming with them. This morning, it almost looked like dragons were battling each other."

"Do you think these islands were connected at one time?" Hector asked. "We saw part of a mural at the monastery."

"Brother Powell and his theories," Tallinn said. "They all started when I told him that we uncovered old foundation stones when the Corps built the lighthouse."

"This lighthouse?" Aislinn asked.

"Yeah. The monks did some digging over the years and excavated remnants of an ancient watchtower and broken bits of pottery on the islands north of here. Probably from a Korellan outpost. What were you doing at the monastery?"

"Helping Francis investigate." Aislinn gulped her tea, delaying breaking the harsh news to the old man. "Are you sure that's all they found?"

"Can't be sure of anything. Why do you ask?"

"Someone plundered through Brother Powell's journals and defaced the mural in the monastery library," Aislinn replied, "but that isn't the worst of it. Tallinn, the monks were murdered. All of them."

Tallinn dropped the tin cup in his hand, and it bounced off the wood floor, spilling its contents. "All of them? How? *Why?*"

Aislinn picked up his cup and sent Hummingbird to the kitchen for a cloth to wipe away the small puddle. Sliding her tea in front of Tallinn, she directed his hand to the handle. "We don't know, but we suspect it may be some kind of demon. The entire compound was desecrated."

"It came on that ship, didn't it?" Tallinn asked.

"Maybe," Aislinn said. "The timing seems right, but the only one who survived is a count from Rhodina, and he's not telling us anything."

Hank shifted in his seat. "I went aboard with Sir Francis' troops and the fishermen. No crew and just the one survivor. But that breech in the hull has me scratching my head. There wasn't any cargo, so what busted out the boards?"

Hector answered, "That's what we'd like to know. We looked around yesterday morning and found gouges in the deck. The monastery's outer wall had similar tracks."

"I saw the marks on deck. Other than how big they were, they looked a lot like the trail left by a fiddler crab."

"They put me in mind of a crab, too," Aislinn nodded to Hank. "Did you notice anything else when you and Francis' men scavenged the ship?"

The apprentice's gaze swept over the visitors. "I take it you did?"

"A revenant," confirmed Hector. "There, and one at the monastery."

"Revenants," the old ranger muttered. "That's not what it is."

"What isn't a revenant, Tallinn?" Aislinn laid a reassuring hand on his gnarled fingers.

"Sounds in the night," he replied. "The hiss of metal on stone; a sound like the grind of clockwork gears out of whack. Is that your demon?"

Hector exchanged a look with Dave, thinking of the petite footprints in the monastery hallway and the monks' cells.

"I don't think so," Hector replied. "The demon left human-shaped tracks. However, the two may be working together."

Aislinn's next question caught him off-guard.

"Have you heard of a dærghenfae roaming these parts? He wears rags and..." Aislinn swallowed hard before she continued, "and he's a vampire."

A chill breeze blew through the house, causing the fire to sputter. Dave and Hector sat up straight. The archer unconsciously rubbed at the scars hidden among his tattoos.

"What's a dærganfae?" Hank asked.

"They live in the Haunted Hills, south of the Alashalian Mountain clans. Most people think they're elves," Aislinn replied, "and maybe they were, in the beginning, but my mother disagrees. According to her, Dærganfae aren't of Gaia."

"What do they look like?"

From the end of the table, Dave's deep voice rolled through the room like a dark harbinger of doom, drawing all eyes to him. "Taller than elves. Reed thin. Pale, like the moon, with hair black as midnight." The archer reached for his flask, cast a furtive glance at Aislinn, and returned his clenched fist to the tabletop.

Aislinn's brow furrowed. "That's right. How...?" Her question died on her lips as Dave turned toward the window with his arms crossed in front of him. Turning back to Hank, she said, "The fae who killed Edge had sharper ears than mine or Hummingbird's. Their most distinctive feature, though, are their eyes: they're completely quicksilver, even the pupil."

"An Alashalian clansman I once knew claimed dærganfae can open portals in bluestone," Tallinn added. "It's what made them such deadly assassins during the Plague War. It was the dærganfae who killed King David and most of the Carolingian royal family. Queen Ambrose was the only one to escape."

"What about a fae vampire?" Aislinn asked.

The old man took a sip of tea, grimaced, and added more honey. Hector began to wonder if he planned to ignore Aislinn's question when Tallinn drew in a deep breath and let it out in a gusty sigh. "There's only one Dærganfae vampire in Parlatheas. He's called Mi'dnirr."

"Who is he?" Aislinn asked. Hector noticed that her clasped hands trembled.

"No one really knows, but I first remember hearing his name during the Plague War, after sickness and death swept through the mountain clans. Word was Mi'dnirr fought Cerdic Uth Aneirin and Rhandall Morghan to a stalemate. They were the wielders of Kingslayer and Widowmaker — weapons forged at the height of Korellan power. After the Plague War, he disappeared. Some say he took over some citadel in the Alashalian Mountains. Others say he roams the Haunted Hills, devouring anyone foolish enough to enter his demesne."

"I've heard that a few vampires can control the weather," stated Hector. "Is this Mi'dnirr one of them? Can he create revenants?"

Tallinn took another sip of tea and said, "Never heard any rumors to that effect. One thing I do know: he's dangerous. Stay away from him. Many a fool has lost their life looking to kill that creature."

"If Mi'dnirr is behind what's happening here in Ruthaer, we'll stop him," Hector replied. "We can handle a vampire."

"And if our village's troubles are caused by more than a vampire or a demon?" Tallinn asked.

"You did the right thing, sending for us. Whatever it is, we'll stop it. Damage, Inc. always finds a way." Aislinn gave the old man's hand a gentle squeeze. "We should get back to town."

Everyone drained what was left of their tea and washed dishes for the old ranger. Aislinn put away the last cup and gave Tallinn a quick hug. "You stay safe up here, old man."

The old seadog returned her hug and said, "You be careful, too, girl. Come back when you can stay longer."

"We will."

As they were heading to the door, Tallinn said, "If you want to know more about Mi'dnirr, ask Francis Courtenay."

Aislinn turned back and gave Tallinn a puzzled frown. "Francis? What makes you think he knows something?"

"Mi'dnirr killed his son three years ago."

The four gathered around Tallinn.

"Francis' son, Evan, came home after a tour of duty in the mountains, driving off Dærganfae invaders. The only thing I can figure is Mi'dnirr followed him home. Probably because of that mission. Evan had been here a month or so when Francis and Father Blackwood found his body just outside of town. I never got the full story, but it shook Francis. He hasn't been the same since."

Aislinn lingered at the top of the steps. With a final hug, she said, "Thank you, Tallinn. We'll talk to Francis."

CHAPTER 12
THE GRAVEYARD

August 3, 4237 K.E.

1:13pm

The sun was high in the sky and the wind had died down to an intermittent breeze. Hector and Aislinn sat opposite each other in the bow, trying not to cook or to get slapped by the jib as the boat tacked. Behind them, Hummingbird loosened a line and the boom swung around to the other side. For a brief moment, the mainsail filled, and they glided toward the pluff mud bank across the main channel. Once there, Dave pulled on the rudder and maneuvered the boat into the wind. Hummingbird grabbed another line, letting the boom swing back, where the sail filled again.

"Can't you make this thing go any faster?" Hector complained.

"You can stand back here and blow," Dave growled.

"No thanks," Hector said.

Their boat drifted past the *Inquisitor*. Despite the cloudless sky, the gaping hole in the ship's side was pitch black, as if the sun feared to send its rays within the hold. Once past, Aislinn broke the silence. "Three years ago, Mi'dnirr killed Francis Courtenay's son, Evan. Now, Ruthaer is plagued by fog, storms, and ghosts. They have a Rhodinan ship with neither cargo nor crew, and someone murdered the monks. What's the connection?"

"They're all dead," Hector answered.

Aislinn shoved him and said, "I'm serious."

"So was I. Mi'dnirr's a vampire. He killed Evan and those monks. Simple."

"What about Margaret Potter, Daniel Tanner, the slave girl, Klara, and the captain? You're telling me he killed them, too?" Aislinn countered.

"Sure. It's possible."

"No, there's something else." She glanced back at Dave and Hummingbird, then lowered her voice. "I didn't say anything before, but the ghosts were in my room last night. They took me to the graveyard."

"They *took* you," Hector said evenly.

"That isn't the worst of it. Here, look at this," Aislinn leaned forward, putting the sail between her and Dave.

"Please tell me this isn't what I think it is," she whispered, pulling back her hair to show Hector her neck.

"*¡Madre de Dios!*" Hector exclaimed.

"*Not so loud!*" she hissed. "I don't want Dave to know." Aislinn wrapped her hand around Hector's wrist and pulled him closer. "He's so high strung, I'm afraid of what he might do."

Hector forced a small laugh and laid his hand atop hers. "Dave will be fine. You shouldn't have kept this a secret."

"Dave? Only if fine means he's foul-mouthed, inebriated, nervous, and explosive. You know he thinks you're full of troll blood."

"Dave thinks I'm full of a lot of things, but he would never hurt you."

"Maybe," Aislinn said, unconvinced.

"So, what really happened last night?" Hector asked.

Aislinn told him everything, and when she was done, it felt as if a great weight lifted from her shoulders. She stared out across the marsh grass and waited.

"I guess, in a way, Mi'dnirr saved you," Hector finally said. "If he hadn't come along, Klara and the gnomes would have buried you alive."

"In a way," Aislinn repeated, "but I was sure he was going to kill me. My connection to Brand seemed to surprise him. The next thing I knew, I was back in my bed."

"We need to take a look at that graveyard."

"What's the point? Between Father Blackwood and Francis' soldiers tromping around all morning, there won't be any tracks worth seeing."

"I want to see the crime scene for myself, and to look at Evan Courtenay's grave before we question Sir Francis. There has to be a reason Brother Powell's journal from three years ago was missing."

CR&SO

1:59pm

Ruthaer's marina held a number of small, flat-bottomed jon boats and narrow punts suited to traversing the river's sloughs and shallow bays, as well as dock space for several large fishing boats. On the opposite shore, an old, rickety wooden pier slumped at the foot of deep, moss-covered steps carved into the granite dome guarding Ruthaer like a sleeping giant. Hector wondered why anyone would take the time and energy to carve the stairs. The ancient risers looked too tall for short-statured gnomes, and he doubted anyone would be foolish enough to use them for transporting stone.

The defaced mural in the monastery library showed the pluton and the barrier islands as a single mass. He tried to imagine an event powerful enough to change the landscape so drastically.

Within a matter of minutes, Dave had their boat berthed and Aislinn hopped out to register with the dockmaster. After collecting their gear, the four headed into town.

A family of ducks scurried out of their way as they crossed the town commons and approached the small church. The rough-hewn granite wall and wrought iron fence extended from the side of the stone building and wrapped its way around the graveyard. A row of triangular cedars with tapered limbs stood sentinel behind the fence, guarding the quick and the dead from each other.

A muscular guard leaned against the arched gateway pillar, his eyes darting back and forth between the graves inside and the people outside. His brow was so furrowed with concentration, his forehead almost touched his chin.

Recognizing the soldier from the previous day, Hector said, "Big Mike, how are things going?"

"Seriously? How can you even ask me that after yesterday? Everybody in town is jumpier than a cat in a roomful of rocking chairs."

"We're here to help," Aislinn reassured the soldier.

Hector nodded. "That's right. We need to take a look at the crime scene."

"No one goes inside. Sir Francis' orders."

"Sir Francis asked for our help," Hector reminded the soldier.

After considering for a moment, Big Mike said, "Go on in." Even though his manner seemed casual, Hector saw the guard relax ever so slightly. It seemed Big Mike numbered among the townspeople on edge.

"Keep up the good work, soldier," said Hector. He gave Big Mike a friendly slap on the shoulder as he strode through the arched gateway. "We'll only be a minute."

A scattering of red cedars and stray pines provided shade and shielded several graves from the view of passersby.

Fifteen plots were demarcated with coped granite border stones and a large family marker. Shorter headstones, many dated June 10, 4212 — the same as the memorial statue for Aislinn's father — marked the resting places of individual family members.

The graveyard stretched back beyond the church, with a short, willow-wythe fence between it and a small rectory. In the far corner, an ancient oak with sprawling moss-shrouded limbs cast a shadow over an unmarked plot with several small tombstones. The tree's roots had disturbed the stones, causing some to lean precariously.

Hector and Dave made for the fresh pile of dirt in the corner while Aislinn hung back, reading the markers. Hummingbird stayed with her, but remained in the narrow path's center, as if afraid the dead would attack if she passed too close to their resting places.

No tombstone stood by the open grave, and Hector could only assume it had been dug for the little girl they found in the marsh. He searched around and found a burnt patch in the grass — Aislinn mentioned seeing a green flash before the gnome's dead body landed at her feet in the grave. Prints from flat-soled sandals like those of Father Blackwood as well as tracks from hob-nail military boots traversed the scorch mark in multiple directions. Hector shook his head in disgust, wondering how crimes in Ruthaer ever got solved with people trampling the evidence.

He jumped down into the grave and searched around. Finding nothing other than loose dirt, he reached up and said, "Dave, give me a hand."

The tall archer leaned down and helped Hector out. "Find anything?"

"No," Hector answered.

"I can go ask Aislinn. She's good at reading tracks. Maybe she can make some sense of this mess."

Hector shook his head. "Don't."

"Why the hell are we even here, then?" Dave asked.

"Because Mi'dnirr was here last night. Right here. I was hoping we'd find a clue Sir Francis and his men missed." He waved a hand at the overlapping tracks all around them.

"Mi'dnirr? Last night? How do you know?"

"Aislinn saw him."

"What the hell was she doing out here without us?"

Hector swept his eyes across the graveyard. Aislinn stood beside a marble headstone between two family plots. The heartbroken longing in her expression pierced his heart. "Aislinn said the dead gnomes Señora Griffon mentioned at breakfast this morning were working with the ghosts. This town has bigger problems than weird weather and a few mysterious disappearances."

"It was stupid of her to come out here alone."

"Drop it, Dave. I'll explain later."

The archer's brow clouded over. "Why do I have the feeling we should get the hell out of this town and not look back?"

"We can't. Aislinn's the client, remember? We stay 'til she says otherwise."

Hector and Dave joined the girls and read the stone marker, "Alaric Yves — May He Rest in Peace. Died June 10, 4212."

"What about Sir Francis' son?" Hector asked.

"Over there," Aislinn replied. She pointed to a plot surrounded by a waist-high iron fence held up by a thick hedge.

Four headstones occupied the space. Judging from the dates on the two older stones, they belonged to Sir Francis' parents. The third stone belonged to Belinda Smith Courtenay and infant, laid to rest in 4221. The final stone read, "Evan Courtenay — Beloved Son. Died August 5, 4234, in his 21st year."

Aislinn pointed and said, "Margaret Potter's grave is there, and Daniel Tanner is over there. Just like the journal said. They each died on the same day as Evan Courtenay, in the two following years."

"Mi'dnirr?" Hector asked. "Maybe he only feeds once a year."

"That doesn't make sense," Aislinn said. "Brother Powell only mentioned fog in his journal, not a vampire. Besides, Tallinn said Mi'dnirr is Dærganfae. Contrary to the assassin rumors, they usually stick to the mountains. Why come here at all? And why start three years ago?"

Hector knelt beside Evan Courtenay's grave. "Aislinn, take a look at this."

Aislinn kissed her fingers and gently touched the top of her father's tombstone.

Kneeling beside the bounty hunter, she brushed her hand over the grass and traced the sunken outline of the grave.

"What are you doing?" Sir Francis' voice boomed across the graveyard. Livid with anger, he gripped his helmet with one hand, swinging it as he walked inside. Big Mike and two other guards ran to catch up.

Before Aislinn could explain, the constable commanded, "All of you, come with me."

Not waiting for an answer, the constable marched them across town, turning many a head. Soldiers and townsfolk alike moved aside to let the group pass. His boots thudded on the bailey flagstones. At the top of the tower entrance steps, a guard snapped to attention and opened the heavy oaken door. Sir Francis led them through the single-story foyer and entered the Great Hall. His metallic footsteps echoed from the rafters. High up near the timbered ceiling, lead paned windows filled the room with light.

Multicolored tapestries decorated most of the left-hand wall, while the right-hand wall, supporting the stairs to the tower, was spotted with wanted posters. A row of scroll-filled niches pierced the wall above a dark mahogany desk. A stack of blank parchments, ink well, and quill occupied the writing surface.

Two rows of tables flanked by wooden benches filled the majority of the room, providing space for about thirty people to gather. High on the far wall, two banners hung above a broad mantle: one the banner of Sir Francis' knightly order, with three golden stags on a blue and white checkered field; the other the flag of Carolingias, emblazoned with a silver dogwood tree issuing from a green hill on a solid blue field.

Below the banners and mantle, an enormous, smoke-stained hearth and fireplace framed the room's head table a step above the main floor. Count Dodz lounged in one of the five chairs facing the room, a sheet of thick parchment in his hand.

"If this is about last night —" Aislinn started.

"I trusted you," Sir Francis snapped, "and you brought a murderer to my town!"

The constable snatched the parchment from Count Dodz and handed it to Aislinn. Hector and Dave leaned in and read over her shoulders. The top bore the official crest of the

Seaport of Rowanoake. It was a letter to Sir Francis demanding he hold one Clem Tyler, also known as Gavin Drake, also known as Dave Blood. It contained a lengthy list of crimes, including the murder of nine soldiers, one officer, and one nobleman: Sir Killian Howard.

Dave lunged toward the door, but several of Sir Francis' men blocked his way. Hector grabbed Dave's arm and jerked him to a stop, trying to prevent the archer from doing anything rash.

Aislinn rounded on Dodz. "This is your doing."

"Aislinn, whether the count brought this to my attention or not is irrelevant," Sir Francis interjected. "Your friend is wanted for *eleven* murders."

Count Dodz' laugh echoed through the room. Before anyone could catch him, Dave broke from Hector's grasp, leapt across the table, and drove a solid right cross against Dodz's jaw. The chair tipped over and the count's arms flew up as he tried to regain his balance. With a loud smack, he landed on his back with his feet up in the air.

Big Mike wrapped his muscular arm around Dave's neck and wrestled him away from the count. He slowly cut off the archer's air supply until Dave stopped struggling.

"I have his quiver, sir," a guard said, handing it to the constable.

Aislinn and Hector both shared looks, already knowing what he'd find.

The constable pulled out an arrow with red fletching and held it up to the sunlight. The hawk's head tip was clean. Next, the constable pulled out one with black fletching and held it up. The tip shimmered with an oily film of poison.

"Lock him up," the constable said.

"No, you can't," Aislinn said.

"Aislinn, he's an assassin. Look." The constable held up the arrowhead for her to see. When he saw the expression on her face, he said, "You knew."

"It's not what you think," Dave said hoarsely. "I'm not an assassin."

"Francis, please don't do this," Aislinn pleaded.

"It's my *sworn duty* to carry out the law. Like it or not, the terms of the Confederation Treaty demand I cooperate with officials from all member countries. Last time I checked, Rowanoake is still part of Gallowen and the Confederation."

Sir Francis clenched the arrow in his fist. "I have no choice but to hold your friend." The constable jerked his head toward a narrow door between two tapestries. Big Mike tightened his grip on Dave and made to leave the hall.

"No. Wait," Aislinn said. "If you lock him up, you have to lock up all of us."

"What?" Hector and Dave said in unison.

Aislinn looked at Hector and said, "We never split the party."

Hector threw her a look that clearly said he hoped she knew what she was doing. He held out his arms and said, "She's right, Constable. Lock us up."

CHAPTER 13
DISCOVERY

August 3, 4237 K.E.

3:30pm

Aaron Ponds sat at a small table with an array of playing cards in front of him. A lit candle sat at the edge. Dark six-foot by eight-foot cells with steel bars set into hard stone lined one side of the room.

Before Sir Francis departed to continue his investigation at the monastery, he ordered the young corporal to keep an eye on their "guests." Their weapons and gear were piled in the corner, in sight but out of reach.

In one cell, Hector rested on the cot with his back to the bars while Dave paced back and forth, grumbling. In the adjacent cell, Aislinn and Hummingbird sat cross-legged on the floor, signing to each other.

"Aaron, we have to pee," Aislinn said.

The corporal looked up from his game. He stopped and started a few times before he finally said, "I can't let you out. There's a bucket in the corner."

"Seriously?"

"Sir Francis' orders."

"Sir Francis said Hummingbird and I have to pee in a bucket with three men watching?"

"Well, no; not exactly."

"Aaron, we're not going anywhere. Hummingbird and I just want to use the garderobe. You can stand in the hall and make sure we don't run off."

The corporal looked through the door to the main hall. His expression made it clear he hoped Sir Francis would return and tell him what to do. "Can't you hold it?"

"No. Hummingbird's really got to go."

Aaron looked at Hummingbird, who squirmed and made a face. "Fine. But no funny business."

"We promise," Aislinn said, crossing her heart.

When they returned, Dave and Hector were sitting at the table holding Aaron's cards. "Your draw," Hector said to Dave. A small pile of silver coins sat between them. Their cell door stood wide open.

"Hey!" Aaron said.

"Good. You're back. Want to join us?" Hector said.

Aaron opened and closed his mouth like a fish. Aislinn and Hummingbird grabbed chairs. When Hummingbird slid her chair over, Hector said, "Grab one for the corporal."

Aislinn gently nudged the corporal toward the seat waiting for him. "Here. You look like you might be getting sick."

"No. This isn't right. You're supposed to be in your cells." The corporal sat down, his eyes darting toward the door.

"New game," Dave said as he dealt the cards. "Ante up. One silver."

Still looking at the open cell, Aaron slowly took a coin from his pouch and put it in the pot. "I'm not supposed to be doing this."

"You're keeping an eye on us, right?" Aislinn encouraged.

"Yeah, but..."

"Pick up your cards," Dave growled.

After they played a few hands, Dave took a swig from his flask and wiped his mouth with the back of his hand. He shook his head at Hummingbird. "Should have remembered the damn girl could read minds."

She smiled sweetly and gathered her winnings. The small pile in front of her had grown steadily.

"What are you drinking?" Aislinn asked.

"What do you want?" Dave responded.

"Do you have tea?"

"Of course not."

Dave rummaged through their stuff and found a tin cup. He spit in it and wiped it with the edge of his seal grey cloak. After inspecting it, he tilted the cup slightly and filled it with a deep red wine.

"Try this."

Aislinn considered the liquid. It had a full-bodied aroma and reminded her of the vineyards outside Orleans in Francesca. She closed her eyes and took a sip. The velvety liquid ran across her tongue and sent goosebumps racing up and down her arms. When she swallowed, she felt her muscles relax and the tension within fade.

Aislinn opened her eyes and said, "Wow. What was that?"

Dave smiled and asked, "What did you taste?"

"Blackberries after a rain. Mixed with red grapes in... a black oak barrel."

Aaron stared at her in amazement and said, "You could taste all that?"

"I could see it," Aislinn said. "Dave, where did you get that?"

"Edmond's personal winery."

"*Dave!*" Hector said, accusingly.

"What? No. It wasn't like that. He gave me a bottle," Dave explained. "We're good."

"*Whew.* You had me worried, amigo," Hector said. "After your escapade in Orleans, you need to mind your P's and Q's with King Edmond. I don't want to lose his patronage."

"Why do you always think the worst?" Dave asked.

Hector's eyebrows crawled toward his hairline, and he gave his friend an incredulous look.

Finding another cup, Dave made to spit in it and Hector said, "No, don't. I'll take my chances."

Dave shrugged. He tilted the cup and filled it from his flask. Aaron gasped. This time, the liquid was a golden color.

"I prefer red, but those Gaels," Dave said, placing the cup in front of Hector.

"Mead?" Hector asked.

"Drink it."

The Espian sipped the fermented honey. He smacked his lips and made an approving sound before taking another swallow.

"Aaron?" Dave said.

"Got any homebrew in that flask?"

"No. Sorry. I have to pour a little in for it to work. Didn't get a chance last night. Why don't you try the mead?" Getting a nod from the corporal, he filled a third cup.

"That flask is amazing," the corporal said. "Can it recreate anything?"

"Most anything, as long as it's mundane. No magical potions or stuff like that," Dave replied. "What about you, Hummingbird?"

She signed something and Dave grimaced. "Savage," he said under his breath.

He found another cup and poured crystal clear water from his flask. Hummingbird sipped it and her eyes went wide. She made a few signs and Dave said, "It's from Ozera."

"Really? Where in Ozera?" Aislinn asked.

"The artesian spring in Sunrise Chapel."

Aislinn studied the archer anew. Sunrise Chapel was an open-air worship space atop Ozera's east-facing cliffs, roughly five hundred feet above the main village. The trail to reach it wound up the mountainside, through prayer gardens, and was meant to serve as a means of meditation. It was not an easy journey. "I didn't know you made that climb after the one time I took you guys." She grinned. "Even after all these years, I don't think Jasper has forgiven me."

"Only because you didn't let him eat first," Hector chuckled.

"Corporal! What's going on here?" Sir Francis bellowed.

Aaron shot up as if his chair had caught on fire and motioned everyone back to their cells. He didn't say anything; he just hung his head low like a puppy thrown out in the rain. He looked so pathetic even Dave returned to his cell without an argument. However, when Aaron closed the cell door, Dave clasped the young man's shoulder through the bars. "The coins on the table belong to Hummingbird. See that they go in her bag, would you?" While his words were friendly enough, his tone held the unmistakable threat of violence.

Returning to Sir Francis, Aaron attempted to explain, but the constable cut him short. "Get out of here."

"Yes, sir." He saluted, threw a heavy keyring on the table, and practically ran out the door.

After Aaron left, Sir Francis took in the table with its pile of money and half-full cups. He cupped his elbow with his left hand and pinched the bridge of his nose with his right. "What am I going to do with you?"

"You can let us go," Hector offered.

Sir Francis didn't respond.

"Come on, señor," Hector urged.

"Did you really kill all those people?" Sir Francis asked.

Dave shrugged. "Maybe."

"Killian Howard was alive when we escaped the riots in Rowanoake," Aislinn reminded him. "I don't think I ever saw him again after he had Hector arrested on those ridiculous insubordination charges."

Sir Francis said, "I heard the Mayor of Rowanoake thinks Dave is the Red Dragon."

"Dave's not the Red Dragon," Hector protested.

Hummingbird signed and Dave answered, "The Red Dragon was a crime lord in Rowanoake." The girl continued to look confused.

"It's a port city in Gallowen, the neighboring country north of here," Hector explained. "When we were there a few years ago, we got accused of being part of his gang."

"That was Robert," Dave grumbled. "You were in jail."

"Was the Red Dragon really a dragon?" Aislinn asked. "I don't think we ever found out."

"No, we never did, but he sure liked to burn things. Set several city blocks on fire, as I recall," Hector said.

"Don't forget the prison break... and the riots," Dave added.

"Stop. Just stop," Sir Francis said. "You're all giving me a headache."

Dave offered him his flask.

"No, thank you," Sir Francis answered without thinking. Realizing what it was, he snatched it from Dave's hand. "Give me that!"

"That's just great, Dave," Hector said. "You pick the weirdest moments to be nice."

"Out of practice," Dave replied with another shrug.

"Francis, the city was corrupt," Aislinn said. "We inadvertently embarrassed one of the councilmen, and things went from bad to worse."

"I can't let you go," the constable said. "Rowanoake is sending someone to pick up your friend. Probably be a few days."

"Thanks, Dave," Hector said.

"Hey, it's not just me. We all have records there, and they'll treat us to a short drop with a sudden stop if they catch us."

Sir Francis plopped down in a chair and said, "I did not hear that."

"Who wanted to come here anyway?" Dave asked.

"I did," Aislinn said. "Ruthaer needed us. Plus, I wanted to fish and to smell the marshes one more time."

"*What?* Are you dying?" Dave asked.

Aislinn leaned her head against the bars. She could feel the others staring at her, waiting for an answer. She'd been avoiding this conversation since joining Hector and Dave in

Orleans. Her feelings for the two Terrans were complicated, and she didn't want to choose between them and Brand, despite what her dragon-brother and their soul-bond demanded. "Brand wants to leave Parlatheas."

The silence that followed was palpable. When Sir Francis sat straighter in his chair, it was like someone cracking a whip.

"Leave and go where?" Hector asked.

"Revakhun Toaglen — the dragon homeland. It's a group of hidden islands somewhere to the east in Tethys Oceanus. He wants to be with his kind," Aislinn said. "Two years ago, when Robert was kidnapped and we went after him, Brand was on the cusp of an oonveytik ssifruen." The draconic phrase slithered over the stone walls and clawed into her companions' ears. "He stayed behind in Ozera and slept through most of his growing pains. Afterwards, he decided he needed to know more about his heritage.

"While we were crossing Altaira, Phaedrus arranged for Brand to meet another bronze dragon. Apparently, an elder female serves as an ambassador to the Confederation of Nations. Last fall, she came to Ozera — with Brand's father. He wanted Brand to go with him to their homeland, but Brand refused to consider it until we made it home with Robert. Now..." she let out a ragged sigh and shivered. "Brand is leaving at winter solstice."

"What about you?" Hector asked.

When she didn't answer, Hector repeated his question. "What. About. You?"

"He expects Emä and me to go with him, but I haven't decided yet."

"You can't be serious!" Dave said.

His sudden outburst caught her by surprise, and she looked up to find him retreating to the far corner of his cell. "I haven't decided yet," she repeated, her tone pleading for understanding. "That's another reason why I came. I wanted to get things sorted out."

"And we all ended up in jail," Hector said with a rueful smile.

Sir Francis rose from his chair and came to stand in front of Aislinn.

"I can't let you go, but I don't have to keep you locked up either. You can stay here at the shrievalty in one of the rooms upstairs if you swear to me, on your father's memory, that the four of you won't run at the first opportunity."

"I think the constable is starting to like us," Hector said.

"Don't push your luck."

Aislinn reached out a hand to her childhood friend, who took it. "Francis, Ruthaer needs our help. You know it; I know it. We can't provide that help locked up in here. We won't run. I promise on my father's memory we *will* figure out what ails this town and do everything we can to end it."

The constable raised an eyebrow at her. The fear in his eyes gave her pause. It wasn't exactly the promise he'd asked of her, but was it more than he bargained for? Taking back his hand, Sir Francis gave her a tiny nod and reached for the jail keys.

When Aislinn stepped out of her cell, Dave grabbed her by the wrist and pulled her around to face him. His whiskey-colored eyes captured her with their intensity. She met his gaze at first, but then had to turn away, her heart torn by the choice Brand wanted her to make.

Rather than let her go, Dave pulled her close. When he spoke, his voice was soft so only she could hear. "Never split the party."

CHAPTER 14
DEATH IN DISGUISE

August 3, 4237 K.E.

7:50pm

The sun hung low in the sky, casting a red glow over Ruthaer. Shadows from the buildings darkened the dirt road, but it wasn't enough to fend off the oppressive August heat. People gathered on their porches, most discussing the dreadful events at the monastery. Sweat soaked their clothes, but it was still cooler outside than inside.

Allyrian spotted Corporal Ponds leaving the shrievalty and sidled up next him. "Aaron, where ya headed?" she asked.

"Hi, Ally," he said absently to the teamster's daughter. "Nowhere, I guess. Been cooped up most of the day and wanted to stretch my legs."

She took Aaron's hand in hers and said, "Why don't we go to the river? Maybe go for a swim?"

Aaron shook his head, "I'd need to change and..."

Allyrian stopped him with a finger pressed to his lips and waited. Slowly, realization dawned.

"Ally?"

She rose on her toes and brushed a kiss on his cheek. "Why not?" she whispered in his ear. Under her hand, he shivered.

His Adam's apple bobbed as he swallowed hard. "What about your father? He'll kill me if he catches us."

"Don't worry about him. He's been tied up all day."

The corporal didn't quite run, but it didn't take him long to guide her to a secluded spot where thick-bottomed trees and springy willows lined a river-bend, hiding them from the road.

She watched with amusement as the young soldier turned his back to her while he stripped off his uniform and draped it over a limb. He still didn't look at her as he waded into the river. She could practically taste his nervous excitement.

Allyrian licked her lips, wishing she had the luxury of time to truly savor his innocence, but the sun would set soon. She peeled her dress off and dropped it into the leaf-litter before sliding into the black waters. Despite the summer heat, the river carried a delicious chill.

Allyrian waited, only the upper half of her face above the dark water. The soldier surfaced and drew in a deep breath before turning to her. She raised one hand above the river surface and crooked a finger at him.

He drifted toward her but stopped just out of reach. "Ally, are you sure?"

Smiling, she closed the distance between them. "Absolutely," she whispered. Her fingers twined through his hair and pulled him closer so she could wrap her legs around his hips.

She kissed him.

The purity of his spirit was sweeter than honey on her tongue. The demoness kissed him harder, drinking his energy into herself.

When only the barest flicker of life remained in him, she drew back and gave him a lazy cat's smile. At the sight of her wings and the sharp points of her short horns, he tried to pull away, but it was too late.

The bitter tang of fear tainted the air. The fiend's smile died. Even if she didn't have other plans for Aaron, she wouldn't feed on him again. She despised the taste of fear.

"Who... what... are you?"

The creature who looked like Allyrian Carmichael shook her head and drove a stolen arrow into the dying soldier's gut. His eyes flew wide and he gasped with pain. She held him until the light in his eyes dimmed and his lids drifted shut, then let his body drift away.

CR80

9:19pm

The doors to the Great Hall burst open and three soldiers rushed in carrying Aaron's naked body on an impromptu stretcher made from a long cloak. A flicker of flame from the broad fireplace lit their grim countenances. Aislinn moved to intercept the trio, leaving Hector and Dave near the wall of posters.

"Place him over here near the fire," Aislinn said, directing them to the long table at the head of the room. The soldiers laid Aaron down and his head lolled to one side. His lips, cheeks, and fingers had a distinct bluish cast. Blood seeped from the puncture wound under his ribs and trailed down his side, pooling under his back. "It looks like he's been shot."

Sir Francis heard the commotion and came downstairs. "Why did you bring him here?" he asked. "Where's Father Blackwood?"

"We couldn't find him, sir," one of the soldiers answered.

Aislinn felt the corporal's skin. It was cold and clammy. He lived, but just barely. Hector handed her his shirt, and she pressed it against the wound.

Aislinn turned to Sir Francis. "I need several buckets filled with water, clean cloths, thick thread — or strands from a horse's tail — for stitching, and a needle."

Sir Francis gestured to one of his men, who raced out the door. He turned to another soldier and asked, "What happened?"

"We found him floating in the river, sir."

Moving Hector's shirt aside, Aislinn probed the wound with her fingers and felt something hard beneath the surface of the skin. "I need more light."

Sir Francis snatched a lantern from the wall, lit it, and held it over the table. Aislinn spread the wound with one hand and dug two fingers into the hole. "Come on, damn it." Blood gushed as she slowly fished an arrowhead and nub of a shaft out of Aaron's gut. She laid it aside and began praying. A dim blue nimbus surrounded the body. She prayed harder, pouring her strength into Aaron.

"Aislinn?"

"Something's not right. He's still having trouble breathing." Aislinn studied the body, grateful the flow of blood had slowed to a trickle.

The front door opened, and Father Blackwood rushed across the hall. Behind him, two soldiers carried the items Aislinn requested.

"Where were you, Father?" Sir Francis asked.

"I was out in the woods, collecting herbs. What happened?"

While the constable and priest talked, Hector rinsed the arrowhead in one of the buckets. "Dave!"

The archer snatched the black metal from Hector's outstretched hand and said, "That's not possible. I counted my arrows this morning."

"Check your quiver anyway," Hector demanded.

"What is it?" Aislinn asked.

Dave held up the broken arrow. The hawk's head pattern was plainly visible.

"How did that get in my corporal?" Sir Francis asked.

"Don't know," Dave mused.

"Dave, black or red?" Aislinn asked. He didn't answer.

"Black or red!" she shouted.

"Black."

"Give me the antidote. He'll die without it."

"There is no antidote," Dave said evenly. "I mixed it that way on purpose."

Aislinn grabbed him by the arm. "Dammit, Dave! You're immune to it."

"Yeah, sort of. Still makes me sick."

"What is it?"

"Curare," Dave answered. He pushed Aaron's gut, working the stomach muscles. The puncture reopened and a steady flow of blood seeped out of the wound.

"Dave! What are you doing?"

"Like you said, he'll die," Dave responded, pressing on Aaron's stomach again. More blood bubbled up, and Aislinn tried to staunch it with a fresh cloth. "Curare freezes the muscles. He can't breathe."

"But doesn't your poison kill quicker than this? I thought it stops an animal's heart."

"It's supposed to. The river probably watered it down."

"I will not let him die," Aislinn said.

She grabbed Hector's hand and placed it back on the cloth. Next, she took out her wheel-cross and laid a hand on Aaron's chest. She closed her eyes and prayed, "Deus, obsecro aufer toxin." Father Blackwood placed his hand over hers and joined in on her prayer. The blue nimbus returned and enveloped the entire table. It grew brighter and brighter, forcing everyone to look away.

The blue glow faded and only the light from the constable's lantern remained. The light formed an imperfect circle around them, leaving the edges, corners, and ceiling of the Great Hall in shadow.

"It's done," Father Blackwood said with a sigh of relief as he stepped back. Everyone let out the breath they held, watching Aaron's chest rise and fall and rise again.

Aislinn brushed a gentle hand over the young man's wet hair. "That was too close. We need to wrap him in a blanket and move him closer to the fire."

"Hey," Hector said, "what happened to the fire?" Smoke from the embers in the fireplace wafted lazily. The room fell quiet. Aaron's ragged breathing was the only sound.

Hummingbird rose from her seat on the hearth and crept closer to the table, giving the shadows a worried look.

"What is it?" Dave asked.

Fear flickered in her aqua-colored eyes.

A loud crash at the front doors startled them. Another crash, and the doors flew open. The wood frame splintered, and the upper hinges tore free. A chill wind rushed inside, rustling the tapestries and banners. It carried with it an eerie chant from outside. *Whip-poor-will...whip-poor-will...whip-poor-will.*

Fog crept into the Great Hall. It slunk along the floor, keeping to the darkness and forming a misty wall. As it rose, tormented faces appeared within, twisted in silent screams. Disembodied heads floated higher. Otherworldly hands probed the surface of the light as if it were a physical barrier.

Everyone drew weapons and formed a tight ring around the constable and his lantern. Pale figures with ragged wounds swirled in the mists floating above them — some human, some not. They wielded ancient weapons, pitch black against the grey fog. The largest apparition reared up and struck the light with its blade, sending up a flash of aethereal sparks. The lantern flickered in response.

"How much oil do you have in that lantern?" Hector asked.

"I didn't check," Sir Francis replied.

"This is worse than last night," Aislinn observed. "I don't remember seeing warriors."

"I've never seen anything like this," said Father Blackwood, his words laced with panic.

"Sir?" one of the soldiers said.

"Steady, Henry. We'll get through this," Sir Francis said in encouragement.

Another flash of aethereal sparks erupted from the far corner. Dull grey lines spider-webbed outward, as if the light had cracked. Again, the lantern-light wavered.

"What the hell are the ghosts doing?" Dave asked.

"They're trying to break through the light," Aislinn said.

"That doesn't sound good," Dave replied.

"Father, get ready. We can't let the light fail."

The priest nodded but did not speak. He clutched his wheel-cross in a quaking fist.

Above them, a black shadow shaped like an axe struck the light. Long grey lines raced along the surface. Another blow, this time to their left, and the spreading cracks connected. The lantern's glow dimmed, and the shadows drew closer.

"What are your names?" Hector asked the four soldiers. "If we die tonight, I want to know who you are."

"Henry, sir," one replied. He wore an open-faced helm and had a smear of Aaron's blood across the front of his surcoat. He held his longsword out with both hands and jumped every time something struck the wall of light.

"Sean," said a bear of a man with a green anchor tattooed on his upper bicep. He wielded a hand-and-a-half sword one-handed and carried a small, round, wooden shield in the other.

"Sergeant Miles Billingsly," said the oldest man. Of the four, he appeared the calmest. He carried two, thirty-inch long gladiuses that could have been Korellan. His greying hair and the scars on his dark skin spoke more about his fighting skills than his rank ever could.

The last was Jared, a young man with frizzy red hair who'd been with them at the monastery. He wore a black leather jerkin that looked to be more a jumble of patches than actual armor. He held a longsword in a shaky hand and his wide eyes darted around.

At the intersection of two jagged grey lines, the tip of a black sword jabbed into the light. A towering apparition worked it back and forth. Not gaining purchase, it reared back and struck again and again. On the last strike, the tip plunged deeper and a small chunk of light broke away, creating a hole. Darkness flowed in like smoke.

Instead of phantoms shrouded in mists, they caught glimpses of warriors, their skin and armor varying shades of grey. In their hands were weapons of steel, bloodied from battles long past.

"The hollow men!" Father Blackwood exclaimed in a choked whisper. Grey warriors swarmed the hole, showering them in aethereal sparks.

"Together," Aislinn said

Father Blackwood's gazed jerked about, frantically following the phantom attackers, but he nodded and replied, "Together."

The fracture grew and the surface of the light turned opalescent from all the damage. Shoulder to shoulder, the two clerics held their wheel-crosses high and shouted, *"Per inlustret lumine!"*

Bright white light lanced out, scorching the grey warriors. The creatures jerked back, and the hole sealed with a resounding thunderclap. The phantoms fled as light filled the Great Hall.

After they were gone, Sir Francis asked, "Everyone good?"

"We're alive, sir," Henry said, amazed.

"That we are, son; that we are," Sir Francis said, patting him on the back.

Sir Francis turned to Sergeant Miles and said, "Geoffrey was on river watch. Take Sean and go with Father Blackwood to make sure he's alright."

"Yes, sir," said the old sergeant, and the three ran upstairs.

Aislinn held her glowing cross high and slowly traveled across the room toward the foyer. Dave and Hector were a step behind her, weapons ready.

Sir Francis handed his lantern to Hummingbird, who stayed behind with Henry and Jared to watch over Aaron, and hurried to catch up with Aislinn. She had stopped just outside the door on the top step, her light a mere candle in the overwhelming darkness.

Shimmering fog swirled in the small bailey, and a figure appeared at its edge. She wore a low-cut dark dress with a belt of silver moons wrapped around her slim waist. Thick waves of jet-black hair framed a face the golden hue of desert sand. When she smiled, her ruby lips parted, revealing sharp, pointed fangs.

Aislinn gasped. "Lady D!"

CHAPTER 15
THE LONG NIGHT

August 3-4, 4237 K.E.

11:06pm

Two arrows with black fletching streaked across the yard. With inhuman speed, the vampire shifted back and to the left, letting Dave's arrows fly past. They hit the outer wall of the bailey; the shafts broke and bounced off with a clatter.

"Archer, as direct as always. I've missed you." Lady D's dark eyes sought Dave's, but he averted them, staring at her feet. Although her voice was as soft as velvet, her words carried across the courtyard. "No matter where you roam, your blood calls to me. It whispers of the longing in the darkest reaches of your heart. Come to me. Let's turn the river red."

"Never. Again," Dave grated, nocking two more arrows to his string.

Hector shouldered his way onto the stoop to stand between Dave and the vampire. "Señorita, it's nice to see you again!" he shouted.

"Saludos, cazador," she replied, shifting her attention.

Unlike Dave, Hector stared boldly into the vampire's eyes. "You may look like Lady D, but you are not her." Hector held up his scimitar and let the light at his back shimmer over the silvered steel. "I killed Lady D with this sword. I chopped off her head and threw it in a lake of boiling acid, then burnt her corpse and scattered the ashes to the four winds."

The smile on the vampire's lips slipped away, replaced by a look of sheer hatred. Hector descended a step, as if daring her. He gave the woman an obvious once-over, and his expression filled with contempt. "You look more the devil's whore than the warrior I fought. Are you picking out your own clothes or is someone doing that for you?"

"Hector?" Aislinn questioned. "What the hell are you doing?"

Slicing the air in front him with his blade, Hector continued, "Besides, if you really were Lady D, you would have no power here. I took her fangs when I broke her sword."

"Cazador, I will feed you your friends, piece by piece," the vampire screamed in rage, "and you will beg me to let you die."

"¡Venga!" Hector challenged. "¡Te mataré de nuevo!"

The temperature in the courtyard plummeted, and for the briefest of moments, the darkness coalesced into the form of a man behind the vampire. Malevolent red eyes glared at Hector.

"Your mask slipped!" Hector taunted.

Lady D seemed to calm, and her lips curled in a cold smile. Her eyes never left Hector's as she whispered to the darkness.

In answer, loud screaming from the barracks shattered the night. Frantic soldiers staggered into the courtyard beset by milky-eyed phantoms.

Sir Francis rushed down the steps, and Hector caught his arm before he stepped into the darkness.

"You can't go out there," Hector said. "Aislinn's light is the only thing keeping them at bay."

"I can't stay here and do nothing! Those are my men."

Another scream erupted from the barracks. Sir Francis jerked away from Hector and plunged into the shifting darkness. Aislinn and Dave rushed to join Hector as he followed.

With an exaggerated wave of her arm, Lady D reared back and threw something as she shouted, "Nigra pice!"

A black, viscous liquid coated Aislinn's fist. It ran down the braided leather to her wheel-cross and snuffed out the light. Fog rushed in around the group, filled with Lady D's laughter.

"Shit! When did she become a spell caster?" Dave asked.

Aislinn flicked her wrist, then scrubbed her hand and wheel-cross against her pants, but the tarlike substance held fast.

Countless spectral shapes armed with weapons blacker than the void between the stars formed around Lady D, some recognizable as men, most not.

Too far from the steps to head back into the tower and too far from the entry to the barracks, Dave, Hector, Aislinn, and Sir Francis formed a circle and took up defensive stances. Though each of their weapons were different, faint runes of magic inscribed on the surface of their blades glowed softly in the aethereal fog.

"I really wish you hadn't pissed her off," Aislinn said, holding her sword in one hand and the tar covered cross in the other. Every so often, she flicked it.

Grey creatures charged across the courtyard. Behind them, Lady D calmly climbed the steps into the tower.

"Aislinn?" Hector said.

"We have to do this the hard way!" she answered.

More phantoms appeared, rising into the air above the others like a swelling wave bearing down on a defenseless shore.

The four braced themselves, swords ready. As the phantoms drew closer, their hollow eyes blazed with an evil, expectant light.

With a silvery flash, ghostly shapes materialized and formed ranks between the living and the oncoming evil. Instead of smashing into Damage, Inc. and the constable, the spectral wave broke on a wall of ghosts.

Hector blinked and found himself and Dave defended by ghostly men and women who shone with their own inner light. Some wielded swords, some carried pitchforks, and others brandished shovels. They struck at the phantoms, driving them back. The two men were swept along in the fight, driving the evil before them to the gates of the shrievalty.

Lady D rushed out of the tower, chased by even more ghostly men. Her eyes burned with hatred as she took in the scene in front of her. In her hand, she carried a narrow, wooden box with the Order of the Golden Stag's crest emblazoned on the top. Behind her, incorporeal townspeople swiped at her with their makeshift weapons. Without looking back, she raised her arms and vanished.

CRSO

11:28pm

Her wheel-cross still stuck to her hand, Aislinn crossed swords with one dark spectre after another. Although she felt the weight of each blow, there were none of the normal sounds of battle. No shuffling of feet or gasping of breath — just a pervasive silence. At least the phantoms suffered real wounds from her blade. In return, their weapons left burning black stripes like frostbite on her skin and sapped her vitality.

The ghosts which had pursued Lady D out of the tower flew down the steps and joined the courtyard battle. Their weapons cut through the grey men, trailing rainbow-hued sparks.

Yelling, Aislinn slashed a spectral shape across the abdomen. Its entrails turned to smoke, and the apparition dissipated. Three more phantoms took its place, and Aislinn was hard pressed to fend off their stygian blades.

Cold sweat dripped from her skin even as her sword whipped back and forth. She whirled, dodged, and struck like a madwoman, but the three pressed closer. Planting her right foot behind her, she leaned way back, avoiding the swift tip of black metal.

A ghost appeared on her left, just in time to turn an attack from her blind side. Its inner light drove back her opponents, allowing her enough time to recover. Hope flooded through her. Together, they pressed forward, and another apparition turned to smoke.

Some of the men from the barracks braved the fight, but having no magic, their weapons simply passed through the grey men without harming them. Aislinn watched from the corner of her eye as the spectral shapes swarmed them, feasting on the easy targets.

The enchanted runes on Sir Francis' sword flared as he cleaved a spectral head. "Men, to me!" he commanded and charged toward the barracks, followed by a company of ghostly warriors. They broke the grey men's flank, driving them away from Ruthaer's defenseless garrison.

CR&SO

3:06am

Dave and Hector fought at the gate, their enchanted blades brutally efficient. The fog grew thick about them, separating them from the others. Surrounded by ghosts and phantoms, they passed into the grey world of the Luminiferous Aether.

The night wore on and their line pushed deeper into the mists. They lost track of how many fell to their blades.

Panic swept through Dave when he cast a glance over his shoulder and could no longer see the shrievalty tower. The mist had them trapped.

"Bloody hell!" Dave swore between sword strokes. "Now, I know how a cork feels."

"What do you mean?" Hector huffed beside him.

"Aren't we just plugging a fucking hole?"

Hector looked around. After a moment, he yelled, "Pull back! They're drawing us in." The ghosts around them responded to Hector's command and, inch by inch, retreated.

Taunting laughter echoed, seeming to come from everywhere at once, and the grey men surged forward, pressing the ghostly defenders. The mists grew more solid but shouts from the bailey occasionally made their way through.

The fighting grew frantic in the mouth of the shrievalty's gateway, now transformed into a portal between the aethereal and mortal realms. Standing between the grey men of the Luminiferous Aether and the world of flesh and blood, Dave and Hector took turns at the front line. Ahead of them, the ranks of the dead seemed infinite. The fog was awash with both grey men and nightmarish, otherworldly creatures.

Time lost all meaning as creature after creature pressed forward, intent on gaining access to the living world.

One charged toward them, looking as though it belonged in an undersea grotto. Arms like lead, Dave slashed with his sabre. His opponent dodged the attack and swept his hooked blade toward the archer. A touch of black frost kissed his chest and his whole body spasmed in pain. Hector leapt and parried the grey creature's next attack, deftly slicing through its wrist.

Dave whipped his sabre through the neck of the spectral creature, and it melted into harmless vapor. Hector and Dave stood ready, shocked to find no new horror waited to take its place.

A hint of pearly light touched the fog. Patches of color floated in the mist. It was like looking through a shattered rainbow. Near the barracks, Dave saw the glimmer of Sir Francis' blade, but the figures around him wavered in and out of focus.

On the far side of the bailey, Aislinn fought back to back with the ghost of a middle-aged man only slightly taller than her. The two swayed back and forth in the distorted air, as though they had fought together countless times, perfectly paired. Something about the ghost's posture, the set of his shoulders as he swung at another opponent, seemed familiar.

"Hector, look."

The bounty hunter held up his hand for silence.

Something new moved in the night. A menace so terrible, it drove off the horde of grey men. As it drew closer, fear spread through his entire body. It clenched his heart in a tight fist threatening to squeeze the life from him.

With a rush of ghost-wind, a winged reptilian shape sailed overhead, dwarfing the shrievalty. It turned the fog red as it circled once, then headed east toward the ocean. Others followed behind it, their silent formation drifting just above the treetops.

Boom!

The sound of a drum broke the silence of the dead.

Boom!

Its regular beat vibrated the ground and shook mortar loose from the walls.

Boom!

The remaining phantoms in the bailey turned toward the noise. Not looking back, they fled toward the river and disappeared.

Boom!

The fog thinned, revealing an army of humanoids: dark olive skinned, ape-like orcnéas, dark-furred dreyri, and the towering, muscular forms of eotenas. The monstrous ranks marched down the dirt road, armored for war, carrying black banners with red skulls that fluttered in the dead air.

Dave swallowed the fear gripping his throat and whispered, "Are they real?" Hector grabbed him by the arm and retreated to the center of the bailey where the others had gathered.

The host outside passed by as if it didn't see them. Battalions of humanoids marched through obstacles with only the occasional tinkle of wind chimes to mark their passage. Minutes seemed to stretch to hours and still they flowed past.

"Where are they going?" Aislinn whispered. She held her cross close. The dark night slowly retreated, and the tarry substance covering her hand evaporated.

The leather-clad ghost who had been fighting alongside Aislinn said, "They march to the sea to fight the old ones who died at the Praesidium."

A red shadow passed overhead and worked its way back to the river. The ghost drifted toward the shrievalty gate. Aislinn gripped her sword and stepped forward as if she meant to charge the horde with him. Dave grabbed her from behind and wrestled her back, turning her around. She thrashed and jerked in a bid for freedom, but Dave kept her pinned against him.

"Let me go!"

"No. Stay." His eyes held hers, willing her to listen.

"Was that a red dragon?" Hector asked.

"Yes," the ghost answered. He turned away from the gate and caught sight of the struggling pair. Momentary surprise gave way to a wry smile.

Dave scowled over Aislinn's shoulder at the ghost. "Do I know you?"

The ghost raised a ginger colored eyebrow. "No, I'm just a fisherman."

The eastern sky began to take shape through the fog, and one of the ghosts called, "Alaric, dawn approaches!"

Aislinn gasped and spun free of Dave's faltering hold to face the spirit. "Isä?" He was already growing transparent under the brightening sky.

Alaric smiled. "Aislinn, look at you..."

She closed the distance between herself and her father's spirit. "Isä! Don't go."

He raised a hand to her cheek and gently touched it. "I love you."

"I love you too, Isä," Aislinn said as her father faded away in the first rays of dawn.

CHAPTER 16
PRAESIDIUM XII

August 4, 4237 K.E.

5:09am

Flight-master Tealaucan Rathaera walked the ramparts, staring out over the fog-shrouded ocean toward the morning horizon, breathing in the salty breeze. He stood just under seven feet tall and his muscular body glinted with a metallic sheen. Covered by fine bronze scales, he wore no armor, just close-fitting leather breeches and a massive two-handed sword strapped to his back. Xemmassian lettering stitched into the leather sheath read, "Per Mare, Per Aerem."

Earlier that morning, scouts had returned, bringing word Praesidiums V and VI had fallen. The Dark One's army slaughtered every man, woman, and child. Those here at Praesidium XII were the last of their people — all that remained of the Xemmassian culture — and soon the tide of evil would come for them, too.

He prayed to Xardus for the strength and cunning to defeat their enemy. The Great Dragon knew his people's pleas for help from the elder council had fallen on deaf ears. Neither Aurum nor Argent, Azure nor Vert, would take wing in what they viewed as a conflict betwixt Xardus and his dark brother. Teal cursed the dragon elders for fools.

A sense of déjà vu washed over him. Racked by flashes of memory, Teal realized he'd lived this day countless times, unable to change the outcome. He fought to clear his vision, wondering if his newfound awareness would allow this time to be different. Teal turned his back to the sea, letting his gaze sweep over his home. In his heart, he knew the answer was no. It would end exactly as before, and sadness saturated his soul.

His draconic bond-mate, Tarnillis, perched on a stone platform behind him, her head towering seventy feet above the battlements. Assembled in the field below was his Flight: a dozen battle-hardened dragons — some with riders and some without — cobbled from the far reaches of the land. Teal knew them all, but not well. The cursed war with the Dark One had robbed them all of family and friends and strove to steal their futures. He could only hope some would escape the coming battle.

"Evil blots the western horizon," the dragon rumbled. Smoke poured from her nostrils and her claws scored the stone. "Gules and Glacies hath joined causes with Obsianus. 'Tis a Gule which doth lead the way." Through their mental bond, he saw the fast-approaching swarm of ruby, obsidian, and frost dragons flying low over the fog shrouded mainland.

Teal raised his hand. A nearby soldier lit the signal fire and thick, black smoke roiled upward from tar-soaked wood. All down the crescent-shaped barrier island, greasy plumes rose skyward from evenly spaced towers set into the long wall.

In the courtyard, fog swirled. Something about the pearlescent grey vapor struck him as wrong. Xemmassian women scooped up their children and fled into the two-story, colonnaded basilica, heading to the Sanctuary. Teal watched them go, realizing with a start that the figures were semi-transparent.

More images bombarded Teal — bodies strewn across the courtyard and into the basilica under a grey sky. He shook his head to dislodge them. Ghosts or not, he would defend his people.

Those without children manned the walls with ballistae. Spears with barbed heads lay stacked beside them. At the main gate, soldiers closed the door and set a stout timber bar reinforced with bands of bronze into the brackets.

"Tarnillis, to war." The dragon lowered her neck and Teal climbed aboard the waiting saddle. Spreading her leathery wings, she sprang into the air. Exhilaration mixed with fear as he beheld the thundering swarm of evil dragons with his own eyes. Approximately four-score surged toward the Praesidium. Behind him, his Flight followed his lead and launched into aerial battle formation. Farther down the island, two other Flights formed up to meet the oncoming enemy.

Jagged bolts of onyx-colored lightning streaked out of the fog. With a belch of fire and black smoke, the main door into the Praesidium exploded into a thousand splinters. Screaming men and women lay amid the wreckage, their bodies torn and broken like the gate. Healers and their helpers moved from person to person, dragging them to shelter.

A shout rose from beyond the basilica, and Teal looked westward. His horror grew as a mob of humanoid creatures charged through the fog, across the top of the pluton, and onto the bridge connecting the outpost to the mainland. Like a black wave of boiling flesh, they crashed against the shattered Praesidium wall and poured inside.

Signaling "Defend" to his flight, he tapped the base of Tarnillis' neck and had her circle toward the pluton. When she was within range, Tarnillis roared. A pulsing blossom of electricity streaked through the air and struck the bridge. Designed to fail in the event of an attack, the elaborate stone and timber viaduct exploded into flame, engulfing the orcnéas, dreyri, and eotenas caught mid-span and transforming them into living torches. Burning, shrieking attackers toppled into the 200-foot wide gorge and the rumbling boom of thunder knelled their deaths.

Tarnillis banked and prepared for another attack, drawing energy from the agitated air particles flowing over her metallic scales until a glowing nimbus surrounded her and Teal. A streak of dark red shot beneath her, slicing her vulnerable underbelly in passing. Ruby colored scales shimmered as the enemy dragon rolled and turned in a tight corkscrew to attack again. With another roar, Tarnillis redirected her attack toward this new target. She spat out a ball of white-hot electricity. For a heartbeat, it hung suspended above the rising smoke, concealing her attacker.

Out of the churning cloud of ozone, a ruby dragon plunged toward them with its front claws outstretched. Leather straps of a riding harness crisscrossed the creature's broad chest, but Teal couldn't see its rider.

Before Tarnillis could respond, Teal reached through their bond. "Hold your position."

At the last second, the ruby dragon changed direction and dove below the burning bridge, giving Teal and Tarnillis a clear view of the enemy rider. A bronze-scaled face Teal knew as well as his own glared back at the flight-master. Dressed in the black robes of a sorcerer, the other rider raised a fist alight with malignant energy. Teal and Tarnillis flew into the gorge and gave chase.

Although he'd relived this battle countless times through the centuries, the shock and pain of betrayal was as sharp as ever, and Teal found himself shouting, "Zalar! What have you done?"

Teal's brother had left their home years before to study at Val Magus with the mages of the Korellan Empire and never returned, until today. Deep in his heart, Teal held a flicker of hope he could turn Zalar back from the evil path he flew and maybe — just maybe — doing so would end this purgatory.

The two streaked out of the gorge and high over the mainland. In the air above the Praesidium, bronze dragons and their Xemmassian kin struggled to save their home from the invading horde. Fire, ice, and lightning surged between the dragons. Everything and everyone unlucky enough to be caught beneath the aerial combatants were scorched and burned.

Teal and Tarnillis slowed to watch three dragons locked in combat crash through the basilica roof. Dust rose from the toppled building and obscured their home. Up and down the great stone island, the ground shook and cracked under the impact of falling dragons.

Appalled by the shear ferocity of the battle, Teal flew in a daze. Too late, he came to himself and was defenseless against the bolt of black energy streaking toward him with a ruby dragon in its wake. Tarnillis roared in pain when the two clashed and began to fall. Folding her wings, she dug her claws into their enemy's gem-like scales and used her weight to drag it down. The ruby dragon tore itself from Tarnillis' grasp and blasted fire into her face and chest.

Trailing smoke and droplets of molten bronze, Tarnillis plummeted toward the forested ground. Teal could still feel the beat of her heart, and he called desperately to his mate through their bond. Loblolly pines became giant spears that grew larger and larger in his sight. He called to her again and felt a stirring of consciousness. Tarnillis' wings snapped open and they shot over the treetops, showering the forest floor with needles and branches.

Teal twisted in his harness. Zalar and his mount sped after them, liquid fire dripping from its open maw.

The flight-master pictured his plan in his mind, scene by scene. Tarnillis answered in kind, offering alternatives that would make them seem more desperate while forcing their enemy to slow his pursuit. Satisfied with their plan, she banked tightly, grunting with pain as her scorched chest pulled with the effort.

Caught by surprise, Zalar and his gem-toned mount flew by and lost distance.

With a flap of her mighty wings, Tarnillis accelerated toward the carnage at the Praesidium. At the edge of the great pluton she dove, and they flew back into the gorge separating the Praesidium from the mainland at full speed. The walls became a stony blur. Along the bottom, a series of half-flooded caves led to the ocean: the homes of the dragons.

Zalar knew this game. He and Teal had played it as children. Then, the first to reach the open ocean on the Praesidium's far side won, and Teal was always faster. Now, he, Zalar, would be the victor. He urged the ruby dragon into the gorge and, when Teal disappeared into a cave, he followed. Light from bioluminescent fungi glimmered in bits of exposed quartz along the granite walls as the two hurtled through the caves, one directly behind the other. They flew just above the still water, the tips of the dragons' wings leaving tiny ripples on its dark surface.

Hot on Teal's tail, Zalar's heart raced. They were so close. Closer than he'd ever been before. The caves and passages linking them twisted and turned, and Teal pulled away. Striking the ruby dragon with a scourge made from black energy, Zalar spurred his mount onward, each turn darker and narrower than the last. Gaining inches on the bronze pair, they passed the island's midpoint and entered a series of passages that spiraled upward, away from the water.

Zalar separated from Teal at a downward sloping passage. With a slap of his scourge, Zalar leaned forward and the two dove into it. Light rippled over the glistening walls, and his dragon continued its dive toward the sea. They leveled out at the bottom and shot through the exit into a glowing fog bank. Light and mist filled their eyes, temporarily blinding them.

Poised above the cave exit, Teal climbed free of his riding harness. When Zalar and his ruby dragon flew out, he leapt onto the enemy dragon's back. Instinctively, the red veered upward into the grey clouds, and Teal clutched a fistful of Zalar's robes.

"Brother! Stop this madness!" Teal shouted. "'Tis your home, our family and friends, below us!"

Zalar sneered at Teal. "Dost thou not understand? The Dark One hath won! Join him or die!"

"Even as a hatchling, thou didst always surrender afore the fight did begin in earnest," Teal said.

"You cannot imagine the power. We can have the world."

"I had all of the world I did want. Thou art destroying it! Thee and this gule."

Zalar laughed a cold, mirthless laugh. "Then perish like the rest, fool."

"Not without thee," Teal replied. Releasing Zalar's robes, he unsheathed his sword. Just as the ruby dragon twisted, trying to throw him off, he drove the long blade hilt deep between the dragon's shoulder blades, severing its spine. The dragon roared in shock and pain. Its suddenly limp body hurtled toward the fog-shrouded sea.

Zalar launched himself at Teal and grabbed him about the throat, a spell on his lips.

"Brother..." Teal gasped. His fist still clutched his sword's hilt, but the blade was bound in bone and useless.

The Xemmassian traitor tightened his grip and Teal felt cold blackness encroaching on his consciousness. Letting go of the sword, Teal grabbed Zalar by the throat with both hands, and together they fell from the ruby dragon's back. The flight-master squeezed with all his might until he felt the subtle snap as he broke his brother's neck.

Over the blood pounding in his ears, he heard Tarnillis' cry of pain and despair. He knew she would not reach him before he hit the ocean surface, and at his height, it might as well be stone. Below him, the fog churned. The first ray of dawn shot over the horizon in a flash of emerald green as he entered the swirling vapor. With a prayer to Xardus to rain eternal vengeance on the evil that destroyed his home, Teal knew no more.

CHAPTER 17
AFTERMATH

August 4, 4237 K.E.

5:36am

"Aislinn. Aislinn!" Hector called.

She stood stock still with her hand up, facing the sun.

Dave reached for her but thought better of it at the last second. Muttering a curse under his breath, he dropped his hand and strode to the tower, where Hummingbird met him at the door.

"Are you alright?" he asked.

Hummingbird's fingers flew from to sign to sign, trying to tell him everything she witnessed. He caught about every third word, but it was clear she was unhurt, and Lady D had not reached Corporal Ponds. She kept repeating, "And they were good ghosts."

Sir Francis pushed past them with a half-dozen men behind him. Dave followed the soldiers into the Great Hall to dig through his pile of belongings for his flask. The building held an unnatural chill, and he let the fiery liquor warm his gut. Spying the blackened hearth, the archer dug flint and steel from his pouch and made himself busy. By the time the constable's men came downstairs bearing the bodies of Sergeant Miles, Sean, and Geoffrey from the roof, Dave had a fire blazing.

The soldiers laid the bodies side by side near the door, waiting for Sir Francis to come down and tell them what to do next. Dave looked around and wondered what became of Father Blackwood. *'Creepy bastard,'* he thought, *'probably hiding.'*

Turning his attention to the fallen men, he knelt and made a ward against evil. There were no defensive wounds, no blood on any of their bodies. Although he wanted to look away, he couldn't tear free of the dead men's gazes. Their extremities — lips, ears, noses, and fingers — were raw and blackened by rot.

Unconsciously rubbing the scars on his neck, Dave glanced at Hummingbird behind him, and the horror etched on her face. "Come on, kid," he said and sent her ahead of him to find Hector and Aislinn.

Dave stopped in the doorway to stare out over the surrounding wall. From his vantage point, he saw men and women wandering the streets, shock and disbelief displayed in their every movement. Some called out to friends and neighbors, knocking on doors and peering in windows, searching for the quick and the dead. Most ambled toward the church, probably not even aware of what they were doing. Spotting Hector, Hummingbird, and Aislinn in the bailey, he gave them a quick nod and aimed toward them.

A hysterical woman with red-rimmed eyes raced inside the walled compound, yelling for Sir Francis. She stopped briefly in front of Dave, seeking reassurance — something — from him, but his glare made her move on.

Outside the gate, men strained to maneuver a flatbed wagon with a dark blanket thrown over the back. Leather straps and buckles along the yoke and tongue jangled with every step they took. The wagon hit a pothole, and the contents shifted, exposing the pallid arm of a child. One of the women who followed rushed forward and gently pushed it back. Another wagon had stopped farther up the street. Men and women ferried bodies from its back into the Meeting House.

"That building's going to fill up," Hector mused.

"Where are the horses?" Aislinn asked.

They all turned toward the stables where the flies were just starting to congregate.

"Dead," Dave replied.

"All of them?"

"¿Qué coño paso?" Hector asked. "Why are some people dead and some not?" He left the bailey and went against the tide of people in the street; Aislinn, Hummingbird, and Dave trailed behind. They found Mr. and Mrs. Griffon on their front porch, holding each other, dazed but alive. Dark circles around their eyes gave testimony to a long night.

Aislinn laid a hand on the matronly woman's arm and said, "Mrs. Griffon, are you alright?"

She flinched as if seeing Aislinn for the first time and said, "Oh, honey, I'm glad to see you this morning."

Mrs. Griffon let go of her husband and straightened her apron. "Do you want your old room?"

"No, ma'am. Not right now," Aislinn said. "Do you need anything?"

"We're fine," she said. "Last night..."

"I know, Mrs. Griffon," Aislinn said softly.

Hector asked, "What about your guests, señora? Have you seen any of them this morning?"

Another wagon went by with still more bodies, and Mrs. Griffon's mouth fell open. "That's Rhonda's family." She ran off the porch followed closely by Mr. Griffon.

∞

7:17am

"Aislinn, see if you can find anything that may have marked this inn, " Hector said. "Something that kept those folks alive."

The bounty hunter turned to Dave and gave him a nod. The archer raced inside and up the stairs. "Hummingbird, help Aislinn." The petite elf nodded and closed her eyes.

While everyone went to work, Hector stood outside the doorway, thinking. Above the door were two rusty horseshoes — one turned up, the other down — each held in place with seven silver nails.

Hector stepped inside and motioned for Aislinn. "Take a look at this."

She came over and studied the horseshoes.

"Are they magical?" Hector asked.

"No," Aislinn said. She looked across the street, and sure enough, many of the doors had horseshoes over them.

Hector followed her gaze. "So, what's special about them?"

"There's a legend," she replied, "about a monk who tricked the Dark One and nailed a horseshoe to his foot. The Dark One writhed in pain and begged the monk to remove the shoe. The monk agreed to release the Dark One only if he promised to never enter a place with a horseshoe over the door."

"And it *worked*?" Hector asked.

"Look around. Something saved those people," Aislinn replied.

"What about you? Weren't you attacked by those same spectres?" Hector asked. "Why weren't you protected?"

Aislinn and Hector turned back to the horseshoes over the inn's door. "Señor Griffon rehung the horseshoes yesterday morning," said Hector.

The two looked at each other and said, "Dodz!"

They rushed upstairs. Each bedroom door hung open, except the last, where Dave stood, back to the wall, sabre in hand. His other hand grasped the doorknob. Though his eyes focused on them, he remained completely immobilized.

Hector shook his head and grinned. "Amigo, you shouldn't stand around with your hand on another man's knob like that. People will talk." He burst into laughter. Aislinn gasped and covered her mouth with both hands, but soon joined in the laughter. Dave's eyes filled with an odd mixture of frustration, anger, and helplessness, which was completely at odds with the rest of his stoic expression, and it made them laugh harder.

"Dave, you would never make a good thief," Hector finally gasped. Aislinn erupted in a new round of laughter, carrying him with her. Tears streaming down his cheeks, Hector spotted Hummingbird crouched at the head of the stairs. The confusion and hint of fear in her expression burned away his humor. "It's alright, chica, we aren't loco."

"That depends on who you ask," Aislinn laughed.

"You're no help," Hector replied. He eyed the door and Dave's predicament. "We may not get in there today. Maybe we should find that bar wench from the other night. I bet she'd be willing to see if a kiss could break the spell."

Aislinn shook her head. "Oh, no. The last time you sicced a strange woman on him, Robert and I had a hell of a time convincing him not to kill you."

"We have to do something," Hector protested. "There's no telling how long he'll be stiff without help."

Aislinn rolled her eyes. "Enough, already! I'm pretty sure I can help him."

Hector gave the archer a speculative look. "I can't tell you if Dave's safe to touch or not. He might explode."

"I'll take my chances," said Aislinn.

CRSO

7:43am

Dave's eyes shifted to Aislinn. She took out her wheel-cross with one hand and placed the other over his heart. Muscles quivered at her touch, sending his heart racing and his pulse pounding in his ears.

"You get so wound up," Aislinn said with a smile. She brushed her thumb over the eye of the Gael dragon tattoo stretching from his left pectoral over his shoulder. "You really need to release some of this tension. It's not healthy."

She began praying, and warmth spread from her fingertips over his skin. Life slowly returned to his arms and legs. As soon as he was able, he released the knob and stepped away from both the door and from Aislinn.

"You shouldn't have touched me," Dave groused. "The spell could have trapped you, too."

Hector nudged Aislinn. "Now that he's gone soft, you want to help me with this wood?"

"Hector!" Aislinn exclaimed and flushed red.

"You were the one willing to touch him when he was stiff," Hector said with a grin. "But seriously, there may be a glyph or something on the door. That's more your department."

Aislinn narrowed her eyes and stuck her tongue out at him, then gave him a playful elbow in the gut. "Step aside." She held out her cross and prayed silently. After a few moments, she said, "It's safe. Whatever magic was there is gone."

Hector opened the door slowly, revealing a room with motes of sunlight filtering through the curtain. Other than the bed and dresser, it was empty. The only sign anyone had been there was a three-foot diameter circle of fine, white sand on the floor.

"The putz is gone," Dave growled.

Careful to avoid the circle of sand, the four went through the room but didn't find anything. Eventually, they worked themselves back to the floor.

"What is it?" Hector asked kneeling for a closer look.

"Magic," Aislinn answered. "As a guess, I'd say it opened some sort of gate or doorway, but you'd be better off asking Jasper the next time we see him."

"Where do you think it goes?" Hector asked. He dug into one of his belt pouches and pulled out a tiny glass bottle with a cork. He used the tip of his dagger to fill the bottle with sand, then sealed it and tucked it back in his pouch.

"If it is a portal, it could open anywhere," Aislinn said.

"Could he come back?" Hector asked.

Aislinn shrugged.

Dave scraped his foot across the sand, breaking the circle. "Not anymore."

CRSO

8:00am

Fatigue settling in from the long night, Damage, Inc. went back downstairs to the empty dining room. While the others drifted toward a corner table, Aislinn went to the kitchen and found four mugs. She returned to find Dave already had his flask in hand. "Water, please," she said as she placed the vessels before the archer.

Dave fixed her with a flinty glare and took another long drink.

"Don't give me guff. After last night, we all need to drink water, even you."

Muttering incoherently, he filled three of the mugs with water from his flask before raising it to his lips again. The harsh, burning scent of grain alcohol drifted on the air.

Aislinn wrapped her fingers around his wrist and jerked the flask away from his mouth, spilling whiskey in the process. "Water, Dave."

"Dammit, woman! Let me be!"

"No. We all look out for each other, remember? Especially when the other can't see what's best for them. Just like this morning in the bailey," she added softly. "Now, drink some water so we can catch a nap before the next disaster strikes."

The archer's glare faded. Finally, he filled the fourth cup and took a swallow. Hector and Hummingbird let out the breaths they were holding, and Aislinn sat down.

Hector interlaced his fingers behind his head and leaned back in his chair. "The murders, Count Dodz and his shipwreck, a ghostly army, the fog. Where do we start?"

"Sir Francis and Father Blackwood," Hummingbird signed. "They have a secret. I sensed it the other day, before we went to the monastery. Yesterday, in the graveyard, Sir Francis hid his fear and sadness behind anger."

"We were looking at his son's grave when he found us," Hector said. "Do you think what you sensed was related to Evan Courtenay's death?"

The elf's narrow shoulders twitched in a half-hearted shrug. "I blocked Sir Francis out of my senses. His emotions were so strong, I felt like I was drowning."

"You and Aislinn can talk to him again this afternoon," Hector decided. "Between the two of you, you should be able to get answers out of him."

"Hummingbird doesn't need to poke around in people's heads," Dave snapped at their leader. "No telling what she might get exposed to."

"Dave's right," Aislinn agreed. The groan and squeak of another canvas covered wagon passing filled the room, temporarily cutting off the conversation. "If I have a chance, I'll try to speak to Francis alone this evening. As for the ghost army and the fog, they're tied together. The borders between this town and the Beyond have thinned, allowing us to see into the Luminiferous Aether, and vice versa."

"Why here? Why now?" Hector asked.

Hummingbird straightened and signed, "They are echoes of the past. What my grandmother called Phantasma."

"Phantoms?" Hector said. "You mean ghosts."

"Not necessarily," Aislinn said. "Places can retain the memory of past events, especially if they're emotionally charged. Fear, anger, and powerful love seep into the earth and stones, even buildings, and sometimes the living feel echoes of it. Normally, it manifests itself as an eerie feeling, or simple goosebumps. However, if the event is powerful enough, it can anchor people — their spirits — preventing them from passing on. They get stuck between Heaven and Hell."

"Is that what we fought last night?" Dave asked.

"I believe so," Aislinn said. "Sister Inez in Ozera once told me the trapped spirits don't even know they're dead. They just keep reliving the same moment over and over. Forever."

"Yesterday," said Hector, "you thought someone might have caused the borders to thin. Do you still think that's possible?"

"After what we faced last night, I don't think a person would be powerful enough. At the very least, we're looking for someone with an artifact."

Hector asked, "What about the horde just before dawn? Do you know any legends or myths that explain that? If what you said about trapped spirits is true, it has to be something regional."

Aislinn shook her head. "There hasn't been a humanoid army like those ghosts since the Dark One and his Sha'iry priests waged war against Korell more than three thousand years ago, and that was far west of the White River, on the northern border of what's now the Espian Empire. There was nothing in the Carolingian histories taught in Ozera. No mention of any battles happening here in Ruthaer before the pirates attacked."

"Something happened," Hector said. Scratching idly at the stubble on his chin, he stared into the distance. "I'd wager the monks found relics or an artifact on those barrier islands, and they were killed for it. It's the only thing that explains the destruction of Brother Powell's mural and the missing journal."

"The fog and disappearances have been happening for months, according to Tallinn and Aaron," argued Aislinn. "If the monks had an artifact causing these problems, they wouldn't have kept it secret. They'd have sent for help from York or Ozera."

"So how do you think it's all tied together?" asked Hector.

She shook her head tiredly. "I don't know. There are too many disparate pieces." She raised her hand and ticked off each item using her fingers. "The murders at the monastery, three deaths exactly one year apart, ghosts in the fog, disappearances, Dodz and his shipwreck. Last, but certainly not least, was Lady D really here last night, or was it her ghost?"

"It was her." Dave reached for his flask. He stopped when he saw Aislinn's eyes narrow and her brow draw down. "But what we saw at the monastery wasn't Lady D. Vampires don't waste blood. Plus, she never made revenants that I remember."

"That was not Lady D last night," Hector scoffed. "Nothing comes back after you cut off its head — not even a vampire."

"Trolls do," said Dave.

Aislinn rolled her eyes. "Altaira is on the other side of the world from Parlatheas. How could anyone impersonate Lady D? We're the only people on this continent who know anything about her."

"The only ones *we* know of," Hector argued. "Gaia is a large and mysterious world, Aislinn, full of magic and miracles, but Lady D is *dead*."

"Who was it then?" Aislinn said.

Hummingbird signed, "A woman trapped inside her own mind. When she came into the tower, I felt her rage and frustration. A powerful shadow clung to her. It dominated her."

Hector nodded. "It lost control for a few moments when I taunted her in the bailey. She must have been in a towering rage to push the shadow out like she did."

"By the way, that was stupid," Aislinn put in.

"It worked, didn't it?" Hector asked.

"You almost got us all killed."

"What about Mi'dnirr?" Dave asked.

Aislinn shifted nervously in her seat and put her hand on her neck. "I don't think so."

"Why not?" Dave pressed. "He killed Evan Courtenay."

Aislinn looked to Hector for help, but the bounty hunter stayed quiet. He raised his eyebrows and turned both hands up. She could almost hear him saying, "Tell him."

Hummingbird put her hand to her mouth and her eyes grew wide.

Dave slapped his hands on the table and said, "This shit's not funny. What aren't you telling me?"

Aislinn flinched at the tone of his voice. She slowly gathered her thoughts and said, "I met Mi'dnirr the night before last. In the graveyard."

"You said she *saw* him," said Dave, pinning the bounty hunter with a glare before turning his scowl on Aislinn. "What the hell were you doing out there alone?"

"Fighting for my life," she replied. "The ghosts in the fog tried to kill me."

"So, he is the one causing all this shit."

"No, he's not."

"Damn it, woman, why are you defending a fucking vampire?"

"Because I'd be dead right now, if not for him." Aislinn glanced at Hector again before reaching up to pull her hair back with a trembling hand.

Dave spotted the bite marks and jerked up from his chair, knocking it over. Looming over the table, he yelled, "Did Mi'dnirr do that?"

"I think so, but I'm not absolutely sure. It's only the one bite, so it's nothing, right?"

"It's not nothing! A damn infernal vampire bit you!"

"I knew he would act this way," Aislinn said staring pointedly at Hector, but the bounty hunter simply motioned her on. She took a deep breath and explained, "I thought I was having a nightmare. I saw the little girl, Klara, in my room. She was a revenant. Next thing I knew, grey men were dragging me out of the inn to the graveyard. Although I didn't see them until after the fact, there were gnomes there, waiting with Klara. The ghosts and the gnomes were going to bury me alive. Mi'dnirr killed them all. He saved me."

"He didn't save you; he marked you! Mi'dnirr put a sarding slave mark on you so he can find you later."

"Dave," said Hector, "the point is he didn't kill her. While his motives may be suspect, he's not the one behind all this. He's not the one making these revenants."

The archer glared at Hector and accused, "You knew."

"Dave." Aislinn tentatively touched his clenched fist, her eyes and voice pleading for understanding. "You of all people know what it means to be bitten. I am terrified of what Mi'dnirr might make me do... and of what you or Hector may have to do to me." She closed her eyes for a moment, struggling to contain the tears threatening to spill forth. She rubbed her sleeve across her face before meeting Dave's angry gaze. "When I die, *promise* me you or Hector will take my head before I rise." Her last words, though spoken in the barest of whispers, cut through the room like a razor.

Dave's features softened, and he reached back to straighten his chair. He sat down and covered Aislinn's hand with his. "You aren't going to come back as a vampire. Ozera's library only had one treatise on vampires, but Phaedrus assured me the information was accurate. It said a vampire has to completely drain you and feed you some of their cursed blood before your heart stops. Mi'dnirr didn't do that, but he's in your head now. You'll hear his voice in your sleep, maybe even when you're awake, and yes, he can and will make you do things. You're strong, Aislinn, you can fight him. Unfortunately, the only thing I've found to drown out Lady D's voice is drinking."

Dave leaned back in his chair, and quiet settled over the Inn. Finally, he said, "Damn. Two vampires. If they're not working together, then this is all about who has the biggest dick."

They blinked at him, uncomprehending.

"Don't you get it?" Dave asked. "This is about territory. Lady D and that shadow we saw with her, they're carving out a piece of Mi'dnirr's demesne for themselves. Last night, they sent him a message — don't fuck with us."

CHAPTER 18
GRAVEYARD DEAD

August 4, 4237 K.E.

9:04am

"Hector, what are we doing with these shovels?" Aislinn asked with a yawn. They wound their way through town from the mercantile, each with a new shovel in hand.

"With so many dead, they'll need extra gravediggers," he answered. "We're going to help."

Aislinn stared daggers at the back of Hector's head.

"I dare you to hit him," Dave murmured.

"I heard that!" Hector snapped.

The street was almost deserted. The few townsfolk they passed were so wrapped up in their own personal tragedies, they paid no heed to Aislinn and her companions. Up ahead, Big Mike stood guard at the graveyard with a bloodstained bandage covering his forehead. He wrapped his meaty hand around the hilt of his weapon when he spotted them.

Dave held out his cupped hand to Hector, but the bounty hunter shook his head. "No, we'll do this my way," Hector said.

"It'll be easier my way," Dave suggested.

"Shut up," Hector hissed. He opened his arms wide as he approached and said expansively, "Buenos días, Big Mike! Nice to see you survived."

"Sir Francis said you might come back," he said, eyeing them warily. "You four need to get in your boat and go back where you came from before this town's curse gets you, too."

Dave brought up his fist to his mouth and coughed. Big Mike slapped at his neck and picked out a tiny needle. He looked at it questioningly for a moment before his knees buckled and his burly frame began to collapse.

"Dave!" Aislinn said, rushing forward. She wrapped her arm around Big Mike's torso and lifted, grunting under the weight.

"What?" Dave replied innocently as he lifted from the other side. Mike's head lolled back and forth. He blinked slowly and opened his mouth to say something, but no words came out.

"I had this," Hector muttered as he tromped through the archway in a huff.

"My way was faster," Dave said.

"Your way caught the mountain on fire," Aislinn reminded Dave.

"Still faster," Dave said defensively.

"And the hay field the time after that? Just be sure you don't set Ruthaer on fire."

Hummingbird kept a watchful eye for signs someone noticed what they were doing. As soon as everyone was through, she closed the gate behind them and took up a lookout position.

Dave and Aislinn sat Big Mike under a tree and tried to make him as comfortable as possible.

"He's going to be *so mad* at you when he wakes up," Aislinn said to Dave as they walked away. She cast a furtive glance toward the great oak off in the distance and the pile of dirt beside it. The open grave sent a shiver down her spine.

"Hey, it's better than my original plan," Dave said.

"Which was?" she asked.

"Hit him with the shovel."

Aislinn stifled a laugh and said, "I'm glad you actually put some thought into it."

Dave looked at her askance but didn't respond.

They caught up with Hector standing by Evan Courtenay's gravestone, the head of his shovel already buried in the sunken loam.

"Gravediggers, huh?" Aislinn asked.

Hector shrugged. "This one's empty. So are Margaret Potter's and Daniel Tanner's. Might as well start here."

"You don't know that for certain," Aislinn replied. "We're already on thin ice with Francis. Desecrating his son's grave will make things worse."

"Humor me. I'll apologize to the constable if I'm wrong," said Hector, "but I'm not wrong."

Aislinn and Dave picked spots near Hector, and the trio started digging. Fortunately, a cluster of bushy cedars stood between them and the street, hiding their work from the casual observer.

The morning air transitioned from hot to sweltering. Sweat rolled down their backs as the pile of dirt grew taller and the hole deeper.

Aislinn sat with her feet dangling into the grave and wiped her brow with the back of her wrist, leaving a gritty streak. Hector and Dave were chest deep in the hole.

"Hector, are you sure about this? If you're wrong..." She left the last word hanging.

Hector stabbed his shovel into the ground and leaned against it with both hands near the end of the handle. "Only one way to be sure."

Dave scooped another shovelful of dirt and threw it over the side. Using the instep of his boot to gain more purchase, he plunged the blade of his shovel into the soil, and it made a dull thud.

Instantly, Hector moved into action and began clearing off the coffin. All that remained of the upper third of the lid was jagged splinters around rusted nails. Aislinn leaned forward, one hand on Dave's shoulder for balance, and they watched Hector scrabble around in the dirt inside the coffin.

"Evan Courtenay isn't here," he announced.

A shadow crossed over the grave, catching everyone by surprise. They looked up and saw Father Blackwood staring down at them with haunted eyes.

Hector said to him, "I assume you already knew."

Aislinn wondered if the priest would reveal the secret he kept. She and Dave shared a quick glance, then propped their shovels in the grave's corner.

"Yes, I knew," Father Blackwood admitted, "but it's not what you think. Come inside and let me explain."

The priest offered his hand to the bounty hunter, who took it. Dave whistled once he and Hector were out of the grave, and Hummingbird darted along the church wall to meet them at the gate in the rectory's willow-wythe fence.

Father Blackwood studied each of their faces. "Did you truly come here to help Ruthaer?" When each of them nodded, he led them out of the graveyard and around to the north side of the church.

Surrounded by a quaint, herb-filled garden, the tiny vestry hunkered against the chapel. Its hip roof extended over a raised stoop flanked by two timber posts.

After crossing the rectory yard, the priest held open the narrow door, which led into a short hall. Straight ahead, an archway gave them a sideview of the altar. He motioned toward a door in the right-hand wall and led them into his office.

Aislinn studied the cramped space. On the left side, sandwiched between two ornate wardrobes made from dark walnut, a shell-encrusted wheel-cross hung above a small counter with a washbasin and ewer. Along the right, shelves filled with a hodgepodge of books, scrolls, and loose parchment flanked an unlit fireplace.

Father Blackwood settled behind a plain wooden table with his back to a stained-glass window depicting a Korellan knight on a pale stallion slaying a ruby-colored dragon with a long golden spear.

There were only two chairs. Hector pushed them aside and all four stood in front of the priest.

"Padre, what's going on in this town?" Hector asked.

"The boundary between this world and the Beyond is breaking down," Father Blackwood answered. "The ghosts of our past sins are converging on Ruthaer."

"Lady D was no ghost," Dave growled.

"Lady D?" the priest asked.

"The vampire in the bailey last night," Hector said. "We've encountered her before."

"Ah, I see," Father Blackwood replied. He took a deep breath and said, "We've had the fog for several years now, but —"

"Since Evan Courtenay's death," Hector interjected.

Aislinn turned to Hector and said, "Let him finish." Turning back, she said, "Father, please, start from the beginning."

"The beginning..." Shoulders hunched and elbows on his desk, Father Blackwood pressed his palms together as if he meant to pray. "Evan took after his father. After his mother passed, he lived in the Shrievalty with Francis and the soldiers. No one was surprised when he left for York to become a career soldier in the queen's army. He sent letters to his father through the church, and Francis shared them with me. Evan did well. He moved up the ranks, and being a knight's son gave him certain opportunities, such as having his own command. Francis was so proud.

"Evan's first assignment as commander was to stop a dærghenfae uprising. They were coming down out of the mountains, raiding the western border. They slaughtered entire families and burnt their homes to the ground. In his letter, Evan said his company tracked the raiders back to their camp and destroyed it. Less than a handful escaped. Needless to say, Queen Ambrose was pleased."

Father Blackwood's visage clouded over as he continued, "I think he must have attracted someone else's attention, though, because his next letter was more guarded. He wrote that some*thing* was following him." The priest slapped his palm on the table. "Not some*one*, mind you. Not a jealous rival or a disgruntled soldier. Evan's last letter said he was heading home, but he never made it." He covered his eyes with one hand as if to block the memory from his sight and heaved a sigh.

"Father Blackwood, Tallinn told us Evan was home for a month or more before Mi'dnirr killed him," Aislinn said. "What really happened?"

"Evan never made it home. His horse showed up riderless at the shrievalty, wild-eyed with fear and mouth dripping blood-flecked foam. Francis insisted I join him in the search. We found Evan on the side of the road, two miles beyond the monastery. By the time we arrived, the vultures had already started feeding."

Father Blackwood hands began to shake as he whispered, "There was no blood. None at all. We should have known better."

"Mi'dnirr killed him, and you didn't take his head, did you?" Aislinn asked softly.

"How could we? Evan was Francis' only child."

"So, he came back as a vampire?" Hector asked.

"No. Don't you *see*? I tried to save him, to call his spirit back from beyond the veil."

"What!" Aislinn exclaimed. "Didn't you know what you were dealing with?"

"Not at first, but you *must* understand. After Francis' wife died, Evan was all he had," Blackwood pleaded. "I had to try something. Anything. What I did worked. He came back, and not as a vampire. Unfortunately, the thing Evan became is far *worse*."

Raising his face toward the ceiling, Father Blackwood mouthed "Forgive me," over and over.

"You stupid fuck," Dave said.

"Dave!" Aislinn reprimanded.

"Don't you get it?" Dave countered. "The lackwit turned to the Dark One."

Aislinn's chin dropped. Tears streamed down the old man's cheeks. "How could you?" she gasped.

"I didn't intend to. All I wanted was to help my friend. He was overcome with grief, and I couldn't give him what he wanted most without help." The cleric hung his head. "I would do anything for Francis."

"Even sell your soul," Aislinn said, her voice flat. "So then, what is Evan?"

"We... We don't know. Not exactly." Father Blackwood rubbed a nervous hand over his glossy pate. "Brother Powell believed Evan was something akin to a ghūl, but more powerful. The fog and the phantoms obey him."

"Does Sir Francis know?" Hector asked.

"Of course he knows! Admitting to himself that Evan was no longer the kind-hearted son he raised nearly destroyed Francis." Father Blackwood sighed. "You see, at first Evan didn't act evil. He was the young man we all knew and loved." The unspoken "but" hung between the priest and Damage, Inc. while he gathered his thoughts.

"It was two, almost three, weeks before I *knew* something was wrong. It was late when a sound in the graveyard woke me; the moon was nearly gone from the sky. From my window, I could see wisps of fog hanging over the graves. We'd buried Ogden Brooks that morning, and I assumed it was an animal I heard." A tear slid down the haunted priest's cheek. "It was Evan out there, digging. I caught him..." He choked back a sob. "I caught him gnawing on the dead man's arm."

Aislinn and Hector exchanged looks of disgust. "What happened next?" she asked.

"He attacked me. I hit him with my walking stick and escaped into the church. Evan couldn't enter, but I couldn't get out and go to Francis for help. When the sun rose, Evan was gone. Ogden's grave had been refilled and, other than some scratches on my arm, there was no evidence anything had happened.

"Evan gave no indication that he remembered the night before. Days passed. Ruthaer became plagued with mishaps and nocturnal scavengers, but nothing pointed to Evan. Then a soldier went missing in the night. When they found his body, everyone called it an animal attack, but I knew it wasn't.

"I had the body taken to the Meeting House. The sun was setting when Francis and Evan answered my summons. I confronted them with the soldier's wounds, which could only have come from a human mouth. Father and son denied the evidence, of course. But, as the sun set, a change seemed to wash over Evan. The color bled from his eyes, and his skin glowed with corpse-light. He laughed as he confessed to killing the soldier."

Father Blackwood eyes grew distant as he recalled that fateful day. "Evan pulled an ivory dagger, a spoil of war taken from the dærganfae, and attacked us. In the ensuing struggle between father and son, the blade ended up in Evan's heart. He didn't bleed — not a single drop. It was unnatural.

"The next day, we buried Evan beside his mother. We blamed Mi'dnirr, telling everyone the vampire had killed him. I took precautions — anointed him with holy oil, laid a blessed cross upon his chest, adorned his coffin with holy symbols. None of it worked. That very night, he emerged from his grave and fled into the forest.

"Francis and I finally tracked him down, but we didn't dare bring him back to Ruthaer. So Francis and I begged Brother Powell and the others at the monastery for help. They trapped Evan within one of the monastery's storehouses while they sought the means to undo his curse.

"Francis stayed with him at the monastery, praying for a miracle. Later, he told me Evan had moments of lucidity. His son truly wanted to undo the evil I'd wrought, even if it meant his own death. Unfortunately, the monks could neither undo the Dark One's curse, nor lay Evan's soul to rest.

"Instead, Brother Powell and the others found a way to imprison Evan where no one would accidentally stumble upon him. It was a secret the monks kept from everyone, Francis included. However, they didn't know there was a price to be paid.

"The next year, on the anniversary of his death, Evan's spirit appeared to Francis and me, demanding payment — a life to feed upon — to vouchsafe the town's safety. For two years, he was satisfied with one life, one kill," the priest explained. "But this year is different. He's come early, and he's getting stronger with each passing day. I fear, before all is said and done, Evan intends to open the gates of Hell and drag this town inside."

CR&SO

1:02pm

Allyrian flitted from house to house like a mayfly. She studied the grieving families with a somber expression, but inside she reveled in their misery. The charnel stench from the Meeting House hung thick in the air and seemed to cling to anyone who had been inside. She followed one couple for a while, then, losing interest, moved on to another.

The few remaining soldiers helped empty the corpse wagons while others searched door-to-door for survivors. Allyrian saw two guardsmen heading toward her home and decided to tag along. They knocked on the door and shouted for her father. When no one answered, they tried to open the door.

"It's locked," Allyrian said.

"Ally, we didn't see you," one said. "We came to check on you. Where's Mr. Carmichael?"

"We're fine," Allyrian replied, looking vaguely down the wide gravel and shell lined street. "My father left to get help."

One of the soldiers spied the teamster's carriage house and asked, "Can we borrow your wagon? Did your horses make it?"

Allyrian didn't hear their questions. Another consciousness brushed against hers. She shook her head, trying to dislodge the alien presence. It pushed harder, dimming her vision.

When she came to, one of the soldiers had her by the arm. "Are you sure you're alright?" he asked.

Allyrian pushed him away and replied, "I'm fine."

A voice whispered inside her head, and with it came glimpses of her past life, before betrayal cast her into the abyss, and she became a succubus. The weight of years crushed down on her and she felt a human-like anxiety. Hugging herself, she fought the self-doubt and loathing building inside her. Behind the soldiers, Allyrian caught a reflection of her true self in the sidelight window beside the front door.

She cast about and spotted a solitary figure. The person stood in the center of the street like a harbinger of death, dressed in ragged, black robes. Though his head was covered, his fierce, colorless eyes bore into hers. The few passersby instinctively moved around him, but no one else seemed to see him. Fear knifed through her.

It was Mi'dnirr.

The soldier grabbed her arm again, tighter this time. "I said I'm fine!" Allyrian yelled as she lashed out and struck him across the mouth. He flew back and landed hard. Blood trickled from his mangled jaw.

The other soldier's eyes went wide in shock, giving her a fleeting second to escape. There weren't many people around them but there were enough. Allyrian dodged the soldier and fled down the street. As word spread, others joined in the chase. Rather than risk being cornered, she fled east into the forest.

Shouts rose up behind her, but she ignored them. She could only see the man in dark robes. Allyrian never actually saw him move, but he kept appearing at the edge of her vision, driving her forward.

The clamor from Ruthaer diminished, and tall oaks closed about her, blocking out the sun. Finger-like branches grabbed at her as she ran, ripping her clothes and shoes. She cast a quick glance over her shoulder. Mi'dnirr was right behind her.

She tripped over a hidden root and fell headlong amongst the leaves and detritus. Crabbing backwards on all fours, Allyrian retreated from the dark fae approaching her. Madness filled his quicksilver eyes.

"I know who you are!" Allyrian yelled.

"I know who *you* are," a whispered voice echoed in her mind. Her back to a tree trunk, she fought to hold her human form. His presence wormed its way deeper into her consciousness, and something inside her broke. Her bat-like wings, tail, and horns slowly took shape.

Mi'dnirr grabbed her by the throat with one hand and drew her close, then pressed his other hand to her temple. She slapped at him, but his arms were like steel. Ethereal fingers stabbed into her skull, and pain wracked her body.

She slashed and clawed at the cursed vampire, tearing away his mask. A scream rose involuntarily as she caught sight of his horribly scarred face. Inside her mind, she battled the dærganfae for her very being. He penetrated deep into her psyche and dug through memories from both her life on Gaia and her time in the abyss. Wavering images of victims, past and present, swam into her vision. She pushed them away but more surfaced — both friends and enemies from the distant past when she was human.

Panic knotted in her chest when she realized what Mi'dnirr sought.

Sunlight dappled the eerily quiet forest floor. Like undead statues frozen in time, the two held each other in an odd embrace, locked in their internal struggle.

Allyrian's head wrenched back violently, and she fell. Mi'dnirr knelt over her and spoke her true name. Helpless to defend herself, he ravaged her mind, tearing at her consciousness. Spittle ran down the edge of her mouth as she stared blankly ahead.

Mi'dnirr flipped her over and pinned her to the ground. In one swift motion, he ripped off her tail, root and all. Next, he placed a knee on her spine, gripped her wings, and tore them away, exposing quivering back muscles. Last, he broke off her horns, leaving gaping holes in her scalp.

The vampire rose to his feet. The succubus lay unmoving, her steamy black blood soaking the ground, withering all it touched. Without her horns and wings, she was little more than human, and she was dying.

The staccato barking of dogs bounced off the trees, and behind it, voices carried with the wind. Men were coming. Mi'dnirr gathered his trophies and disappeared.

CHAPTER 19
AN ACCIDENT

August 4, 4237 K.E.

1:38pm

Lying on his back, Teal woke to a world shrouded in thick, cottony fog. He lay on a bed of pine straw and leaves, surrounded by a cluster of tall, vague shapes. After several heart-pounding minutes, his mind finally recognized the dim shadows as a pine copse.

An image of dawn's green flare as he plummeted toward the sea with his traitorous brother flashed before his mind's eye. Pain lanced through him. His eyes and jaw clenched until the spasm subsided. He'd slain Zalar and the ruby beast he rode, but what of the battle?

Teal reached for Tarnillis through their bond. Empty silence greeted him. Agony seared his soul. His thoughts railed against the silent gods, demanding, then begging, for answers. Had they won? Had they lost? Where was Tarnillis?

A faint rustle of leaves distracted him.

Not thirty feet from where he lay, a twelve-point buck took a tentative step. It dipped its head and drank from a babbling brook. The fog behind it thinned.

His throwing spear rested against the trunk of a nearby pine. His hunting knife lay along his hip in its belt sheath. With the discipline of an expert hunter, Teal eased into a crouch. A long-sleeved, hooded leather jerkin covered his scales, and fingerless gloves enclosed his hands. He didn't recall putting on his hunting leathers or entering the forest. As he fought to remember where he was and how he got there, a hollow and thin feeling blossomed in his gut. Food. How long had it been since he'd eaten?

Teal shifted his stance and brought up his spear. His muscles tensed as he readied the weapon, paused, and then let fly. Barking echoed in the far distance. The deer's head jerked up and the animal leapt away. Quick as lightning, the spear shot through the maze of tree trunks and vanished in a swirl of fog. A heartbeat later, it reappeared, lodged in a nearby tree.

Teal swore silently. Dogs meant men from the village weren't far behind. While he didn't have anything against humans, per se, he didn't have much use for them either.

The local villagers spoke in a strange, uncouth tongue they called Glaxon, rather than the Korellan he had learned in his youth. He had only a passing understanding of the language and, more oft than not, their meaning escaped him. It made Teal glad his job required little interaction with them.

A dog bayed and the others broke into an excited chorus of barks. Were they on the trail of his buck? The flight-master had no desire to confront the humans. He retrieved his spear and raced ahead.

The wind shifted and with it came the smell of blood. At least Teal thought it was blood. It had the same coppery tinge, but it also held the barest odor of brimstone. He followed the scent, keeping ahead of the barking. Like a shadow, he stalked through the trees in silence.

The smell grew stronger, and he spotted a human female lying face-down on the ground. A gnarled nest of tawny hair concealed her features. Her clothes were in tatters, and it looked as though a bear had attacked her. Wary, he scanned the area for signs of her attacker. Above him, boughs wove together, forming a natural canopy and blocking out most of the sun's rays. Turning his attention to the forest floor, he saw no tracks, no obvious spoor.

Worry for the female overcame his caution. Laying his spear aside, he knelt beside her and examined her wounds. They were grievous. Severe lacerations marred her back and lower spine, and it looked as though someone had scalped her. He placed his large hand close to her mouth and nose. Miraculously, she still breathed. Under his calloused fingertips, her skin was cold and clammy.

The barking grew louder as the dogs closed on them. Teal looked back the way he had come. By the sounds of it, he had less than a minute before they arrived. Even with his hunting skills, he wasn't sure if he could escape their notice. Still, Teal could not, in good conscience, leave her.

Under the voices of the baying hounds, he heard the distant boom of surf against cliffs. Teal looked back at the young woman. If he could get her to the sea caves, they stood a chance. With all the care and tenderness he could muster, he rolled her onto her side. Her expression sent shivers down his spine, and he almost dropped her.

Like the flesh of a newborn maggot, her colorless cheeks glistened under a mixture of spittle and dirt. A gash of a mouth hung open over a slack jaw, but it was none of those things which struck his soul. It was her wide, violet eyes fixed on the horror of her last vision. Something so terrible she would never be able to unsee it, even if she were to live forever.

Teal brushed his hand over her eyes, closing them, and then hoisted the girl over his shoulder. For a moment, the world shimmered. The sound of the dogs vanished mid-bark, replaced by the booming of surf. His vision cleared. A dozen yards away, verdant trees with softly glowing leaves gave way to stark silver cliffs silhouetted by a brilliant, azure sky.

"Xardus, help me help this child," he prayed, and raced through the trees toward the sea.

Laughing gulls wheeled overhead in the salty air. A narrow, rugged path led down the cliff-face to a wide ledge. As far as the eye could see, an opalescent blanket of fog obscured the sea and surf. Teal picked his way downward, holding his burden against him. Blood soaked through his leathers to coat his arms and chest. He could only hope he wasn't doing the girl more harm than good.

He finally reached the antrum he and Tarnillis called home. Sunlight warmed the sand at its entrance. Teal tried again to reach out with his mental bond but could not sense the dragon's presence. For the first time since he reached adulthood and took his oath-bond with Tarnillis, he was truly alone.

Teal eased the human down onto his bed fur and removed the remnants of her dress.

His eyes widened with shock.

On either side of her spine, gaping wounds surrounded by tattered flaps of skin revealed torn muscles and scapulae with socket cavities for wing joints. Another wound gaped at the base of her spine, as if she'd lost a vestigial tail. He wondered what she was, and if this was why the humans pursued her. Too many feared those who were different from themselves.

Could she be dragonkin? In all the history of the Xemmassian race, only a handful were born with wings. He'd heard of a few other beings with them as well, but she didn't really resemble any of those creatures. She looked too... innocent.

He shook himself. The child was dying, and he was cloud-gathering. Teal stood and walked farther into the cave. A hollow low in the rock held a chest, and he dragged it over beside his patient. Inside, he found a bone needle and strips of bandage, as well as a ball of wax and spool of heavy thread.

"I hope, for thy sake, thou dost not wake 'fore I am done," he said, then set about the grim task of cleaning and stitching her wounds.

By the time he finished, the early afternoon sun slanted into the cave mouth, warming the sand near the entrance. Thankfully, the girl slept through the operation. Teal gathered the edges of the furs and folded them across her now bare form, tucking them around her to help preserve whatever body heat she might have left, then lifted her in his arms and carried her into the sunlight.

He wondered again who and what she really was. She seemed little more than a child, even by human standards.

Sitting there with her in his lap, with the sun's rays wrapped around them and the glowing fog spread beneath his feet, it felt both strange and right at the same time. He leaned back against the cave mouth and basked in the sun's rays. His thoughts drifted. The feel of the cave and the weight in his arms faded, and Teal slept.

CRSO

1:51pm

"Henry, she's over here!" the huntsman called out. His dogs circled the body on the ground, alternating between whines and barks.

Henry ran faster. His sheathed longsword slapped his leg with each step. He still wore his surcoat with a smear of Aaron's blood across the front. Behind him, Jared navigated the fallen branches and underbrush with muttered curses. Henry shook his head and was about to say something, but stopped when he saw Allyrian.

Her dress a tattered ruin, she lay face-down, without a mark on her. The huntsman rolled her over. No wounds — nothing. She had a peaceful look about her, as if she were sleeping.

"God's teeth, Oscar, is Ally dead?" Jared asked.

"No, just unconscious," replied the old man.

"Maybe she tripped and hit her head," Henry offered.

Jared rubbed his fingers through her hair searching for lumps or anything that might give them a clue as to what happened. "I don't feel anything."

"The only tracks are hers and ours," Oscar said, circling the site. He glanced at the shredded state of Allyrian's dress, then made a sign against evil while muttering a prayer.

"Let's make a litter and take her to Father Blackwood," Henry said.

☙❧

2:23pm

A sharp tap on his head wrenched Hector from exhausted slumber. He blinked owlishly at an old woman with a pinched face and sour expression wielding a folded fan. Aislinn slumped against his shoulder, sound asleep.

Despite the boiling summer sun, it remained chilly inside the stone and mortar church walls. Evenly spaced stained-glass windows lit the nave in hues of green, orange, red, and blue. Above, light brown pegs dotted every joint in the dark timber trusses and purlins. At the east end of the church, small steps led to a red oak table covered in a deep green cloth fringed in gold. To its left, a prayer rail and kneeler separated the sanctuary from an ornately carved ambry containing the collection plates and a small bottle of blessed wine. A lectern carved with reliefs of fish and shells stood to the right of the altar. Behind them, a large wooden wheel-cross hung from the wall.

A few of the elderly townsfolk with nowhere else to go huddled in pews, hands clasped before them in prayer. Near the hallway leading to the vestry and the back door, a wrought iron votive stand held dozens of lit prayer candles.

Snores echoed through the room.

"Your friend should leave," the old woman hissed and pointed to the pew where Dave sprawled. "It's disrespectful. And it's unseemly for that little girl to sleep under him on the floor," she added.

Already drifting back to sleep, Hector nodded and muttered at her in incoherent Espian.

"Bah! Father Blackwood will hear about this," the woman threatened.

It seemed to Hector that he had closed his eyes for only a second when the door to the church burst open. Dave jerked awake, rolled off the pew in a mad scramble for weapons, and landed hard. Hummingbird bolted upright like a startled cat and hit her head on the bottom of the stout wooden pew.

Henry and Jared carried a young woman inside on a makeshift litter. Behind them, a crowd gathered.

"Father Blackwood!" Henry yelled.

The door to the vestry opened and the priest stumbled out. He looked haggard and worn, with dark circles under his eyes, but squared his shoulders to meet the newest disaster.

"Ally's hurt, and we didn't know where else to take her. We couldn't find her pa."

"It's fine. Bring her in here," Father Blackwood said. "Lay her on my desk." He threw Aislinn a pleading look before he disappeared back inside.

"No rest for the weary today," Aislinn said.

"How long did we sleep?" Hector asked.

Aislinn shrugged and threw her hand over a jaw-popping yawn. "Ugh. A couple of hours, maybe." She stifled another yawn. "I'd better go help Blackwood. No telling what trouble he'll be tempted into next."

Hector trailed behind Aislinn and found Jared leaning against the wall.

"Helping hold up the building?" Hector asked with a smile.

Jared yawned and returned the smile. "I guess so."

"Who is she?" Hector asked.

"Allyrian Carmichael, Aaron's sweetheart. Her pa, Garret, drives the wagon to and from the quarry."

"The quarry at the dome across the river? Where the gnomes found dead in the graveyard the other morning worked?"

"The same."

Hector rubbed at his chin. "How long before the sun goes down?"

"Not long enough." The haunted look in the young soldier's eyes spoke volumes.

∞

2:34pm

"Pardon me. No, ma'am, I don't know what's happened,

but if you'll let me through so I can help Father Blackwood..."
Aislinn threaded her way through the crowd of parishioners gathered in the hallway and vestry. The priest met her halfway, ushering the church elders back into the sanctuary. He carefully closed the vestry door behind them.

Aislinn and the priest examined Allyrian, looking for anything that might explain her condition, but there wasn't a mark on her — no wounds, no bruises, nothing. Taking out her wheel-cross, Aislinn held it over Allyrian's heart and placed her right hand on the girl's forehead. Nothing happened.

A frown formed as Aislinn studied the girl, seeking a reason why her healing spell wouldn't work.

"Is something wrong?" Father Blackwood asked.

Aislinn worried her bottom lip between her teeth while she considered the possible causes of the girl's condition. "That was weird."

Sir Francis burst into the room. Deep lines scored his face and his eyes looked sunken. "Cecil?"

The priest rushed to intercept him. "Francis, what are you doing here?"

"She attacked one of my men," Sir Francis said. "I need her awake."

"She's under a spell," Aislinn said. "There's nothing I can do until we figure out how to work around it."

"That's not good enough," Sir Francis said with heat in his voice.

The priest reclosed the door and gripped the constable's arm.

"Cecil, this is all my fault. All of this," Sir Francis whispered. His broad shoulders slumped, and his countenance became one of defeat.

"We can still save Ruthaer, Francis," Aislinn said, "but we have to stop Evan to do it."

Sir Francis straightened and blinked at her as if seeing her for the first time. He turned back to Father Blackwood and accused, "You told her?"

Father Blackwood gave him a grim frown and said, "They figured it out on their own. I didn't have to tell them."

"They?" Sir Francis said, alarmed. "Who knows about Evan?"

"Just my friends," Aislinn said.

Sir Francis studied her for a few seconds and said, "Where did the little girl I once knew go?"

Aislinn's eyes grew distant. "Time marches on, Francis. I grew up a long time ago." Her eyes refocused and she asked, "Where is Evan?"

"I wish I knew," Sir Francis answered.

A crash from the chapel ended their conversation. Sir Francis threw open the door and strode to the altar. Big Mike lay amongst several overturned pews. Dave stood over him with a calmness about him that belied the scene. Beyond the wreckage of their fight, the church doors hung open. Those who had sought refuge earlier were gone.

"Sergeant!"

Big Mike rubbed his jaw with his meaty hand. The pews rocked precariously and every move he made caused them to shift. Dave grabbed one to steady it, and Hector grabbed another.

"Sergeant, what happened?" Sir Francis asked.

Getting to his feet, Big Mike said, "They dug up Evan and took his body." His words landed in the chapel like an open basket of snakes.

Sir Francis took a deep breath and stared hard at Hector. "Did you find what you were looking for?"

"Señor, we had to know," Hector replied.

"You had no right!" Sir Francis yelled. "I should have never let you out of jail."

"You have a responsibility to these people to keep them safe. They deserve to know what sort of monster is out there." Hector's words were soft, but they cut through the air like daggers. "How many more have to die before you face the truth?"

"That's my son you're talking about!"

"Not anymore. Whatever crawled out of that coffin is not your son," Hector said. "It's something evil, and it's bent on destroying this town and you with it."

"No, you're wrong," Sir Francis protested. "Evan isn't evil, he's cursed. He loves Ruthaer, and he knows we're searching for a way to help him."

"¡Idiota terco! ¡Nos matarás!"

"Hector!" Aislinn interposed herself between the frustrated bounty hunter and her childhood friend, then took the older man's hand. "Francis, Evan is going to tear you down and kill you because the evil inside him can't bear the love he felt for you," she said softly.

"But you don't know it's him out there," the constable countered. "That was a woman who attacked the shrievalty last night."

"Get your head out of the pluff-mud, Francis! Brother Powell and the other monks are dead," Aislinn snapped. "It's past time for you to face the fact that Evan and his minions are responsible."

"You were on the steps with us last night," said Hector. "Didn't you see the black shadow clinging to Lady D? *That* was Evan, guiding and controlling her."

Sir Francis opened his mouth to say more but stopped. Instead, he said, "Mike, rebury my son, please."

"Sir? He's not there," Big Mike said. Confused and still a bit groggy, the sergeant waited, expecting an explanation from his commanding officer.

"Just do it."

"Yes, sir." The sergeant trudged away. As he reached the door, Dave joined him. Big Mike paused, giving the archer a suspicious look.

"We'll help," said Dave. He passed the soldier and turned toward the churchyard with Hummingbird trailing him like a shadow.

Big Mike rubbed his jaw again and followed them out. After the door closed, Jared asked, "Do you think they'll hurt each other?"

"Not permanently," Hector replied. "You have to understand, that's as close as Dave gets to a peace offering."

Aislinn drew Sir Francis back to the altar, and they knelt together at the prayer rail. Father Blackwood disappeared back inside the vestry, leaving Henry and Jared to help Hector set the pews aright.

"What am I going to do?" Sir Francis asked after finishing his prayer.

"Well, first, you need to save the town," Aislinn said.

"How am I going to do that? Night's almost here and there's nothing I can do to stop it... to stop Evan."

"Have everyone hide inside houses with horseshoes over the door," Aislinn said. "Or find enough horseshoes and nails for every door. It might not save them all, but I think it will help."

"Horseshoes?" Sir Francis asked.

"We noticed earlier, only the public places, like the shrievalty and barracks, and houses not protected by horseshoes were attacked."

The constable considered her words carefully, then nodded.

Hector took a seat nearby and said, "We need to take the fight to Evan. There are too many people who can get hurt if we fight him here, horseshoes or not. Do you know where to find him?"

"No, but I haven't looked," Sir Francis answered. He drew in a deep breath and sighed. "Brother Powell and Brother Quintus insisted I couldn't know. They didn't want me to be tempted or coerced into freeing Evan."

"They were killed to keep that secret," Aislinn said. "Blackwood told us the monks had Evan confined, but he still returned and claimed lives. How was that possible?"

"They bound Evan's body but, over the years, he changed," said Sir Francis. "Now, he's as much spectre as man."

"If the monks couldn't lay his spirit, how can we?" Hector asked.

Aislinn cupped her chin in her left hand, with her index finger pressed to the tip of her nose as she pondered everything they'd learned that afternoon. She pointed to Hector. "The combination of Mi'dnirr's attack and Father Blackwood's deal with the Dark One must have turned Evan's body into an anchor, tying his spirit to the mortal realm."

"So, if we find his body, we can sever his link to Ruthaer," Hector said. "The problem is, we don't know where to start."

"The map in the library!" exclaimed Aislinn. Sudden certainty made the bronze flecks in her green eyes sparkle. "Tallinn mentioned Brother Powell and the other monks digging, looking for evidence of a settlement on the barrier islands. What if they found something, buried chambers or passageways that convinced them the pluton and the islands were once connected like on the mural? If the monks trapped Evan on the other side of the river, between the quarry and the islands, I bet the ruined part of the map showed exactly where and how to reach him."

Hector thought about the gnomes helping Evan. "Sir, it's too late to go out there today. Is it alright if we start looking for Evan at the quarry tomorrow?"

The constable nodded and said, "I'll gather some volunteers and we'll head out together."

"No, sir. I think just the four of us should go. Let us get the lay of the land, so to speak," Hector said. "We'll leave at first light."

"And tonight?" the constable asked.

"We hunker down and weather the storm," Hector answered.

CHAPTER 20
LADY D

August 4, 4237 K.E.

11:00pm

Night fell, bringing strong winds that howled through abandoned streets and crashed against the buildings. Wooden walls creaked and groaned under the onslaught. Windowpanes rattled in their frames.

Phantoms shrieked in frustrated fury as they stole handcarts and rain barrels, flinging them down the road to batter anything they encountered. Small wind chimes made of glass and shells snapped from their hooks and vanished into the night. Larger bronze chimes, strung on heavy twine, held tight and rang out in a sonorous chorus. The warning bell atop the Meeting House clanged wildly, as though a horde of imps tugged upon its rope.

Those families who survived the previous night's horrors huddled in their homes, daring neither to sleep nor to look out their windows for fear of what might be lurking there. Although the wind raged like the fiercest of hurricanes, no rain fell from the heavens. The villagers took it as proof supernatural forces were at work. They prayed by turns for deliverance from the storm and that their homes would withstand the battering.

Within the thick masonry walls of the church, the sick and the injured lay in the pews along one side of the chapel where Aislinn and Father Blackwood could tend to them more easily. Only the exceptionally lucky were able to sleep through the noise.

On the sanctuary's other side, Sir Francis and his remaining soldiers kept vigil. The majority of them were young and traumatized by what they witnessed within the shrievalty barracks. They sat, shoulder to shoulder along the wall, too nervous to have their backs to the open room. Many had their hands over their ears to block the sounds leaking under the church doors and through the eaves. Every new rattle or moan made the solders flinch and twitch.

Sir Francis paced beside them, offering words of encouragement. Each new noise outside drew his eyes to the windows, where darkness seeped into the stained glass, dulling its colors and obscuring the images depicted.

CR♥SO

1:25am

Dave knelt before the fireplace in the vestry, tending a meager flame beneath the black kettle hanging inside. Every once in a while, he snuck a sip from his flask. Hummingbird waited in the doorway, staring at the young woman lying on the priest's desk like a princess under an evil spell.

'*Come to me.*'

Dave looked around at Hummingbird and asked, "Did you hear that?"

She shook her head.

Dave stoked the fire and checked the water in the kettle. The bundle of herbs floating on top gave off a faint minty smell, but the water had yet to steam.

'*Come to me.*'

Dave surged to his feet, holding the poker like a sword. He stared at Allyrian, but there was no sign of life there other than the gentle rise and fall of her chest. His suspicious glare turned to the wardrobes, and he snatched open their doors. No one hid inside.

Worry crept over Hummingbird's features and she signed, "Are you alright?"

Shaking his head, Dave returned to the fireplace and checked the water again. A sharp itch spread from one of his many ink-covered scars at the base of his throat. He scratched at it unthinking, but then caught himself.

"Shit," Dave said. "Go get Hector."

Hummingbird signed, "What is it?"

"Just get him!" Dave rounded on her, his eyes fever bright. Hummingbird dropped her cup and ran.

'*How long has it been, my archer?*' the voice asked.

Dave closed his eyes and saw Lady D. Like the day they met, she wore chain and plate armor and carried an antique flamberge that shone with an ice-cold light — the same sword Hector broke. She brought up her weapon and saluted him before taking a fighting stance.

Steam whistled from the kettle, snapping him out of the vision. Dave snagged the fireplace crane with the poker's curved hook and swiveled it from the fire.

Visions swam into his head. He felt her arms wrap around him. She pressed her naked flesh against him. The bottomless depths of her black eyes seemed to swallow him whole. '*You may call me Ymara,*' she purred. Her teeth sank into the base of his neck, and warm blood trickled down his chest. A shiver rippled through his core as she lapped at it with a cat-like tongue. Though he tried with every fiber of his being, he could not stop; he wrapped his arms around her and lost himself.

'I always knew where you were,' Ymara whispered inside his head. *'Did you think you could escape me so easily? You will always be mine.'* A spasm of equal parts pleasure and pain shot through Dave's chest as she bit him again.

CRSO

1:31am

Dave and Hector erupted from the vestry, tangled together as they wrestled. Dave pushed away from Hector and threw a wild haymaker. Hector dodged back and slid underneath Dave's guard, landing two solid punches of his own. The tall archer doubled over.

"Hector! Dave! Stop!" Aislinn yelled. "What are you doing?"

Dave's eyes were cold and emotionless. The bounty hunter backed away with his fists up. "Whatever I have to," Hector said. "She's got him."

Blood drained from Aislinn's face as fear and understanding dawned in her eyes.

Dave rushed Hector, throwing him back into a pew. Before Hector could get up, Dave pinned him down, punching him hard across the jaw, again and again. Amid the tattoos circling his neck and shoulders, the scars of old bites glistened ghost white.

Several guards clambered to their feet, including Big Mike, but Aislinn motioned for them to stay back. "Don't interfere. Hector knows what he's doing."

"He's getting killed," Sir Francis said.

Hector kneed Dave in the groin and rolled under a pew. Instead of following him, Dave dashed for the front door.

"Stop him!" Hector yelled.

Big Mike planted himself before the church doors, and Dave slid to a stop. Taking advantage of the moment, Hector leapt over several pews, plowing into Dave's back. The two landed in a heap, and their gear scattered across the floor, including the round balas ruby brooch they had discovered on the ship.

Dave twisted around with a flash of silver in his hand. Hector reached out and grabbed for a weapon, but only found the brooch. With a grunt, Dave plunged his dagger into Hector's chest. Blood flowed out and Hector's body went limp.

Nobody moved. Around the chapel, mouths hung open. Soldiers and townsfolk gaped in horror.

His hands red, Dave shoved the bounty hunter off him. When he did, the brooch fell from Hector's lifeless hand and landed on Dave's chest. A brilliant glow ignited within the ruby, casting blood red light throughout the room.

"What have you done?!" Sir Francis exclaimed.

Captivated by the brooch, Dave sat up, holding it in front of him. Slowly, the dawning realization of what he'd done replaced the cold blankness of Lady D's control. His knife clattered to the floor. Still gripping the brooch tightly, he rolled Hector over. A bloody stain spread over his tunic.

"You killed him," Big Mike accused.

"Stay back," Aislinn said. She rushed over, grabbed Dave's chin, and forced him to meet her gaze. Satisfied by what she saw, she used Dave's knife to cut away Hector's shirt and reveal a deep puncture. She laid her hand over the wound and prayed. Unlike the evening before with Aaron, no divine light answered her prayer. The blood seeping past her hand slowed, then stopped. Dave looked from Hector to Aislinn, his fear and pain as clear to her as if he'd spoken.

"He'll be fine," she assured him. Hector's unnatural blood prickled her palm, and she fought the urge to pull her hand away.

"He's dead," Big Mike said.

"Just wounded, not dead," Aislinn corrected. She felt a twinge of guilt, lying to the soldier, but it was better that than explaining the truth of Hector's 'condition.' Beneath her hand, she felt Hector's silent heart stutter, then beat. He drew in a ragged breath. She clenched her wheel-cross tight in her left hand and breathed a silent prayer of thanks.

As those around them watched, Hector's eyes flew open and he sat up, causing many a gasp. Aislinn's hand fell away from his chest, revealing smooth, unscarred skin.

"Dave?" Hector asked.

"Still here," replied the archer.

Dave helped Hector to his feet, and only Aislinn heard Dave whisper, "Troll blood."

As if Dave offered him an apology for their fight, Hector nodded with a smile and clapped the archer on the shoulder before murmuring, "Not troll blood — I'm pure bred Espian, and don't you forget it." Growing serious, Hector pointed toward the brooch and asked, "What's that?"

Still gripping it tight, Dave replied, "It's from the shipwreck. Must have fallen out."

"Can I see it?" Hector asked, holding out his hand.

"No. I don't think so," Dave said. "It's the only thing keeping me from rushing out the door."

"How does it work?" Hector asked.

Dave shrugged. "Don't know. Don't care."

"You'll have to find a chain or something," Hector said.

"Why?"

"I doubt it will work in your pocket. It probably needs to touch your skin."

Aislinn unclasped a gold necklace from around her neck and threaded it through the loop of the brooch. The finely crafted links looked like tiny oak leaves joined tip to stem.

Dave's expression turned dubious. "Will the chain hold? I don't want it to fall off."

"My mother gave this to me a long time ago. It's held up so far," she answered, reaching up to put her arms around Dave and fasten the necklace. When he drew back from her hands, she saw the self-loathing in his eyes. "Hector already forgave you," she whispered. "Now forgive yourself. You can't help the things *she* makes you do."

Dave held the brooch against his chest, turned and knelt so she could fasten the necklace from behind. Hector studied Dave for a moment and said, "One thing's for sure. Lady D is back from the dead."

"Yeah," Dave said. "That, and she's working with Evan."

"What do we do now?" Aislinn asked.

"We kill Evan, and we kill her — again," Hector responded. "But this time, we'll make sure she stays dead."

CHAPTER 21
TRIP TO THE QUARRY

August 5, 4237 K.E.

9:26am

"It's an easy job on the coast," Dave grumbled as he rummaged through their boat's aft storage locker. Swapping his quiver for another, he took off the cap and looked inside. A simple ring cut from glossy obsidian and marked with runes of magic was secured to the underside. He placed it on his right index finger and then dove back into the compartment.

"Dave, come on. The fog's burning off and I want to get to the quarry before lunchtime," Hector said from the dock. Behind him, Aislinn and Hummingbird discussed route options with Sir Francis.

Finally, Dave came back up with a pair of worn, leather archery bracers. He didn't offer any explanation; he just cinched the straps tight on his wrists and slammed the lid closed.

"We'll find a couple of missing people and then go fishing, she said," Dave muttered as he twisted the lock and the compartment disappeared.

"What was that?" Aislinn said. "I didn't hear you."

"Nothing," Dave replied, knowing full well those elf ears of hers heard him just fine.

Sir Francis left them alone at the docks to check on the town. It seemed Aislinn's idea about the horseshoes worked last night, but he wanted to be certain. A smattering of people milled around, collecting debris and boarding over windows. Others carried what they could and left town, not looking back.

A single cow wandered the street, lowing forlornly until a boy ran up, looped a rope around its neck, and led it away. The breeze shifted, carrying the stench of the Meeting House to the waterfront.

"Where to, amiga?" Hector asked.

"I had planned to take the stairs," Aislinn pointed across the river, "but Francis didn't recommend it. He suggested we either take the road past the monastery to the bridge and loop around, or cross upriver about a mile and take a footpath along the bottom of the dome.

Hector asked, "What's the quickest way to the quarry?"

"The footpath," Aislinn said.

Dave unpacked the oars, kept one for himself and handed the other to Hector. While they took their positions, Hummingbird and Aislinn unwound the fore and aft mooring lines. They tossed them onto the deck and pushed the boat off the dock as they came aboard.

Once past the marina, the river's swift current caught them and tried to take them out to sea. Heaving on the oars, Hector and Dave forced the boat upriver. With each stroke, white caps formed along the bow. As the two found their rhythm, inches of progress became feet and a small wake trailed behind them.

The sheer granite wall of the plutonic dome remained starboard, and Dave wondered what geologic event could have caused such a formation. Although the coast continued to be rocky cliffs north of Ruthaer, they were primarily clay, shale, and sandstone. There was nothing else like Ruthaer's dome and barrier islands for hundreds of miles.

On the aft bench, Hummingbird gazed off the port side at grey cypress columns and their fang-like knees rising out of the black water. She dipped her fingers in the cool river, creating tiny ripples on the glassy surface. A curious alligator materialized inches from her fingertips. Wide eyed, Hummingbird snatched her hand back inside the boat, and the gator slipped beneath the water without so much as a ripple.

Surrounded by nature, the four settled into a comfortable silence as they travelled. The fresh morning air carried the scent of spawning panfish. Both Dave and Aislinn eyed the shore for the perfect place to fish. Without a word, one of the two would nod toward the other and point out a fallen branch sticking up out of the water or a tiny slough barely visible amongst the trees where the water eddied.

A triangle of grassy bank appeared between the river and the rock wall, and they paddled the boat closer to it. Farther ahead, short scrub trees found purchase at the water's edge. Aislinn pointed. On the other side of the underbrush, the bank opened up and revealed a natural inlet. A patch of stubborn fog shrouded the shore, but as they drew closer, they spotted a narrow trail hugging the base of the granite dome and disappearing into the woods.

10:13am

When the bow bumped the bank, Aislinn hopped out carrying the anchor. She walked uphill at an angle, trailing the line behind. At the base of a tree, she dropped the anchor, flukes down, and stepped on its stock to bury the sharp bills in the loam between two roots. Once the boat was secure, everyone checked their equipment and piled out.

At the trailhead, Aislinn brushed away some leaves and studied the earth. At first it looked like a game trail, but as she cleared more of the detritus, faint footprints came to light: some adult sized, some smaller.

"These tracks must be from the gnomes," Aislinn said, pointing to a particularly small set of prints. "Maybe even gnome children."

"Are they recent?" Hector asked.

"At least a few weeks ago," Aislinn answered, "maybe older."

"The morning we went to see Tallinn, señora Griffon said two gnomes were found dead in the graveyard," said Hector. "How do you think they got into town? I don't see a boat."

"They probably used the road. The Queen's Coastal Highway crosses the Emmassa just west of the monastery. A side road from the north gives teamsters access to the quarry," Aislinn replied.

"Jared told me Allyrian Carmichael's father drives a wagon for the quarry. Do you think he brought the gnomes to town?" asked Hector.

"Maybe. It's odd that we didn't see Mr. Carmichael at the church, especially with his daughter being there. We should definitely speak to him when we get back," said Aislinn.

"What about the larger tracks?" Hector asked.

Aislinn shifted around and followed a set of footprints to the river. "At least one set of heavy prints, and one, maybe two sets of lighter prints. One male and two females? It's hard to tell. They start here beside this depression. Probably from a small boat. Smaller than ours."

"A man and a woman; are they still here?" Dave asked. His dark eyes scanned the trees for someone waiting in ambush.

"I bet its Dodz and Lady D," Hector said. "There are plenty of boats they could 'borrow' in Ruthaer, although I can't imagine him rowing. Let's keep our eyes and ears open, just to be on the safe side."

"Guys, the other boat is *gone*. Besides, we don't know Dodz is Lady D's thrall," Aislinn said, but Dave's look suggested he thought it more likely than not.

"He didn't act like a vampire's servant," said Hector, "but he did have a bite mark."

She shrugged in return and started down the path. Behind her, Hector and Hummingbird walked single file. Dave took up rearguard with a black fletched arrow nocked and two more in the curl of his ring and little fingers. Unlike the arrows Sir Francis saw, the ones Dave used for game hunting, the barbed heads of these black arrows were horizontal to the ground, like the line of a man's ribs. They also lacked Dave's typical hawk's-head design.

As the four moved farther from the river, the prodigious shape of the plutonic dome blocked out the sun. Its shadow blanketed the forest, and the morning air grew cold as dew clung to their clothes. The ground became boggy, forcing the trail to hug the granite wall, which seemed more a block of ice than earth. Dark stains marred its surface and water constantly dripped from the various outcroppings.

The snapping of a distant twig brought up Aislinn's fist, and everyone stopped. Already on edge, the four scanned the woods, searching for anything out of the ordinary. They were painfully aware that, just because you didn't see anything, it didn't mean nothing was out there. She gave it a minute or so before motioning everyone to continue.

After a quarter mile, they rounded the end of the dome and moved away from the wetlands. As they walked, the trail grew firmer and more used. Between a pair of sprawling oaks, the trail split, and Hector called for a halt. Aislinn knelt and said, "The human prints go that way." She pointed to the trail closest to the dome.

Dave stepped close to Hector and whispered, "We're being watched."

"Where?" Hector whispered back.

Dave nodded toward an oak in the distance. Thick green foliage obscured most of the dark, twisted branches, but near the upper reaches, a single leafless branch pointed toward the granite dome. Rising from the center of the bone-like limb was the silhouette of an ash-colored eagle with a tall crown of ragged feathers adorning its head. "I noticed it when we stopped."

Hector turned his back to the raptor and stepped next to Hummingbird. "Do you see that águila?" he whispered.

Casting a quick glance over his shoulder, Hummingbird signed, "It may be the same one I saw in the marsh when we first arrived."

"You think its Dodz in disguise?" Dave asked.

"Amigo, you've got Dodz on the brain," Hector replied with a smile. "No. I don't think it's him, but then again, you never know. Considering the disappearing act he pulled from the inn, he could have any number of magic items, including one that allows him to shape-change." He turned back to Hummingbird. "I've never seen an eagle like that before, have you?"

Hummingbird shook her head and shifted to place Hector more squarely between herself and the shadowy bird before signing, "Whatever it is, it's not natural."

CR8O)

10:42am

Hector glanced at Aislinn, who still knelt in the trail, staring at the eerie raptor, her expression blank. "Come on, let's get moving."

As if some silent message had finished passing between bird and half-elf, the crowned eagle unfurled broad wings, revealing bands of light grey feathers, and launched itself into the air.

A noticeable shiver swept over Aislinn, and her eyes focused on Hector. "What happened to the dagger Evan took from the dærganfae? The one Father Blackwood said ended up buried in Evan's heart when he attacked Francis."

"¿Qué? What are you talking about?" he asked, taken aback by the odd question.

"It just suddenly occurred to me," she replied. "Father Blackwood didn't say what happened to the blade. I think that's why Mi'dnirr's still here; he wants that dagger. It's important to him."

"I still say this is about territory," Dave said. "If Evan had returned as a vampire, he would've been Mi'dnirr's to command. Thanks to Blackwood's meddling, not only is

Evan a free agent, he's powerful enough to capture and command Lady D. What if he does the same to Mi'dnirr?"

"How do we know he hasn't?" asked Hector.

"Because Mi'dnirr saved me from Klara and the gnomes in the graveyard," Aislinn replied. "Father Blackwood said Evan controls the phantoms and the fog, so Mi'dnirr must be working against Evan. He could even be a potential ally for us."

Hector crouched beside Aislinn and studied her intently. "Cariña, you're defending Mi'dnirr again. Is he talking to you, putting ideas in your head?"

"No," she answered. Her quick response was hard and full of confidence. As her thoughts reflected inward, her voice softened, "At least not that I can tell." Fear clouded her expression. "But then, he wouldn't let me tell you if he was, would he?"

"We won't let him take you, Aislinn. I promise." He took her hand and pulled her up as he stood. "Now, one problem at a time. Let's concentrate on the quarry and finding Evan's lair. Todos estén alerta."

Hector followed the trail with the human prints. With each step, the air grew muggier and the shadow of the dome receded.   Ground gently rising, the forest opened up. Majestic pine trees with wide trunks reached skyward and blanketed the forest floor with orange pine straw that choked out the underbrush. On the right, deep vertical scores striated the sheer face of the granite wall. Along its base, small pools of water trickled into tiny streamlets leading back toward the river.

Rounding a sharp corner littered with small moss-covered boulders, Hector found himself at the bottom of thirty-foot tall scaffolding made from wooden poles lashed together with thick ropes and intermixed with an odd assembly of pulleys and gears. A series of planked ramps crisscrossed their way up the stone wall and appeared to be slick with grease. Cut blocks of granite rested at the bottom, ready to be loaded. Above them on a towering tripod, a heavy block and tackle dangled in the sunlight.

Like the first slice in a loaf of bread, a single, vertical crack within the rock face paralleled the edge of the scaffolding and ran all the way to the top. Along the quarry floor, roughhewn terraces attested to the progress the gnomes had made into the dome.

On the north side of the quarry, a kettle of vultures circled in the clear blue sky above a neighborhood of diminutive houses with grassy roofs. Instead of cutting straight across the open ground, the four backed into the woods. Maintaining strict silence, they used the trees for cover and took the long way around to the gnome village.

An intricate wood and metal trellis connected twelve houses like a clock with a common well in the center. Directly above the well, a metal spire cast a shadow, pointing to one of the houses like a large sundial. Built to resemble caves, each home had walls of blue granite laid with pearly white mortar, and a low-pitched roof covered in bright green grass. The sod roofs were well manicured with just the occasional weed. Below, a garishly colored front door flanked by sidelight windows faced the well. The homes at twelve, three, six, and nine o'clock had a smaller second floor that stuck above the green roof. A round window peeked out from under the high roof, overlooking the trellis.

In the road beyond the twelve o'clock house, the source of the vultures' attention came into view. A heavy-built wagon hosted a half-dozen quarreling birds vying for access to the body slumped in the driver's seat. More birds hissed and fought over the dead horses, who lay tangled in leather traces. Clouds of droning flies surrounded the bodies.

Other than the carrion birds and insects, nothing moved. With the backdrop of the dome, the place felt abandoned.

Alternating between marveling at the trellis and dreading the corpse on the wagon, Hector hesitated before moving to the road. He motioned for Aislinn to join him, letting the others stay behind to cover them if needed.

Hector pulled the collar of his shirt over his nose in a vain attempt to block the stench surrounding the wagon. "Mr. Carmichael, I presume. I guess now we know why he didn't come to the church to see about Allyrian."

Aislinn covered her nose and mouth with one hand and battled flies with the other as she studied the body. Dried blood covered the front of his shirt. She avoided looking at his pecked-out eyes and hollow cheeks; instead, she focused on his neck. "His throat's been slit. He hasn't been dead for long. Might have been yesterday or the day before."

"Why kill him and then just leave the body and everything out here in the open?" Hector said more to himself, flipping a tarp off the empty wagon bed.

"Dead men tell no tales," Aislinn suggested.

Hector scanned the quarry and asked, "Do you think he stumbled across Evan and Lady D?"

Aislinn shielded her eyes as she searched the scaffolding. The road led to the far end of the stone terraces and stopped at the tripod with the block and tackle.

Hector let his gaze wander over the quarry, the road, and the village. The uneasy feeling someone was watching wormed its way through his brain. He tapped the wagon to get Aislinn's attention. She started to turn toward him, but her eyes jerked back to the quarry.

"Did you see that?" she asked.

"See what?" Hector asked, staring in the same direction Aislinn did. His unease solidified into a zing of fear. He grabbed her by the arm and yanked her down into the wagon's shadow.

"Come on," Hector said as he crouched and ran to the side of the twelve o'clock house where Dave and Hummingbird waited.

"What did you see?" Aislinn asked in a whisper.

When they reached the others, Hector said, "It's a trap."

"Sir Francis is the only one who knew we were coming here." Dave peeked around the corner of the house and said, "I don't see anything. Are you sure?"

"No," Hector replied, hesitantly. "But that doesn't mean I'm wrong."

"I saw a flash of light under the scaffolding. I'm sure of it," Aislinn said. "Something's out there."

"Gnomes or that bird?" Dave asked.

Hector shrugged. "No se, amigo. I just had the feeling something evil was watching us."

"If it's not the gnomes, then where are they?" asked Aislinn.

Hector jerked his thumb toward the twelve o'clock house and said, "Let's check inside just to be sure. Dave, stay here in case our watcher makes an appearance."

Dave motioned for Hummingbird, and the two slipped into the shadows.

Hector reached for their chosen target's doorknob before remembering Dave's predicament at the inn. He took a half step back and signaled Aislinn to check for magical traps. Seconds ticked by, then she stepped to one side, back to the wall, and gave him the go ahead.

He pushed open the door, and the top struck a tiny bell, setting it jingling. Hector grabbed it and muffled the noise. He slowly took his hand away, silently cursing the bell. Aislinn's stifled laughter burned his pride.

Stooping down as they entered the gloomy living room, they were hit by the rank scent of decay that filled the house. Hector took out his bone tube and shined the light around. A female gnome with curly, brown hair slumped in the center of the room facing a worktable, her wrists strapped to the arms of her chair. Each of her long, delicate fingers lay on the floor beside her feet. The hazy film of death coated her eyes.

Hector and Aislinn searched the small house. As far as they could determine, the female gnome had a mate, an elder parent, and at least three children, but there were no signs of them. In a matter of minutes, the pair stood in the living room once again, trying to make sense of what had happened.

A three-foot square copper frame with various sized gears of gold and bronze hung above the worktable. A bronze pendulum ticked off each second, and bright silver hands marked the time. A battered container the size and shape of a lady's hatbox sat on the table, its lid pried off to reveal wires, gears, and thin shafts fused together in a tangled nest. A stack of small metal gears and coils of thin wire occupied the rest of the worktop, but the material and workmanship were not the same as the ruined original. Glossy black armor plates lay under the table. Each sported a gaping hole.

"What is this stuff?" Hector asked. He picked up one of the smaller gears and held it against the contents of the damaged box. Unsatisfied, he sorted through the gnomes' toolbox until he found something to pry out one of the fused gears.

"Whatever it was, this gnome was killed because they couldn't fix it," Aislinn said. "There's at least a few days between the first and last of her finger wounds."

"Yuck," Hector said. "Here," he handed her the broken-toothed gear, "have you ever seen anything like this?"

Aislinn rubbed it between her fingers and held it up in the sunlight. "It feels like pottery, or maybe shell of some sort. Is the box the same?" she asked.

Hector pulled the container into a shaft of sunlight. Its deep black surface seemed to drink the light.

She handed back the gear and picked up one of the partially melted plates. "This is different, oily, like chitin on a beetle," she said, "but too thick... almost like dragon scales."

"Dragon scales? Black dragon scales?" he asked, pocketing the gear.

"I said almost. It isn't, though."

"Are you sure?"

"Positive," Aislinn nodded. "Look here, where it's melted." She used a jackknife to scrap at the edge. "Shine your light here. It looks a bit like rough glass, right? Dragon scales have fibers, like your fingernails."

Hector shook his head. "How do you know this stuff?"

"I grew up with a dragon, remember? Brand doesn't shed like a snake or lizard. His scales grow with him, like a turtle or maybe a fish. Still, Brand loses a few here and there that eventually regrow. As for the chitin," she shrugged, "crabs, shrimp, and bugs are all covered in the same stuff."

Hector huffed a frustrated sigh. "I guess we have to hope we find a gnome who can tell us what happened here."

"What now, fearless leader?" Aislinn asked.

"Let's find Evan and Lady D. They've got to be here, somewhere."

CHAPTER 22
CHASING A NIGHTMARE

August 5, 4237 K.E.

12:15pm

Someone or some*thing* cried out from the shadows clinging to the quarry scaffolding.

Hector and Aislinn crouched between two houses, Dave and Hummingbird across the alley.

"That sounded like a child," Hummingbird signed.

"Dammit," Hector said.

Hector was right about the trap. Not that Aislinn had doubted him earlier; she just hoped he'd be wrong this time.

They waited in silence, but the sound did not repeat. Hector raised his eyebrows, meeting the gazes of each of his companions, and received a determined nod in return.

"On three, then," Hector said. "Aislinn, you lead. Take us where you saw the flash of light."

"One."

Aislinn said a short prayer.

"Two."

Hands gripped sword and dagger hilts to keep them from banging against legs.

"Three."

They raced out of the gnome village toward the scaffolding. It was open ground between them and the quarry face, so Aislinn struck out at an angle toward the left side where the wooden ramps would provide partial cover.

Ducking underneath the nearest one, Aislinn put her back to the cool wall and waited. Within a few heartbeats, the others joined her, their breaths coming quick. She slid out her longsword.

Bow in hand, Dave scanned their back trail, looking for a target.

Silence settled around them.

Keeping within an arm's length of the wall, Aislinn crept through the worksite, Hector and the others hard on her heels. She dipped under taut ropes and stepped across diagonal braces. All the while, doubt gnawed at the edges of her confidence. Everything was so quiet. She wondered if she had imagined the flash of light.

She paused and glanced back across the quarry at the cluster of houses, gauging angles and positions. A little farther, she decided. Another half-dozen paces later, she stepped around a vertical outcrop and stopped beside the mouth of a narrow crevice tall enough for Dave to walk through upright. Aislinn traced the jagged edge of the opening, noting powdery white wounds in the weathered granite. She pointed it out to Hector and made a diamond shape with her thumb and forefinger, which she spread apart, mimicking an enlarged opening.

A single off-centered gouge marred the crevice floor. It resembled the mark of a pickaxe. Images of both the shipwreck and monastery flashed in her mind's eye, and she regretted making that joke about a giant tree crab.

Aislinn motioned everyone back. Before she could voice her suspicions, a soft moan escaped the mountain. Faint sounds of scuffling movement followed.

Hector pointed to his eyes and then to Aislinn. She shook her head and nodded toward the sun. Until their eyes had time to adjust, whatever waited inside had the advantage.

Picking up a fist-sized chunk of rock, Hector handed it to Aislinn. When she didn't move fast enough to suit him, he gestured for her to hurry.

Aislinn set her jaw and raised an eyebrow. She knew what he wanted, but it irritated her that he expected the Eternal Father to obey *her*. She waited until he shuffled from one foot to the other and had the good sense to look embarrassed. Taking out her wheel-cross, she whispered a prayer over the rock until it glowed brighter than a campfire. She handed it back, stepped around Hector, and nudged him forward.

CR8O

12:29pm

Hector tossed the glowing rock inside the crevice, waited a heartbeat, and darted inside.

The others rushed after him and slammed to a stop in a cramped maze of shattered stones. The sun at their backs filled the space with ominous shadows. Hector retrieved the glowing stone and picked his way through the obstacle course.

The path twisted and turned before opening into a natural chamber thick with moist stalagmites and stalactites. Aislinn touched his shoulder and pointed to a muddy footprint. Hector nodded and followed the tracks. Here and there, he pressed bits of red wax into cracks to mark their path.

Another fissure served as a short tunnel into a larger chamber.

Three gangly gnomes hung naked from the wall, their hands and feet tied to iron spikes. Hector held up his light, and the gnomes shied away from it, shutting their eyes tight. One made protesting noises through cracked lips as he struggled against his bonds. Trails of dried blood crusted the prisoners' chests, arms, and legs.

"This is Lady D's doing," Dave said. His growling voice echoed through the cavern.

"We can't cut them down, can we?" Hector asked.

"No," Dave said. "They'll turn against us."

"We can't just leave them," Aislinn protested.

"We're not," Dave said, thumbing the jewel at his throat. "We're going after their mistress. They'll never be free until she's dead."

Movement on the far side of the chamber attracted Hector's attention. He raised the light in his hand in time to see a dusty cloth drop to the floor, revealing a cluster of gnomes wearing muddy leather aprons, caps, and goggles with thick red glass lenses. The light refracted from brass gears and silver wire on small, intricate crossbows. The gnomes fired, ratcheted a lever on the underside of the bow, and fired again. It took half a moment for Hector to realize the boxy shapes on top of the weapons were ammunition magazines.

A cloud of tiny darts filled the air, aimed at the intruders' legs. Hector and Aislinn swung their blades back and forth in a vain attempt to sweep the projectiles from the air. Hummingbird scurried back into the narrow tunnel mouth.

Dave fired into the group, killing his first target. With the speed and accuracy of long hours of practice, he sent one arrow after another at their attackers, but the darts kept coming. Dave killed two more before the gnomes ran out of darts and retreated into another tunnel.

"Dave, what's on this dart?" Aislinn asked, picking one out of her leggings. The tip had barely scratched her, but the skin around it was already red and irritated.

Dave picked up a dart, examined its color, and sniffed the dark stain on its tip. "Poison sumac," he said. "It'll itch but shouldn't kill you."

"They're trying to keep us alive," Hector said.

"More slaves for Evan and Lady D," Aislinn surmised.

A trickle of dirt was the only warning they had. A nightmare creature, blacker than the depths of the sea and far larger than it had any right to be, lashed out at them from the cavern wall above.

Hector shoved Aislinn aside just as a scythe-like foreleg gouged into the stone floor where she had stood a moment before. He tossed the glowing rock in his hand to Hummingbird and melted into the shadows at the base of the wall directly under the monster.

"What the hell is that?!" Dave asked. He dove in the opposite direction, rolled, and came up firing into the joint between the creature's underbelly and one of its long, thin walking legs. The thing shifted toward him, and the arrow shaft snapped.

Trying to draw the thing's attention away from his friend, Hector slashed at its thorax, but his scimitar barely scratched the armor plating.

Aislinn rushed forward and jammed her sword into a leg joint. Something inside gave with a loud crack, and the creature jerked out of reach.

Hector felt a sharp sting in his leg. He risked a glance down and saw the end of a dart. The gnomes had returned and were firing on them again.

"Retreat! Retreat!" Hector yelled.

Dave shot another gnome, giving Aislinn an opportunity to dash out the entryway to join Hummingbird.

Hector jabbed at the creature on the wall and charged out of the room. Behind him, curses poured out of Dave's mouth in a torrent. Ahead, Aislinn and Hummingbird battled a pair of gnomes intent on preventing their escape. Still cursing, Dave crashed into Hector.

"Aislinn, get a move on! We're about to be up to our asses in Lady D's minions," Dave shouted.

Jaw clenched, she smacked a gnome with the flat of her sword. The short, stick-thin man flew out of sight, but the sound of his head striking stone echoed back to them. Before their other attacker could react, Aislinn snatched her hatchet from her belt and clocked him on the head with the flat poll. He fell to the floor in a boneless heap. Together, the four friends hurtled into the next room.

They raced through the forest of stone teeth toward the exit. Behind them, the wall of the chamber exploded in a rain of whizzing shrapnel. Hector turned back despite the sting of sharp rocks lashing his exposed skin, determined to defend his companions' escape route. The sound of scraping metal and grinding gears echoed from a gaping hole in the rock wall, reminding him of the wrecked Rhodinan ship. Spindly black legs clutched the lips of the stone mouth and pulled forth a vile and twisted shape.

Now that it was eye-level, he got a good look at the nightmare creature. What he saw reinforced his impression of the thing being the freakish offspring of a spider and a praying mantis. Neither arthropod nor arachnid, yet bearing traits of both, its pickaxe-sharp claw-tips chipped gouges from the floor. Chitinous exoskeleton plates covered most of its body, except for one area where it was missing a leg. There, iron pins held hardened leather over the gaps. The collection of items in the gnome's workshop suddenly made sense. The creature was a clockwork construct.

Fiery light flickered within its body, leaking out at joints and through a row of spiracles along its bulbous, upturned abdomen. A crushed and twisted metal framework hung from its back, making Hector wonder if the creature once had wings. He tried to imagine what could possibly have captured, much less harmed, it.

The giant bug crashed through a cluster of stalagmites and columns, sending another cloud of dust and shrapnel in their direction. It held its spade-shaped head canted such that it seemed to be watching both the floor and the ceiling at once. The bounty hunter paused, curiosity demanding a closer look.

On the side of its head, three multi-faceted, black diamond eyes of differing sizes glittered with inner fire. They aimed toward the floor and its fleeing prey. Two nubs protruded from its forehead where a normal insect would have antennae. The other side of its face was a mass of cracked and rippled shell. Globs of waxy tissue welled up around three cracked and cloudy eyes.

With its undamaged foreleg, the creature lunged and slashed at Hector. He barely got his scimitar up in time to deflect it. The leg crashed down like a sledgehammer and drove him to the ground. He rolled back over one shoulder and came up in a crouch. Aislinn and Dave charged past him.

Aislinn plunged her longsword into the joint at the base of the foreleg she damaged earlier. She pried at the limb, exposing thin, wire-like tendons. Beside her, Dave slashed at the joints of its nearest walking leg with his sabre. The cavern shook and a fist-sized stone struck the creature's broken antennae, another hit above its flickering eyes. The spider-mantis jerked and flailed. Chance blows sent Dave and Aislinn careening through the debris.

Hector came up under the creature's spider-like mandibles. His scimitar glinted in the light as it sliced one clean off. Black, viscous liquid sprayed from the wound and spattered his jerkin.

The creature bucked and smashed into the cavern ceiling. With arms over their heads, the four ducked and dodged through the ensuing shower of granite chunks to the relative safety of the far wall.

Black from the creature's fluids, Hector watched the wounded monster skitter away into the darkness. "Well, I think we can safely say we know what busted out the *Inquisitor*'s hold," he said, catching his breath. "Everyone alright?"

"More or less," Dave replied. He held his bow in one hand and dug in his belt-pouch for a new bowstring with the other.

While he was distracted, Aislinn slapped her palm to his back, and deep blue light flared between them.

"Dammit, woman! That hurt!" Dave shouted.

"It wouldn't hurt if you held still long enough for me to tend this gash," Aislinn replied.

Dave opened his mouth to retort, but Hector cut him off. "Let's go after it."

"Are you crazy?" Aislinn asked.

"It's wounded. You saw," Hector said.

"Yeah, I saw. It nearly killed us."

"But it didn't," Hector said with a sly smile.

Aislinn threw up her hands, knowing that look in his eye.

"What about the child we heard earlier?" Hummingbird signed.

"We're here to find Evan and Lady D," Dave grumbled. "Not fight some damned bug or rescue gnomes."

"We can't leave a child trapped here," Aislinn said with a sigh. "Besides, what better guardian for Evan and Lady D's lair than a creature like that? We must be getting close." She gestured at Hector with her longsword. "Lead the way."

⊗⊗

12:47pm

Light stone held high in his left hand and scimitar held low in his right, Hector reentered the chamber where the three gnomes hung from the wall. Passing them by, he followed the spatters of black ichor through tunnels and chambers, both natural and tool carved. Shadows flowed over and around grotesque feldspar shapes as the bounty hunter delved deeper into the pluton.

Dave watched the play of light and darkness, searching for lurking danger overhead. Although he recovered some arrows, his supply was dangerously low. Out of two dozen black arrows, only six remained, alongside three with bright orange fletching he carried for emergencies. He had a bad feeling he was going to need them today.

After what seemed like hours, Hector finally came to a stop on the lip of a small chasm. A narrow ledge sloped down like a natural ramp along the right-hand wall into the darkness. Dave took up a position off to the left so he could see both ahead and behind them. Hector, Aislinn, and Hummingbird crouched low, peering into the murky depths.

"Damn," Hector swore under his breath.

Dave glanced down into the hole. Twenty feet below, an adolescent gnome peered up at them from a wide opening with large, milky eyes. Glistening grey mud saturated his clothes and covered his slender body. The darkness shifted and a second child jerked the first out of the light.

Aislinn drew Hector and Hummingbird back from the ledge, closer to Dave, so the four could come together in a loose huddle.

Dave nodded to the pickaxe-like gouges covering the walls. "That giant bug's down there somewhere with those children," he said softly.

"Did you see that one's eyes?" Aislinn asked. "They were like the ship captain's."

"That's Evan's doing," Hector said.

"What do we do?" Dave asked.

Hector turned to Hummingbird and asked, "Is there anyone alive down there?"

The tiny elf closed her eyes and her brow furrowed in concentration. When she opened them, she nodded and signed, "Three still live, but they're weak."

Dave gripped Hector's arm and said, "Probably bitten."

Hector nodded and said, "Maybe, but what if they aren't? We're their only hope of making it out of here, amigo."

Dave released his grip on Hector.

One by one, they eased their way down the slope behind their leader. Dave held a black arrow against his bowstring. Cold sweat beaded on his forehead. At the bottom of the narrow ramp, a low opening in the rocky wall gave access to another chamber. The floor dropped off a shallow ledge and sloped deeper.

An iron ring set in the floor held the knotted end of a heavy hemp rope looped around the necks of nine children. The three closest to the iron ring lay curled in tight fetal balls, their eyes clenched shut, seemingly unaware of the newcomers' presence. The others hissed and spat at the pale light Hector carried, arms raised to shield their milky eyes.

Her hands shaking, Hummingbird pointed to the three children and signed, "They're still alive. Very frightened."

"Can we cut them loose without releasing the rest?" Hector asked.

Aislinn traced the rope from child to child and shook her head. "I don't think so."

"Can you create another light rock?" Hector asked. "I've got an idea."

Aislinn picked up an egg-sized chunk of quartz and prayed over it. Within seconds, it glowed, doubling the brightness in the room.

Hector pointed toward the three children on the ground. "Put it between them and the others," he instructed. With his glowing stone still in hand, he worked his way around the other side of the milky-eyed group, forcing them to close ranks and capturing them within the overlapping light spheres. Pulling against the rope, the six children spat and clawed at the light.

Aislinn stepped into it, brandishing her wheel-cross. Her eyes fixed with steely determination, she repeated, "Cineres cineribus, pulverem pulveri."

Blue light lanced out from Aislinn's cross, illuminating the six children. They shrieked and cried out as the light burned away their skin and sinew. When she finished, all that remained of the six children were piles of dust. "Requiescant in pace," she whispered, tears sliding down her cheeks.

As soon as the blue light died away, Hector and Hummingbird cut the bonds away from the three remaining children. The two boys, feeling Hector's gentle hands, looked up and quickly wrapped themselves around their savior. The girl remained curled up tight and Hummingbird picked her up.

Dave checked the children's necks, shoulders, and arms, and sighed in relief. They appeared free of bite marks.

"I don't care what it takes," Aislinn said. "We have to destroy Evan Courtenay."

"Let's get out of here," Hector said, trying to extricate himself from the boys' grasps and get them to walk. "We'll worry about Evan after we get these niños somewhere safe."

Dave passed the shining quartz to Aislinn, and they turned to leave. Hummingbird stood with her back to the exit, the girl in her arms.

Above her, the cursed and crippled spider-mantis clung to the wall, its scythe-like foreleg poised to strike.

Dave drew and fired an arrow even as Aislinn dove for Hummingbird. The creature's foreleg plunged down. Aislinn crashed into Hummingbird, knocking the young elf and the gnome girl to the floor. Instead of catching Hummingbird, the foreleg struck Aislinn in the back and punched through to the other side.

The foreleg bore Aislinn's impaled body into the air like a stuffed toy to hang before the monster's blazing black diamond eyes. The creature shifted. A side leg shot down and pinned Hummingbird to the floor, snapping her collarbone and several ribs. She let out a blood-curdling scream as the creature yanked its leg back. Pushing with her good arm, she rolled over on top of the little girl.

Dave's arrow shot true, striking the creature in the mouth. Its head reared up as it bit down on the shaft, and it dropped Aislinn's body. Red blood dripped from the thing's leg to pool on the muddy floor.

Hector shoved aside the gnome boys and charged. He swung his scimitar and struck the creature's wounded foreleg. Dave fired again, his arrow catching the beast where its foreleg joined the thorax. The shaft snapped when it moved, but the arrowhead remained lodged inside, impairing the leg's movement. A shriek of metal on metal split the air. The creature stuttered and dropped to the floor.

Yelling, Hector held his scimitar with both hands as he beat aside an attacking leg and darted closer to the beast. The pickaxe tips of its secondary legs slashed the bounty hunter, but Hector ignored the gashes across his chest and back. He stabbed his scimitar deep into one of the cracks where a leg joined the creature's thorax. Wires broke with a twang, leaving the leg limp.

Dave let loose three more jet-black arrows. Each buried itself in the creature's joints, making the stuttering movement worse.

Hector ripped his scimitar free, dodged another attack, and plunged his blade into one of the bug's walking legs. He leaned into it, levering it down like a prybar. The enchanted steel sliced through cables and chitin, and the leg dropped to the floor.

Wounded and oozing viscous, oily fluid, the bug slipped and fell from the rocky ledge, rolling deeper into the chasm. With a metallic sounding shriek, the creature rounded on them.

Dave raced toward it, an orange-fletched arrow with a glowing ruby head already against his bowstring.

"No!" Hector yelled, but the archer ignored him.

The arrow streaked through the cavern. It hit the spider-mantis in the joint between its thorax and abdomen. The ruby tip erupted in a teeth-rattling explosion, and a ball of fire engulfed the clockwork bug. The ceiling turned white-hot and the rock began to melt. His obsidian ring glowing, Dave stood at the edge of the flame, unharmed, with his sabre ready. Waves of heat shimmered about him, causing his sweat to steam.

An ominous rumble emanated from the cavern walls. Hector grabbed Dave and hauled him back by the arm. Dave whipped around, his eyes wild with rage.

Molten rock fell from the ceiling like rain, and the whole room shook.

"We have to go!" Hector yelled.

Dave shook his head. He had to be sure the creature was dead. He turned to enter the flames surrounding it.

"Aislinn!" Hector yelled over the din of collapsing stone. "We have to get her out of here!"

Seeing the destruction in the cavern for the first time, Dave sheathed his sword. He moved past Hector, crouched, and drew Aislinn up in a warrior's carry. He ignored the stinging burn from his wounds and the warm blood sliding down his back. His eyes moved to Hummingbird's limp form.

"I'll carry her!" Hector yelled. "Get these kids moving!"

Dave nodded and herded the gnome boys up the slope out of the cavern. Hector grabbed Hummingbird and slung her across his shoulders, freeing his arms to pick up the little gnome girl.

They clambered out of the gorge through a cloud of hot, choking dust.

Using Hector's bone tube for light, they followed the trail of red wax back through the caverns. Dave felt Aislinn's warmth slip away and his insides went numb. Trying to keep the demons in his head at bay, he kept his eyes focused on Hector's back, but with each step, he knew.

Aislinn was dead.

CHAPTER 23
BRAND AWAKES

August 5, 4237 K.E.

1:30pm

Pain.

It seared through Brand's chest, making it impossible to breathe.

The nightmare didn't want to release him, even as his mind screamed for consciousness. He dragged one eye open, his ponderous body heaving with the effort to draw in air. A single gem glowed softly in its niche near the cavern entrance. The shadowy image of a giant black insect with glowing eyes filled his vision, and fear coursed through his veins. Coins and gems shifted in the sand beneath his scaled belly as he struggled to free himself from sleep.

The pain seized him again, searing through his chest and back. His stomach spasmed and clenched tight, forcing out the remnants of his last meal. He convulsed and spat out globs of fish and green bile. Brand sucked in a single ragged breath before his stomach spasmed again and his heart constricted, as if it meant to never beat again. He needed help.

He reached for Aislinn through their bond with all of his heart and soul, and only emptiness greeted him in return.

NO!

Ghostly images from the strange dreams he'd been having hovered on the edges of his mind, and one tried to whisper the truth. His roar of denial echoed through the cavern and tunnels.

Brand heaved himself up and lurched toward the cave entrance, only to crash against the wall.

"Eternal Father, don't let her die before I find her," he prayed. He plucked his platinum ring from a narrow ledge and clutched it in a taloned fist, reading the pulse of three rings near the eastern coast.

Aislinn went to Ruthaer to help Tallinn. Brand wedged the signet ring onto his smallest claw and stretched his aching muscles. They cried out for another week's rest, but it was time he didn't have. Nothing was going to take her from him.

He launched himself from the cliff, gathering a static charge from the air as he fell. Energy sparked and crackled over his scales. He snapped open his wings and shot across the valley, blowing leaves and pine needles from the trees. Lightning exploded in the sky over Ozera, and thunder shook the ground in the wake of the dragon's passage.

CHAPTER 24
PICK UP THE PIECES

August 5, 4237 K.E.

1:56pm

Sweat and tear streaked, Dave and Hector, along with two bleary-eyed gnome boys, stumbled into the sunlit center of the quarry. Dave let Aislinn's body slide forward until he held her cradled against his chest, willing the sun to warm her, to feel the beat of her heart against his skin.

White-hot rage seethed in Dave's gut. His mind replayed the final moments before that hell-spawned bug ambushed them. This was his fault.

His bow slipped from numb fingers to clatter on the stone ground. The archer's legs buckled, and he fell to his knees. He leaned forward and gently laid Aislinn beside his bow. When he looked down at her face, horror coursed through him. Aislinn's unseeing eyes stared back, and he couldn't look away. They reflected the loathing and condemnation he felt. *You did this to me.*

᎒᎒

1:58pm

Hector eased down onto his knees beside a shallow puddle and lowered the little girl and Hummingbird to the ground side by side. The gnome boys hovered around him, so he set them to dabbing the little girl's lips with water.

He pressed his palm to Hummingbird's wound and pulled an iron vial from his belt. "Hummingbird, wake up. I need you to drink this healing potion," he said. When she didn't respond, he pressed his fingers to her neck, studiously avoiding the pool of blood forming beneath her. A weak, erratic pulse brushed his skin. Hector closed his eyes and said a silent prayer of thanks. He opened them again in time to see Dave drop to his knees.

Scrambling over the short distance, he knelt beside Dave. At first, his mind refused to believe what his eyes told him. Then reality crashed down on him. He stared down at Aislinn's body and went numb. Slowly, Hector tucked the vial back into his belt pouch. Taking a deep breath and letting it out through his nose, Hector placed his hand on Aislinn's eyes and closed them.

"She's gone, Dave." Hector reached toward his friend's shoulder but stopped. There was so much blood on his back. Hector couldn't tell if it was Dave's or Aislinn's.

"I know," Dave replied, not looking up. Black, greasy hair hid his face as he tried to brush away the dirt from Aislinn's cheek. "She deserves better."

"Amigo, we need to get Hummingbird to town. She's hurt," Hector said.

"It should have been me," Dave said. "I was supposed to be the rear guard. I let it get behind us."

"Dave!" Hector said, grabbing his upper arm. "Hummingbird!"

Despair filled his friend's eyes. "We can't save her. We're not healers; not like..."

Hector thought a moment and said, "Nunca te rindas."

"Hector?" Dave said warily.

The bounty hunter slapped Dave on the arm and walked to Hummingbird. Gaps in his torn jerkin revealed fresh skin underneath. His wounds from the creature had already healed. As he walked, he rolled up his sleeve. When he reached the young elf, he took out his knife and knelt beside her on the rocky ground. In a swift motion, he cut the laces of her armor, peeled it away, and slit open her undershirt sleeve.

"Hector! What are you doing?" Dave demanded as he moved beside his friend.

Positioning his elbow over Hummingbird's wounded shoulder, Hector clenched his teeth and cut into his forearm. A thin line of blood trailed down to his elbow.

"Hector?"

"Be ready."

"Ready for what?"

"How should I know? I've never done this before."

A drop of blood fell from Hector's elbow and landed in Hummingbird's wound, followed by several more. They both watched and waited.

When nothing happened, Hector pulled away his arm and let his blood drip on the ground.

"Maybe you didn't give her enough," Dave said.

"I think I saw a sewing kit in the boat," Hector replied. "Maybe..." his voice trailed off as he saw flickers of light arc along the edges of the girl's wound. Before their eyes, her skin began to knit itself together, and Hector let a smile escape.

Suddenly, Hummingbird stiffened. Every muscle in her body contracted. They both fell back when she turned sideways, then violently twisted back the other way. Her legs came up, held for a moment, and rammed back out again. Froth bubbled up from Hummingbird's mouth and her head shook back and forth. Back arching, her eyes fluttered open, revealing only white.

"Shit! Help me!" Dave said, grabbing the knife out of Hector's hands. He captured Hummingbird's shoulders and dragged her head into his lap.

Hector straddled the convulsing elf and pinned her arms between his knees. Together, they pried her mouth open and jammed in the knife's hilt. Another seizure attacked Hummingbird, and her teeth clamped down on the leather wrapping.

Several more seizures wracked her body, and the two did their best to keep her from hurting herself. After several agonizing minutes, her body relaxed, and the knife fell out when her mouth went slack. A ragged breath escaped her, and Hummingbird lay completely still. Dave looked at Hector. They shared the same dread: they had killed her, too.

Hector ripped a strip off the tail of his shirt and wiped the foam from Hummingbird's chin. Her normally tan skin looked ashen, making the red whorls and white dots across her forehead and cheeks stand out more than normal. He placed a hesitant hand against her throat and waited. Eventually, he was rewarded with a weak but steady pulse.

Hector looked down at her wound. A red, striated pucker marked where the creature had impaled her. "At least she won't bleed to death between here and Ruthaer."

The two looked at Aislinn.

"What do you think?" Dave asked. The hope in his voice was raw and pain filled.

Hector held out his hand, and Dave returned his knife. With infinite care, they removed the formed leather that should have protected Aislinn. Hector took a deep breath in an attempt to steady his nerves and slit open her homespun shirt.

Of all the horrible things he'd seen in his life, none hit him as hard as the wound in Aislinn's chest. Fighting back tears that threatened to blind him, the bounty hunter held his arm over Aislinn's gaping wound and sliced deep. Blood streamed down his arm in a crimson cascade.

Hector and Dave waited, but Aislinn didn't respond. More drops of blood fell, and still the two remained.

A cloud blocked out the sun and moved on. As if in response to the sunlight, a multitude of tiny dancing sparks like phosphorous in ocean waves flickered across Aislinn's bloodstained body. Hector watched with rising hope. Flesh and bone fused together, leaving a fractal pinwheel of red, fern-like scars centered near her heart, spreading over most of her torso and throat.

Dropping to his knees, Dave slid an arm underneath Aislinn and held her up. Her cold body hung on his arm like a rag doll. With a hand supporting the back of her neck, he touched his forehead to hers.

Hector felt along Aislinn's throat, searching for the pulse-point below her jaw. After a moment, he dropped his hand. "Dave," his voice cracked, and he heaved several ragged breaths before he could speak, "it didn't work."

The archer gripped her tighter and began rocking back and forth.

"Come on. Let's get back to Ruthaer," Hector said.

As the archer moved, fresh blood seeped from his upper back where the creature had scythed off a section of his skin. Blood ran down his arm and mingled with that already saturating Aislinn's clothes. From there, it seeped into the legs of his pants, leaving a dark stain.

"Dave, you're bleeding!" Hector exclaimed.

There was no reaction from the archer. He just continued rocking back and forth.

"¡Maldita sea, Dave!"

Hector looked around and spotted a rain barrel at the corner of the closest house. Mumbling to himself in Espian, he left the grieving archer. The barrel was just under a third full, and it was cold. Hefting it up, he carried it back.

"Dave," Hector said, sloshing the water in the barrel.

Not getting a response, Hector heaved the barrel, splashing the water on Dave's back. The archer let out a harsh gasp and Aislinn's body slid from his lap.

Planting both hands on the ground, Dave spun and gave off an animalistic growl. Red-rimmed eyes filled with fury, he lunged at Hector.

Hector threw the barrel at him. Dave batted it away, dropped his head, and slammed his good shoulder into Hector's stomach, wrapping his arms around Hector's knees.

"Dave," Hector grunted as he doubled over and landed on his butt. The two slid across the quarry floor a few feet before Hector worked his arms around Dave's torso. Using Dave's momentum, Hector rolled back, lifting and twisting in one motion. Dave's long legs scrambled for purchase but slipped as he tried to hang on. Catching him in a half-nelson, Hector got behind him and pinned his head to the ground.

"Dave, listen to me! She's *dead*."

Dave pushed up with his free arm, his muscles straining. "It's my fault."

Hector gritted his teeth and pressed the side of Dave's head back down to the ground. Dave coughed and a cloud of dirt sprayed out.

"It's Lady D's fault. It's Evan's fault."

"But —" Dave started.

"The ship — remember the ship and the hole in the side?"

Dave relaxed but Hector didn't let up.

"That creature came on the same ship with Count Dodz and, I imagine, Lady D. Don't you see? Ruthaer was a trap from the beginning. They brought that bug here to kill us, and it almost worked. I'm sure of it," Hector said with a lot more confidence than he felt inside. "You good?"

After getting a quick nod, Hector cautiously untangled himself from Dave and watched his friend sit up.

"You threw a fucking barrel at me," Dave said, brushing himself off.

Offering a hand up, Hector said, "Yeah, I did."

CHAPTER 25
CONFESSIONS

August 5, 4237 K.E.

2:29pm

With the quarry behind him, Dave stood over Aislinn's body, thumbing the balas ruby at the base of his throat. Hector's torn and dirty shirt hid most of the angry red marks covering her torso, but the frond-like ends of the red, swirling scar spread above the collar and were visible around her waist, where Hector had torn away the shirttail. He was acutely aware of the strips from Aislinn's ruined shirt binding his shoulder. They clung to his wound like a second skin, but he refused to drink their one healing potion. He knelt to lift her over his good shoulder when Hector stopped him.

"Get Hummingbird."

Dave threw him a questioning look.

"It'll be better for Hummingbird if she wakes up with you carrying her."

Nodding, Dave moved to Hummingbird, and gently scooped her up with both arms. He let her head rest against his shoulder as he shifted her to a more comfortable position. When he did, he caught a whiff of lavender soap and his heart lurched. The nagging temptation of his flask crept into his mind, and he almost laid Hummingbird back down.

'*Put your flask away. I need you sober.*'

Dave jumped at the sound of the voice and searched for its source. His gaze settled on Aislinn. He recalled their conversation at the lighthouse, and her fear. Closing his eyes, he tried to block out the visions in his head and squeezed Hummingbird tighter.

CREO

2:31pm

Hector watched Dave from the corner of his eye as he cradled Hummingbird against his chest. If he didn't keep the archer aimed at a target, the man would likely tumble beyond anyone's ability to help him.

He gathered the tiny gnome girl in his arms. She scarcely weighed more than a human toddler, spindly and fragile as a bird.

"Dave, will you carry her, too?" Hector asked.

"Sure, whatever," Dave mumbled.

Hector nodded and laid the sleeping child on Hummingbird's chest. He wrapped the elf's arm over the girl and stepped back. Coated in dust and blood, the three of them looked like a poster for a disaster relief charity.

Hector hefted Aislinn's body into a warrior's carry. The two boys huddled in his shadow, casting fearful glances toward the cave, yet trusting him to take them to safety.

He took a stumbling step and spied the red stain seeping through the bandage on Dave's left shoulder. Guilt settled on his heart, heavier than a second body on his shoulders. For the first time, the strange gift that healed his wounds in minutes or hours instead of days or months was a curse rather than a blessing. He wanted — no, *needed* — physical wounds to mirror the agony in his soul, yet he had none. Pushing those thoughts aside, Hector asked, "You ready?"

Dave gave the quarry a once over. Growling something inarticulate, he headed out.

They picked up the trail and retraced their steps from earlier. Neither spoke. Hector walked in a daze, his thoughts tangled and drifting. When they finally arrived at their boat, it took him a moment to recognize where they were.

With the gnome girl settled in the bow and Aislinn and Hummingbird lying on a bed of sailcloth at the bottom of the boat, Hector pulled on his spare shirt before unwrapping the bandages around Dave's shoulder. The saturated cloth stuck to the seeping wound, and when he removed it, fresh blood gushed out. He whistled and said, "You need stitches."

Dave gave him a slight shrug.

Rummaging through Aislinn's medicine bag, Hector came up with a small jar. "Sit down. This may sting a bit."

Dave eyed the bounty hunter warily. "Are you sure that's the right jar? The stuff Aislinn uses on trees is in a jar just like that one."

Hector popped open the lid and sniffed its contents. "Smells right to me. Besides, what's the worst that could happen?"

"I start growing bark, asshole."

Hector forced a laugh, thinking Dave was joking.

The archer's scowl deepened.

"Here, you read it," Hector said, handing Dave the lid.

Dave took it and squinted at the fine script. Shaking his head, he gave it back to Hector.

"Do you want me to try it?" Hector asked.

"Hell, no," Dave said, standing up.

"Sit down. At least let me rewrap your shoulder. We can always get Father Blackwood to look at it."

Dave flinched and snarled, "The hell you will."

"Sit," Hector repeated. "I meant we'll see if Father Blackwood can read the writing on the lid."

After Hector finished, he brought in the anchor and gave the gnome boys each a paddle. Seating one boy starboard and the other port, he launched the boat from shore and let them guide the boat out into the river current while Dave manned the tiller. The swift water quickly caught them and carried them downstream toward Ruthaer.

Hector stood by the mast, watching the dapples of afternoon sunlight dance over the water's surface. A light breeze whispered through the trees, and he worried about how he would break the news to Aislinn's mother. Then he thought about Brand and wondered if the dragon already knew. He clenched his fist around his signet ring to activate the tracking spell. A knot of worry formed in his gut. The signature of Brand's ring was already moving toward Ruthaer.

Dave's voice broke through his thoughts. "You really think this was a trap all along?"

Hector nodded. "I do. If for no other reason than finding Lady D here waiting for us."

Dave white-knuckled the tiller and spat. "Bitch. She knew where I was the whole time."

"That," Hector conceded, "and I expect she got her hands on the same navigation charts we did. Plus, we camped each night, while she probably came straight here."

"How in the hell did Evan get control of her? It just doesn't seem possible."

"That's the question, isn't it?"

The docks at the marina came into view and Dave adjusted the tiller.

Hector studied the activity along the waterfront. He contemplated dumping the gnome children on the docks and letting the current carry them out to sea. He and Dave could sail up the coast to Port Remley or back south, across the border to Santa Casilda, and find a healer for Hummingbird. They might find a mage who could open a portal to Ozera, home to one the continent's most powerful priests — one powerful enough to call Aislinn's spirit back to the land of the living. He'd give anything... The shadow of the shrievalty passed over them and he caught himself before he finished the thought. *'No, not anything.'*

Someone onshore spotted their boat and pointed. A crowd started to gather.

Hector's gaze drifted down to the two women and the little girl at his feet, but what his mind saw was Aislinn standing in that cave, weeping for the murdered gnome children whose bodies she had destroyed and determined to fight the Dark One himself, if necessary, to end Evan Courtenay's evil.

The bounty hunter swallowed the lump in his throat and slipped a silver necklace out from under his collar. *'We will finish this for you, cariña, and get you to Ozera when it's over,'* he silently vowed. He sealed the promise with a kiss on the gold and silver crucifix before dropping the chain back under his shirt.

Jared and Big Mike caught the ends of their mooring lines and helped them off-load the gnome children. Hector stepped out onto the dock and took Aislinn, then Hummingbird, from Dave. The two soldiers offered to help, but the bounty hunter waved them away with a curt gesture.

The crowd in the street grew, jostling and murmuring, speculating on what happened. Although no one tried to stop them, the press of bodies slowed their progress toward the chapel.

The distinctive clank of Sir Francis' armor cut through the clamor, and he cleared a path without saying a word. The look in his eye was enough.

Father Blackwood hurried down the church aisle to meet them, bearing a basket filled with bandages, herbs, and ointments.

Dave ignored the priest, striding past him to the altar. He cleared the red oak table with a swipe of his arm, knocking two candles and a thick tome to the floor with a clatter, and laid Hummingbird down. Glaring up at the dark timber wheel-cross, Dave growled, "Heal her. Heal them both."

"It doesn't work that way," Father Blackwood said softly.

"The hell it doesn't," Dave snapped. "I've seen it. Why won't your Eternal Father help Hummingbird and Aislinn?"

"Son —" Father Blackwood said.

Dave shoved him aside and yelled, "I'm not your son!"

Sir Francis caught the priest before he fell and took a step toward Dave.

Hector pushed in front of the constable and held Aislinn's body where Dave could see her. "Keep it together," he said. "Keep it together for her."

Dave shook as he said, "It should have been me."

Handing Aislinn to Sir Francis, Hector grabbed Dave by the arms and said, "I know how you feel, but it wasn't you. It wasn't me. It was *Aislinn.* You have to live with that, and so do I."

"We've seen miracles. *Real miracles.* Why can't *He* perform one for her? Just this once."

"Let me take a look at them," Father Blackwood offered. "Maybe there's something I can do."

Dave and Hector rounded on the priest. "No! Don't touch them," they commanded. Their combined voices echoed from the rafters.

"Why? Let me try to help," the priest said.

Hector said, "You're not the only one who's made a deal with the devil."

A hush fell on the chapel as Hector continued, "Because of what you did to raise Evan from the dead, we wouldn't know if it's the Eternal Father or the Dark One doing the work. And if El Diablo is involved, the consequences would be dire."

"But Father Blackwood is a good person, he's helped a lot of people since then," Sir Francis protested.

"Doesn't matter," Hector replied. "I'm not willing to take that chance."

"Me neither," Dave said.

"Even if Hummingbird dies," Sir Francis said, looking at the young elf on the altar struggling to stay alive.

The constable's words stung, but Hector's voice remained calm. "*Especially* if she dies."

Father Blackwood clutched his basket of bandages tighter. "Well, what *can* I do?" he asked. "I won't just stand here and watch her die while this man bleeds on the floor," he added, nodding toward Dave.

Hector reached into the bag slung across his shoulder and held up a tiny jar. "Can you read this? I'm hoping it's healing ointment."

CXSO

4:00pm

Teal opened his eyes. The first thing they focused on was a stained-glass window. The sun illuminated a white knight slaying a ruby dragon, making the vibrant colors glow. Teal lay on top of a hardwood table. A pair of cabinets flanked a washstand on one side of the room, and shelves held leather-bound books on the other. Through the door crack, he heard several voices speaking Glaxon.

He felt as though he slept over-long, recovering from battle, betrayal, and his own near-death. The memory of a vision drifted through his mind, and he wondered what made him dream of a human girl.

Teal tried to sit up, and a sharp pain spiked through his head. He reached to rub his temple, but when he saw his hand, he stopped. Gone were his bronze scales, along with his talons. Smooth, tanned skin with tiny, pale hairs covered fine-boned hands and arms.

He hadn't survived the battle. He'd been reborn — as a human. Shock overcame the pain in his head, and he sat up, letting the thin sheet covering him slip down to his lap.

"By Xardus' great horned head, 'tis a cruel jest!" he muttered. Long, tawny hair the same as the girl's in his dream slipped forward over his shoulders, obscuring breasts. Teal shook his head. Human body or not, he had to get home. Someone there could help him. He slid from the table, only to become tangled in a tattered dress. He fell and landed hard on the stone floor. Pain coursed through his body; it was all he could do not to vomit.

Teal tore the dress away from his chest and arms, clutched the edge of the table, and pulled himself upright. The dress slid down his quivering legs to pool around his feet. His balance felt wrong.

A child's shriek jolted through his head like lightning. Teal jerked his gaze up to the door, where a small male gnome screamed something inarticulate while pointing at him.

"Ally's awake!" male voices shouted beyond the door. Someone was coming.

Grabbing a spindle-backed chair, Teal smashed the stained-glass window. The sound of metal-shod feet pounding on stone sent adrenaline streaming through his veins. He snatched a purple robe from an open cabinet and draped it over the windowsill.

The shouting escalated.

Teal heaved himself into the window frame and jumped. The sting of glass scraping his arm and pricking his bare feet was both new and unpleasant. He shoved back a mass of thick, tawny hair, feeling it run through his fingers for the first time. Naked and unarmed, he bolted through the graveyard.

CR8O

4:03pm

Hector leapt through the shattered window after Allyrian. A blood-flecked footprint in a bare patch of dirt made him pause. Although the track was a bit larger than he remembered from the monastery, the toes and heel bore the same distinctive shape. The gnome boys' screams drifted out the vestry window, insisting the fleeing girl had helped kill their parents. The knowledge that Allyrian played a part in the chain of atrocities leading to the day's disaster sent rage seething through Hector's veins. He sprinted after her. In the street, Sir Francis shouted for men to cut off Ally's escape.

CR8O

4:14pm

Teal darted inside a gable-roofed smithy to avoid the mob of humans seeking him. The forge was cold despite the tools and materials at hand. Teal hefted steel rods of varying sizes, trying to find a suitable weapon. None of them felt right. His mind gravitated toward the heavier pieces, but his human body wasn't nearly strong enough.

Yelling attracted his attention, and he saw a swarthy human armed with a scimitar heading his direction. He needed Tarnillis; he needed his body back. He cursed his current condition. However, there was one thing about his new form he did like. It was nimble. He scurried up into the workshop's rafters and ran along the timbers to the far end. A small window afforded him a view of the forest. Was he facing east or west? Not knowing if it was morning or afternoon, he couldn't tell.

Down below, the swarthy human crouched low as he followed Teal's blood-spotted footprints. Teal had never seen his like before. He had the olive complexion of a Korellan but was darker. The hunter had shoulder-length, black hair pulled back into a single queue, giving him the look of a rogue rather than a warrior. Appearances aside, Teal sensed the human was an experienced fighter.

More people arrived, cutting off his exit. Some broke away from the crowd and found a ladder.

Looking back out the window, Teal spotted a rope dangling from the peak of the ridge. A moment before the ladder clattered against the timber framing, he leapt and grabbed hold of the rope. People milled about on the ground. One saw him and shouted, pointing at him with an accusatory finger.

Shinnying up the rope, Teal heaved himself over the roof rake. He ran on the wooden shake-covered ridge to the other end and caught a glimpse of the river and the granite dome on the other side. *'There it is,'* he thought. He knew where he was. He even knew the village, though it looked different. *'How much time has passed since the battle?'* he wondered.

Shouting below snapped him back to his present predicament. His chances to escape were diminishing. He needed to go north — to go home.

Taking a deep breath, he hurtled down the roof in a sliding run. At the eave, he jumped with all his might. He flew across the small gap and landed on the neighboring roof on all fours. His skin scraped over the wooden shakes until he finally slid to a stop. Moving one arm and the opposite leg in tandem, he crabbed his way up the roof and streaked down the other side.

The villagers' shouts lingered near the smithy. Instead of jumping to the next roof, he aimed lower and flew toward the wall of the building across the alley. The ball of his foot impacted with the clapboard siding, his knee bent, and he bounced back across the alley. Each time he flew a little lower, but his momentum never slowed. Six feet from the ground, he leapt at a soldier blocking his way, and planted the unfortunate man into the ground.

Straddling the unconscious soldier, he took the man's sword and tossed it away.

CRSO

4:17pm

Hector glimpsed Allyrian's backside as she jumped out the smithy window. He raced outside, but by the time he got out there, she was already disappearing over the neighboring roof.

"Damn, she's fast," he said to himself. He rounded the corner and caught sight of Allyrian racing away. A soldier lay flat on the ground, looking as if he broke her fall. Hector spared him a quick glance to make sure the man was alive before chasing the girl again.

Allyrian ran north toward the river. The bounty hunter gained ground, but only because each time she slipped through the crowd, it slowed her down.

She looked over her shoulder as she landed on the closest dock. Hector saw a mixture of surprise and confusion in the girl's expression. Before she could run again, he leapt, sword-point aimed at her lower back.

Allyrian swayed to one side, avoiding the blade but not the bounty hunter. They crashed to the boards in a rolling slide.

Hector came out on top, without his sword. She shoved up from the deck and tried to buck him off, but he slammed an elbow between her shoulder blades. The girl collapsed against the boards.

Hector grabbed a fistful of her hair, jerked her head back, and pressed his dagger to her throat.

"Don't move, puta," he snarled into her ear. His muscles quivered under the mix of rage and adrenaline surging through his veins, and he fought the temptation to slit her throat for what she did at the monastery and the quarry.

Chest heaving with each breath, Allyrian looked at him askance. "*Why dost thou and these others hunt me?*"

Hector blinked hard. Her accent was odd and the language rare. In all his travels, he'd encountered only two others who spoke it: Aislinn and Brand.   He met her unflinching amethyst gaze, and his anger drained. It had to be more than a coincidence.

"Aislinn?" Hector asked in a tremulous voice.

"*Kindly remove thy weapon from mine neck, hunter.*"

The girl watched him, her freckled face a mirror of his own confusion. Over the murmur of the crowd, he heard Sir Francis' footsteps on the dock.

"What did you say?" Hector asked in the same language she used.

"*Remove thy weapon. I shall not run.*"

After sheathing his scimitar, Hector pulled the girl to her feet.

"What language is that?" the constable asked.

"Dragon," the dumbfounded bounty hunter replied.

CHAPTER 26
DANIEL TANNER

August 5, 4237 K.E.

4:35pm

"She says her name is Tealaucan Rathaera, last Flight-master of the Twelfth Praesidium, whatever that is."

"Didn't Alaric's ghost say something about humanoids fighting the *old ones* at a place called the Praesidium?" Sir Francis asked.

Hector nodded, then listened to the girl speak again, brow furrowed in concentration. When she finished, he grunted and shook his head. The budding hope he felt on the dock withered and died. "She claims she's some kind of dragon-kin called a Xemmassian."

Allyrian sat in a ladder-back chair in the main room of the shrievalty, wearing an ill-fitting dress. She refused to speak Glaxon, and only responded to questions Hector put to her in dragon. Despite the chase she led Hector and the townsfolk on, she made no further attempt to escape. Instead, she watched Hector and Sir Francis intently, as if she could make them release her through sheer force of will.

Sir Francis shook his head. "Hector, I don't care who or what she says she is. That's Garret Carmichael's daughter. I've known the child her whole life. Her parents spoiled her rotten, but I never dreamed she'd come to this, attacking one of my men and accused of murder."

"Did she speak dragon before?" Hector asked.

"No," Sir Francis said, his confident demeanor wavering somewhat. "But speaking dragon does not excuse her from the crimes she committed."

"Agreed, but *something* happened to her after she hit that guard yesterday. With all the strange things going on around here, we can't rule out the possibility that we're not talking to Allyrian Carmichael."

"You think she's possessed?"

Hector shrugged. "Maybe she's a good actress, but where did she learn to speak dragon?"

The shrievalty's makeshift door crashed open. "Sir! You need to see this," Big Mike called.

"What is it?" Sir Francis replied.

"We searched the Carmichael house." Big Mike appeared to be at a loss for words. "It's a mess, sir."

Sir Francis motioned to two soldiers and said, "Let's go. Bring her with us. Hector, you too."

The streets swarmed with agitated and angry people. More than a few carried weapons and openly glared at Allyrian.

Snatches of conversation reached the bounty hunter's ears. "She attacked Billy and broke the boy's jaw... Gafan and Micha's sons say she killed their parents... Mark my words, she summoned the fog and the ghosts..." Hector wondered if Sir Francis and two green soldiers would be able to stop the growing mob if they decided to hang the girl.

Hector remained quiet, following Allyrian and the guards who gripped her thin arms while they marched through the streets of Ruthaer. She looked neither right nor left, spine stiff and head held high, like a soldier in a parade. He wondered if she understood her peril. The testimony of a pair of hysterical children aside, there was nothing to suggest she had anything to do with the recent murders, other than the similarity of her footprints to those at the monastery. However, one thing was clear. If they found any evidence, her execution would be swift.

Sir Francis turned right onto a wide gravel street. In front of a two-story tabby shell and timber mansion, several soldiers in blue and white surcoats formed a semi-circle, struggling to keep the growing crowd on the street side of a narrow flower garden. Curious neighbors spilled past the edges as they stretched and strained to see through the gaping front door on the veranda. A shaft of sunlight struck the ornate sidelights, turning the glass into rainbow colored mirrors. Heavy storm shutters hid the first-floor windows while a pair of high-peaked dormers watched the smaller houses across the street, giving the home a look of indignant surprise.

A guardsman staggered out the door. He made it halfway to the street before he collapsed to his knees and vomited amid particolored lantana flowers. Sir Francis passed the young man without speaking.

The slaughterhouse stench hit them at the foot of the porch steps. Hector tugged his collar up over his nose, but it was little help. He doubted anyone would live in this house again.

"Stay here," Sir Francis commanded.

When Big Mike stooped down to assist the sick soldier, Hector slipped around Allyrian and her escorts into an enclosed foyer. Straight ahead, grand stairs with dark wood balusters curved up to the second floor. Beside the stairs, a hallway led to more rooms. To the left behind a partially open door was a formal parlor filled with Francescan furniture and oil paintings in ornate frames.

On the right, a wide archway opened into a ballroom illuminated by thin streamers of sunlight leaking through the shutters. A stone fireplace dominated the back wall. Sir Francis stood in the center of the room, staring at the broad mantle. "Get her in here," he boomed.

Allyrian took a cautious step inside the ballroom. Her two guards remained in the foyer, hands on their weapons. Hector and Sir Francis studied her reaction as her eyes roved over the room and settled on the mantle. Nine human hearts sat in a row, separated by thin tapir candles. Blood had stained the timber in a half-circle under each organ like a row of demented doilies. The girl's spine went rigid, and her eyes widened. Her mouth twisted in a moue of disgust before she schooled her expression.

"What manner of deranged creature stalks this village, hunter?" she asked.

"That's what we're here to discover," Hector replied, bending down to inspect the fireplace. He gently raked the cold ashes in the grate with a long-handled poker. Aside from a few lumps of charred wood, he found nothing else.

A side door opened, spilling lantern light across the ballroom, and two guards with kerchiefs tied over their noses and mouths joined them.

"Anything?" Sir Francis asked.

"You wouldn't believe me if I told you, sir," Henry said in a muffled voice. "Best to see for yourselves."

The house's stench became a physical thing as they followed the guards to the master bedroom. Blood spattered sheets draped over the side of a four-poster bed. A single, man-sized handprint stained the floor near a porcelain bathtub, sitting in the corner. Crusted, brown smears marked the tub's lip on one side, and a thick layer of coagulated blood coated the bottom. Next to the tub sat an ornate dresser and mirror. A single unlit candle rested on top.

"What happened here?" Sir Francis asked, his eyes wide in horror.

Hector didn't answer. Instead, he turned to Allyrian. "Is this your house?"

The girl frowned. *I have told thee, hunter, my home is the Praesidium. This lodging and the horrors it holds art as new to me as to thee. Please, I must return hence and see to mine people. Wherefore didst thou bringeth me hither?*"

"Because Sir Francis and most everyone in Ruthaer thinks you're responsible for this mess," Hector replied.

"*By my troth, I have ne'er been here! Nor have I committed any of these atrocities we see before us. Xemmassians art a gentle race. This is the work of the Dark One.*"

"Gentle? Allyrian, I think you and I have different meanings for that word," Hector said.

"*Hunter, my name is not Allyrian. It is Tealaucan, but thou may call me Teal.*"

"Teal," Hector repeated. "Take a good look at yourself in that mirror over there, then follow me."

Hector stalked into the parlor and pointed to an oval portrait hanging on the wall. In it, a man and woman sat in brocaded chairs, and their teenage daughter perched on a low bench between them. Turning to the young woman trailing in his wake, he said, "Recognize her?"

She studied it for several long minutes, brow furrowed. "*Whither art this child's parents?*" she asked. "*What did happen to her that I now inhabit her body?*"

"Your parents are dead," Hector replied. "As for you..." He grabbed her wrist, his dark eyes boring into her amethyst ones. "Convince me you aren't their killer."

"*I know not what oath or action might convince thee of the verity of my words, but for the nonce, mine word is all I can offer thee.*"

The hiss of something soft sliding over stone drew Hector's attention to a dark hallway that ended at a door. It stood open the barest sliver. He signed to Teal to stay behind him, then pointed to her, his own eyes, and then the door. When she nodded, he eased into the hall and beckoned to Sir Francis, Henry, and Jared, who had followed them.

"Was there anything upstairs?" Hector whispered.

"No, sir," Henry replied. "Just furniture."

"What about the kitchen?"

"Nothing odd," Jared said. "Normal kitchen and pantry stuff. Why are we whispering?"

"I heard something," said Hector. "I think someone's in there."

Jared and Henry glanced at each other and shook their heads. "We didn't check the well," Henry said.

"Let's go look."

The single-story kitchen, while attached, lay at the back of the mansion and had the feel of a recent addition. A soot stained fireplace took up one wall and held grilles, tongs, and three different sized cauldrons. In the middle of the kitchen was a large bar with a granite top. Above it dangled an array of utensils. Off to the side, the pantry was the size of a bedroom. Inside, a wooden bucket and rope lay next to the short brick wall surrounding the well and buttery alcove.

Hector searched the floor and shelves around it, noting various cured meats and multiple casks of ale and wine. Taking out his bone tube, he shined the light down the well and saw a flicker of motion. Finding a loose bit of stone, he dropped it down the shaft and listened. It landed with a soft thump, bounced, and hit the water with a loud plop.

The scrabbling sound of claws on brick echoed up to him. Hector took a step back and drew his scimitar. The thing that crawled out of the well bore only a passing resemblance to a human. Tattered clothing clung to rotten, suppurating flesh. A smear of old blood covered its mouth.

As soon as Hector's light struck the creature, it vanished. It reappeared in the kitchen behind Henry and grabbed him around the throat. It latched onto his shoulder with a mouth full of rotten, jagged teeth. Henry screamed and tried to twist from the creature's grip.

Sir Francis smashed his gauntleted fist into the side of the revenant's head with a sickening crunch. It lurched back, letting Henry go, and disappeared.

"Jared, we need more light!" Hector yelled, retreating to the parlor.

"Got it!" he replied. Passing his lantern to Teal, Jared dashed outside, shouting for soldiers to bring light as he ran.

Hector and Teal stood shoulder to shoulder, searching the shadows for danger.

"I think you'll live, Henry," Sir Francis said, checking the bite wound, "but you're going to have a scar."

Drawing his sword, Henry smiled and replied, "That's fine with me, sir. Women like scars."

Sir Francis shook his head. Turning his attention to Hector he asked, "What was that?"

"A revenant. Evan creates them."

Suddenly Teal's lantern went dark, and the thing reappeared. Instead of attacking, it remained in a shadowy corner. Flanked by closed shutters, milky white eyes glowed eerily in the partially obstructed light. Its mouth worked up and down as if it were trying to form words.

"Daniel Tanner?" Sir Francis said in shock. A gasp escaped the soldiers and the more brazen of the townsfolk gathered at the foyer.

The revenant turned toward Sir Francis and said, "It's been a long time, Father."

"Evan? What...what have you done with Daniel?"

The revenant smiled. "Aren't you proud of me? I have given life back to this man."

"What you're doing is evil, Evan. Release him at once," Sir Francis commanded.

"Oh, I will. But first, I wanted to let you know this fledgling is ready to leave his nest."

"Leave?" Sir Francis said. "You can't leave. The monks bound you to this place."

"Father, the monks are dead. I killed them, just like your sacrifices to my bondage. One life a year, all for nothing."

Henry looked at Sir Francis, confusion and shock warring on his young face.

"Evan, don't do this. We have not broken our side of the pact," Sir Francis pleaded.

"I will break mine. I have found the key to my freedom."

"What have you done?" Hector demanded. Charging forward, he held the point of his weapon to the creature's neck.

The revenant emitted a grisly laugh that came across as more a wet cough. "Bounty hunter, I have heard much about you." Shifting its weight, the revenant slapped the weapon aside and struck Hector across the cheek, leaving four thin scarlet lines. "But this is not about *you*," it hissed.

Jared burst into the parlor carrying another lantern. The creature hissed and drew back. Taking advantage, Hector sliced open its abdomen with his blade. Black ooze seeped from the wound, filling the room with an overpowering reek of death. Jared gagged and coughed, causing the light from his lantern to flash around erratically and snuff out.

Everyone stood blinded for a brief moment. Only the dusty rays of sunlight streaming through the louvered windows provided any illumination.

Free of direct light, the creature clawed for Hector's neck. Teal grabbed the iron poker and jabbed it deep into the revenant's eye. The soft flesh burst like a pus-filled pore and white gore leaked from the socket.

"Goodbye, Father. The next time we meet I will kill you," the revenant gurgled as it slumped forward and fell to the floor. Hector moved to one side to avoid the falling body and chopped off its head in one swift stroke of his scimitar.

A grizzled old man with leathery skin blocked Sir Francis' path when they emerged from the Carmichael mansion.

"Hew..." Sir Francis started.

The old man held up his hand and said in a broken voice, "Francis, I have considered you a friend for a long time. Until today."

"Hew?"

"My wife, Margaret, do you remember her? Was she part of this deal you made with the devil?"

"Not here. Let's talk somewhere else," Sir Francis said, noting the shift in the crowd around Hew.

"No, here's fine." Hew Potter poked Francis in the chest and said, "You tell everyone here why my wife had to die. Is she still out there somewhere — like Daniel?" Hew balled up his fist and struck Francis across the jaw.

The knight stood there and took it. He didn't even try to avoid the blow.

"Daniel and Margaret, they volunteered," Sir Francis said softly.

"What? Why?"

"They were sick, dying, Hew, and they felt their sacrifice could help the town."

"So, what? You find someone who's sick and give them to your son?"

Sir Francis blanched. After a moment, he said, "Yes. Something like that."

Hew opened his mouth to say more, but Francis interrupted him. "You have to believe me. There was no other way to stop Evan. He would have killed us all."

"But she was my wife."

"You've been trying to hide this from everyone," said a giant of a man with stone-dust permanently embedded into his thick, calloused hands. "You should have sent a message to the Queen."

"Caradoc, I couldn't..." Francis faltered.

"Evan is no longer your problem," Hector said from behind Sir Francis. "Dave and I will find him and kill him."

"How are you goin' to do that?" Hew asked. "From what I hear, Alaric's daughter is dead, and your elf is soon to follow."

"We'll find a way."

"You don't even know where he is," said another of the townsfolk.

"He's on the other side of the river. Probably one of the barrier islands."

"You could spend years searchin' those islands," Hew said. "I know 'cause I've fished them my whole life. There's nothin' out there."

"Hunter, if I understandeth their words correctly, thou search for someone near mine home. Perhaps I can be of assistance."

Hector turned and relayed what she said to Sir Francis.

"North of the river, near the ocean, lies a fortification named the Praesidium. Mayhap yond is whence this fiend lies imprisoned."

When Hector finished translating, Hew said, "Allyrian lies. There is no such fort. She's just tryin' to escape."

Murmurs of agreement rose in the crowd.

"She's the one responsible for the fog!" someone shouted from the rear of the crowd. "She should be hanged!"

"Hold your tongue, Eryl!" Sir Francis bellowed. "There'll be no hangings."

"Francis, you lost the authority to tell us what to do when you killed my wife," Hew said.

Sir Francis gripped the hilt of his sword and said, "I am still the constable and responsible for the Queen's justice."

"Then do your job," someone shouted. "She killed our kin."

"No one dies today," Sir Francis said, releasing his hilt. "We'll take her to the Shrievalty and send word to the Queen."

"You can't do that," Hector said. "If Allyrian's working with Evan, she'll escape. If not, the phantoms in the fog will kill her."

"He's right!" someone yelled. "She'll use the fog against us! Hang her now before the sun falls!"

At a sign from Sir Francis, soldiers formed a line on either side of the constable and created a path through the crowd. Angry shouts rose up, but no one broke their formation.

"Everyone! Calm down. Caradoc's right," Sir Francis admitted. "I should have sent word to the Queen sooner. I'll send word to Port Remley immediately, but we must hold out until help arrives."

"It's too late, Francis!" Hew accused. "The fog has us trapped. Those families what tried to leave this morning found fog blocking the way in every direction! It's like the world just ends. We're all going to die."

"Help is coming!" Sir Francis insisted. "As it happens, the city of Rowanoake is sending a ship. They should arrive within the next day or two. Until then, keep the peace, and I promise I will turn in my sword."

"What if they can't get through the fog?" someone asked.

"They will," replied Sir Francis. "Jared, Henry, bring the prisoner."

The two grabbed Allyrian roughly by the arms and followed the constable to the Shrievalty.

CHAPTER 27
THE DEAD WAKE

August 5, 4237 K.E.

5:12pm

"This whole town has gone loco," Hector said as he stomped into the church. The sight that greeted him caused the bounty hunter to bite his tongue.

Groans of sorrow filled the chapel. Parishioners who sought a meaning for the last few days lined the pews. Most had family members at the Meeting House waiting for burial. Hector scanned the crowd, noting the lone figure on the front pew where Aislinn's body lay. Corporal Aaron Ponds sat beside her, his head bowed in sleep.

At the altar, Dave leaned over Hummingbird with a small spoon and dribbled broth into her mouth. He pushed an unruly tangle of hair from his face and waited. A fresh bandage covered his wounded shoulder. Mrs. Griffon stood beside him with a bowl, tears glistening in her eyes.

Father Blackwood left a grieving mother, joined Hector, and whispered, "He hasn't left her side. I asked Mrs. Griffon over to help, but your friend is making it difficult."

"Padre, I'll see what I can do," Hector replied.

Mrs. Griffon met Hector when he walked up to the altar and wrapped him in a motherly hug. "I'm so sorry," she murmured in his ear. Her tears spilled over, seeping into his jerkin.

"Gracias, Señora Griffon. Please, let me talk with Dave."

Mrs. Griffon handed him the bowl of what smelled like weak chicken broth then, with a quiet sniffle, stepped away.

"¿Qué pasa, amigo?" Hector said, positioning the bowl so Dave could reach it. Dave dipped his spoon, letting most of the liquid fall back out before giving it to Hummingbird.

"Broth's getting cold. I hate cold soup. I told that woman to warm it."

"Dave, Hummingbird's unconscious. She doesn't know."

"But I know."

Hector watched his friend for a long moment. Taking a deep breath, he whispered, "This town's falling apart."

"Let it. They all should have run for the hills at dawn."

"A bunch of them tried. The fog has the town cut off by land and sea. The only way out now is to destroy Evan Courtenay and Lady D."

Dave grimaced and pressed the heel of one hand to his temple. "Fuck! I just want Ymara out of my head."

Hector's hands curled into fists at his side, and he took a half-step back. "You can hear Lady D?"

Dave shook his head and ran a thumb over the ruby at his throat. "Not clearly."

"I take it, if you remove the ruby, she knows where you are."

Dave looked up, a haunted look in his whiskey-colored eyes. "She knows where I am — ruby or no ruby."

"What about the other way around?"

Dave's expression turned confused.

"If you take off the necklace, could you find her?"

"Are fucking nuts?"

"No, I'm serious."

Dave thought a moment and said, "I don't think so. When we arrived, I had no clue she was already here waiting on us."

"What if you think about her? Try to find her," Hector suggested.

Dave shook his head. "As soon as I do, she'll have direct access to what I'm thinking — among other things."

"¡Maldita sea!" Hector swore under his breath.

"Did you catch Allyrian?"

"Sí," Hector said. He watched Dave dribble more broth into Hummingbird's mouth, noting the extreme care his friend took each time he fed her. Waiting until he was done, he said, "She speaks dragon."

The spoon stopped midway between Hummingbird and the bowl. "What?"

"There's something strange about her," Hector mused. "I think she may know where Evan is hiding. Or at least, she knows the lay of the land."

"Where is she?"

"In jail."

"That figures. Nothing is ever easy, is it?"

☙❧

5:28pm

The top half of the sun hovered just above the tree line when Dave and Hector crossed the road and entered the Shrievalty. Soldiers cleaned out their last few belongings from the barracks and prepared to join their families or move to the chapel. Small talk between soldiers was almost nonexistent, giving the courtyard a somber feel. Outside the stable, a short, stocky horse with grey and white dapples nosed her tether in a half-hearted attempt to escape.

Hearing Sir Francis' voice booming from the main room, Hector and Dave strode up the steps and inside. The constable sat at his desk talking with a skinny teenager with dusty yellow hair wearing farmer's clothes. As they crossed the room, Hector realized it was one of Anne Farigest's boys.

"Luke, I need you to go farm to farm," Sir Francis said. "Call in everyone you can find to the Gryphon Inn or to the church. Tell them... tell them I said to bring every spare horseshoe they can find. We'll nail them above the windows and doors on the inside of the buildings as an extra precaution. No matter what happens, what anyone hears tonight, everyone must stay inside. Don't even look out the windows."

The young man swallowed and said, "Yes, sir."

Sir Francis stood up and clapped the boy on the back, "Ride hard, Luke. Everyone needs to be indoors before sunset. Goodspeed."

The youth ran out the hall and disappeared.

"El niño is young to bear so much responsibility alone, señor," Hector said.

Sir Francis turned his red-rimmed eyes to the pair and said, "I don't have a choice. Luke has the last horse this side of the Emmassa River, and he knows everyone. I don't dare try to send him to Port Remley for help. Not with the fog surrounding us."

"It would be at least three days before anyone could reach us from Port Remley, assuming they could get here," Hector said. "By my reckoning, the ship from Rowanoake should be here mañana or the day after."

Sir Francis rubbed his tired eyes and said, "We need the Queen's support — not pirates."

"Sometimes having a couple of desperados can be helpful," Hector said with a sly grin.

Sir Francis narrowed his eyes at the two warriors. "What do you have in mind?"

"First, we need Allyrian."

"Absolutely not," Sir Francis said with a swipe of his hand. "I have enough trouble holding this town together as it is. Letting her go would be crazy."

"We need her help to find Evan."

Sir Francis let out a long sigh. "I can't."

"You must."

Stepping closer to Hector, Sir Francis said in a low voice, "Look, I've already betrayed this town. You heard Hew. If I do what you ask, I'll turn those few who are on my side against me."

"If you don't do it, you'll condemn every remaining soul in this town to become revenants. Isn't that what you were fighting against in the first place?"

Sir Francis' voice broke as he said, "But my son. What I did. There's no going back."

"Forget what you and Blackwood did. Your responsibility is right here, right now. Whether they know it or not, these people need you. They need a leader."

Shadows crept across the Shrievalty floor and a cold shiver went up the constable's spine.

"Listen. Resorting to the Dark One to bring your son back from the dead was wrong; it was evil. To stop him, we need to know where he is. By some miracle, Allyrian knows where to look, and if you leave her here, either Evan will take her, or he'll kill her. Either way, it does us no good."

"And if I say no?" Sir Francis asked.

A dangerous glint crossed Hector's eyes as he said, "Say yes, señor." Behind Hector, Dave's presence suddenly loomed in the room. Looking as though he was making another deal with the devil, Sir Francis nodded.

CR80

6:01pm

Jared and Henry flanked Allyrian as they marched toward the chapel, followed by Sir Francis, Hector, Dave, and a half-dozen soldiers with no family in town. Some townsfolk muttered as they passed, but most remained fixed on watching the sun as they hurried to prepare for another terrifying night besieged.

The crowded chapel smelled of fear when they entered. People in the aisle shifted around to let them pass. When they did, a gnome child screamed and pointed at Allyrian.

"Murderer!" someone shouted.

The crowd's fear quickly turned to anger. Men rose from the pews as women herded their children and the elderly away from the threat in their midst.

"All who seek refuge from evil are welcome here!" Father Blackwood shouted over the din. He went from family to family speaking words of faith and hope. While the priest calmed everyone, Henry and Jared pushed their way to a seat on the opposite side of the chapel with Allyrian between them.

"Big Mike, is the vestry window covered?" Sir Francis asked.

"Yes, sir," Mike replied, "and we hung horseshoes over the opening, inside and out, like you asked."

CR&SO

11:00pm

Darkness had settled in the streets of Ruthaer like a midnight thug awaiting his next victim. Thick fog swept in from the river and rolled across the ground. It filled empty buildings and continued through town until it found homes with life still in them. Light peeked out from covered windows, and the grey mist oozed along its borders, caressing walls of tabby and wood. Probing tendrils sought for a weakness as they tried to reach those within.

Whip-poor-will...whip-poor-will...whip-poor-will.

The eerie cry reached weary hearts, driving away sleep. Families huddled together around fireplaces, praying for deliverance from the evil at their doorsteps.

Whip-poor-will...whip-poor-will...whip-poor-will.

Inside the Meeting House, hoarfrost coated the glass windows as the temperature plummeted. The fingers of a corpse twitched, followed by another, and then another. Movement spread throughout the room and, one by one, the dead opened their milky eyes and sat up.

"Come out my children," a voice called from the fog. "It's time."

Men, women, and children, two-score in all, shambled toward the exit. The door burst open like a festering wound, releasing the dead. They joined the phantoms in the fog and spread out, each driven by a nameless hunger within.

CR&SO

11:25pm

Screaming shattered the night. In the chapel, those who dozed bolted awake, wide-eyed and gasping. The screaming cut short, leaving behind a palpable silence.

"That came from next door," Sir Francis said, finding his voice.

Big Mike stood at the broken window in the vestry and looked out through a narrow gap in the wood planks. White-eyes glared back at him. He gasped and fell back, slamming into Father Blackwood.

"Father, there's... there's something out there."

Hector stepped in from the hallway and joined the priest and Sir Francis at the window. Nothing was there.

Something struck the front door hard, jarring the wood frame.

Dave handed his spoon to Mrs. Griffon and eased out his bow.

"Men, form up," Sir Francis ordered, his sword ready.

The door shook again and nearly broke from its hinges.

"Father! Come out," called Evan's voice. "Meet my children."

Something heavy hit the base of the door with a wet thud and blood pooled on the threshold. "Help me!" a woman's voice gasped from the other side.

"Open it!" Sir Francis commanded.

"No, don't," Father Blackwood pleaded, but a soldier opened the door anyway. Widow Brooks lay on the stoop. Many of the bones in her body were broken, causing her arms and legs to form unnatural angles. Her clothes were blood-soaked from dozens of bites.

Sir Francis peered into fog awash with ghosts and revenants. Among the latter, he recognized several of the dead townsfolk they had laid in the Meeting House. With blood coating their mouths, they stood shoulder to shoulder in front of Lady D. Some grasped a struggling man or woman and gnawed on the fleshy parts of an arm or shoulder.

"Evan, stop this," Sir Francis said, stepping over Widow Brooks. "If you want me, I'm here. Let these people go. I will not fight you."

A handsome young man coalesced in the fog. He wore a glowing blue and white surcoat with three golden stag heads. At his side, he carried a blackened sword.

"Another deal, Father?" Evan said.

"My life for those here," Sir Francis replied. "Isn't that what you want?"

"Francis!" Father Blackwood called out from the door.

A malicious smile crossed Evan's face, and he said, "You have no idea what I want. No idea the power you and Father Blackwood have given me."

The young warrior raised a gloved hand and after a moment, the sound of scrabbling carried from the graveyard. A groan cut through the stillness and Ogden Brooks crawled from his grave. Filled with an unholy glow, his decomposed body stood up on wobbly legs and shambled toward his wife's broken body on the church doorstep.

"See what I can do," Evan said. "I brought her husband back."

Sir Francis left the chapel and walked forward, his arms spread to each side. He stopped in front of his son and said, "Let them go, Evan. These were your friends and neighbors. Let the dead rest and the living put this terror behind them."

Ϟ℔ϟ

11:39pm

Dave held his bow ready, but Hector waved him down.

"I can take him," Dave grumbled.

"Dave, look at him. I mean *really* look at him."

The archer's scowl deepened when he realized Evan was no more solid than the fog. "*Shit.* How do we kill it?"

Hector leaned closer to the archer and said quietly, "Find its source and destroy it."

The priest shoved past them and ran to the edge of the churchyard. "Francis, no!" he shouted.

But it was too late; Evan grabbed his father by the throat. Sir Francis' skin turned black around the ghost's fingers. The constable's legs buckled, and Evan let him fall to his knees. Black rot continued to spread to his nose, lips, eyelids and other thin-skinned areas as more tissue died. Through it all, Sir Francis kept his eyes fixed on Evan's. There was neither hatred nor guilt in the look he gave his son, only an infinite sadness. Finally, the pain was too much, and the knight screamed, even as his tongue rotted away.

"Somebody, do something!" Big Mike shouted.

Dave whipped up his bow, drew, and fired in a single fluid motion. The black-fletched arrow slammed into Sir Francis' back. The heavy arrowhead and half-inch thick shaft dented, then pierced, the constable's plate armor, delivering its lethal poison to the suffering man's heart. His voice choked off mid-scream. Sir Francis slumped forward, with only the metallic sound of his shifting armor and the eerie chant of whippoorwills to mark his fall. The black fletching of Dave's arrow stuck straight up from his back and pointed toward the night sky.

Evan's face twisted into a mask of fury. "Kill them! Kill them all!" Fresh screams rose from the prisoners held by Evan's undead minions in the street.

Dave took another arrow from his quiver and aimed for one of the townsfolk being eaten alive. Before he could shoot, Father Blackwood raced to Sir Francis' side. He knelt beside his friend, oblivious to Evan standing right there. Gripping his wheel-cross, the priest held it up.

❧

11:44pm

"Stupid priest," Evan said. "Your power is gone."

Ignoring Evan, Father Blackwood's voice rang out in a prayer for forgiveness — not for himself but for Sir Francis, for Ruthaer. Dim at first, Father Blackwood's cross glowed with a pale blue light. It grew stronger until it enveloped the whole town, blinding those within its borders. Horrible cries filled the night, but no one dared move.

Using his hands to block some of the light, Hector tried to see, but all he caught were glimpses of dark silhouettes fleeing. The light from Father Blackwood's wheel-cross winked out, and he had to wait for his eyes to adjust. He closed them tight and opened them again. When he did, pale white light illuminated the yard in front of the church, and it took him a little while to realize it was coming from the moon.

Healed by Father Blackwood's prayer, the townsfolk in the churchyard stood dazed, but the revenants who had captured them were gone, along with Evan and Lady D.

Hector and Dave rushed down the steps to Sir Francis and Father Blackwood. The archer removed his arrow and turned over the constable's body. The man's skin was hard and cracked where it wasn't consumed with rot.

Hector laid a hand on the priest's shoulder, then jerked it back. The padre knelt on one knee and looked toward the heavens. Closed in a fist, his left hand covered his heart. His right hand held his wheel-cross high in the air for all to see. His robe and skin were stark white with glittering veins of silver and blue.

The priest had turned into pure marble.

CHAPTER 28
SIR WILLIAM HOWARD

August 6, 4237 K.E.

8:00am

Sunlight glimmered through the stained-glass windows. Only a few townsfolk remained in the sanctuary. On the front pew at the end farthest from the vestry hall, Big Mike and Jared slumped on either side of Allyrian. Where the central aisle met the altar, Dave sat on the other front pew, his long legs stretched across the walkway. Behind the altar, Hector slept in a chair from the vestry with his head resting beside Hummingbird's. An empty soup bowl sat on the floor at his feet.

The fingers of Dave's right hand brushed the top of Aislinn's head. "What do you want us to do?" he whispered. "Hector wants to take you to Ozera, but we can't drag you all over God's creation. I won't let them feed you to the worms — I can't let you go."

The church door swung open, filling the sanctuary with glaring sunlight. A tall, husky-built youth with a shock of sandy-brown hair hurried inside.

"Hank, what news?" Jared asked.

"Sails in the river mouth," he announced. "A single ship. They've dropped anchor and are launching longboats as we speak."

"Who is it?" Big Mike asked.

"Rowanoake."

Hector yawned and knuckled his eyes. "How late did we sleep?"

"Mid-morning," Dave replied, gathering his weapons. "We need to get out of here."

Hector rounded the altar. "And go where, amigo? They'll have the river blocked, and the two of us aren't going to out-row a longboat full of sailors. The only place to go is into the woods. There's no way we'll make it, carrying the girls."

"There's no fucking way I'm going back to Rowanoake," Dave said.

Meeting Hank in the aisle, Hector clasped the young sea ranger's hand. When Hank saw Aislinn and Hummingbird, he stopped short. "I'm so sorry. Let me know what Tallinn and I can do to help."

"I appreciate the thought," Hector said, "but I'm afraid it may be too late. If Rowanoake has boats in the water then you're stuck here, too. I doubt they'll let anyone leave town. Probably even ask for tribute."

A big smile lit up Hank's face. "They couldn't stop me if they tried. Tasunke's old but he's still faster than any rowboat."

"You rode the winged horse?" Hector asked.

"Of course."

"Could you carry Aislinn and Hummingbird back to the lighthouse?"

Hank studied the two petite bodies and seemed to weigh them in his mind. "Sure, but wouldn't it be easier to leave them here? They'll be safe in the chapel."

"Easier, maybe, but not safe. I need you and Tallinn to take care of them and keep them out of Rowanoake's reach while we sort out Ruthaer's ghost problem."

"What about us?" Dave asked.

"Don't worry, I have something else in mind for us." Turning to Big Mike and Jared, Hector said, "Gentlemen, I know we haven't been on the best of terms, but we need your help getting out of here."

Big Mike scowled and shook his head. "You're wanted men. What do you expect us to do?"

"For one thing, don't hand us over to a bunch of pirates," said Hector.

"Why not?" Jared asked.

"We're your best hope for saving Ruthaer," Hector replied.

"Father Blackwood and Sir Francis saved Ruthaer last night," Big Mike said. "Evan Courtenay is gone."

"He's not gone. Just driven away for the time being," Dave said, touching the balas ruby. "We have him on the run, but if we don't finish him off, he'll come back."

"And I doubt Rowanoake will care if Evan destroys this town," Hector added.

Big Mike frowned. "You're just trying to weasel your way out of going to jail."

Mrs. Griffon stepped from the shadows of the vestry hall and joined the two soldiers. She laid a hand on each of their arms. "I heard what you said, Michael Christopher Hart, and you should be ashamed of yourself. Despite being strangers to our town, they've stood between us and evil more than once since they arrived. I'm just an old lady, but I trust these two a lot further than anyone from Rowanoake. I say we gather those we can and help them."

Big Mike mulled over the innkeeper's words. He glanced over at Hank.

"Tallinn trusts them," the young sea ranger replied.

The burly sergeant turned back to the bounty hunter. "What do you have in mind?"

After explaining his plan, Hector ran his hands through his hair and tied it back. "Let's go see who Rowanoake sent to pick up Dave."

CR80

8:37am

Two longboats bearing Rowanoake's colors came rowing in like an invading army. Six to a boat, the sailors each wore a red button-up shirt and a black, peakless-cap sporting two silk ribbons. The single officer riding in the rear boat's bow dressed similarly, except his black cap bore the brass insignia of a sea serpent coiled around a fouled anchor.

Their leader stood at the bow of the foremost boat, wearing a stark white surcoat adorned with a fierce, currant-colored sea serpent coiled around a fouled anchor with its mouth agape and poised to strike. Where visible, his steel plate armor gleamed in the morning light. In one hand, he carried a horsehair-plumed helmet and the other rested on the hilt of his sheathed sword. Hair the color of spun gold framed his cleft chin and strong, handsome features in a glowing halo-like nimbus, but his dark, Gael blue eyes were cold and aloof.

Hew Potter stood alone on the waterfront pier. He glanced over his shoulder at the small group of his neighbors clustered at the edge of Fisherman's Wharf before turning toward the foreign knight and his crew once again. The old fisherman wiped sweaty palms on his pants legs and tugged at the hem of his best jerkin one last time.

The sailors pulled back on their oars, and the lead boat gently glided into the marina. Just as the hull scraped the dock, the knight leaped onto the planks, along with two sailors armed with cutlasses. While the sailors tied off the boat, he strode up to Hew.

"Milord William," Hew said, "your reputation proceeds you."

Ignoring his offered hand, the knight demanded, "Where is Sir Francis?"

"Dead, sir," Hew replied. "He died last night."

"Is that so?" William's eyes acquired a wicked glint as he surveyed the crowd. "Where are they?" Seeing Hew's confused expression, he repeated, "Where are Dave Blood, Hector de los Santos, and Aislinn Yves?"

"In the chapel, Milord."

"They should be in jail. How did they get here?"

"Sir?"

"Dammit, man! Did they come here by horse or by boat?"

"B...b...boat, sir," Hew stammered and pointed to their sailing skiff.

Turning to the nearest crewman, William ordered, "Confiscate their boat! We're taking it with us."

The sailor saluted smartly and replied, "Aye, sir."

"Milord, Queen Ambrose —" Hew started.

"What about your Queen?" William focused his blue eyes on Hew.

The old man quailed under the young warrior's venomous glare. "The men you came for are Carolingian prisoners. You're not supposed to take them without official permission."

"Are you going to stop me?" William asked, a mirthless smile forming at the edges of his mouth.

"Well, no, sir."

"Then I have your permission," William said. He scanned over the crowd and asked with a nod of his chin, "Is that the chapel?"

"Yes, sir."

Handing his helmet to a nearby sailor, the knight from Rowanoake marched toward the church with a half-dozen sailors trailing behind him. "What became of the garrison?" he asked Hew, who hurried to keep up.

Hew summarized the events of the past few days as best he could and ended with a recount of the phantoms vanishing.

William stopped at the marble statue of Father Cecil Blackwood. "Do you expect the fog to return tonight?"

"I don't know," Hew replied. "Milord, you'll need to leave men here to protect us in case the ghosts return."

The cheerless smile returned to William's lips. "Didn't you say this is the Queen's country? She can protect you." He climbed the chapel steps and threw open the door. Crossing to the altar, he shoved aside Mrs. Griffon and surveyed the room.

An ugly lividity rushed up the knight's throat and flooded his too-perfect appearance. "They're not here!" he shouted. He clenched his mailed fist and was about to stalk away when his eyes settled on the tall girl sitting beside Jared.

"Who is that?" William asked.

Hew replied, "Allyrian Carmichael, daughter of Garret Carmichael."

"Soldier, why are you here and not working?"

Jared stood at attention and said, "I'm guarding her, sir."

"Is she someone special to deserve a personal bodyguard?" The knight took in the lovely girl with undisguised lust. His eyes roved up and down the curves of her body, noting the ill-fitting dress she wore and the glimpses of smooth flesh underneath. He expected to see the typical adoration most women gave him. Instead, her gaze held only loathing.

"She's killed people, sir."

"This waif?" William said as he approached her. "She looks more the bar wench than a killer. She's not even bound." Unsheathing his blade, William said, "Girl, are you a killer like he says?"

With a defiant jut to her chin, Allyrian remained silent. William gripped the hilt of his sword tighter as he glared into her amethyst eyes. "Answer me, woman, or I will surely be your executioner."

"Foul and uncouth flesh-monger," she replied in halting Glaxon, "thou art a coward."

Rage blossoming anew, William loomed over the girl and raised his sword.

CR§O

8:41am

Dave and Hector let the river current carry them toward the marina. Using hollowed-out reeds to breathe, they drifted along just under the surface of the black water and aimed for an algae-coated piling supporting the closest dock. Under the cover of the low planks, the two split up. Hector headed to the other side of the marina, while Dave glided toward the nearby fishing boats.

Hector slowly worked his way past another row of pilings to the Rowanoake longboats. All around, sailors wearing red shirts scurried about under the disgruntled scrutiny of the officer. Careful not to splash, Hector stayed within the shadow of the dock as he swam closer to one of the longboats. Out of the corner of his eye, he watched two sailors follow the dock master to Dave's skiff, leaving four sailors to guard the docks.

Hector sank deeper and drifted under a longboat. In one hand, he held a T-shaped corkscrew and began drilling tiny holes into the wooden hull.

❦

8:55am

His blade held high, William reached for a handful of Allyrian's hair. She wrenched back with all her might, tipping over the pew. Sailors crowded the doorway as Allyrian rolled away from William and crouched next to Jared. With a not too gentle rip, she handed her dress to the slack-jawed soldier, and like a tigress, she leapt onto the upright of the nearest pew. It tipped over as she bounded to the next one, and the next, toppling the pews like dominos. Finally, she landed on one with someone sitting in it. Using their weight for counterbalance, she jumped and grabbed the bottom chord of the timber roof truss.

"Somebody, catch that bitch!" William yelled.

Rowanoake sailors spread along the aisles with drawn cutlasses, stabbing at the naked woman overhead. Allyrian ran along the timber beam and jumped to the next roof truss away from the sailors, clutching the king post.

"Find me a crossbow!"

"Sir William!" a sailor shouted as he ran into the chapel. "Our boats! They're sinking!"

With a final scathing look aimed at Allyrian, William ran outside and watched in disbelief as a fishing trawler drifted downriver, followed by another. Sailors in red shirts huddled on the dock with their weapons drawn, staring into the water.

Leaving two sailors at the chapel, William led the others back to the waterfront. "What the hell is going on?" he yelled.

The officer took off his hat and wrung it with both hands when he answered, "It's one or two men, sir. They're in the water."

"You bloody idiot, this is Dave and Hector's doing."

Big Mike ran up with several soldiers. "Milord, they're making a run for it up stream. Look."

William turned around and saw two men in a narrow boat steadily paddling at an angle toward the opposite shore.

"Leftenant! Commandeer boats and get our men on the water. Catch them!"

CRASO

9:03am

Jared waited at the chapel's rear door as Hector and Dave crossed the rectory yard, soaking wet and grinning. He put a finger to his lips and surreptitiously pointed back toward the sanctuary. "Two sailors from Rowanoake are inside, trying to catch Allyrian for Sir William. She's up in the rafters. Naked."

Hector nodded and slipped past Jared. Using only hand signals, he laid out his plan for Dave before easing along the wall toward the front entrance. He crouched low, keeping the pews between himself and the sailors.

Allyrian jumped from truss to truss, leading the sailors away from the church doors. Above the altar, she swayed toward the vestry hall, then suddenly spun and leapt toward the front entrance. The sailors raced down the center aisle.

Hector waited between two pews near the center of the sanctuary.

When Allyrian reached the truss over his head, she turned back toward the altar once again. The pursuing sailors skidded to a stop on the worn stone floor.

Hector jumped the rearmost sailor from behind and wrapped an arm around his neck. The man bucked and they fell among the pews. Holding on, Hector squeezed tighter.

The sailor's eyes bulged, and he turned scarlet. Fighting for air, he clawed at Hector's arm. With a final shudder, the sailor went limp.

Closer to the altar, Dave crossed swords with the other sailor. Steel on steel rang out. Dodging the swipe of the cutlass, Dave struck his opponent, crushing the man's nose with the guard of his sabre. Blood spattered and mixed with the tears that streamed down the sailor's face. Hitting him again, Dave pulped his nose and knocked him unconscious.

"Sorry about that," Hector said with a wince.

"Don't worry, we'll take care of them," Jared said.

"Gracias. Where's Mike?"

Jared smiled. "He's leading that ogre and his men away from town in pursuit of Henry and Aaron. Somebody mistook them for you guys. Hurry. I don't know how long they can fool Sir William."

Hector looked up and saw Allyrian watching him from the rafters, naked as the day she was born. "We're getting out of here."

The nimble girl jumped down. "I need a weapon."

"You need some damned pants," Dave snapped.

Tossing the girl one of his daggers, Hector said, "Come on."

☙❧

9:13am

Mr. Griffon led the small group across town. Each wearing a hooded peasant's cowl, Hector and Dave carried a rolled-up tapestry while Jared and Allyrian, dressed in a spare uniform, marched beside them.

At the docks, two sailors from Rowanoake stood guard. Mrs. Griffon was offering them something to eat from a basket she carried in the crook of her arm. Upriver, two commandeered jon boats carrying William and the other sailors were rounding a bend into the shadowy edge of the forest. One of the sailors held up his hand at Mr. Griffon's approach. "This area is off —"

Dave shifted the tapestry on his shoulder, brought up his fist, and coughed. The sailor fell to the ground. Before the other crewman could raise the alarm, a tiny, yellow tufted dart took him down as well.

Mrs. Griffon handed Allyrian her basket. "You'll need this."

"Thank thee, gentle lady," Allyrian said.

Mrs. Griffon turned to Hector and drew him close in a farewell hug. "I don't think that's really Allyrian," she whispered in his ear. "You watch yourself."

"I will, Señora Griffon," Hector said, returning her hug.

"You're not coming back, are you?" she asked, watching Dave help her husband and Jared gently load the tapestry into their skiff.

"No, señora."

Mrs. Griffon squeezed him again and said, "Well, give Dave a hug for me."

"I'll try, señora," Hector replied with little conviction. "You take care of yourselves."

Pulling away from Hector, she said, "Get out of here before they figure out what happened."

CHAPTER 29
A DAVE PLAN

August 6, 4237 K.E.

9:16am

Stripped to his waist, Dave cast off while Hector pulled the line to raise the mainsail. Caught in the swift current, the skiff took off like a shot. Allyrian found a stable spot near the bow of the boat and held on. Dave adjusted the tiller and steered the craft downriver toward the ocean. Once settled, he retrieved his bow and quiver of arrows from the rolled-up tapestry near his feet and set it beside him.

The late morning sun glinted off the water. As he gauged distances, Dave's dark eyes became tiny pinpricks. With both the wind and current behind them, they cut through the water, throwing whitecaps in their wake.

"Head toward the lighthouse. We need to talk with Tallinn before going after Evan. I'm hoping he and Hank can point us in the right direction," explained Hector. "You think we can get there without getting trapped?"

"Don't worry. I have a plan," Dave replied.

Worry crept into Hector's eyes as he gazed at the archer. Before he could say anything, shouts carried to them from upriver.

One of the crafts filled with Rowanoake sailors emerged from the dark edge of the woods. Sunlight struck William's armor, turning it into a fiery beacon. The knight leaned forward with his foot on the gunwale and pointed toward their skiff.

"William Howard," Dave spat. "Every bit as vain and stupid as Killian."

Hector twisted in his seat and grinned. "Looks just like his brother. What's he doing here?"

"Considering that letter Rowanoake sent Sir Francis pinning Killian's death on me, who did you expect to come after us? Here, you steer," Dave said as he grabbed a line and eased down the sail a bit. The skiff slowed and the rowboats quickly gained ground.

"Dave, what are you doing?" Hector asked.

"Letting them catch up. I don't want to disappoint William."

"What do you want me to do?" Hector asked, laying a reluctant hand on the tiller.

"The tide's turned. Stay close to the left bank, and don't run us aground."

"What about me?" Allyrian asked.

"Stay out of the way," said Dave as he picked up his bow and quiver. The archer nocked a hawk's head arrow, aimed at the lead jon boat, and let it fly. It hit the hull just under William's foot with a loud thunk.

Crying out, the knight stepped back hard. With the sudden shift in weight, the boat lurched, and the knight lost his balance. He fell amongst his men just as another arrow zipped over his head. The arrow buried itself into the shoulder of one of the rowers, who let go his oar and lost it in the water. Everyone aboard searched frantically for cover from incoming arrows, causing the boat to rock side-to-side even more, and the starboard gunwale kissed the water.

"Fool should know better than to wear heavy armor in a boat," Dave muttered, taking aim again. This time, he shifted to the adjacent boat and fired; the hawk's head erupted out of the back of the officer's throat with a spray of blood. Pandemonium ensued. Sailors jumped into the water.

Their splashing attracted several alligators sunning on the shore. With a shove of their clawed feet, they slid down the muddy bank and slipped into the murky river. The archer watched sailors treading water as the current carried them and the officer's bleeding body toward the sea. One sailor cried out, then flailed at the water and vanished under a reptilian body; a dark cloud of bloody water replaced him.

CRSO

9:20am

Stepping closer to the mast, Dave pulled on the line to raise the sail again. The wind caught the skiff, and she leaned hard-over while shooting forward.

"After the next bend, aim for the Rhodinan ship," Dave said. He held on to the mast, lost in thought with the wind blowing through his greasy hair.

"You do remember that there's a huge hole in the side," Hector said, adjusting the tiller to keep the skiff parallel to the river's shore.

An errant cross breeze caught the bow, and the jib broke loose. "Humming..." Dave started. Taking a deep breath, he collected himself and yelled, "Allyrian, get off your ass and stay that line!"

"My name is Teal, as I have told yon hunter more than once."

"Allyrian, Teal, whatever the hell your name is, when I give an order on this boat, you jump to it!"

The girl glared at the archer but grabbed the flapping rope Dave indicated. With tension back on the line, the jib billowed, and the craft sped up again.

"Since when did you start understanding us?" Hector asked her.

The tall girl thought a moment as she looped the line around the cleat and said, "I did understand some of thy tongue from the start, mainly those words like unto the Korellan taught in my youth, but also some from my time as flight-master for the Praesidium. These other words have come to me in bits and pieces. I learned some during the parlay at the manor, and more whilst everyone spoke at the chapel. It seems I learn more, the more I hear."

They rounded the next bend in the river, and the wrecked Rhodinan galleon came into full view. "Hector, take us alongside," Dave said.

"Aye, aye, Capitán," Hector said, exaggerating his Espian accent.

"We need to do something about Rowanoake. Can't keep one eye on them and find Evan Courtenay with the other," said Dave to himself, as if sorting through his thoughts. "If I'm right, William's ship should be waiting at the end of the river." After studying the river current and gauging the tide, a roguish expression crossed his face.

"Dave, what's going through that head of yours?" Hector asked.

"Let's get to the Rhodinan galleon," Dave replied. "Teal, help me furl the sails."

The skiff drifted past the galleon's stern and came to rest several yards past the spot where the keel touched bottom. It had been only four days since they were last here. Four days since — Hector shook the thoughts from his head and lowered the anchor.

Dave had Teal loosen specific lines from their cleats and coil them in neat piles. "Hector, you and Teal, pay attention.

I want you to be able to do this without me." Making sure both could see what he was doing, he undid the lashing at the base of the mast, pulled the pin, and carefully picked it up and leaned it over.

"Where will you be, amigo?"

"Creating a distraction."

After Hector and Teal stepped and unstepped the mast to the archer's satisfaction, Dave frowned at Teal. He stood there for a moment in complete silence. Hector, seeing his friend stuck, asked, "What is it?"

"I need supplies and to know how far William is behind us."

"There's the crow's nest. What's the problem?"

Dave nodded at Teal. "I don't want to leave *her* alone with our skiff."

Teal brought her fist to her heart. "I swear by my troth; I shall not flee."

"Not that we don't trust you —" Hector began.

"— but we don't trust anybody," Dave finished.

"Then let me board yon vessel and attempt to spy 'pon thine enemies," Teal countered.

Hector and Dave exchanged questioning looks then nodded to each other. "Here," Hector said. He pulled a small box from the bow locker and produced a spyglass. "Do you know how to use this?"

"What is't?" Teal asked, extending a hand to take the compacted device.

Hector grinned. "Powerful magic. When you look through it, distant objects seem close enough to touch." He pointed to the galleon. "Climb the main mast to the crow's nest. That should give you cover while you scout the river."

Teal looked up at the ship in confusion.

"The one in the middle," Dave growled and slid over the gunwale into the creek.

Teal followed Dave through the gaping hole in the ship's hull. Hector waited, one eye on the ship and the other on the river for signs of their pursuers. Finally, Teal appeared at the rail overhead and gave him a sharp nod before climbing the rigging. In a matter of moments, she reached the crow's nest and peered upriver, both with and without the spyglass.

Hector continued to watch Teal. Surveying the marsh, she followed the river's course to the anchored ship and the barrier islands. Her mouth dropped open, and Hector could see the horror etching itself on her features. Fear zinged through his veins, and he opened his mouth to call out to Dave before he realized Teal was staring north, beyond the lighthouse. Her gaze followed the cliffs south, horror giving way to a dazed look, and she climbed back to the deck far more slowly than she ascended.

A sharp whistle drew his attention to Dave, waiting at the hole with two small pitch-coated barrels tied together with a length of rope.

"Catch!" Dave called out as he tossed them in the water near the skiff.

"I thought you said the hold was empty," Hector replied, grabbing a gaff.

"It was. I found these on the crew deck. They use this to patch the hull when it springs a leak."

"What are we going to do with them?" Hector asked hauling in the tandem barrels.

"Pay the devil."

CRΩSO

10:16am

Anchored on the south side of the channel, the ship from Rowanoake, the *Fluyt*, squatted in a shallow cove, its rails barely visible above the surrounding cordgrass. Designed for shallow coastal waters, the combination of its broad bottom with a rounded fore and aft made it look like an eighty-foot long bathtub with two masts. Eighteen pairs of oars peeked out of the hull, and a metal-plated battering ram and spar took the place of the bowsprit. Towering over the ship and cove, the worn face of the barrier island leered like the village idiot.

Hidden by cordgrass, Dave knelt in ankle deep water and let the current carry his two barrels downriver. He watched their progress for a moment before moving along the shore to get a better view of the ship.

The clangor of a brass bell rang out. In the crow's nest, a sailor in a red shirt held a spyglass to his eye. Down below, oar blades turned and shifted as unseen mariners took positions on benches. Sailors lined the rails, searching for the source of the alarm.

Still hidden, Dave caught sight of the skiff's white sails out of the corner of his eye and smiled.

The captain stalked across the poop deck to the rail and looked up at the crow's nest. The sailor pointed upriver and held up one finger. The captain aimed his spyglass in the direction indicated, then nodded. Wiping his brow with a kerchief, he ordered, "First Mate, prepare to weigh anchor!"

"Aye, sir," a sailor responded from the main deck.

"Captain, I lost the skiff!" the sailor in the crow's nest shouted. "Their mast just disappeared into the marsh grass." After a moment, he shouted and pointed, "There it is! No, wait. I lost it again."

"How can you lose them?" the captain shouted.

"Their mast just dropped out of sight."

The thump of wood against the hull carried over the water. Sailors at the forward starboard rail looked down, then called to a crewman amidships. He produced a long gaff, leaned over the railing, and snagged the rope tied between the pair of barrels.

The quartermaster saw the commotion and yelled, "Hey! What's going on over there?"

"We found a barrel floating in the water, sir," the sailor replied. "Correction, sir, two barrels. They're tethered together with a rope."

"Well, bring them up, lad. We're about to cast off."

"Aye, sir."

The sailor leaned over farther and began pulling them up. The rope slid through the hook as the weight from the second barrel tugged on the first. He almost had it up when the captain shouted, "Belay that sailor! Drop it back in the water!"

The order came too late. A smoking hawk's head arrow slammed through the lower barrel. The wooden shell exploded, coating the *Fluyt's* hull with a flaming mixture of grain alcohol and pitch. Lines of fire raced fore and aft, and oily, black smoke billowed as the tar-caulked seams in the wood planking caught flame.

Dave watched the spreading blaze and growing chaos on deck. When sailors started jumping overboard, he retreated behind the nearest scrub-topped hillock. Heading south and east to the barrier islands, he kept on the brown paths

Aislinn had shown him and descended into a narrow, oyster lined creek bed.

Thick smoke plumed from the cove. Across the channel, Tallinn's lighthouse stood tall and proud, and Dave used it as a landmark to guide his way. The last thing he wanted was to get turned around, especially considering the anthill he just kicked over.

The tide crept steadily higher the farther he went. He hoped he hadn't mistimed it. When the creek he followed met the cliff-face of a barrier island, Dave aimed south and traveled along a submerged ledge.

Hector waited, knee deep in a nearby tidal creek, with one of the mooring lines wound around his fist. Teal stood at the transom, gripping the gunwale, but her eyes were fixed on the cliffs rising around them.

With the mast folded over and sails furled, the profile of the boat remained below the cordgrass. However, it wouldn't be long before the tide would be too high, and they would be visible to all.

"How did it go?" Hector asked.

Dave shrugged as he trudged into the creek and said, "They won't be chasing us in that ship." He laid his bow and quiver in the boat and grabbed the end of another mooring line. He jerked a thumb toward Teal. "What the hell's wrong with her?"

"No sé, amigo. Está loca."

Frothy seawater sloshed about their legs as they guided the boat into the narrow gap between two of the barrier islands. Wide at the bottom and narrow at the top, the channel looked more like a tunnel with a stripe of golden sunlight above where the two islands almost met. Similar to the channel they used when they first arrived, it became deeper the closer it got to the ocean. When the water reached hip deep, Hector and Dave climbed aboard the skiff. Just as they grabbed the oars, Teal hoisted herself up onto a ledge and edged along the defile.

"Girl, get your ass in this boat!" Dave called.

"I am not a girl," Teal snapped, "and I'll thank thee to keep a civil and courteous tongue in mine presence."

"Teal, what are you doing?" Hector asked. "We need to go."

Teal worked her way along the ledge to an odd patch of blue and green on the cliff-face. Using the hilt of her borrowed dagger, she struck the wall in a circle around the edges of the discoloration. Like a thick piecrust, the patina cracked and fell off revealing a brass placard riveted to the wall. On its surface was an embossed sigil. She traced her finger over the swirling knotwork and bowed her head.

Hector offered her a hand up when she reached the skiff. "What was it?"

Teal didn't answer until she was aboard and seated. "'Twas a doorway, once. Now, 'tis all the proof I have that my people once called these sundered stones home."

CHAPTER 30
HOME IS WHERE THE HEART IS

August 6, 4237 K.E.

11:18am

When the skiff floated out of the inlet, a crashing wave broke against the base of the cliff-face, its spray soaking everyone aboard. Another wave slapped against the hull, and the boat rocked violently as it tried to make headway over the rolling swells. Hector and Teal worked together to lash their gear down tight.

Gritting his teeth, Dave angled the sails to collect more wind, and the skiff shot ahead. It hit the next wave as if it was a ramp, and the skiff flew through the air, trailing sparkling diamonds of seawater. Dave steered the boat north-northeast and increased their distance from the dark cliffs.

Three hundred yards to their left, near the channel mouth, a trail of tarry smoke led back to the cove. There, the *Fluyt* listed heavily to one side, the burning ship's hold apparently taking on water. A pair of longboats bristling with oars glided across the channel as redshirt sailors rowed north toward the lighthouse. On the far side of the cove, sailors clambered aboard a fishing trawler from the commandeered jon boats. Sir William's armor was a blinding beacon as he paced the trawler's deck.

"Dave, you imbécil, what were you thinking?" Hector said when he saw all the activity.

"That William is a vain prick with an ugly tub of a boat." The skiff plummeted into a trough and crested the back of the next wave. Dave grinned maniacally at Hector. "Come on, I stopped him from taking us to Rowanoake."

"How are we going to get to the lighthouse if it's crawling with sailors? What about Aislinn and Hummingbird? They're up there."

Dave was silent for a moment before he replied, "Even if they weren't pirates, Tallinn wouldn't let them in his lighthouse. There's too much bad blood between Rowanoake and the Sea Ranger Corps."

"What are you talking about?"

"Don't you remember? The city uses apprentice mages to keep their beacon lit. Our first week there, Jasper told us every Sea Ranger stationed at the Rowanoake light met with an accident."

"I'd forgotten about that." Hector shook his head at the smoke spire towering over the lighthouse. "You know, Tallinn won't like you burning a ship in his channel."

"Bah," Dave said. "That's nothing. Wait until he hears about all those boats you sank in his river."

"Only two," Hector said defensively.

Dave watched William's crew use oars to push the fishing trawler free of the muddy bank. Sails unfurled and the ship aimed for open water. Both longboats changed course to join the trawler, and together they headed after the skiff.

"You should have sunk more," Dave said, adjusting the jib.

Hector turned and saw the tiny armada heading their way. "Do you think we made William angry?" The knight stood at the prow of the boat gesticulating. Even though they couldn't hear him, it was easy to guess he was shouting for more speed.

Narrowing his eyes, Dave said, "I hope so."

"Can they catch us?" Hector asked.

Dave leaned forward. "They can try." The skiff crested the next swell and a gust of wind caught the sail. She flew down the backside at an angle, throwing off white spray.

Hector wiped seawater from his brow as he scanned the cliffs. Similar to the south side of the channel, the line of barrier islands stair-stepped to the north. Craggy inlets, wide at the bottom and narrow at the top, interrupted their dark, granite face every quarter mile or so. Like a castle wall, the cliffs trailed off into the distance and turned west where they seemed to merge with the mainland.

The bounty hunter turned back to the channel and the lighthouse, matching up what he saw to the map in the monastery. He believed Aislinn was right about the map holding the key to finding Evan Courtenay's lair.

The ghūl was hiding somewhere in those islands.

છ૪ૈ

11:22am

Hand over hand, Teal followed the gunwale forward to sit beside Hector. "Is't thy intent to reach yonder spire?" she asked.

"That *was* the plan before those marineros cut us off."

"Perhaps there is another way."

"What's that?" Hector asked.

"Yon islands are my home. 'Twas my wont to explore them when I was but a youth, and as an adult, it was my job to defend them."

"Those islands?"

"Aye. At the time, 'twas a single island that did tie back to the mainland by an arched bridge. A series of antre near the base once housed our dragon kin. Those antre art thither still, but now they are inlets. If't be they have not moved o'er much, I may can find thee another path."

"Speak Glaxon will you," Dave said. "I can't understand a damn word you're saying."

Hector thought a moment and asked Teal, "Antre? You mean caves?" Seemingly at an impasse, the two remained quiet, vainly searching for the means to bridge the communication gap. Hector looked over his shoulder. The trawler and the longboats were still several hundred yards behind them, but they were losing ground.

"Teal, does it matter which inlet we take?" Hector asked.

"Nay. We can double-back to the antrum we needeth once we art on the other side. But I think yon knight is anticipating our move." She pointed to a longboat veering toward the broken cliff.

"Dave, take us into one of those inlets."

"What?"

"Do it!" Hector commanded.

The memory of their arrival on this god-forsaken shoreline filled Dave's mind. For a moment, he saw Aislinn, rain and sea-spray soaked as she pointed at the cliffs, rather than Hector in the bow. Letting the shiver down his spine subside, the archer adjusted the lines to the sails, and the skiff made a long, gradual arc back toward the barrier islands. At least this time there wasn't an unnatural storm bearing down on them.

Seeing the skiff change direction, the trawler angled to cut them off while the remaining longboat aimed for the closest inlet.

The skiff sliced through the swells at an angle, letting them push the boat toward the cliffs. They passed the third island from the main channel, then the fourth and fifth before Dave swung the boom.

"Hang on!" Dave yelled and planted a foot on the bulwark to brace himself as he pulled on the tiller. With a heart-stopping lurch, the skiff leaned hard-over, and they plunged through a wave. The spray of water scintillated in the sunlight, creating a rainbow over the prow. As they came about, another wave swelled behind them and Dave let it propel them into the inlet.

Already in position, Teal and Hector rowed through the craggy gap. Unlike the south side of the river where there were mudflats and oyster rakes, the north side was a maze of rocky narrows guarded by tall, granite cliffs.

Dave quickly furled the sails and dropped the mast. When finished, he knelt in the bow with his longbow and quiver.

"I hope you have enough arrows," Hector said.

Dave counted. He had ten shots left in this quiver and a dozen left in the other. He'd have to make the most of them.

"Can the trawler follow us in these waters?" Hector asked, looking over his shoulder.

"Maybe at high tide, if they find a passage wide and straight enough," Dave replied. "We still have to worry about the longboats."

With just the dip of their oars to mark their passage, they navigated the twisting inlet. Teal studied the shadow shrouded cliffs, here and there pointing out discolorations and weathered recesses to Hector. They floated under a natural stone arch marking the end of the inlet. Entering another channel that ran north-south, they hugged the sheer face of the barrier island.

Heat radiated from the cliff walls, and Dave blinked away the sweat dripping from his hairline. He drew a faded leather headband adorned with two tiny red feathers from his belt pouch and tied it around his forehead. Instantly, he felt the temperature lower to a comfortable level.

Turning south, they rowed deeper into the maze. Intermittent tufts of brown grass dotted the rocky shores. A white heron stalked along the bank and gave them a sideways glance. The three floated past it, straining to hear sounds of pursuit.

Up ahead, the tip of an island jutted out like a giant foot, with the top of the toes just visible above the dark water. The canal hugged the protuberance, bending first right, then left, ninety degrees.

When the skiff rounded the last bend, they found themselves at the edge of a broad pond. Craggy outlets of various sizes breached the islands and led further into the confusing maze.

"Which way, Teal?" asked Hector.

She pointed to a narrow opening. "Yonder."

No sooner than Hector and Teal dug their oars into the water, William's two longboats popped out of a passage midway between them and their destination. In the bow of the lead boat, the *Fluyt*'s captain shot an accusing finger at Dave.

"There they are, lads! Don't let them escape," he shouted.

Dave's arrow streaked across the water and hit the officer in the heart. With cries of outrage, the lead oarsmen in each longboat banked their oars and snatched up crossbows.

Hector and Teal reversed course. "What now, Teal?" Hector asked, looking for a way to escape. They were at least a mile away from the lighthouse as the crow flies, with three islands still to go. "Things are about to get ugly."

"We needs must retrace our path," Teal said. White stripes crisscrossed the water as crossbow bolts struck around the bow. The last thing they saw as they disappeared behind the giant's foot was the longboats pressing forward.

The skiff retreated into a channel between two barrier islands. Teal had them row about a third of the way in before she stopped and searched the walls.

A longboat appeared at the entrance to the channel. Dave stood and fired two arrows in quick succession, striking sailors wielding crossbows. Shouts erupted across the water as the remaining officer urged the boat forward, but the sailors hesitated. Dave fired again and took down another sailor.

Teal jumped out of the boat and splashed along the ledge of the southernmost island. She felt along the wall, searching.

The second longboat took up a position at the other end of the channel, and its sailors fired their crossbows. One bolt fell short. One struck the wall. Another hit the hull near Dave's foot. "Hurry up!" Dave called, nocking another arrow and aiming at the sailor who had nearly shot him.

Teal struck the wall with the hilt of her dagger and found another bronze placard. Spitting on her hand, she scrubbed away a stubborn piece of patina from the edge. A bolt whizzed overhead and ricocheted off the granite wall, throwing sparks.

Closing her eyes, Teal shoved in the placard and turned it as she said, "Aperire hoc ostium."

Sensing their prey was on the verge of escape, the officer's voice echoed from the surrounding cliffs. "Aft oars, make way! Forward bowmen, look lively! A bonus to the first man to wound the archer!"

"Hurry, Teal!" Hector shouted. "We're about to be boarded!"

Dave fired again, striking a crossbowman. The sailor next to his fallen comrade picked up the crossbow and fired back.

The cliff-face where Teal stood grumbled and shook. Chunks of debris rained down, and thick dust clouded the channel, obscuring everyone's vision. Dave and Hector spit dirt and covered their mouths with their hands. Over the sound of their coughing, they heard water gurgle as it rushed into the widening gap in the wall.

The turbulent current grabbed the skiff and sucked it into the growing maw. As their skiff plunged inside the cliff, Dave spotted Teal on another ledge, her hand already pressed against a thick bronze plate. Her words were lost amid the grumble and shriek of shifting stone. In response, the opening stone door slowed, stopped, and began moving in the other direction. The door closed with an ominous boom and threw the cave into darkness.

Hector took out a thin bone tube and uncapped the end, letting its light refract from the water. Above, wet stalactites dripped onto the black seawater, forming overlapping rings.

Like the cavern where they spent their first night among these islands, the water in this cave lapped against a broad stone landing littered with debris. Fortunately, this one did not contain a dragon's corpse.

Crystals set in the ceiling caught and magnified Hector's light. High on the wall, a bas relief carving circled the room in a series of scenes. In one, human-like shapes sat at the feet of dragons. In another, the dragons and humans seemed to exchange gifts. In still another, small figures rode dragon-back, wielding long spears against other dragons. The enemy dragons bore flecks of shimmering black paint.

"I wish Aislinn and Brand were here to see this," Hector said softly.

Dave grunted in reply but didn't speak. Outside the cave door, the sailors from Rowanoake shouted to one another as they sought a way to follow the skiff.

While Hector and Dave rowed across the cavern, Teal followed the perimeter ledge to the foot of roughhewn steps leading through an archway. There, she crouched near a small pile of white stones. Piece by piece, she sorted them into a rough rectangle on the floor. By the time Dave and Hector reached the girl, she had most of a broken carving reassembled. Despite the missing fragments and pitted stone, it was clearly a depiction of a young dragon perched on the edge of a cliff beside a humanoid warrior.

"This was the home of Flosaeris, mother of Tarnillis," Teal whispered. She ran a fingertip along the carved dragon's neck. Flecks of verdigris clung to both figures.

"Where do the steps go?" Hector asked.

Teal knuckled her eyes before meeting the bounty hunter's gaze. "During my time, they lead to the battlements that once lined the Praesidium."

"Are there caves like this riddled throughout these islands?" Hector asked.

"Aye. They were the homes of the dragons."

Another shout drifted through the wall from outside, accompanied by the clang of metal on stone. "We need to go," Hector said. "We're going to be hard pressed to speak to Tallinn and then find Evan before nightfall."

Teal gave one last look at the broken carving, then stood. "Let me go up and make sure the way is clear." Hector nodded and Teal ran up the stairs. Her soft footsteps echoed as she went.

Dave and Hector plundered the skiffs lockers, picking out what gear they were going to carry, including a coil of rope, and secured the rest.

By the time they were ready, Teal waited at the foot of the ancient stairs. "The way is clear, but 'tis tight as a pauper's purse in places," she said.

The stair spiraled sunwise as it wound higher and higher. Rotten wood and shattered stone littered the first two landings, creating a dark, dangerous obstacle course. At the top, the stair ended inches below a granite lid.

Teal laid the palm of her hand on a nearby placard and pressed. Dirt tumbled down as the lid slid back, pushed by an unseen hand. Sunlight blinded them and they had to blink back dusty tears from their eyes.

Blue skies and stubby greyish-green trees with gnarled branches greeted them. After they climbed out, Teal touched the stone lid. It slid back to its original position and when it did, it took on the irregular shape of a rocky outcropping common to the island top.

Dave made a sign to ward off evil and searched the ground for a placard or other sign that may mark the stairwell. There was none.

CR&SO

1:51pm

Through the trees, Hector spotted the lighthouse tower south of their position, a little less than a mile away. From their vantage point, it was easy to see how the islands stair-stepped up to the largest island in the center of the maze.

As they trekked toward the lighthouse, there was no sign of the civilization Teal said once inhabited this land long ago; no evidence they had ever existed, other than the carvings on the cave walls below. The bounty hunter caught himself staring at the tall girl, wondering how she could know about the caves and stairs, let alone the words needed to call the ancient magic back to life, if she wasn't what she claimed.

An eight-foot gap separated the edge of their island from the next. Seventy-five feet below, one of William Howard's longboats traversed the tidal inlet, its crew unaware of the people watching them.

Teal backed up several feet and, with a running start, hurtled across the chasm. She landed without losing her stride and turned back toward Dave and Hector. The two studied the gap and then looked at each other. With maniacal grins, they charged the edge and leapt.

CHAPTER 31
FLIGHT OF TASUNKE

August 6, 4237 K.E.

2:04pm

After a quarter mile, they reached the second barrier island's far shore and stood at the gap separating them from the lighthouse. Deep rumbling growls emanated from the woods on the other side, and the trees shook. They caught a glimpse of brown fur moving in the shadows.

"Stupid bears," Dave muttered.

A shadow passed overhead, and they looked up to see Tasunke fly low over the trees.

"Do you think they remember us?" Hector asked.

Teal stared wide-eyed at the winged horse. She rubbed her eyes with her fists and searched the skies. Tasunke circled once and headed toward the lighthouse. A pair of bears shambled out of the woods on all fours and sat down with a loud grunt.

"What do you think?" Hector asked.

Dave shrugged, not sure what to make of them. "We'll have to cross eventually."

"Teal?" Hector said.

The tall girl backed away from the gap, holding the coil of rope, and vaulted across. When she landed, the bears eyed her warily. Other than a single muscle twitch to discourage a biting fly, the creatures remained still.

Taking it as a good sign, Hector and Dave leapt across the gap. The trio passed between the two bears, who followed them. They cut through the woods, heading toward the lighthouse. As they went, Dave and Hector repeatedly looked back to make sure the bears kept their distance.

Hank met them at the clearing around the lighthouse. He cocked his head and said, "You've caused quite the stir."

"More than I intended," Hector said. "I assume you and Tasunke didn't have any trouble getting here with Aislinn and Hummingbird."

"We flew north around the quarry and across the islands. No one from Rowanoake saw us." The young Sea Ranger shook his head and sighed. "I'm afraid old Tallinn's heartbroken, though."

"Can we speak with him?" asked Hector.

Hank nodded. "Sure. He's inside waiting for you."

They followed the ranger to the foyer where he turned and said, "If you want anything let me know. I'll be up in the tower. Hopefully, I can spot where those scurvy bilge rats have gone in Hew Potter's trawler."

Hector found Tallinn sitting in a ladder-back chair in the first-floor bedroom. Aislinn and Hummingbird lay side by side on the old man's bed. Tallinn held Aislinn's hand as he murmured a prayer. When finished, he laid her hand gently atop her chest. "What happened?" he asked without turning toward the door.

"Señor, the sounds you mentioned when we were here before — the scrape of metal and grinding gears — turned out to be a huge clockwork-bug. It ambushed us in the quarry while we were looking for Evan Courtenay. Aislinn died trying to save Hummingbird."

"Evan?" said Tallinn. Deep furrows formed on his brow and his shoulders slumped. The old ranger began to shake.

"Yes, sir. Evan Courtenay is the cause of Ruthaer's troubles. He's become some sort of ghūl, and to make matters worse, he has a vampire in his thrall.

"Señor, we don't have much time. Sir Francis and Father Blackwood are dead. Night is coming, and that's when Evan seems strongest."

Taking a deep breath, Tallinn asked, "And Rowanoake?"

"They're after Dave, but William Howard will want to arrest me and take Aislinn's body, too."

"That complicates things," Tallinn said, standing up. After straightening his shirt, he approached the trio. "I can't protect you. Relations between the Sea Rangers and Rowanoake are strained at best. You'll have to leave before you make a bad situation worse."

"We aren't looking for sanctuary, at least not for ourselves. Only information and time. Aislinn trusted you, and I trust her judgment," Hector said. He held his breath waiting for the sea ranger's response.

"I'll help if I can, but it may not be much," Tallinn said finally. Then he turned to Teal, as if sensing her presence for the first time, and asked, "Who's this?"

"Teal, señor," Hector answered.

"Teal," Tallinn repeated as if it was some foreign word. Turning the girl around so he could touch her face, the blind man gently ran his wrinkled fingers across her brow, the bridge of her nose, cheeks, and chin. After a long moment, he frowned and said, "I know you, yet you seem different. Where is Allyrian?"

Teal replied, "I know not, good sir. I must confess, my memories are a jumble. It seems but yesterday my people defended this isle against the Dark One's hordes, yet today my home is sundered and unfamiliar. Beset with peculiar dreams, I slept and awoke as you find me now."

Tallinn mulled over her words and said, "Strange magicks are at work on you. Even though I'm blind, I can see you are not Garret's daughter."

"It was lucky for us, too," Hector said. "She knew a secret way to the island top. It allowed us to slip past William and his sailors."

Tallinn gave Teal another searching look before turning back to Hummingbird. "What happened to the elf-child? She's alive, and yet not."

Dave's jaw muscles tensed. Sensing his friend's struggle, Hector stepped closer to the ranger and said, "The bug-thing nearly killed her. We patched her up as best we could, but..."

Laying a hand on the bounty hunter's shoulder, Tallinn said, "She won't live much longer if she doesn't get care."

"I know," Hector said. "Is there anything you can do?"

"I'm sorry. What ails her is beyond my abilities," Tallinn said.

Hector turned to Dave and said, "Take Teal and let me know when William's men head this way." With a curt nod, the archer grabbed Teal by the elbow and led her outside.

When they were gone, Hector said, "Señor, the three of us are going after Evan Courtenay. Come Hell or high water, we intend to stop him and the vampire in his thrall. What we need is a starting point to ferret him out. You told us Brother Powell and the other monks did some digging on these islands. Do you know where?"

"Mostly here, around the house, but Hank saw them north of here a few times, from the top of the lighthouse. He said they were on the biggest island, in the middle of that watery maze. It has a lake on top. I still don't know how they climbed up there."

"Gracias, señor. If we're lucky, Teal can find us a path." The bounty hunter fought the urge to stare at the two elven women but found his eyes returning to them. "Tallinn, I know you said you can't offer Dave and me sanctuary, but we need you to take care of Hummingbird and Aislinn while we go after Evan Courtenay. If we don't make it back..."

Tallinn ran his hand through his sparse hair and replied, "I would still need to hide them. Sir William and his men will search the entire island looking for you, and I can't stop them."

"Damn Dave and his plan!" Hector said, slamming his fist on the bedroom door frame.

"Your past has caught up to you."

Hector gave the ranger a puzzled look, uncertain what he meant.

"Ruthaer's not a bustling seaport, but I still get news of goings-on up and down the coast. You and your team may have saved a councilman's son, but you embarrassed several other councilmen in Rowanoake, including Sir William's father."

"That was an accident," Hector protested. "We didn't know the pirate treasure belonged to Councilman Howard's grandfather." A faint smile touched Hector's lips as he remembered the look on old man Howard's face when he found out his ancestors really were pirates. Of course, that's when everything turned sour for Damage, Inc.

"Be that as it may, when you add in the Espian riots Rowanoake claims you started, the prison-break, and a girl on dragon-back sinking ships in the city's harbor, it's no wonder you've a price on your heads. The ruling elite of Rowanoake will never forgive what you did. I don't think they'll ever stop hunting you."

Palms pressed to his temples, Hector stared up at the ceiling. "I get tired of running, señor. Dave and I both do."

Tallinn's grip on Hector's arm was like iron. "Then go home. Find a woman and raise fat kids."

"We can never go home," Hector whispered. Even saying the word shook the bounty hunter.

"Why not?"

Hector looked down at Hummingbird and Aislinn, resting on the bed — one near death and the other... For the first time, it started to sink in. Hector slammed his fists against the wall. When he spoke, all the sorrow in his soul escaped through his voice. "Dave and I lost our homes years ago, but we... *I* felt like we finally had a new one. We created our own familia. Now it's gone."

Pulling away from Tallinn, Hector walked to the window overlooking the forest. He drew in a deep breath of salty air. "Tallinn, I'm afraid I'm turning into Dave. Everything I had, all I ever wanted, has been taken away, and all I have left inside is venganza."

The old man pondered Hector's candid words. He remembered the little girl Aislinn had once been, her constant, irresistible attraction to trouble, and thought, perhaps, he understood a little bit about her friends. Making up his mind about the bounty hunter, the ranger said, "The wind speaks of something terrible coming this way, and it has all the animals afraid. Some say it's a dragon and the Dark One himself has sent it to finish you."

At first, Hector didn't react, and Tallinn had doubts if the bounty hunter had even heard his words. Then Hector turned away from the window. The light from outside rendered him in silhouette, but Tallinn didn't need to see. He could hear the subtle trace of hope in the other's voice when Hector said, "It's Brand."

"Aislinn's dragon? How can you be sure?"

"It's not the Dark One," Hector stated. "It's Brand, and he's coming for Aislinn. The best thing we can do is stay out of his way and hand her to him when he gets here. He could take Hummingbird to Ozera as well. If anyone can save her and bring Aislinn back to us, its Phaedrus and his clerics."

Tallinn scratched his chin and said, "If you're certain, I'll talk to Hank and Tasunke. Maybe we can meet the dragon midways."

As if he had heard his name, Hank burst through the door and said, "Sir William is on his way up the stairs. What do we do?"

Hector and Hank ran out of the keeper's house carrying the girls. At the foot of the steps, the young ranger passed Hummingbird to Dave, then raced back inside and up the lighthouse stairs. With a pack slung over his shoulder, Tallinn exited at last, and Hector, Teal, and Dave followed him toward Tasunke.

"We have to get out of here," Dave said. The bounty hunter laid Aislinn face-down across Tasunke's shoulders, took the rope from Teal, and cut a short piece off the end. He bound Aislinn's hands and feet together under the horse's belly, just behind the forelegs.

Tallinn held Tasunke's head in both hands and whispered in the horse's ear. They seemed to be having some sort of debate. When Tallinn finished, Tasunke eyed the ranger and gave him a blatant look that said, "You're crazy!"

Belying his age, the ranger leapt on the horse's back. Dave lifted Hummingbird into Tallinn's arms. "Be careful with them, old man," he said.

"We will," Tallinn said, giving Tasunke a reassuring pat on the neck. Tasunke stomped the ground, obviously irritated he wasn't getting a say in the matter.

Everyone turned when the restless breeze delivered indistinct voices from the stairs.

Hector placed a platinum signet ring smaller than his own into Tallinn's hand. "This is Aislinn's. Brand will use it to find her, so keep it safe and be sure you give it to him." He watched the old man slip the ring over the first knuckle of his pinky and wedge it against the second knuckle. "Vaya con Dios, señor,"

"Good luck, bounty hunter," Tallinn replied. With that, the ranger pressed in with his knees and Tasunke responded with a short whinny. Keeping his wings tucked in, the horse started at a trot. Tasunke lowered his head and galloped toward the ocean, each step kicking up a spray of dirt. Just as they reached the edge, the horse spread its wings and dove off the island. A couple of heartbeats later, the winged horse soared skyward. It banked north and headed toward the mainland.

"There they are!" shouted a redshirt sailor from the top of the stairs.

All three fugitives ran. Hector didn't look back; he didn't want to know how many chased them. All he knew was they had to get away. They flew through the woods, dodging roots and branches that seemed to cling to their every move.

Behind them, the lighthouse swept a crimson beam across land and sea, signaling for help.

The sailors' shouts grew fainter as Hector, Dave, and Teal ran, but not enough to allow them to slow. Throwing all caution to the wind, they leapt across the gap between the first and second barrier islands and continued running.

A bear's roar echoed from the trees, followed by a man's scream. Dave scanned the woods behind them. "Seems like the bears liked us after all," he said.

Teal took the lead and together they crossed the second island, retracing their steps from earlier that day, pushing themselves to continue outdistancing Sir William's men. After they crossed to the third island, the sounds of pursuit faded away, and the trio stopped to catch their breath.

Overhead, the westering sun silhouetted an ash-colored eagle as it followed them. Hector's brows drew together. "There's that bird again. What do you think it's after?"

The raptor lit atop the tallest tree and stared down at them with baleful eyes.

With a deep thrum from his bow, Dave released his arrow. It shot straight and true. Before it reached its intended target, the eagle's form blurred and reappeared on another branch. The arrow flew past and disappeared. The faint clatter of it striking tree limbs reached them.

Dave had another nocked and ready.

"Don't waste your arrows," said Hector.

Reaching back into his quiver, Dave said, "I've got one I know will work."

"Let it go."

"But that could be Mi'dnirr."

Remembering how Aislinn reacted when she saw it and what she said, Hector replied, "Dave, what if it's helping us?"

"Vampires only help themselves."

"If that is Mi'dnirr, he wants Evan gone just as much as we do. You said so yourself."

"Then why doesn't he get off his ass and do something?"

"Maybe he can't. Maybe Evan's hiding somewhere Mi'dnirr can't reach him."

"That's a lot of what ifs and maybes, even for you."

"Think of it anon, for we must hurry," Teal said. "Darkness shall fall ere long and the matter of Evan will not wait."

Dave relaxed his bow, but by his expression, it was clear he questioned Hector's judgement.

Giving the eagle one last look, they raced onward. The sun's burnished face perched on the horizon when Teal finally found the stone lid over the stairs and placed her hand on it. The ancient door slid back in response to her words, and they disappeared inside.

CHAPTER 32
BRAND

August 6, 4237 K.E.

5:36pm

The rush of wind over Tasunke's wings and past Tallinn's ears deafened him. The old sea ranger's world was a fuzzy, white blur. He held Hummingbird tight against his chest, her thin body wedged between him and Aislinn's form bound over the winged horse's withers. Tallinn silently prayed to the Eternal Father he and Tasunke could keep up the pace.

On his finger, Aislinn's platinum signet ring pulsed with magic. They were drawing closer to the dragon. He squeezed Tasunke with his knees, and they altered their course to meet it.

Without warning, Tasunke's wings stiffened and he banked hard. Tallinn leaned forward as they made a wide spiral. A ball of white-hot light streaked past, and thunder boomed, making Tallinn's heart skip. Tasunke neighed and tossed his head, protesting both dragon and the danger it posed.

"I don't care if you think he's huge! We promised to bring these girls to him. Now get down there!"

The two circled through a wreath of smoke and landed. The clearing surrounding man and horse smelled of scorched earth and ash, but Tallinn heard no tell-tale crackle of fire in the trees. The entire world held its breath. The white blur of his vision turned to bronze. Tallinn slid from Tasunke's back, still holding Hummingbird.

"Brand!" the old ranger called.

Electricity fizzed and spat. The bronze shape shimmered and faded, and he heard human-sounding footsteps. The ring on his finger told him Brand was near, but his cloudy sight could not find the dragon. Suddenly afraid he'd made a mistake, that he'd misread the magic in Aislinn's ring, and this unknown person meant them harm, Tallinn lifted Hummingbird back onto Tasunke. "Protect them. Leave me, if need be," he told his steed and turned to face the newcomer, ready to fight. "Stay back," he demanded.

"Back off, old man," the stranger said in an elven accent.

Tallinn reached toward the voice, but the unknown elf evaded him. Tasunke's feathers rustled as the hippoætós spread his wings.

"Brand! Where are you?" the old man called again. Waves of sorrow struck him as raw sobbing erupted beside him. His gut tightened, and he had a hard time finding his voice. Only then did Tallinn realize Tasunke hadn't fended off the elf. Instead, he'd let the stranger draw close enough to untie the rope securing Aislinn on his back.

Tallinn gripped the elf's bare shoulder. "I told you to stay back."

"Let me be, Tallinn," the elf said as he grasped the old man's wrist and pushed his hand away. The stranger had a warrior's grip, but there was a subtle gentleness to it, as if he was trying not to hurt the lighthouse keeper.

"Who are you?" Tallinn asked.

"I'm Brand." He pulled Aislinn from Tasunke's back and knelt there with her across his lap.

"Brand... How is it you have a man's form?" Tallinn asked.

Brand gave no answer. Shuddering gasps escaped him as he wept over Aislinn's still form.

The ranger's curiosity faded, replaced by a dull, hollow ache. Steeling his voice against his own emotions, he said, "Now is not the time for grief."

"She's dead! Can't you see that?" Brand demanded.

Gripping Brand's shoulder, Tallinn crouched beside the elf and said, "Young man, stop looking at her with your eyes and look at her with your heart. There is a chance we can save her!"

Brand rose to his feet and moved away, taking Aislinn with him.

"Brand, don't give up on her."

Brand stopped and said, "Give up on her? I would have moved the ocean for her. And now she's dead. I no longer feel her inside my soul. Do you have any idea what's that's like?"

"Yeah, I know exactly what it's like to lose something that's part of you. And there's not a day that goes by that I don't wish I could have it back."

After a pause, Brand said, "Tallinn, what happened? Your message said people had disappeared from Ruthaer, and some monk thought they had been murdered. Aislinn, Hector, and Dave should have been more than a match for a situation like that, especially if the local constable worked with them."

Tallinn nodded. He stared off into the distance, fighting the voice inside him — fighting the guilt. "I wanted her to come home, not understanding what truly plagued Ruthaer. I'm so sorry."

"I wanted her to come with me to the Dragon Isles and meet my father," Brand replied. "If I'd had my way, she, Emä, and I would have been long gone before your message reached Ozera." Grief overcame Brand, and he struggled to regain his self-control. "The thought of leaving our friends, especially Hector and Dave, tore her up inside. She tried to hide it, but, deep down, I knew she didn't really want to go away.

"My oonveytik ssifruen — my growth sleep — was almost upon me. I was tired and irritable. When she said she needed to talk to Hector and Dave before she decided, I lost my temper and demanded she be ready to leave at winter solstice. We argued, and she left me in Ozera." His voice cracked, and he tried to stifle another sob.

"And now? Will you go without her?" asked Tallinn.

"I don't know," he groaned. "I've lost my guide."

Tallinn walked toward Brand. "What does your heart say?"

"It says I'm dying without Aislinn, Tallinn. She's gone forever, and I'm the one who drove her away."

"Let's give Phaedrus a chance. He and his healers are known to work miracles."

"What if they can't bring her back?"

"That's in the Eternal Father's hands, not ours, Brand, but we can help Hummingbird. She needs a healer, and I'm afraid she doesn't have much time left."

"The little bird's wings are broken," Brand murmured. "Where are Dave and Hector?"

"Hector promised Aislinn they would save Ruthaer. They're supposed to meet us in Ozera afterward."

The crackle of electricity and the scent of ozone filled the air, and the large bronze shape reappeared. A sonorous reptilian voice said, "Let's go, then. If you carry Hummingbird, I'll take Aislinn."

With a flap of his wings, Brand launched himself into the air. Tallinn climbed onto Tasunke's back and shifted

Hummingbird so she was astride in the circle of his arms. He gripped a fistful of mane and said, "Follow the dragon."

Brand and Tasunke flew into the sunset, wings beating in a desperate race to outrun Death.

CHAPTER 33
ENTER THE PRAESIDIUM

August 6, 4237 K.E.

6:43pm

Cliff walls surrounded them on all sides as the skiff glided silently in the slack waters. Following Tallinn's instructions, Teal and Hector steadily rowed toward the middle of the maze while Dave knelt at the bow.

Like the other channels, these twisted and turned upon themselves. In some places the dark stone walls were close enough on either side to touch, yet in others they drew back in rounded hollows. The shadows grew deeper, and a clammy fog began to rise off the water. There were neither fish nor birds in these channels, yet Hector felt the prickling sensation of someone watching.

Teal said, "All these were once antre and halls. As a youth, I would oft ride Tarnillis and race mine brother to see who couldst reach the ocean first."

"You mentioned Tarnillis earlier. Who was she?" Hector asked.

"The dragon with whom I shared an oath bond," Teal replied. "I know not what became of her."

"What about your brother?"

Teal dipped her oar into the water. Tendrils of fog swirled about it like the tentacles of an octopus. "I slew the traitor ere I died."

Dave and Hector stared at the tall girl for a moment. Hector opened his mouth but closed it again without speaking. Dave shrugged and turned away.

"There 'tis." Teal pointed to a sheer cliff-face rising from a dense fog bank.

"That's not creepy at all," Dave muttered.

Keeping the skiff within an oar's length, Teal had them paddle around an island larger and taller than the others. Hector suddenly felt they were in a moat surrounding a castle's keep. Time and again, he scanned the island's upper reaches, searching for a defender on the walls, expecting to be challenged with each passing minute.

The hull of the skiff bumped up against a submerged rock, and Teal called for a halt. Using the end of her oar, she scraped away some of the slime. Even in the dim light, its smooth surface looked more like the eroded tip of something carved rather than a natural formation.

"What used to be here?" Hector asked, noting how the channel had opened up like a vast chamber.

Working the skiff around the rock, Teal said, "This was where dragons and Xemmassians did speak their oaths to one another, where unions were formed, and bond-mates presented themselves to the Praesidium."

Dave hung over the side, helping Teal steer past the formation. Hector dipped his oar into the water and struck something solid — a landing of some sort. Teal jumped out and waded to the cliff-face in water up to her waist. In the growing darkness, it took her several minutes of searching to find the placard marking the entrance, and several more to clear away centuries of salt rime and corrosion with her dagger. Placing her palm on it, she said, "Apertus amici pacem."

Rolling fog cascaded out as the stone door ground open. Teal guided the skiff inside the flooded cavern and closed the door.

Hector took out his bone light. The beam struck the wall and refracted in a plethora of sparkling colors. Crystals seemed to grow from every surface, like the inside of a colossal geode. The chamber was enormous and had enough space to fill it with all the people and animals of Ruthaer and have room to spare.

"Holy shit," Dave swore. "We could buy half the continent with all these gems."

Still guiding the skiff, Teal followed a submerged ledge around the cavern. Hector panned his light around. At first, his mind couldn't grasp what he saw resting on ledges and protruding from the water. It looked like stacks of bleached wood. Most pieces were long, but some were short, some curved and others not.

Then it struck him. They were petrified dragon bones.

A pair of boulder-like skulls blocked Teal's path. Like a statue, she remained frozen in place, staring at the ancient bones. Her lips compressed into a thin line. One minute passed, then two. Finally, she reached out and laid a trembling hand on one of the skulls. "The Praesidium fell," she murmured. A shiver passed over her, and she stepped around the skulls.

Hector shined his light and followed a series of steps out of the water. From the upper landing, a broken skull leered back at them. Beyond it were brittle pieces of more skeletons. However, these were humanoid, albeit larger and more impressive than the average human. Their skeletal hands clutched oversized, verdigris crusted swords.

Hand over hand, Dave lowered the anchor and caught one of its flukes on a crusted-over ribcage. After giving it a tug, he walked the boat, checking hatches and lashing down the oars. Last, he gathered his remaining arrows into one quiver at his hip. With longbow in hand, he jumped onto the ledge and joined Hector and Teal.

ᘒᘓ

7:19pm

Teal remained at the foot of the stairs. Ahead of him, the remains of his people littered the steps. The hunter's meager light did not penetrate more than a few feet into the darkness overhead, leaving further horrors hidden from the flight-master's now-human sight. His mind raced as he recalled his final of battle. Their enemies vastly outnumbered the Praesidium's defenders. Had they lost everything to the Dark One's followers that day?

A sense of desperation pounded in his veins, a driving need to find some clue as to the fate of his people. Teal took the steps in bounding leaps, skipping treads in his haste. He bolted down a stone corridor, with the hurried footsteps of the hunter and the archer echoing in his wake.

Weird, dry fog swirled around their feet, clutching their legs with icy fingers as if to hinder their progress. Hector's light swung into each side passage, but Teal ignored them. Avoiding the ever-growing number of dusty skeletons in the hall, he moved with a definite purpose.

Teal raced up another set of spiral stairs, followed a short hallway, and entered a long, vaulted chamber. Their features and detailing chipped away by crude hands, alternating caryatid and telamon pillars along either wall guarded alcoves lined with dust-filled shelves. Only the sporadic glint from flecks of gilt hinted at the artistry lost.

Thick fog clung to the chamber, and Teal waved his arms to clear it as he worked his way around piles of broken bones to the opposite end. There, a wall of blackened stone marred by deep grooves and gouges barred his path.

"What's behind it?" Hector asked.

Instead of answering, Teal placed his palm in a small hollow and said in a shaky voice, "Apertus amici pacem."

The wall split in the middle, and two, thick stone doors grated open toward them. Cold fog spilled out, and with it came the musty scent of dry bones.

CRSO

7:35pm

With his scimitar held tight, Hector followed Teal into a broad, octagonal room. The fog thinned in patches, revealing three other doors that led out of the room, each facing one of the cardinal directions. More fog receded, exposing piles of skeletons lying at the base of the walls. Smaller in stature than the ones in the corridors and vaulted chamber, they wore the remnants of moldy clothing and huddled together in small clusters.

As they moved inside, ghostly hands reached out for them. Dave swatted at them with his longbow, but the hands turned to fog and flowed around the yew.

With a gasp, Teal fell to her knees beside a pile of bones. The skeletons were all jumbled together, and it was impossible to tell how many there were. "Every man, woman, and child," Teal whispered. Grief twisted her features and burst from her body in an echoing roar. "Xardus, why?"

Hector asked, "What is this place?"

Tears streaming down her face, Teal said, "They did take refuge here during the battle."

Hector's brow furrowed and he turned in a slow circle, trying to understand what he was seeing.

Teal clenched her fists and said, "Dost thou not understand? The Dark One's minions could not breach the doors! These were the last of mine people, and they were trapt here, forced to choose betwixt starvation and self-murder."

Hector made himself look at the different skeletons. On Teal's other side, Dave did the same. Even with the toll of time, held hands and the remnants of infants in their mothers' arms grew clear. The horror of it seeped into the bounty hunter's marrow.

A faint laugh mocked them.

Hector and Dave stood back to back with blades drawn. Teal looked up and asked, "What was that?"

"Evan," the men replied in unison.

Teal wiped her eyes and climbed to her feet. Her eyes lit on a vacant wall niche. Frowning, she searched through the fog, moving it to and fro with a wave of her arm, revealing more empty slots and hollows. "They're missing," she said. In front of her were a series of recesses in the wall of varying sizes. Most were empty but some held the remains of hardened leather scroll cases.

"What's missing?" Hector asked.

"Someone hath taken the treasures of the Praesidium," she said, moving down the wall.

Hector and Dave hurried to keep up. The fog grew thicker the farther they went, masking the shapes of ghostly humanoids and other *things*.

"Teal, slow down," Hector cautioned.

"'Tis all gone, all of 't. The history of our people, our culture, 'tis all gone," the tall girl said. Driven by despair, Teal moved deeper into the fog, repeating, "'Tis all gone." The indistinct image of a tall, broad-shouldered warrior shimmered around the girl's statuesque form.

Taking a deep breath, Hector caught up to Teal and slammed her against the wall. The ghost-possessed girl spun toward her attacker, ready to fight. Quick as lightning, Hector caught her by the throat with his forearm and pinned her in place. Fierce, tear-stained amethyst eyes met Hector's steady gaze. From the corner of his eye, Hector caught sight of Dave, longbow in one hand and his sabre in the other; his normally tanned face was white as a sheet.

Teal blinked and then relaxed. "I offer my most humble apology. 'Tis much to take in."

Hector didn't let up. Instead, he added a little more pressure and hissed, "Look around you."

Teal looked past Dave and Hector, and her eyes went wide. Somehow, they had moved beyond the walls of the octagonal room and into a hallway. Her pulse skittered and beat against Hector's arm. The room they had just exited disappeared, replaced by swirling fog.

"What's going on, Teal?" Hector asked. "The walls are fading away."

"I know not," Teal answered.

"Was there anything in that room that could have caused this?"

"I did know some of the treasures kept there, but naught of any power. We mostly did use that room to house our ancient histories."

"Think," Hector said, his eyes boring into hers. "What could have been in there? What could Evan Courtenay use to breach the barrier between our world and the Luminiferous Aether?"

Teal gave Hector a blank stare and replied, "I confess I know not this aether of which you speak."

Releasing Teal, the bounty hunter swore in Espian. He gesticulated with one hand and muttered, "This *detestable* fog."

Faces leered at them through the swirling clouds and the temperature in the hallway seemed to drop twenty degrees.

"It's not fog; it's the gates of hell," Dave muttered.

Rubbing her throat, Teal said, "Auguratus, a soothsayer, did use an artifact called the Orbuculum. He died before the Great War."

"What did it look like?" Hector asked.

"'Twas a sphere of green crystal about so big," Teal said forming a circle with her hands. "'Tis the only thing I can think of, but 'twas inurn'd with him."

"A crystal ball?" Dave scoffed. "*Really?*"

Hector waved Dave back and said, "How did it work?"

"There were a few amongst us born with the sight, and Auguratus was one of the most powerful," Teal explained. "He would peer into the center of the Orbuculum and go into a trancelike state. A scribe did record all he said or did. 'Twas gibberish more oft' than not, yet some few of his prophecies did come to pass. 'Twas his bodement that foretold the fall of our race."

"Did this soothsayer talk with the dead?" Hector asked.

"I ne'er took part in the ceremonies, but 'twas common to meet with Auguratus should someone recently dead leave something unresolved."

Dave edged closer and said, "We need to get moving. Evan's here, somewhere."

All around them, the uncanny mists swirled and the shapes inside became more solid — more lifelike. Hector swore he could hear the creak of leather on leather when something walked past him.

"Which way do you want to go?" Dave asked.

Hector looked back the way they came and then up the hallway where the fog grew thicker. "That way," he said, pointing toward the wall of fog.

As the three walked down the hallway, the sound of fighting drifted toward them. Several translucent humanoid shapes rushed by. One brushed against Hector's arm, and his hair stood on end; another ghost shouted, "The gules have broken through the mure. Protect the Sanctuary at all cost." Teal had spoken the same language when he first captured her.

Hector, Dave, and Teal entered the fog bank. Another group of humanoids charged past, their forms seeming solid. They stood just over seven feet tall with muscular bodies that gave off a bronze sheen. The last thing Hector saw before they disappeared was the massive two-handed swords strapped to their backs.

CHAPTER 34
THE MISTY ROAD

August 6, 4237 K.E.

7:48pm

Hector rushed through the wall of fog after the retreating figures. When he emerged from the other side, he stopped cold. Mangled bodies — draconic humanoids covered with bronze scales — littered the floor. Rivulets of dark, red blood ran out from under them and pooled on the stone. Farther down the hall, the clangor of metal striking metal echoed loudly.

Armed with only a dagger, Teal made to run ahead, but Dave caught her by the arm. "Think about it," he growled.

"Those are my people," Teal said.

"This battle already happened," Dave said, "and you lost."

Teal opened her mouth to speak but Hector beat her to it. "Dave's right. The only ones out there we need to worry about right now are Evan and Lady D."

Dave pushed one of the bodies with his boot. "You may want to rethink that. This corpse seems real enough to me."

Teal grasped the hilt of a massive broadsword, thought better of it, and took an oversized dagger from a fallen Xemmassian instead. She added its sheath to her borrowed belt, opposite the blade Hector gave her that morning.

Hector picked his way through the dead, careful to not slip in the blood. Teal and Dave followed in his footsteps. Steadily moving toward the sounds of fighting, they went up a flight of stairs and down another corridor. The fog ebbed and flowed, giving the halls a surreal quality.

"Now I understand why Jasper called this the Misty Road," the hunter muttered as he swatted at an incorporeal hand reaching toward his throat.

Sconces of glass lit their way, as if they had travelled back in time. However, the light only revealed more horrors of battle. When they came to an intersection, Hector signaled a halt. "Teal, do you recognize any of this?"

"Aye. Though I know not how, we are a level above the Sanctuary. The entrance to the basilica lies yonder," Teal said and pointed to the right.

The hollow echo of booted feet answered Teal's words. Dark grey fog swirled, and a cluster of orcnéas charged toward them.   The humanoids ran hunched over, making them more apelike than human. Heavily muscled, they wore blood-spattered chainmail shirts and carried curved falchions, along with small, wooden shields.

"Stay behind me," Dave said, sweeping up his bow. His sabre was back in its sheath.

Long hair trailing behind her, Teal dodged past the archer and raced up the wall two steps before bounding off toward the opposite side. Three impossible seeming steps along the wall and she was past Hector, gaining speed. With the momentum of a hurtling comet, she plowed into the lead orc, planting her foot into its solar plexus. The orc's arms flailed as he toppled backward, striking the two orcs directly behind him and causing them to stumble.

Not stopping, Teal slit the first orc's throat with her dagger and struck another across the eyes. She kicked off the wall with one foot and leapt over the outstretched blade of the next orc.

To Dave, it seemed as if the orcs moved in slow motion around the girl. She bounced off one and then the other, stabbing one in an exposed armpit, slicing another across its groin. With bellows of rage and pain following in her wake, she didn't stop until all five lay writhing or dead. She turned back then, a fierce grin on her freckled face.

A sixth orc materialized behind Teal, his falchion reared back.

Dave drew and fired the arrow he'd been holding. He had the satisfaction of seeing Teal's eyes widen in shock as the arrow streaked past her face. Black fletching sprouted from the orc's forehead, and the hawk's head arrow exploded out the back of its skull. The orc fell and its head smacked the floor with a loud, wet crunch.

"Está muy asqueroso," Hector said, as he stuck his scimitar into the heart of one of the wounded orcs.

Dave lowered his longbow. "Not bad for a ghost," he said while retrieving his gore-smeared arrow.

Shouts at the far end of the hall preceded the pounding of iron-shod footsteps coming toward them.

"This way," Hector said. He ran the opposite direction from which the orcs came, directly into a growing patch of roiling fog. The air grew colder the farther they went.

Another step and the walls seemed to fall away. It felt like they had left the Praesidium.

Dave recalled their fight outside the shrievalty, and he knew: they had entered purgatory.

Hector's light only illuminated a few feet ahead. Faces in the aether reappeared: grey men who hungered for their flesh.

"You sure you want to go this way?" Dave asked, his breath coming out in clouds.

"No," Hector replied, "but it's the only way that makes sense. The other way took us back to the battle at the Praesidium, and we already know how that went. Teal, you still with us?"

"Aye," she replied.

"Stay close. I don't want to lose anyone in the aether," Hector said.

The landscape shimmered and shifted as they walked. A touch of warm air slid over Dave's skin, bringing with it the salty tang of the ocean. Tall spiral fluted columns materialized out of the darkness on either side, forming an open hall. Above, a stormy grey sky appeared through gaps in a cracked and broken ceiling. Left to the ravages of time, the vast, two-story building seemed more like a crumbling mausoleum than a place where people had once gathered.

"The basilica, I presume," Hector said. He played his light over the remaining stone and woodwork and gave a low whistle. "¡Caramba! Monarchs would bankrupt their kingdoms trying to recreate something this fine."

More than fifty feet high, the basilica's roof sailed up in the air atop two long rows of stacked columns which flanked the center aisle like an honor guard. A tile mosaic, once rich with tones of dark and light brown, covered the floor. Under a dome at the end, a semi-circular dais bore the marble feet of a half-dragon statue shorn off just above the ankles. The rest of it lay broken in chunks.

Teal knelt beside a section of pitted and chipped marble where the statue's head should have been. Countless foul symbols scored its surface, rendering it unrecognizable. Teal laid her hand upon it, murmuring to herself in draconic. For a moment, it was not the tawny-haired girl Dave saw, but Aislinn kneeling in prayer.

Again, a faint laugh mocked them.

"Fuck this shit," Dave said turning in a circle. "Evan's playing with us." His eyes came to rest on Hector, who was scratching his chin and staring at the archer with a calculating look.

"What?" Dave demanded.

"I need you to concentrate."

"Bloody hell. No! I am not doing that!"

"It's the only way," Hector said. "Otherwise, we'll walk the Misty Road until we starve, then our ghosts will keep walking, from one end of purgatory to the other."

"Hector, I'm not doing it. I'd rather die here than be Lady D's slave," Dave said.

"I'll be right here with you. Look, I'll take the ruby off you, count to ten, and put it back. It's that simple."

"The last time she got in my head, you almost died. A lot can happen in ten seconds."

Hector shook his head. "Not this time. I promise."

Dave contemplated the shapes drifting in the fog. Rubbing his thumb up and down the ruby's facets, he closed his eyes and said, "Okay. But count to five and do it fast."

"Teal, hold his left arm so he doesn't smack me with his bow," Hector directed. The bounty hunter clamped one hand around the wrist of Dave's sword arm and pinched the silver brooch with the thumb and forefinger of the other. He locked eyes with Dave and asked, "Are you ready, amigo?"

"Shtupping bastard," Dave said.

"Uno..."

In a flash, Dave saw Lady D. She reclined naked on a chaise-lounge drinking from a bejeweled cup. Sitting up, she beckoned to him with a pale hand bearing a ring connected to a heavy wrist cuff by a steel chain. Warmth spread from his gut and he felt his knees go weak. Part of him wanted to give in, to let her feed on his blood.

"I'm going to kill you," Dave growled.

Ymara crooked her finger at him, and he walked toward her like a boat pulled to the dock. Dave bent down and felt her lips touch his ear.

"Set me free," she whispered.

Dave jerked back, falling on his butt. He reached to his neck and let out a sigh when he felt the brooch once again.

"Well?" Hector asked, standing over him with a concerned look on his face.

"She's this way," Dave said and led them through another swirl of mist. Behind them, the basilica melted back into the aether.

An arrow shot from his own bow, Dave aimed straight for a crumbling, three-foot high wall surrounded by gnarled trees, twisted with the agony of age. It guarded the top of a narrow stairwell, similar to the one Teal used earlier to reach the island tops. Beside it, the stone lid lay smashed to pieces.

"I do not know this place," Teal said.

Hector turned in a slow circle, playing his light across the uneven ground. In the distance, frog eyes glimmered in a stagnant lake. "This must be where Brother Powell and the other monks entombed Evan Courtenay."

Dave stepped over the wall and looked down into the shaft. Suddenly, the steps disappeared and there was no bottom, only a deep, dark chasm exuding the charnel scent of death. "Son of a Bitch! Where did the stairs go?"

"I bet they're still there," Hector mused. "Evan's using the aether to hide them."

"You sure?"

"Consider it a leap of faith," Hector said.

"Yeah, right. We should have brought the rope."

"If it be true Evan doth not wish to be found, wherefore did he not conceal the way complete?" Teal asked.

"It's a trap," Dave answered.

"He's not really trying to stop us," Hector replied. "He's testing our resolve."

"Still a trap," Dave muttered.

"Of course it's a trap, cabrón."

"Did you just call me a goat?"

"Something like that."

Dave looked over the edge again and said to Hector, "You go first."

"Fat chance," Hector replied, joining him. "Together?"

"This is going to suck," Dave said, securing his gear. He tossed a silver coin to Teal, who deftly plucked it from the air. "For the Ferryman."

Before Teal could respond, the two jumped.

With his heart in his throat, Dave fell hard and fast. Not able to see, he tried to count aloud, but the rushing wind swept away his words. The darkness weighed down on him, and Dave had trouble focusing. All he could see in his mind was the ground rushing up to meet them, and their crushed bodies.

They fell farther down the shaft and the aether slowly thickened about them. It wrapped them in its cold, clammy embrace, giving Dave the impression they had fallen into the moist nose of a dog. The fog tightened its grip, slowing their descent. On the count of five hundred, Dave landed on his feet with Hector beside him.

After catching his breath, the bounty hunter took out his bone tube and lit the small antechamber. In front of them, the carved wall resembled the entrance to a temple. Half-columns protruded on either side of two imposing stone doors, their bronze handles bound together with an intricate knot. Knuckles of brown clay inscribed with strange sigils rested over each of the handles.

A few seconds later, Teal appeared beside them, her face flushed with excitement. "Thou art both mad as Martius hares. I did think we would perish," she said, her hands on her knees.

"Still might," Dave replied. "The night ain't over yet."

Panning his light around, Hector aimed it overhead. There was no chasm above them, no tunnel or stair, only smooth, dark grey stone. Opposite the sealed doorway, his light revealed a single step half-buried in the roughened wall. It seemed the monks had shaped the rock around it to close off the exit. They were sealed inside a granite tomb.

Wiping the cold sweat from his forehead with the back of his hand, Hector approached the knotted handles. "Teal, do you recognize this place or these symbols?"

"The portal to yon tomb, aye, but not the binding 'pon the door, nor the symbols carved therein."

What at first glance appeared to be twine, turned out to be braided gut and sinew, bound together in an inseparable mass by the drying process. Shining his light on the rope, Hector followed it back and forth, as it intertwined around the handles several times before the ends finally came together in a blood knot. He frowned and shined his light on the crack between the doors. Shut tight, they revealed nothing of what lay beyond.

With a dissatisfied grunt, the bounty hunter took a few steps back to study the doorway again. On the architrave above the door, some ancient hand carved an inscription in strange symbols composed of thorns, blades, and geometric shapes.

"Auguratus — etiam ultra mortem futura prospicit," Teal translated. "Yea unto death doth he foresee the future."

"What the hell does that mean?" Dave asked.

"I think it means he saw us coming," Hector replied.

Dave gave him a narrow-eyed scowl, uncertain if Hector was joking or being sincere.

"Hold the light," Hector said to Teal.

Taking his knife from his belt, Hector placed the tip near the end of the blood knot. Closing one eye and holding his head back, he touched the blade to the rope. With a loud *Pop!* the knife blade sparked blue fire and an arc of electricity shot up his arm. Hector jerked back his hand but then, gritting his teeth, he reached forward with his knife. A thick haze of ozone surrounded him as he carefully sliced through the gut. When done, he let out the breath he had been holding. He unthreaded the loose ends and let them dangle from each handle while keeping the clay seals intact.

"By Xardus, how is that possible?" Teal asked, her mouth hanging open.

"Troll blood," Dave answered.

"Foresooth? His countenance doth not tell it."

"Dave!" Hector reprimanded. "That's enough. Both of you, get ready."

Weapons out, Dave and Teal prepared themselves for what might wait beyond the doors, then gave the bounty hunter a curt nod. Hector grabbed the bronze handle with both hands and pulled. It opened without a sound, as if someone had maintained the hinges through the long years. A cloud of dust plumed up with the sudden shifting of air.

Hector motioned for Teal to shine the light into the room. Rotten furniture and other sundry items filled it wall to wall like some long-forgotten apartment. His nose twitching, Hector unsheathed his scimitar and picked his way across the musty room. At its center, shattered lengths of iron chain lay amid the busted remains of a coffin. Hector bent down and picked up one of the planks that had served as the lid. He blew off the dust, revealing a portion of the Order of the Golden Stag's crest.

Dropping the piece of wood, Hector moved to the stone door at the other end of the room. Once there, he held up his finger for the others to stay quiet as he leaned in close. After several long minutes, he straightened and placed his free hand around the bronze handle. Again, he waited for Dave and Teal to be ready and then yanked open the door.

A miasma of rot and corruption rolled across the threesome, turning their stomachs. Hector grimaced and released the handle to back away before he noticed the seven-and-a-half-foot tall monstrosity at the threshold. Bits of flesh clung to its bones, giving it a humanoid shape, but it was impossible to tell what it had been before death. An unholy light lit its dark sockets and oily ichor issued from its open maw as it raised its skeletal arms to attack. Behind it, more zombie-like creatures shambled forward.

"¡Madre de Dios!" Hector exclaimed, trying to slam the door. The creatures pushed back.

Drawing an orange fletched arrow, Dave charged the opening and jammed the ruby arrowhead into a glowing eye socket. With a quick spin, he put his back to the door and began to count.

"Dave!" Hector said through gritted teeth. "What did...?"
Whumph!

The door exploded off its hinges, throwing the two across the room in a shower of broken stone. They cut a swath of destruction through the moldy furniture and landed amongst charred bits of bone and wood. Small clumps of red and yellow flames licked hungrily at the walls and ceiling, adding burnt flesh and singed hair to the already fetid air.

Curls of steam still rising from his hair, Dave sat up and gave Hector one of his crooked grins. The bounty hunter punched him in the arm and said, "¡Estúpido! ¿Qué diablos estabas pensando!"

"You know you're speaking Espian," Dave commented, still smiling.

"¡No puedo creer que me hayas prendido fuego!" Hector yelled, slapping at the small fires on his shirt and pants.

"Teal," Dave said, ignoring Hector's rant, "you alright?"

"Aye, but let us not do that again," Teal said. Soot covering her face, she ran from fire to fire, putting them out.

After making a final sweep, Hector retrieved his light from Teal and knelt beside the doorway before flashing the pale beam inside. Black smoke hugged the scorched ceiling above piles of charred, smoldering bones. At the bottom of the left-hand wall, jagged stone chunks marked the edges of a hole large enough for a person to crawl through.

"Teal, do you recognize any of this?" Hector asked.

"Nay, 'tis as unfamiliar as yon chamber behind us. But if this be the resting place of Auguratus, no one has been here for many a year, even in my time."

"This place just doesn't feel like a tomb," Hector said.

Dave squinted at his companion and leaned away from him. "You been hanging around in tombs?"

"*No.* Don't be ridiculous."

Dave shrugged. "How else would you know what a tomb is supposed to feel like? Besides, what about this stuff?" he said, gesturing to the bones and old furniture.

"Maybe it all belonged to this Auguratus, but it seems odd for him to be buried with junk." Hector frowned as he continued, "Or to have a room guarded by undead monsters."

"Who I blew up," replied Dave. "Besides, it probably wasn't junk when they buried him. He was ready for the afterlife, like a pharaoh, or a Viking jarl."

The bounty hunter looked askance at Dave but didn't say anything. Instead, he covered his mouth with his hand and crouched-walked into the room. Not waiting for Dave and Teal to catch up, he laid flat and shined his light into the small hole, revealing a dark corridor beyond.

"Where do you think it goes?" Dave asked, sabre in hand.

"No idea."

After scrambling through, they followed the corridor until it turned right. Waving them back, Hector poked his head around the corner. Thirty feet farther along, a ten-foot high by four-foot wide bronze door etched with the same type of symbols they saw over the tomb's entrance blocked the passage. Affixed at the eye level of a half-dragon was a round glass porthole. Below, a verdigris-covered fist projected from the door, holding a thick, vertical rod. Equally spaced on all four sides of the door, bronze bars sank deep into the stone.

Hector handed his light to Dave and said, "You're tall."

"I hate doors," Dave growled. Holding the light above his head against the dusty glass, he gripped the edge of the porthole, stretched onto his tiptoes, and peeped over the lower rim. "It continues on the other side, but it slopes down."

"How far down?" asked Hector, wishing he were taller.

"Can't tell. It goes beyond the light. Seems to curve as it goes."

The two backed away from the door. Hector studied the runes and asked, "Teal, what does this one say?"

"Auguratus did commission the building of the sardāba beyond in the Korellan year 1125," Teal read. "'Twas once a utility entrance to one of our cisterns." She brushed past the men, wrapped her slim hands around the rod, and tried to turn it sunwise. Nothing happened. Closing her eyes, Teal strained harder. Dave joined her, and something inside the door gave with a loud metal-on-metal screech. The verdigris fist at the handle's midpoint rotated, and the bronze bars slid back with a clank.

With a loud hiss of stale air, the door opened, and dust blew from the seams. Hector snatched his light from Dave and shined it ahead, but nothing came rushing at them. Everything remained as quiet as a tomb should be.

"I'm sure that woke the dead," Dave quipped. Hector and Teal glared at him with narrowed eyes; clearly, his joke was not funny.

They had only gone a few steps down the ramp when the door slammed shut and the matching fist-clenched rod on their side snapped back to its original position.

Dave made a sign against evil.

Hector led the way, hugging the inside face of the curved passage and keeping his light pointed at their feet. Despite his efforts, Dave knew it was a beacon in the stygian darkness.

"Set me free."

Dave looked around, but Teal and Hector made no signs they had heard anything. He gripped the brooch around his neck. "Work, dammit."

"What was that?" Hector asked.

"Nothing," Dave said. Even to his own ears, his voice sounded strained.

"Dave?" Hector asked.

"She's here."

"Who?" Teal asked.

"Ymara... Lady D... she's close."

"How do you know?" Hector asked.

Dave pointed to his head. "I can hear her."

"How much farther?"

Dave squeezed his eyes shut and gritted his teeth. "Can't talk. She's trying to fuck with my head."

"Entendido, mi amigo. Let's go kill this puta again."

CHAPTER 35
SHATTERED WINDOWS

August 6, 4237 K.E.

11:00pm

Weapons out, the three burst through the arched opening at the end of the sloped hallway into an immense cylindrical space decorated with more strange runes. Hector shined his light up in search of the ceiling, but the chamber stretched beyond its piercing glow. On the opposite side, stacked stone steps accessed an observation balcony. A thin layer of wispy fog covered the tiled floor.

Hector took a step toward the center and involuntarily gasped as waves of bitter-cold air seeped up from below. His breath clouded with each exhalation, and hoarfrost danced along the edge of his scimitar like spidery veins.

"Welcome to my home." Evan's voice echoed from the shadows. "It was used as a cistern at one time, but someone was kind enough to plug up all the inlets." The undead knight appeared on the balcony. He wore ceremonial plate armor with a high gorget. Tucked in the crook of his arm was a crested, closed face helm. Over his armor, his blue and white surcoat — though ragged and ripped — still bespoke his military rank. At his belt, he wore a hand-and-a-half longsword with a blackened stag's head on its pommel.

Scars disfigured Evan's once handsome face. Unlike his ghost form outside the churchyard, his decaying body bore little resemblance to his father. Most of the scars were old, but a few seemed fresh. Like those of his revenants, his eyes were solid white, and they glared at the pale light emanating from the bone tube in Hector's hand.

With one smooth motion, Dave unslung his bow and nocked his last ruby-tipped arrow.

Ymara's voice slithered into his mind. *"Free me, my archer."*

Dave searched the balcony. She stood concealed in the shadows, but it didn't matter; he knew where she was. He saw her in his mind and wrestled with the involuntary desire building inside him. His arrow shifted from Evan to Ymara, then back to Evan.

Ymara stepped up behind him, sliding her hands over his hips and around his waist. She worked her lips along the base of his neck, while her fingers teased the inside of his waistband.

"Stay with me tonight."

"No! This isn't real."

Her nails traced fire up either side of his spine to his shoulders. She nipped his ear lobe, sending pain and lust through his body. "Are you certain?"

"Get the hell away from me, monster," Dave said, trying to push her from his mind. He gripped the brooch in the hollow of his throat, and glimpses of the cistern broke through the spell.

Evan clenched his gauntleted fist and then flung his arm forward, fingers splayed, as if casting sand at the interlopers in his demesne.

Mist cascaded down the wall. Out of it sprang a dozen undead sailors, wielding long knives, belaying pins, and cutlasses. Hector and Teal whipped around with scimitar and dagger, striking and thrusting to keep the revenants at bay.

Dave remained frozen in place by his internal struggle; his bow aimed toward the balcony.

Hector and Teal moved in a slow orbit around him. Revenant sailors circled like sharks, feinting and attacking from opposite sides, growing ever closer.

The archer focused on Ymara standing on the balcony, somehow seeing her pale skin and ruby lips with greater clarity. Behind her, he spotted a discolored patch of mortar on the wall. A thin rivulet of water trickled from it.

The ruby-tipped arrow streaked toward the balcony. With inhuman speed, the vampire shifted back and to the right, letting the arrow fly past. But it wasn't aimed at her. The arrowhead hit the discolored plug and exploded in a ball of fiery fury.

Shrouded in smoke and flames, Lady D hurtled off the balcony. Chunks of mortar chased her through the air and rained onto revenants and humans alike. At the explosion's center, water sprayed from a crater in the newly exposed stonework.

Crack! The entire cistern shook, knocking Hector, Dave, and Teal off their feet. Water geysered into the shaft. The pressurized spray ate at the rock around the mouth of the inlet, opening the hole wider.

As water rained down, the curtain of grey mist parted, then evaporated. Warm water swirled about the legs of undead sailors, who shrieked and writhed as they dissolved. Some fell over to disappear completely while others remained upright, striking at the dark liquid as they fought the pull of the aether.

Hector panned his light around and found Lady D on her knees with her hands covering her face. Blood streaked down her forearms and dripped off her elbows to mingle with the rising water.

Ears still ringing, Dave sat up. At his feet, dull light pulsed in the muddy, blood-tinged water, and he felt Ymara's call. With a trembling hand, he lifted a bone mask from the water. Bits of bloody meat clung to it. Transfixed, he held it in front of him and watched the gore slide off. Etched into both the inside and outside surfaces, glowing sigils twisted and writhed, making it seem alive.

"*At last!*" Ymara's exultant cry rang through his mind, muffling the roaring water. "*Join me, archer. Together we can slay the foul creature who dared entrap me.*"

Dave dropped the mask like a hot coal. "Lady D! She's a fuckin' haunted mask!" he yelled over the din.

"Ha! Told you I killed her!" Hector exclaimed, grabbing Teal's hand and helping her up. He flashed his light up on the balcony, but Evan Courtenay was nowhere to be seen. He turned his light on the kneeling woman. "So, who was impersonating Lady D?"

The woman from the balcony lowered her hands. The vampiric mask had ripped away the skin from her face, exposing a quivering mass of gruesome muscle and sinew. Not sparing a glance for Hector or Dave, she clambered up the stairs.

Slashing with their blades, Hector, Dave, and Teal mowed down the wailing revenants between them and the steps, sloshing through the water as it climbed higher up their legs.

While Dave and Hector fended off the remaining undead, Teal scampered up the damp treads. Once she was halfway, Hector started up, leaving Dave to take out the last attacker. The archer thrust and parried, seizing every advantage the creature gave him, but not killing it.

"Dave!"

"I'm thinking!" the archer replied.

"Well, quit thinking and come on!"

With a vicious strike to the neck, he parted the last revenant's head from its shoulders. The thing's body collapsed and fizzed to nothing as it hit the water.

Ymara's voice whispered at the edges of his mind. Gritting his teeth, Dave waded back to the dully glowing mask. He fished it out of the muddy water with his blade and struck it repeatedly against the wall with all his might. The last remaining vestiges of skin and blood dislodged, but the bone remained unmarred. Dave swore under his breath as Ymara's laughter echoed in his head.

"Come on! We have to get Evan!" Hector yelled from the balcony; his light illuminated the length of the stairs.

"Hold on!" Dave said, as he worked loose a drawstring bag from his belt. He jammed the haunted mask inside among his spare bowstrings and arrowheads then knotted it to his belt. Flickering light burst overhead, and Hector's light vanished. Certain he would regret his decision to take the mask but terrified of what could happen if he left it behind, Dave raced up the stairs.

Sickly yellow-green flames licked the ceiling of the observation balcony. They briefly lit up the cistern before guttering out, only to flare again moments later.

Dripping wet, Dave caught up with Hector and Teal taking cover behind a stone column flanking the melted remains of a bronze door. At each green burst, they leaned back, keeping their distance.

"Who'd have thought?" Hector whispered, answering Dave's unspoken question. "The woman who wore Lady D's mask is a sorceress."

"The same one who escaped us back in Santander?" asked Dave.

"Could be."

"And her demon?"

They both looked at each other, recalling what they had seen at the monastery.

Dave snuck a glance down the hallway and saw Evan flailing at the green flame with his sword. Each time he struck it, a portion died out, but with a word, the sorceress cast another gout of fire at the knight. Green tongues licked over moldering tapestries, casting weird light and flickering shadows over the combatants.

"Did you see her face?" Dave asked. "It looks like the mask ate it."

Hector nodded and said, "I imagine she got more than she bargained for from whoever gave it to her."

"Depends. She got to be Ymara while she wore it," Dave said, uncomfortably aware of the relic in his belt pouch. "I think Evan was an unexpected monkey wrench in her plans."

"Judging by how intently she's trying to kill him for us, I think you're right," Hector agreed.

The sorceress faltered and the green flames clinging to the knight snuffed out, replaced by the revenant's ghostly glow. With a bare hand, Evan grabbed her by the throat.

"Now's our chance!" Hector whispered. He surged to his feet and led the charge down the hall.

The sorceress' neck and bloody face began to harden and turn black, just like Sir Francis. Her legs buckled, and Evan let go. Turning his attention to the trio rushing toward him, he donned his gauntlet. Green flames from the tapestry covered walls reflected in Evan's armor, intensifying his otherworldly appearance.

Hector aimed low with his scimitar, while Dave went high.

Never raising his weapon, the knight shifted his stance and disappeared.

"Shit! He's like the *Inquisitor's* captain!" Dave said.

The two stood back-to-back, circling with their swords out. Teal quickly joined them, a dagger in each hand.

Evan Courtenay reappeared with his sword raised and slashed toward Dave.

The archer fended off the attack at the last second with a life-saving parry and a flurry of counterstrikes. Teal took two quick steps and jumped. She kicked off the wall and flew toward Evan's back with daggers ready.

Again, the knight disappeared.

Teal's momentum carried her into Dave and sent them both tumbling to the floor. Hector stood over them, scimitar flashing in the green fire.

"How do we stop him?" Dave grunted, pushing Teal off him.

"The sorceress," Hector answered. He grabbed the small iron vial from his pouch and rushed to her side. The lighting made it difficult to judge, but even though the rot had spread, it looked like it hadn't penetrated as deep as it had with Sir Francis — at least not yet. With Dave and Teal standing over him, Hector lifted her head and poured the contents from his vial down her throat.

She sputtered and coughed but managed to get some of it down.

Evan appeared before Teal, his sword already in motion. With a shout of defiance, she twisted to avoid the knight, but his blade cut across her back and shoulder. She arched her spine and stumbled forward. Dave whipped around sabre-first and struck the knight where his pauldron met his gorget. The sword bounced off with a metallic ring.

"Damn that's some thick armor!" Dave yelled, swinging again, trying to keep Evan from finishing Teal.

"Aim for someplace thinner!" Hector shouted back over the din of swordplay.

"Aim for some place thinner," Dave mimicked. "He's a poxy *knight*, you halfwit!"

Evan feinted right with his blade. Dave chased it and was rewarded with a left cross from the knight's gauntleted fist. Stars exploded in his head as he slid across the floor.

While Teal dragged the sorceress clear of the fight by the arm, Hector leapt up with his scimitar and slashed first left, then right. The knight countered, then caught the scimitar in his gauntleted fist. Forcing the blade up, he stepped in and stabbed the bounty hunter in the gut, twisting and driving his sword in all the way to the hilt before yanking it out.

Hector reeled back and looked down. Blood poured from the wound. Crimson rivulets slid down his pants to pool at his feet. One hand pressed to his stomach, Hector collapsed to his knees. His saturated shirt clung to his skin. A moment later, he sprawled on the floor.

With a yell, Dave charged the knight. His sabre moved so fast, only glimmers of it were visible in the green light. Evan staggered back under the onslaught. The sabre found small gaps in the plates, but it wasn't enough. Evan's armor kept him from being cut to shreds.

The knight countered with a couple of quick strikes of his own, putting distance between the two. Evan swung his sword in a wide arc and hit the guard of Dave's sabre so hard the archer's hand went numb from the impact. The weapon dropped to the stone floor with a loud clatter.

Jumping on the knight's back, Teal jabbed her dagger into his visor. Evan roared and flung the tall girl away by the scruff of the neck. Teal hit the wall with a loud smack and lay senseless where she fell. A trickle of blood from her scalp ran along her hairline and mixed with that from the wound on her back.

"Enough!" Evan yelled. Mist rose up and more revenant sailors appeared. Dave picked up his sabre but made no move to strike.

"Bring them," Evan Courtenay commanded before turning to march down the hallway.

In pairs, the revenants dragged Teal, Hector, and the sorceress down the hallway by their arms. Dave turned to watch them go, but the wet trail of Hector's blood drew his eyes and held them prisoner. He couldn't tear them away until the last two revenants blocked his view, replacing it with the sickening sight of their ravaged faces and milky, hunger-filled eyes.

Dave stepped back and raised his sword, but the revenant sailors didn't attack. One motioned with his arm toward Evan and waited. Sliding his sabre into its sheath, Dave placed his hands behind his head and followed.

They entered a nine-sided chamber, newer than the cistern but still ancient. Tall, gold-framed mirrors covered eight of its walls. Instead of reflecting what was inside the room, they showed Ruthaer and the surrounding lands through the ages — one showed the Praesidium as it had been in Teal's day and another showed the islands as they were today. Some mirrors had buildings and people in them, some showed only trees, and others reflected weird creatures from a distant time. The same grey mist bordered them all.

The room appeared to have been someone's home at one time. Moldy, rotten pieces of furniture lay scattered about. In the center stood a small three-foot high by two-foot square table intricately carved from dark wood. A gold filigree, octolateral stand decorated with silver whippoorwills set equidistant about a pair of rings supported an eight-inch diameter, glowing, crystal orb made from a single piece of smoky green beryl.

The Orbuculum.

Beyond the table was an ornate sarcophagus, its heavy, stone lid cracked open to reveal the skeletal remains of a half-dragon — Auguratus, the soothsayer Teal said owned the orb, Dave surmised. The coffin looked as if someone had shoved it aside to make room for the table.

Tossing his helmet to the side, Evan said, "What do you think of the view, Dave Blood? Or should I call you Clem Tyler?"

"Teal's dagger must have hurt," Dave replied.

Evan raised his hand to the deep gouge in his cheek. "I don't feel pain like I used to. It's one of the gifts bestowed by Cecil's meddling to please my *father.*" When he said the last word, his mouth twisted as if tasting something bitter and foul. "But I don't heal — I am destined to rot away like this ancient furniture."

A red shadow blotted out one of the mirrors, and with it came a feeling of dread. Curved, ivory claws scraped the glass surface, but couldn't break through the magical barrier. The claws withdrew, and a monstrous golden eye with scarlet flecks surrounded by ruby scales filled the mirror. The fire inside the slit pupil illuminated the whole room.

Evan's milky eyes narrowed, and he said, "Now that my father and Cecil are gone, all that remains is Mi'dnirr." Clenching his fist, he hissed, "He will pay for what he did to me." Evan glanced toward a narrow, wooden box engraved with the crest of the Golden Stag.

Dave realized it was the same box Lady D took from the shrievalty the first night the ghosts attacked them. He wondered what it contained, then remembered Aislinn's bizarre comment about the dærganfae dagger on their way to the quarry. "What are you planning to do with us?" he asked.

"Make you my servants," Evan answered as he walked toward Hector, removing his gauntlets.

The two revenant sailors nearest Dave grabbed his arms and held him in an iron grip. Their icy touch burned his skin. He shoved against one and then the other, trying to break free.

"The great bounty hunting team, Damage, Inc. I watched you stumble about in Ruthaer. At first it was Aislinn's faith that drew my attention. The way she destroyed the *Inquisitor*'s captain truly was impressive. Then I saw you try to heal her at the quarry. A shame what happened. Tell me, did you feel her life ebb away or was she already dead?" Evan grabbed Hector by the throat and lifted him to his feet. Black rot spread from the knight's hand and wormed its way into the bounty hunter's flesh. Hector kicked and bucked as Evan ripped open his shirt and dug his fingers into the half-healed wound.

"I saw her skin knit back together, and I want to know." Pulling the bounty hunter closer, Evan whispered, "Can your blood heal me?"

Hector spat in his face.

"Get your fucking hands off him!" Dave yelled. Straining, he pulled harder against his captors, forcing them to take a couple of steps toward their master.

Evan smiled, revealing jagged, yellow teeth, and probed deeper. All color drained from Hector's face. He tried to scream but the rot stole his voice. When Evan withdrew his hand, it was dark red with thick gore. Bringing it to his lips, he licked Hector's blood from his fingers and a shudder of ecstasy ran through him.

"The irony is, if you hadn't come to Ruthaer, I wouldn't have been able to kill the monks and escape this prison. Tell me, did you recognize the sorceress, Consuelo, without her vampire mask? Probably not. There's not much left of her now. She and her pet demon meant to ambush you, but Consuelo was weak. I bent her to my will and made her my slave." He peered intently into Hector's eyes and asked, "What became of Magali? I sent her to kill you, but that was before I realized it was you who had the *real* power."

Fueled by hate, the sorceress rose to her knees and launched a ball of sizzling, black energy at Evan's back. It hurtled through the air and melted a hole in his armor, scorching his undead flesh. Evan staggered and turned to face his attacker.

Hector grabbed his knife and stabbed it into the knight's neck. He reared back to strike again.

Evan flung Hector against the wall and charged Consuelo. "Your spells have lost their strength, sorceress."

Hector struggled to his feet. He held his knife ready and took a shaky step toward the knight.

The sorceress saw him and gurgled, "Break the mirrors! His spirit is bound to them!"

Evan jerked back around when Hector smashed the mirror next to him with a piece of furniture. Tiny fragments of blue and green light tinkled and chimed as they fell to the floor.

"You will pay for that!" Evan yelled. In one swift move, he unsheathed his sword and slashed the sorceress across the abdomen, spilling her intestines. He disappeared before she hit the ground.

"Hector, he's vanished!" Dave yelled, still struggling against the two revenants pinning his arms. Out of the corner of his eye, he spotted a mirror that reflected their room. "He's in the mirror!"

With the rot still spreading along his neck and torso, Hector grabbed a chair and threw it at the mirror. Falling to a knee, he caught himself by grabbing the metal frame of a chaise lounge.

The glass spider-webbed and Evan reappeared. His mouth compressed with concentration, the knight made a series of complicated gestures and spread his fingers wide. The Orbuculum floated above its stand and ethereal mist poured into the room.

Dave freed himself from one of his captors and snatched his sabre from its sheath. The other wrenched the archer's arm back and sank its broken teeth into his injured shoulder, sending a spike of pain down his side.

"I will destroy Ruthaer and everyone in it!" Evan cried out. "Once they are gone, I will be free of Brother Powell's binding. Everyone will become my thrall — even Mi'dnirr."

The town appeared in one of the mirrors. It was twilight and tiny figures raced home. Evan reached toward the mirror with the dragon's eye and mimed pulling something out. The eye and the red scales surrounding it turned hazy and dissolved into countless motes of light, which surged out of the glass, spinning and whirling like a cloud of angry hornets as they poured into the Orbuculum. With the slither of steel on leather, the undead knight redrew his sword and pointed it at the mirror of Ruthaer. Red mists billowed out of the orb and floated across the room.

"Hector! You have to stop it!" Dave yelled, slicing through the lower thigh of the revenant biting him. Sinew and decaying muscle parted, and the creature collapsed, dragging its nails down Dave's arm.

With the undead creature clutching him, Dave watched as Hector looked from the mirror of Ruthaer toward the Orbuculum and back again. Pain twisted the bounty hunter's features. His chest heaved as his lungs fought the effects of the necrosis eating away at his throat and airways, and Dave could only hope Hector's dubious healing gift would still be able to bring him back.

Within the red mists, a small red dragon formed. It flew toward the mirror and the unsuspecting town lying beyond its surface, growing larger with each flap of its wings.

Hector's gaze darted back to the orb floating in the center of the room. Lurching to his feet, he gave Dave the barest of nods, then dove toward the table. His injured state skewed his aim. He sailed past the small table, and his fingertips brushed the Orbuculum. The beryl orb flashed, then dropped to the floor, rolled across the room, and smacked against a mirror frame. Unable to stop himself, Hector landed in the open sarcophagus.

With a furious roar, the dragon dissipated in a fiery cloud of orange, yellow, and red before settling to the floor and evaporating.

Pushing away his captors, Dave cleaved the fallen revenant's head from its shoulders and disemboweled the other. The remaining seven lumbered toward him, mouths agape. Behind them, he spied Teal. Her amethyst eyes glittered in the unnatural light before the creatures closed on him, blocking his view. Dave thrust his sword into the nearest one and moved on to the next, fighting his way to the sarcophagus.

Holding his sword out in front of him with both hands, Evan stood guard over the Orbuculum.

A mirror shattered, followed by another. Teal lifted a moldering chair, heaved it at another mirror, and raced across the room.

"NO!" Evan shouted. He flung his sword end-over-end. As she neared the next mirror, the horns of the stag-head pommel caught Teal in the hip, knocking her against the wall. Several revenants rushed toward her, like buzzards to a feast.

Evan placed the beryl orb back in its stand. It floated up and again mists poured from the walls. Grey shapes coalesced and became the solid forms of murdered townsfolk.

Bloodied and bruised, Dave struggled against the rising tide of revenants. He slipped in a pool of his own blood and jagged fingernails tore across his ribs. From the corner of his eye, he saw Evan lean over the sarcophagus. The knight's head tipped to one side, as if he couldn't understand what he was seeing within the box.

Hector suddenly sat up and thrust a slender, ornately inscribed dagger at Evan. The knight leapt back, narrowly avoiding the silver tip. The bounty hunter held the blade aloft and shouted, "*RUPTUS!*"

Lances of hot, white light shot out from the blade and shattered the remaining mirrors. Shards of glass scintillated in the blinding light as they rained down like tiny gemstones.

The Orbuculum rose higher and its glow grew brighter. Cloudy swirls inside darkened and churned as if it held a tempest.

Evan turned wide, panic-stricken eyes to the mist collecting about his feet. The orb's light grew brighter, and grey hands reached up from the growing aether, latching onto the knight's legs. "No! You will do as I command!" he shouted. More hands reached up and Evan slowly sank into the floor.

All around, grey hands appeared, pulling the revenants down into the misty floor. The creatures screamed and fought against the hands, to no avail.

"*NO!!!!!!*"

Evan reached for the sarcophagus, vainly struggling to remain above the mist, but it would not be denied. With a surge, it rose up and devoured him, cutting off his scream.

The Orbuculum dropped into its cradle and the light winked out.

CHAPTER 36
SHAPES IN THE FOG

August 8, 4237 K.E.

1:32pm

"We'll roar across the salt seas/ Until we strike soundings in the Channel of Old England/ From Ushant to Scilly is thirty-five leagues!

"Now let every man toss off a full bumper/ And let every man drink off a full glass/ And we'll drink and be merry and drown melancholy/ Singing, here's a good health to each true-hearted lass!

"We'll rant and we'll roar like true British sailors/ We'll rant and we'll roar across the salt seas/ Until we strike soundings in the Channel of Old England/ From Ushant to Scilly is thirty-five leagues!"

"Now, repeat the first verse," Hector heard Dave say. The singing continued, with a female voice joining Dave's.

"Farewell and adieu unto you, Spanish ladies/ Farewell and adieu to you ladies of Spain/ For we have received orders to sail for old England/ And we may ne'er see you fair ladies again."

Hector opened his eyes, but everything was a blur. A stab of pain burst in his temples and he groaned. It felt as if someone had plunged a stiletto into his head and twisted it. He closed his eyes and waited for the pain to subside.

When he opened them again, they focused on the gentle firelight reflecting off the ceiling. Other details slowly came to him. He lay inside a stone sarcophagus amid the skeletal remains of Auguratus, the half-dragon soothsayer.

"Whence did thou learn this song?" Teal slurred. From the sound of it, she and Dave were close by.

Dave took a swallow of something and replied, "Ever heard the story about the old sea captain who chased a giant shark?"

Hector struggled upright and said, "Dave! What are you doing?" The sudden movement sent the room spinning. Groaning, he propped his elbows on the side of the coffin and cradled his head.

Teal and Dave sat with their backs to the sarcophagus. At their feet, a small campfire built from various scraps of furniture burned merrily. A piece popped and threw sparks into the air.

"Hey, you're alive," Dave said, staggering to his feet. Soiled bandages covered his arms, torso, and shoulder. Hector reckoned the only thing keeping the archer from getting an infection was the volume of alcohol in his system.

The bounty hunter's stomach had a hollow ache. "How long have I been out?"

"I don't know. Lost track of time," Dave replied.

"I'm hungry," Hector said.

Dave offered him his flask, but Hector waved it off. "I said I'm *hungry*, not thirsty." The archer shrugged and took another swallow.

Hector looked at him askance and said, "You know we're not done. We still have to get out."

"I did findeth a way out," Teal said, then hiccupped. The tall teenager swayed on her feet as she covered her mouth.

"Help me," Hector said, throwing out an arm. Dave grabbed it and hauled the dusty bounty hunter out of the box. "You're going to get us all killed one day with that drink of yours."

"Why do you worry?" Dave asked. "You can't die."

Hector grabbed the flask from Dave and took a swallow. Spicy liquid burned all the way down, leaving a trail of fumes. He made a face and asked, "*¿Qué coño es esto?*"

"Better?" Dave said, stoppering the flask.

Miraculously, the fumes cleared his head, even if the liquor did leave a sour feeling in his stomach. Looking at Dave's bandages, Hector asked, "Did you pour any of that stuff on your wounds?"

"No," Dave replied. "I didn't want to waste it."

Shaking his head at the absurdity of Dave's logic, Hector checked the sarcophagus for his gear and found the ruined remains of the dagger named Ruptus. He didn't know how it ended up here, but he said a small prayer, thanking whoever had left it.

"How did thou know aught of yon dagger?" asked Teal.

"The orb showed me when I knocked it from the air," Hector replied. He surveyed the room. At the edge of the firelight, the sorceress lay in a coagulated pool of her own blood, her mangled face unrecognizable. Of Evan Courtenay, only the knight's sword remained. It lay against the wall with the stag horns on the pommel crusted over in Teal's blood.

"Where's Lady D's mask?" Hector asked.

"I have it," Dave said, his voice sobering. "I also picked up the box Evan and Ymara stole from the shrievalty. There's an ivory dagger inside. Evan couldn't stop himself from looking at it when he mentioned getting revenge on Mi'dnirr."

"Mierda. Sounds like Aislinn was right about Mi'dnirr wanting that blade." Hector checked each of the shattered mirrors before turning his attention to the Orbuculum. The beryl orb lay in its whippoorwill stand as if nothing had ever happened. He stared into the crystal ball. Deep inside, there was a pale green glow. Storm clouds swirled; it reminded him of another time, another day. Before he realized it, he placed his hand on its surface.

The full moon illuminated frothy, black waves lapping against rocks at the base of an old masonry lighthouse. In the distance, the lights of Charleston dotted the horizon. A deep-water boat rocked back and forth beside the pitted remains of a concrete dock that provided the only access to the dark tower.

"This isn't right. Look," a voice said next to Hector. It was Robert, and he was pointing his penlight above the door at a black metal sign that read, "Danger! No Trespassing!"

"Stop waving around the light. Do you want to get caught?" Hector heard a younger Dave say. He carried a black duffel bag over his shoulder — one large enough to conceal a body if needed.

"See? You know this is wrong," Robert replied. Carrying a duffel bag of his own, he stood beside Dave. The resemblance was uncanny. The two could have been brothers, but where Dave was dark and brooding, Robert was fair-haired, with bright blue eyes and a ready smile.

They made an unlikely trio, and tonight, all three wore dark cargo pants, t-shirts, and black combat boots.

Hector was down on one knee with a set of lock picks in his hand. Working the padlock, he said, "Only if we're caught." After an audible click, Hector's teeth flashed in a grin. "We're in."

The door creaked open and Robert shined the light inside, revealing a set of old, cast-iron stairs spiraling up into darkness.

"Do you think it's safe?"

Hector shrugged. "If it wasn't, I think those 'Save the Light' people would have fixed it by now."

With the door firmly closed, the three lit several battery-powered lanterns. They climbed the stairs, all three checking for weak spots and loose railings. The rust coated metal stairs creaked and rattled under their booted feet but held firm to their various testing. Once satisfied, the three friends returned to the base of the stairs where their duffle bags lay side-by-side.

Within the bags were a variety of fencing gear — meshed facemasks, padded jackets, thick gloves, and practice blades. Robert had been in the fencing club the longest and had the most equipment. He could use the foil, epee, and sabre, and was working to master the parrying-dagger called the main-gauche.

Dave had joined the club a little over a year before and was the first member Robert's age in quite a while. Robert had worked with Dave on the rules and forms, and Dave convinced him to expand their practices beyond the strict rules of tournament fencing. Though Dave would never admit it, he shared Robert's love of old swashbuckler movies. The two spent a number of long afternoons working out the choreography of their favorite fights, and then learning the moves.

When Hector joined their group a few months ago, they practiced with multi-weapon forms and techniques gleaned from hours of movie choreography and a variety of fencing books. Hector was naturally ambidextrous and loved their free style practices, where he tended to flail around with a pair of curved cavalry sabres he purchased at an Army surplus store.

Laughter echoed inside the tower amid the clang of weapons and good-natured name-calling. Each battled the other two to be king of the stair, first one on the high ground, then another. As they reached each landing, the fight rotated, forcing one of the boys to back up the stairs while defending against the two below. In their banter, time slipped away.

At the top of the tower, they pushed outside onto the metal balcony hanging just below the lamp room. All three came to a bemused stop when they found themselves shrouded in the soft glow of a thick, chill fog that hid both moon and water. A muffled rumble drifted through the air.

"Is that thunder?" Hector asked, pulling off his mask.

Dave snorted. "Probably some asshole with too much bass in his radio."

"Language," Robert said, giving Dave a reproachful look. He turned to Hector. "The weather report didn't call for any storms this weekend. The tide probably turned while we were inside, and the swells are up." Sweat matting his hair, Robert took off his facemask and glanced at his wristwatch. The glowing face showed it was nearly one in the morning.

Hector leaned against the brick wall and pulled off his gloves. "Well, Robert, are you glad we came?"

Robert laughed ruefully, and then nodded. "I suppose it's fun to break the rules sometimes. I'm not saying I want to do anything like this again soon, considering the price I'll have to pay when I get home, but I've had a good time. What about you, Clem?"

"I hate that fuckin' name."

"Huh?"

"I hate my name."

Robert and Hector exchanged a glance. Dave never talked about himself or his feelings. They could hear from his tone that their friend was in a rare mood.

"Okay," Hector said. "You want us to call you Tyler, like they do in the military?"

"No."

Robert cleared his throat. "What's wrong with your name?"

Dave glared at him. "Clement. Tyler," he said with deliberate slowness. "I got called Inclement or Clementine until I started beating the shit out of people."

A sudden flare from the lantern room overhead knifed through the swirling mass of pearlescent fog. For a moment, all three youths froze, their eyes wide with shock, before flattening themselves against the lighthouse wall.

"That's not good," Dave muttered.

"Amén, amigo," Hector replied. "Mi papa is going to kill me."

From below, the mournful sound of a foghorn echoed through the night.

"What on earth?" Robert said. "When did Folly get a foghorn?"

Hector and Dave shrugged.

A muffled clanking came from the lamp room, followed by footsteps. A rotund man, wearing red robes inscribed with blue and silver sigils, shouldered open the door. His dark hair was shoulder length, and a well-groomed beard and mustache obscured his face, making it difficult to judge his age.

The man stopped in the open doorway leading to the balcony. Holding a clay pipe to his mouth, he stuck his thumb into the bowl and puffed a few times. Within moments, scented smoke swirled about him. He pulled his thumb from the bowl, revealing a small flame that danced along his fingernail.

Robert gasped.

The flame vanished as the newcomer stepped onto the balcony. Taking in the looks of blank surprise on the boys' faces and the blades in their hands, he said, "You're not supposed to be here. Did you put out the light?"

Hector started. Dave had him by the arm and stared at him strangely.

Taking a deep breath, Hector pushed Dave away. "I'm all right."

"You touched the orb," Dave said. "What happened?"

"I saw the three of us at the lighthouse. The night we first arrived in Gaia and met Jasper."

Dave stared down at the swirling green gem. After a moment, he asked, "Could that thing send us home?"

"Would you really want it to?" Hector asked, surprised by the question.

"Me? No, there's nothing for me there, but Robert's another matter." Dave scratched his beard. "Do you ever miss it? All the things we took for granted... the ignorance?"

Hector slapped his friend on the back and said, "Dave, you're mixing up home with youth. Nunca se puede volver atrás."

"No, I guess not. Besides, everybody who knew us probably thinks we're dead." After a moment, Dave asked, "Do we dare leave it?"

Hector studied the orb and its stand. "We have to. I'm fairly certain we'll trigger an aethereal gate if we lift it out of that stand."

"What do we do about it then? I'm not planning on coming back here."

Teal joined them and said, "It should remain hither, sealed away forever. Could we trust the villagers to guard its secret?"

"Yeah, I think they would," Hector replied.

"Well, quit gawking and let's get out of here," said Dave.

CHAPTER 37
VISITORS

August 8, 4237 K.E.

1:47pm

"This way," Teal said, pointing with Hector's bone tube light.

Hector and Dave followed the staggering teenager along the cistern's balcony to the fissure created by Dave's arrow. A thinning rivulet of muddy water trickled out and dripped into the pool filling the room to a few feet below the ledge. A fish jumped, sending ripples in all directions.

Hector stepped over the remaining chunks of granite, mortar, and brick, and peered into the opening. "This tunnel goes on forever."

"It doth reach the surface," Teal replied, and hiccupped again. "In my time, this was but one of many qanāts which fed the cisternae and provided ventilation, though I do confess I know not wherefore someone hath sealed it."

"If you know so much, lead the way, girl," Dave grumbled.

"I did warn thee to keep a civil tongue. Do not insult me again, archer, lest I take thee to task."

"What insult?" Hector asked.

"I did hear the soldiers... Dost the word 'girl' not mean one who is weak and cowardly?"

"No," Hector replied. "It means young female. Like it or not, you *are* a girl. Well, technically a woman, but female. Everybody in Ruthaer saw you naked, us included."

Teal stared down into the cistern water as if she were trying to find something. "I belong neither in this body nor in thy world, hunter. My place is here, among the bones of my people."

Hector grabbed Teal's elbow and forced her to face him. "Whatever else you may be, dead is not one of them. Until we know what part Allyrian Carmichael played in the events of Ruthaer, you *will* continue to travel with us. Now get up that pipe."

Teal's mouth compressed in a thin line, but she nodded. When she disappeared from sight, Hector motioned to Dave. "You're next, amigo."

Dave shook his head. "I'm rear guard. I go last."

"You're also tired, injured, and drunk as a skunk. I'll watch your back this time."

"Art thou coming?" Teal's voice echoed back to them.

"Yeah, keep your pants on," Dave muttered as he entered the pipe.

Hector grinned and shook his head, then followed Dave. The tunnel's rough-hewn sides were moist and held pockets of gritty mud. The climb turned steeper as they progressed, with patches of slime.

"This shit's gonna ruin my bow," Dave cursed. Coated in black sludge, the archer bellycrawled in a vain attempt to keep the bow strapped to his back from rubbing against the craggy, dripping ceiling.

"Keep moving," Hector said.

"Why couldn't we, just once, avoid the fuckin' sewers?"

"Karma," Hector answered. "You're making up for something horrible you did in a past life."

"Yeah, but it seems like putting up with your shit would be enough."

The pipe grew warm. Sweat streamed down their backs and dripped off their faces. Teal and Dave slowed, struggling to push their way upward. Both were panting with the effort, and Dave stopped muttering curses. Hector realized Dave and Teal's wounds, along with the copious amount of alcohol they had imbibed, were taking their toll.

Dave suddenly slid down the pipe several body-lengths before managing to stop himself. Blood seeped from his bandages and mingled with the sweat trickling down his back.

"Can you make it?"

Dave grunted and nodded, but Hector could see his muscles trembling with the effort of pulling himself up after Teal.

After an endless seeming hour of climbing through the pipe, the sweet taste of fresh air caressed their faces. "Wait," Hector called. "Mata la luz."

Tapping on Teal's foot, Dave pointed to the bone tube. She nodded and closed her fist around the end.

At first, there was total darkness, but as their eyes adjusted, they saw a dim ray of light filtering down from above. Teal passed the light back to Hector before scampering up the pipe and disappearing into the sunlight. Dave was not far behind.

Hector slithered out the narrow opening and down a short bank of black mud into a shallow puddle. Dave and Teal stood nearby, letting fresh air wash over them. Short, stubby trees swayed in a late morning breeze, and two herons stalked along the bank, catching frogs.

"You feeling okay?" Dave asked.

Spitting the mud from his mouth, Hector turned and caught Dave staring at him. "Yeah. Why?"

"Your throat and stomach. They're grey."

The bounty hunter looked down at his ripped shirt. A dark grey scar marked where Evan Courtenay had stabbed him. Around it, grey lines branched out like veins. "Huh. How about that? I guess magic blood only gets you so far."

"You still have his handprint around your throat."

Hector reached up and felt his skin. Finally, he said, "Don't worry about me. Let's just get out of here."

"Where to?" Dave asked. Overwhelmed by a jaw-cracking yawn, he tilted his face toward the sapphire sky and closed his eyes. "I could sleep for a week."

"Back to the lighthouse," Hector said. "I want to let Hank know Evan Courtenay and his phantoms won't trouble the town anymore. Plus, we need to deal with *Sir* William."

"Fuck him," Dave grumbled.

"I don't think so, amigo," Hector replied with a smile.

"Let's at least get my boat," Dave said, opening his eyes again. "Do you think Tallinn found Brand and made it to Ozera?

"You tell me. Your ring works the same as mine," Hector replied.

"You do it. Magic makes my ass-hair twitch."

"Don't be ridiculous. Between your sword, those ruby-tipped arrows, and your obsidian ring, you've been using magic all week."

"Do not forget his wondrous flask," Teal added.

"Not one of those things affects my mind," Dave growled.

"Fine," Hector sighed. He concentrated on his ring for a moment, then shook his head. "They're still on the move. Now, how do we get down off this island?" Hector asked.

"Jump?" Dave suggested.

Hector motioned for his companions to get moving. The trio climbed out of the slimy hollow and emerged on the bank, looking more like mud elementals than actual humans.

At the top, Hector asked, "Which way is south?"

Dave studied the position of the sun and pointed. "That way. You sure you want to go back to the lighthouse?"

"Yeah," Hector said. "How far do you think it is to the river mouth?"

"Four, maybe five miles," Dave answered.

"Do you two think you can make it?"

Receiving tired nods from the other two, Hector found a path leading from the pond and set a steady pace through the trees.

At the end of the path, a thick knotted rope attached to a rust-covered spike driven into the rocky ground led to a strip of beach, two-hundred feet below. A maze of channels and tree-covered islands surrounded them. No two seemed to be the same size, and none looked close enough to jump to — at least not the way they had done the day before. In the distance, the lighthouse beam was red.

Dave leaned over the edge of the precipice and asked, "How did those monks ever find this place?"

"Who knows?" Hector gave the spike a sharp kick and said, "Well, it held. Who wants to try it first?"

⊂꙰⊃

3:00pm

The small boat broke through the jagged crevice in the cliff face. Each wave they hit threw a sparkling spray of water into the air. Free of the islands, wind filled the sails and Dave hauled on the tiller, aiming south. Lines in hand, Hector and Teal scanned the horizon.

A galleon lay at anchor not far beyond the lighthouse. Abuzz with activity, sailors climbed the ratlines and walked the yards as they furled the sails. Hector dug out his spyglass. Atop the ship's centermost mast flew the standard of Carolingias: a blue flag with a silver Dogwood tree issuant from a mount vert. Underneath was a smaller flag with a sable lion rampant on a field of gold.

Dave piloted their vessel in a wide arc. "We should have waited for nightfall. What do we do now?"

On the forecastle, a sailor waved at them and used a signal mirror to tell them to come about.

"This will be interesting," said Hector. "Take us to the ship."

"Are you sure?" Dave asked. "We can hide in one of Teal's caves and outrun them tonight."

"That's one of Queen Ambrose's ships. We should be okay," Hector said with more bravado than he felt.

"What about the flag underneath?" Dave asked, squinting at the motto.

"Non revertar inultus," Teal read. "I will not return unrevenged."

"Whose banner is that?" Dave asked, adjusting their course.

"No sé," Hector said.

As they drew close, a sailor tossed Hector a line, and he tied the boat off to the ship.

Dave yelled, "Permission to come aboard!"

"Permission granted!"

A row of armed marines lined the gangway as the three climbed the wooden ladder affixed to the hull and boarded the ship. William Howard shoved forward from their ranks and reached for his sword.

"Sir William!" a tall, lanky man with greying temples shouted. While his embroidered silver and black vest and dusk colored leggings spoke of nobility, his worn, black leather boots told a tale of hard work.

The knight from Rowanoake stopped short, giving the nobleman a vicious glare.

"William," Hector said with a big smile, "it's so nice to see you again. How's your ship?"

Sir William turned several shades of red. "You know damn well my ship's a burnt-out wreck."

Hector made a show of looking over the rail and said, "Oh, there it is."

"Both of you!" the nobleman snapped. "You are guests on this ship. Behave that way or I will have you thrown overboard."

"Yes, Milord," said Hector.

"Milord," Sir William said.

The nobleman approached Dave, Hector, and Teal, and said, "Allow me to introduce myself. I am Lord Roger Vaughn, Viscount of Snowdon." His open countenance and dark eyes held a glint of mischievousness.

Hector gave the nobleman a sweeping bow. "Hector de los Santos, of Damage, Inc., at your service. My companions are Dave Blood and Teal of Ruthaer. Please excuse our unkempt appearance, Milord."

"Milord," William Howard snarled, "these men are base criminals. They have destroyed the sovereign property of Rowanoake." Sir William pointed to Dave and Hector and said, "These two have insulted my family name and are responsible for the death of my brother. I demand restitution!"

Lord Vaughn raised an eyebrow at the young knight and said, "I will hear what they have to say." He turned back to the three newcomers and appraised each of them. When he came to Dave, his gaze lingered. His expression became unreadable as he took in the tattooed man behind the layers of blood and grime.

"Welcome aboard the *Trinity*," he said finally. "Now, can someone explain what happened to this place?"

"Milord, I must insist!" Sir William said.

"Lord Vaughn, if I may," a familiar voice called. Hank stepped clear of a small cluster of ship's officers and pointed at the knight. "Sir William's men attacked my lighthouse. These two," he motioned to Hector and Dave, "have been helping defend the town."

Lord Vaughn raised his hands, silencing them both. Sighing, he turned to Hector and asked, "Did you burn Sir William's ship?"

"Yes, Milord, we did, but I can explain everything," Hector replied.

CHAPTER 38
THE VISCOUNT

August 8, 4237 K.E.

8:11pm

'*Set me free*,' the wind whispered.

Dave's grip on the *Trinity*'s deck rail tightened until his knuckles turned white. Fresh bandages wrapped his shoulder and portions of his torso. His hand trembled ever so slightly as he brought the flask to his lips. Fiery whiskey burned through him, a vain attempt to drown the ghost of Ymara's voice. Melodic laughter only he could hear drifted up from the skiff below.

The upper rim of the sun slipped behind the trees atop the rocky barrier islands, leaving the sky a dark, ruddy orange and the clouds bruised black and purple. Across the ocean at his back, he felt the heavy cloak of night falling over the world.

Atop the promontory, the lighthouse cast red beams out to sea, still signaling for help that had already arrived. A campfire flared to life near the base of the cliff, and he could see the vague shapes of Rowanoake sailors settling in for the night.

Darkness engulfed the Carolingian ship.

'*You are mine, Archer.*' The vampire's voice was stronger. '*Remove that sad, flawed bit of jewelry and take your place at my side.*'

"No, dammit," he muttered quietly. "Stay the fuck out of my head."

'*I know you want me,*' she purred. '*Though you try to deny it, you brought my relic out of that pit because you hunger for the pleasure only I can give you. All you need do is find a host for my mask.*'

Dave took another shot from his flask. "Shut the hell up," he growled a little louder.

"I beg thy pardon?" Teal asked.

He whipped around, his hand reaching for his sabre before he remembered Lord Vaughn's men disarmed him when he came aboard.

"Dammit, don't sneak up on me. What do you want?" Dave glowered at Teal, who stood just out of reach, limned in dim lantern light. She'd changed out of her mud and gore-stained clothes into a bright blue sailor's tunic and black pants. The sea breeze played through her long locks, turning them into a mass of writhing golden tentacles.

"The viscount desires we join him for supper. Hector hath finished his account of our deeds, with some little help from the young lighthouse keeper and the town guard called Big Mike."

The lanky bowman turned back to the rail and his contemplation of the darkness. "I'm not hungry."

Teal joined him at the railing. "I do not think it wise to decline this invitation, despite the inevitable presence of thine enemy."

"I don't care what you think."

"Thou shouldst care what yon nobleman thinks of thee. I do believe 'tis he who shall decide our fate this night."

"Hector will convince him to let us go."

"William hath demanded we three be hung from something called a yardarm," Teal replied.

"That sorry son of a bitch." Dave waved his flask at the furled sails above the deck. "See the spars those sails are tied to? That's a yard. The arm is the bit at the end over the rail."

Teal's amethyst eyes darted up and back. "Who was this girl whose body I now inhabit? Why doth all and sundry, save Hector and thee, wish her dead?"

Dave shrugged. "Damned if I know." He cut his eyes toward the strange girl. He drank deeply and swiped his mouth with the back of his hand. "Are you really a ghost?"

Teal held out a hand toward the flask, and Dave handed it over. She tilted it back and swallowed; a shudder rippled over her lithe form. "Aye, I suppose so. The mouldy bones of mine people in the caverns and halls we traversed yestereve did speak of many long centuries since my race passed from these lands." She raised the flask again before passing it back.

"So, what, you were some kind of lizard people?" Dave asked, remembering the scaly skinned warriors they saw in the unnatural fog and the ghostly shape that had surrounded the girl in the Praesidium's haunted halls.

"We were dragon-kin," Teal said. "Children of Xardus, created to be the bridge betwixt our bronze kindred and the humans of Gaia."

"Lizard men," Dave said again with a nod. He glanced at Teal. "Lizard women," he amended.

"Dragon-kin," Teal insisted. "Xemmassians. And I am not a woman, appearances to the contrary."

Dave shrugged again. "Whatever."

"Come. Let us not make our host send someone to fetch us."

Dave huffed in exasperation. "They'll probably make me wear a damned shirt."

CRSO

8:19pm

"A man from Santa Casilda arrived with three horses this afternoon," Big Mike said. "He said they belong to you."

"¡Fantástico!" Hector exclaimed. "I expected them three days ago, and was beginning to wonder if they were going to make it." He and the sergeant sat near the end of a long dining table with the ship's officers and guests.

Running parallel to the long axis of the ship, the galley took up the central third of the aftcastle. Rising from the middle of the table, the tar-stained mizzenmast speared through the overhead deck. A row of low cabinets lined the stern beneath a row of windows. Lantern-light shimmered on the glass panes, hiding the darkness outside. A marine in blue and white livery stood between two louvered doors in the port-side bulkhead, and two starboard-side doors flanked a narrow bench.

Conversations ceased when a marine opened the door from the main deck. At the head of the table, Lord Roger Vaughn, Viscount of Snowdon, stood when Teal entered, prompting the other men present to rise as well. The teen stopped, surprise writ over her features.

Dave gave Teal a push. "Let's get this over with," he grumbled. A grey silk shirt concealed his torso and arms, but the laces at the collar were undone, exposing Aislinn's gold oak leaf necklace and the cracked balas ruby brooch resting against his tattooed skin.

At the foot of the table, on the captain's right, the lighthouse keeper's assistant, Hank, gave the latecomers an encouraging nod. His formal white sash, emblazoned with two diagonal tridents over a black tower, contrasted starkly with his dark blue shirt. From the viscount's left, Hector and

Big Mike motioned to a pair of empty chairs. Opposite Hank, Sir William Howard and the *Fluyt*'s jossman glared at Dave as he and Teal made their way to the far end of the table.

"I'm glad the two of you could find the time to join us," Lord Vaughn said. "Teal," he stepped around and slid out the chair on his immediate right.

Teal looked from the older man to the chair and back again.

"Go sit, *girl*," Dave growled in her ear. She shot a glare at Dave, then stalked to her chair.

Hector grinned at the pair as they all took their seats. If he didn't believe Teal was a male spirit in a girl's body, he would almost think Dave had met his match. Almost.

He watched the steward pour golden wine into each of their goblets and waited for Dave's reaction. He was surprised when the archer actually waited for Lord Vaughn to raise his glass and take a sip before reaching for his own. Was Dave becoming *civilized*? The bounty hunter gave himself a mental shake; their situation was still too precarious to allow himself to become distracted.

The door opened, and a team of seamen wheeled in carts bearing covered dishes. With swift efficiency, the officers and their guests were served grilled flounder fillets beside a mound of sautéed summer vegetables.

Dave and Teal both reached for their cutlery just as the chaplain said, "Let us pray."

Hector bowed his head and tried not to laugh. He closed his eyes, and a pair of green, almond-shaped eyes framed by red-gold hair swam before him. He lost track of the ship chaplain's words as he said his own prayer for Aislinn, Hummingbird, and Brand. His attention snapped back when he heard the priest say, "Soþlice," ending the blessing. Hector crossed himself quickly and murmured, "Amén." He opened his eyes and found Lord Vaughn staring at him, his face filled with melancholy.

"My apologies," the nobleman said. "My wife used to end her prayers the same way. I... I haven't seen that gesture in a long time."

"Used to, sir?" Hector asked softly. Warning bells went off in Hector's head. As far as he knew, he and Robert were the only two people in all of Gaia who crossed themselves after prayer. He eyed Lord Vaughn curiously; a niggling suspicion developed deep in his gut.

Instead of answering, Lord Vaughn's eyes flicked in the archer's direction, but then drifted into the distance. Several long moments passed before he finally shivered and returned to the present. "Please, forgive me. I'm starting out to be a poor host this evening."

An uncomfortable silence fell as the nobleman and his guests focused on their dinner. At the other end of the table, Hank and Captain Adams discussed the lighthouse, trade routes, and the present storm season.

"The last few years have been hard, and this one doesn't look to be any better," said the young sea ranger. "We've already had four rough storms come in on us, even though it's early. Tallinn said it wasn't so bad until two or three years ago." He laughed. "The old man keeps telling me they didn't see this kind of weather until I came aboard."

The first mate made a short, dismissive gesture. "The sea is a wild and dangerous mistress. One never knows when she'll turn on you."

"Where is that crusty old dog?" the captain asked.

"He and Tasunke flew north yesterday afternoon to find out if the rumors of a bronze dragon were true."

The captain shook his head and laughed. "Still full of piss and vinegar, isn't he?"

Hank's face turned red, and he glanced down the table at Teal. "Sir," he mumbled from the side of his mouth, "there's a lady present."

"She's no lady," Sir William replied. "She's a criminal like the other two, and a tart besides. She stripped naked in the church in front of the Eternal Father and everyone."

The grey-haired captain's smile vanished. "We are all naked before the Eternal Father, young man, and her lack of education in proper behavior does not excuse us from our obligation to act as gentlemen." He turned to Teal. "Forgive me, miss. I shouldn't speak so crudely about friends or enemies in a lady's presence."

Apparently lost in her own thoughts, Teal paid no heed to the conversation at the other end of the table. Finally noticing the weight of multiple stares, she looked around at the men facing her, then turned to Hector, her confusion clear.

Tilting his head, Hector's eyes darted toward the officer, then back at Teal. His eyebrows went up slightly.

Dave drained his glass, then leaned toward the teenager. "They're waiting on you to accept the captain's apology," he mumbled.

Teal glanced from Dave to Hector, who nodded encouragingly. She cleared her throat. "Thank thee, sir. Thy apology is accepted, though I must confess I did not notice anything untoward from thee."

Lord Vaughn's eyes twinkled, and he hid a smile behind his hand. He turned to the steward. "John, perhaps we should move things along. Some of our guests will need to head home soon." The officer summoned the servers, who replaced the dinner plates with slices of cake and small bowls of iced fruit. "Sergeant Hart, you're the ranking officer of the local shrievalty?"

Big Mike nodded. "Yes, sir. We've lost a lot of good people the past week. Without Sir Francis or Father Blackwood, Ruthaer is pretty much cast adrift."

"How do you feel about being in charge for a while?"

"Me, sir?"

"You can't be serious," Sir William scoffed. "This idiot led me and my men upriver after a pair of fishermen, claiming they were my missing prisoners."

"Who's the bigger idiot," Hector smirked, "the one who leads or the one that follows?"

Sir William lunged to his feet, and his chair scraped loudly over the decking. "I have had it with you! You and me out on deck, right now."

"Sit down!" Lord Vaughn barked. "That's twice I've had to raise my voice at you two. Not another word, or I will have you both clapped in irons and gagged."

Hector took in the anger blazing in Lord Vaughn's leonine eyes and blinked in surprise. Across the table, Dave's scowl mirrored the viscount's. His eyes darted between the two men, noting the lines and contours of their faces, the color of their eyes. He felt his jaw drop as he realized they looked enough alike to be related. Forcing his mouth closed, the bounty hunter stared at his dessert while he tried to put his thoughts and emotions in order.

After Sir William retook his seat, Hank said, "Milord, do you have orders for me? I need to get back up to the lighthouse."

"Keep the lamp red for now," Lord Vaughn answered. "I've sent a report to Port Remley, but we're also going to need transport for young Master Howard's men."

"Milord?" Sir William queried.

"Master Howard," Viscount Snowdon said, "you asserted authority you do not hold in a sovereign nation not your own, refused aid to a community in need, and your men attacked a lighthouse owned and maintained by the Confederation of Nations. Despite what your father and the rest of his peers in Rowanoake may wish, they and you are still subject to the Highlord of Gallowen. Did it not occur to you Queen Ambrose and Carolingias could construe your behavior as an act of war by a foreign nation?"

The young man kept his expression neutral, but a vein in the center of his forehead throbbed with anger.

"This matter will have to go before Queen Ambrose in York. I'm certain she will wish to confer with the Highlord in Tydway before passing judgement," Lord Vaughn continued. "They are likely to view your behavior as an act of piracy. At the very least, your family will have to make reparations."

Hector didn't dare look down the table at Sir William. He bit the inside of his cheek to keep from laughing at the so-called knight.

"Hector de los Santos."

The bounty hunter's head jerked up at the sharp tone in Lord Vaughn's voice.

"I've heard about you and your team. These warrants against you must be addressed. To that end, I will arrange for your transport to Tydway."

"What?!" Hector exclaimed. "Please, Milord, some of my team were injured. We *have* to get to Ozera."

"I'm afraid it may take some time for the council at Rowanoake to present all their evidence to the royal court, Milord," said Sir William. "There are several witnesses who will have to be summoned from Francesca, and with travel times being what they are —"

"I beg your pardon?" Lord Vaughn asked.

"*¡Espera un minuto!* You want witnesses from *Francesca*?" Hector demanded.

"My brother went there to arrest these two miscreants," Sir William told Lord Vaughn. "One of Killian's retainers returned months later, crippled by a shattered knee. He brought us the news of Killian's death. I must be allowed to appear in Tydway and present eyewitnesses. Citizens who can testify they saw Clem Tyler murder my brother."

"I didn't *murder* your brother," Dave growled.

"Killian and his thugs ambushed us while we were working for King Edmond," Hector said. "As agents of the Francescan crown, we were within our rights to defend ourselves. Real witnesses will attest to the fact that Killian Howard and his men refused to withdraw. The governor of Amienes will be able to provide proof that we reported the incident to the local gendarmes and turned over three prisoners."

"The warrant for Killian Howard's murder originated in Rowanoake," Viscount Snowdon stated. He raised an eyebrow at Sir William. "Rowanoake has no authority regarding matters occurring in foreign nations, Master Howard. Only King Edmond or one of his provincial governors can issue a warrant for crimes within their borders. I'll make inquiries, but if the Francescan government determined there was no crime, I'm afraid you'll have to consider the matter closed."

Sir William's jaw clenched so tight, Hector could hear his teeth grinding together. He allowed himself an inward sigh of relief. They had nothing to fear from King Edmond and his governors. He knew for a fact there were no warrants for them in any of Francesca's provinces.

"In the meantime," Lord Vaughn continued, "the four of you will remain aboard the *Trinity* where the captain and I can keep an eye on you. At least until we can send you on your way to trial."

"You have no authority to hold me!" Sir William shouted.

"Oh, but I do," Lord Vaughn replied. "You see, I hold titles in both Carolingias and Gallowen, giving me authority as a representative of both Queen Ambrose and the Highlord. Either you accept my hospitality and stay in one of the forward cabins, or you can sleep in the brig."

"I see," Sir William replied. While the viscount spoke, the knight's demeanor had morphed from vehement hatred to coolly distant. Speaking in a measured tone, he said, "If that is your decision, then I must make arrangements with my men."

Lord Vaughn rose. With a nod toward the knight, he said, "You're dismissed."

"Milord," Sir William said with a curt bow.

As the knight and his jossman turned to leave, Lord Vaughn said, "Captain, have a landing party escort Sir William to his crew's camp and back. Provide him any assistance he requires to get them settled for the night, but he *will* sleep aboard the *Trinity*."

CHAPTER 39
PIRACY ON THE HIGH SEAS

August 8, 4237 K.E.

9:23pm

As the other men filed out of the cabin, Lord Vaughn said, "Hector, remain for a moment."

"Of course, señor," replied Hector.

"John, if you would be so kind, please have a tray of kahve brought in."

"Yes, Milord," the steward said.

Resuming his seat at the head of the table, the viscount turned his chair at an angle so he could stretch his legs. He leaned back with his fingers interlaced behind his head.

Hector waited quietly. The creaks and moans of the rigging seemed to grow louder. Outside the door, he heard the sailors prep the long boat, and the squeal of the block and tackle as it was lifted out over the ocean.

Hector placed his palms flat on the table and leaned his weight against the surface. "Milord, we can't go to Tydway. We need to go to Ozera. Hummingbird and Aislinn will be there, waiting for us."

The door opened, and John walked in carrying a silver tray laden with a pot, a small pitcher of cream, and two ceramic cups. He placed them on the table and filled each cup with a thick, dark brew. The rich aroma of kahve inundated the room. When finished, he bowed and left them alone.

Wrapping both hands around the streaming cup, Lord Vaughn inhaled deeply and asked, "Was it worth it?"

Hector stopped short. "Señor?"

"Banishing Evan Courtenay. Was it worth it?"

"We saved Ruthaer," Hector replied.

"But at what cost? Sir Francis Courtenay, Father Blackwood, and your Aislinn. Maybe even your young elf, Hummingbird."

"Hummingbird and Aislinn are well on their way to Ozera. I *have* to believe Phaedrus and his healers will save them. As for Ruthaer, what would you have had us do, Milord? Walk away? Damage, Inc. never walks away."

"You walked away from Rowanoake."

"No, señor, we *ran*, with nothing more than the clothes on our backs, the weapons on our belts, and the coins in our pockets, and you see what it got us. After all this time, we're still treated like criminals, and taking us before some judge won't change that — even if the Highlord himself presided. William and his family's vendetta against us will follow Damage, Inc. wherever we go. So, you see, going to Tydway is just a big waste of time."

Lord Vaughn straightened. "Actually, it's the quickest way for you and your companions to reach Ozera. Especially if you help us."

Hector quirked an eyebrow.

"Queen Ambrose is pleased with your work here and intrigued by your discoveries. I expect Countess Devon and the *Lady Luck* to arrive tomorrow morning with a team to explore these islands. Once she does, we'll set sail for Tydway, and if all goes well, you can continue on to Ozera. It may cost you a few days, but it's still faster than if you were to cut cross country on horseback."

Hector chafed at the thought of a delay, but he didn't see they had a choice. "What can we do?"

"The Orbuculum."

Hector pushed away from the table. "You want us to go back into those haunted caves?"

"From what you've told me, we can't have an item that powerful fall into the hands of a stranger. Can you imagine what would happen if Rowanoake had it? Or what about this Count Dodz? No one has seen or heard from him since he delivered the message from Rowanoake."

"Do you think he knows about the orb?" Hector asked.

"I can't answer that, but you said his ship brought the sorceress Consuelo here to ambush you. I doubt he did so out of charity. The odds are ten to one he's after something, so the sooner we get the Orbuculum the better."

CRSO

2:00am

The four-bell chime marking the second hour after midnight drifted over the gentle swells rocking the *Trinity*. A waxing crescent moon peeked out from behind a solitary cluster of cottony clouds. Countless stars of varying intensity dotted the night sky, seeming so close a person could almost touch them. Below, the dark ocean reflected light from the large lantern on the poop deck and the smaller lanterns hanging from the *Trinity*'s three masts. In the forecastle, a single porthole shimmered with dim candlelight.

Avoiding the pools of light, a dozen men swam to the ship and gathered about the foreword anchor rope, their faces smeared with black grease. They did a quick head count before four of them swam toward the skiff, trailing aft.

Wrapping his legs around the thick hemp rope, the *Fluyt*'s jossman climbed out of the water, while the remaining seven waited. Lean and athletic, he wore only tar-stained breeches cut just below the knees. In his mouth, he carried a long, thin dirk.

Once past the orlop deck, the sailor reached out and grasped one of the ratlines secured to a narrow ledge projecting from the hull. Between the series of pullies, there was enough space for him to place the ball of his bare foot and stand while he listened to the thud of boots above on the forecastle deck. Taking hold with just his fingers, he moved sideways to the bowsprit and the wooden figurehead — a muscular man with his left hand shielding his eyes and a golden trident in his right.

Holding onto the curved railing that surrounded the *Trinity*'s prow, the jossman waited until the ship's forward sentry walked past before slithering onto the ship. Crouched low, he padded across the short deck. With a burst of speed, he wrapped his left hand around the sentry's mouth and jaw. Wrenching it back and to the left, he buried his dirk into the side of the man's exposed neck and out through the larynx. Blood from severed arteries sprayed the figurehead and rail as the jossman hid the gurgling sentry under the angled bowsprit.

One after the other, the seven seamen climbed over the curved railing. Dressed like their leader and armed with daggers, five of them crept up to the forecastle deck before separating, each aimed toward a specific target. The jossman, with two remaining seamen beside him, waited. Not hearing any sounds of alarm, he opened the hatch into the ship.

Typically reserved for the upper crewmen, the forecastle of the *Trinity* housed four cramped forward cabins. A narrow passageway with a hatch at either end ran down the axis of the ship and separated the rooms into port and starboard sides.

Midway down the passage, a marine stood guard beside a lantern that cast an orange glow on the pine paneling. Stepping inside, the first of the seamen hurled his dagger, lodging it in the marine's throat. The two rushed forward to ease the man's fall while the jossman closed the door behind them. One came up with a set of keys. Their leader unlocked the door of a port side cabin.

Sir William Howard stood aside while the seamen laid the dead marine on the bunk and covered him with the thin white sheet. Motioning to the two starboard cabins, Sir William grabbed the keys and opened the first one.

Teal lay on her bunk fast asleep, still dressed in the clothes she wore to dinner. A seaman crept into the room. She opened her eyes just as he clamped a damp sponge over her mouth and nose. Teal pushed against the seaman's arm, but within a few seconds, her eyes rolled back into her head and she collapsed. Lifting her across his shoulders, he carried her into the passage and out to the prow.

Sir William and the jossman quietly waited at the other starboard door. As soon as the seaman carrying Teal exited, they unlocked the door. The room reeked with the cloying scent of alcohol. Dave lay atop his cot, passed out. On the other, Hector groaned and turned in his sleep, his face clouded in pain.

Sir William reached out his hand, and the jossman gave him his dirk. With an evil smile, he leaned over Hector and whispered, "I want you to feel this." William dropped his forearm hard across Hector's throat.

The bounty hunter's eyes flew open.

The knight from Rowanoake raised the dirk where Hector could see it before slowly pushing the blade between the thrashing bounty hunter's ribs and deep into his heart.

Sir William held the bounty hunter down the few seconds it took for him to fall unconscious. Removing the blade with a wrench, he wiped it on the sheet before handing it back to the jossman.

The other seaman already had Dave over his shoulders, alive but unconscious. The three men exited the forecastle onto the prow with their prisoner.

Midship, fierce flames rose from the long boats. The clangor of the ship's bell rang out, and the pounding of footsteps echoed on the wood deck.

Below, the skiff waited at the anchor rope. The pirates lowered Dave, then shinnied down the line. Amidst the confusion on the *Trinity*, no one saw or heard the seamen row away.

⊂⊃

2:32am

Lord Roger Vaughn's boots thudded across the *Trinity*'s main deck as he strode toward the forecastle, beside himself with anger. Crackling flames rose from the topmost longboat. "Put out that bloody fire!" he ordered.

The command was unnecessary. Sailors poured through the hatches from below to join the night watch's bucket brigade. When seawater didn't douse the flames, four broad-shouldered sailors wrapped in wet blankets raised the burning boat and tossed it overboard. With three longboats stacked atop one another, tossing the uppermost was the only way to save the rest. Roger could only hope the other two longboats were undamaged.

"Milord, Sir William is missing, along with the girl and the archer," a barefoot sailor reported after a hasty salute. "There's more, sir. The bounty hunter's dead. Knife through the heart. They also killed Jenkins, and Parker's missing."

Roger swore and said, "Show me."

The doors to the forward cabins lay open, swinging with the tide. Jenkins' body lay on Sir William's cot, his blood staining the sheets. On the other side of the hallway, Hector and Dave's cabin was a mess. Eyes closed, Hector lay on his back with a puncture wound over his heart. A dark bruise covered his throat and the underside of his jaw. Whoever killed him had done it up close. It had been personal.

The grey-haired captain joined them and said, "Their skiff's gone."

The news was getting worse and worse.

"I take full responsibility, Milord," he said.

"That's not necessary, Captain Adams. I know who's responsible for this treachery. Get the remaining longboats in the water. We're going after William."

"Milord, we have no way to track them."

"I know where they're going."

"Yes, Milord," Captain Adams said with a smart salute.

Lord Vaughn ran a hand through his hair. He knew where they were going but not how to get there. Maybe Hank, the assistant lightkeeper, knew.

As he turned to leave, he glimpsed a spark from Hector's wound. Concerned that William's men had set the beginnings of another alchemical fire before they fled, he stepped back into the room.

Another spark arced across the puncture. Roger Vaughn drew closer. Many years ago, he had witnessed the Highlord recover from a wound that should have been fatal. His wound had sparked and burned as well.

Roger closed the cabin door. In the darkness, the tiny sparks became more pronounced. Taking a seat on Dave's bunk, Roger waited and watched the bounty hunter.

CHAPTER 40
COMPROMISES AND REGRETS

August 9, 4237 K.E.

5:45am

"Wake up, sluga!"

A sharp sting across his cheek briefly replaced the dull ache in Dave's head. He cracked open an eye, and the morning sun pierced his stupor. The ache flared into a stabbing pain as he sought to recall where he was and how he got there.

"Luchnik!"

The archer tried to wipe the sleep rheum from his eyes, but his arms were restrained. A cool breeze caressed him, and he heard the gentle sway of branches. The rough texture of pine bark scraped his back. Sitting on rocky ground and tied to a tree, he caught fuzzy glimpses of brawny sailors stripped to their waists.

"Wake the shlyukha. That will get his attention."

The Rhodinan accent was unmistakable. Still groggy, Dave squinted at the figure standing over him. "Dodz?"

"Give him a moment," said Sir William Howard. "He's coming around."

"Where am I?"

"Don't you recognize it?" Sir William smirked.

Finally managing to open both eyes, Dave gave the area a good look. Twenty feet away, muddy footprints led out of a deep hollow. He was back on the island. "You've got to be fucking kidding me."

There was no sign of Hector, but he saw Teal, still unconscious, lying on the ground, her wrists and ankles bound by a thin wire that bit deep into her flesh.

Sir William knelt beside Teal and gripped a fistful of blonde hair. He raised her head and turned it to face Dave. "She's absolutely beautiful — almost angelic."

"You better not have hurt her," Dave said, straining against the ropes holding him.

"Hurt her? No, we're here to hurt you."

"You bastard! Where's Hector?"

Sir William let Teal's head drop and took a step toward the archer. "I killed him, just like you killed my brother."

Shock coursed through Dave and his eyes flew wide. "No."

"Sir William! Do not upset the archer. We need him."

The knight from Rowanoake dipped his head in a short bow and replied, "Of course."

Impeccably dressed in a silken tunic and breeches that bloused over the cuffs of leather boots, Count Dodz crouched and reached for the brooch hanging in the hollow below Dave's throat.

Dave jerked back and sunlight glinted off the oak leaf necklace. Dodz slipped two fingers behind the chain and gently tugged the clasp around to where he could see it.

"No! Don't!" Dave said, renewing his struggles against his bonds.

Dodz touched the balas ruby with its jagged black flaw. Letting it go, he brushed cool fingers over the glistening scars on Dave's throat. "Ymara speaks to you, da?"

Dave grew deathly still. "You know?"

"I was Ymara's thrall for a time," Dodz replied, "but now, I think, she has found another."

"Fuck you."

Count Dodz smiled a cold smile, revealing white teeth that seemed to glisten with an icy frost. "We want you to retrieve the Orbuculum."

"The hell I will. Get it yourself."

The smile never left as the count said, "Wake her."

Two of the seamen grasped Teal by her arms and picked her up. Sir William took a vial of smelling salts from his pouch and waved it under her nose. She spasmed and shook as if electricity coursed through her body.

"Unhand me, vile heathens," Teal said, her draconic accent thick. Eyes flashing, she tugged against the two seamen, tossing them this way and that.

The jossman's knuckles crashed against her face in a backhanded slap. "Be still, girl."

Sir William walked behind her and snatched down her trousers. When he rose, Teal bucked and struck Sir William with the back of her head.

"Harlot, you're going to regret that!" Sir William said through clenched teeth. Blood covered his nose and mouth. He grabbed a handful of her hair and yanked her back. Pressing against her backside with his body, he said, "Which of you two will go down there and bring us back the Orb? Make your decision quick."

"You might as well kill us," Dave said. "There's no way we'll do anything for you."

At a nod from Sir William, the jossman punched Teal in the gut. She let out a hoarse cough and gasped for air. Teeth bared, she kicked at her tormentor, but the men holding her kept their grip and started laughing. The jossman struck her in the face, busting her lip. She eyed him with a dead calm and spit blood in his face.

All the while, the count remained in front of Dave, watching him jerk against the ropes with interest. "You wish to save the girl, da?" Count Dodz asked. "Bring us what we want."

The jossman shifted and there was a meaty thud. He struck her again and again. Each time, Teal let out a reluctant grunt.

With the count in front of him and the men holding her, Dave couldn't see what was happening. Fresh blood ran down his arm where the wound on his shoulder had ripped open. Not caring, he tugged harder. "Leave her alone, damn it!"

Count Dodz replied, "We will. All you have to do is say you'll go down there. It will all stop."

Dave looked from the count to the men surrounding Teal. "All right. I'll do it."

The smile on the count's face broadened, and he said, "Sir William."

Teal slumped forward between the sailors holding her arms, sweat dripping from her hairline. Blossoming bruises marred her face, and blood dripped from her bound wrists. The knight from Rowanoake stepped out from behind her, wiping the blood from his face with a silk handkerchief.

"You'll go down there with four of my men," said Sir William. "I expect them to come back alive."

Teal looked across at Dave, her lips swollen and bloodied, and mouthed, no.

Count Dodz laughed as he removed Dave's restraints. "No tricks. I would hate for something to happen to your friend."

"When this is over," Dave said to the count, "I'm going to cut out your heart and eat it."

Dave led the jossman and five sailors across the muddy hollow to the cistern's inlet. "This thing's slicker than chicken shit, and twice as messy," he said. "Took us an hour or more to climb out yesterday. I don't want you lot sliding all over me, so keep on your asses and brace against the walls with your feet on the way down."

The jossman scowled at Dave but nodded his acceptance of the instructions. "Gills, Salter, you two stand watch here. This bloke comes out without us, you bash his head in."

Dave eased into the tunnel mouth, braced himself, and scooted forward until he started to slide. The light behind him flickered and shifted as the four sailors from Rowanoake followed. In a matter of minutes, the light died altogether.

"Stop a minute, lads," the jossman ordered. "That goes for you, too, archer."

Dave grumbled but waited, knowing Teal would be the one to suffer if he failed to follow orders.

The jossman lit a small handlamp and shined it down the muddy shaft. "How far does this go?"

"All the way to hell," Dave replied.

They continued down for another ten minutes before their lamplight breached the cistern and reflected off the dark pool of water. Dave crawled from the pipe and strode across the balcony. The men behind him hurried to catch up.

Green and purple light flickered from Evan Courtenay's lair, reminding Dave of the unnatural storm which nearly drowned Damage, Inc. He stopped in the doorway, unwilling to approach the pulsing green orb and its whippoorwill stand.

The jossman shoved Dave. "There it is, lads," he said.

In response, the three sailors grabbed Dave and wrestled him to the floor.

"Fuckers," he said as he punched one and tried to roll. The jossman stomped the archer's side, bursting open the wound there like a ripe grape. His breath whooshed out, and Dave gasped. The others took turns kicking him.

"Grab his necklace," ordered the jossman. "The count wants it."

One of the seamen rolled Dave onto his stomach and snatched at the necklace. Despite his repeated efforts, the gold chain would not break.

"Maybe you should cut off his head," someone said with a laugh.

The seaman planted a knee on Dave's spine. Rough fingers parted the necklace's hoop and toggle clasp, freeing the balas ruby brooch and strand of golden leaves. "What about him?" he asked.

"Leave him," the jossman said. "We'll have the hole plugged before he comes to."

Turning toward the orb, one of the sailors produced a canvas sack.

The jossman poured a flask of brine over the orb's surface, and the swirls inside slowed, then stopped. "Be careful. The count said we still shouldn't touch it."

CREO

6:00am

Lord Vaughn crept along a narrow path bordered by waist-high grass, scrub oaks, and short, twisted pines, sword in hand. Behind him, a score of sailors hand-picked from the combined crews of the *Trinity* and Countess Devon's *Lady Luck*, along with Big Mike and a handful of soldiers from Ruthaer, slipped through the island's undergrowth, silent as wolves on the hunt. Shortly after topping the cliff, they'd caught two of Sir William's sailor's napping.

Their deaths had been swift.

A dozen yards later, Lord Vaughn caught up to Hector, leaning against a tree. Sweat dripped from the bounty hunter's forehead, and he clutched his chest. Although his knife wound had closed, he was still weak. The grey handprint and yellow-green bruising on his throat looked ghastly in the morning light.

"I should have left you on the ship," Roger said.

"That pendejo took Dave and Teal, Milord," said Hector. "I'm going to rescue them." Grim determination gave his voice a hard edge, and he pushed himself away from the tree onto the path.

"Alright, bounty hunter. Lead us to this lake of yours."

CREO

6:25am

'Archer.'

Pain became his entire world as Dave struggled to move. He tasted blood in the back of his mouth, and the floor beneath him felt wet.

'Archer.'

'Fuck,' Dave thought.

'I can help you.'

'Ymara, get out of my head!'

'We are bound, you and I. You struggle against it, but our relationship could be mutually beneficial.'

'There was nothing good about being your slave.'

'I gave you pleasure as my slave, archer, but that time is past. As my partner, I can give you more. Take my strength, I give it to you freely. Take my will to live, it is yours as a gift.'

'Bitch, there's always a price.'

'Archer, I am not the monster you think I am.'

'Yes, you are.' Dave tried to ignore Ymara and force his abused body to move.

'Then lie there helpless while those men ravage that girl and Dodz takes up my mask.'

'What?'

'Dodz knows you have my mask hidden in your boat. He hears me, senses my presence, just as you do. That's why those men took the necklace.'

'Why don't you just control me like you did at the chapel?'

'I offer the power to defeat your enemies, archer. The choice to accept my gift is yours.'

"Do you have everything?" the jossman asked. His light sparkled from broken bits of mirror, sending shadows creeping and lurching around the room.

Two seamen nodded. "Yes, chief," one replied, as he slung the sack with the Orbuculum and its stand over his shoulder.

"Where's Mr. Wynn?"

The two seamen looked around. "He was here just a moment ago," the second man replied.

"Mr. Wynn!" the jossman called. He panned his light to the bloodstained spot on the floor. "Where's the archer?"

Dave growled as he launched himself from the shadows and flew at the seaman holding the sack. He crashed against the man's chest, ripped out his Adam's apple, and leapt onto the next seaman before the first realized he was dead.

The archer slammed his next target against the open sarcophagus, breaking his spine across the stone lip. The man whimpered and clenched his eyes tight. Dave bared his teeth in a savage snarl. He gripped the man's head with claw-like hands and broke his neck with one swift wrench.

The jossman let out a strangled cry and raced from the room. Dave's eyes glowed amber and his growl fell silent as he chased his prey. He could smell fear in the air, and his blood pounded in response.

Man and predator burst onto the balcony over the cistern mere steps apart. The jossman slipped and slid through the mud slick below the inlet shaft. He made it partially inside before the archer grabbed his ankle and yanked him out again. Dropping his lamp, he kicked the blood-covered archer dead center with his free foot.

Dave fell back a step and assumed a half-crouch, watching for the moment to strike. Moisture trickled from his mustache to his lips, and he licked it away; the copper tang ignited a new kind of hunger in his belly. The scars about his neck and shoulders sent pulses of burning energy through him.

"Mercy!" cried the sailor.

Dave held no mercy in his soul, only death for his prey. He lunged.

The prone man came up, dirk first, and sliced through Dave's forearm. The archer didn't stop. He grabbed the jossman by the throat and breeches and threw him headfirst into the wall of the cistern. The man bounced off and landed at Dave's feet. The archer grabbed his stunned prey beneath the jaw and lifted him bodily from the floor. He smashed the man's head against the rock wall, once, twice, thrice, until the jossman lolled like a broken doll.

'Do it!'

Opening his mouth, Dave brought the jossman closer. He could taste the coppery blood. He wanted it. All the rage from seeing what they had done to Teal built up inside him. Visions of Hector, Hummingbird, and Aislinn swam before him. All dead.

"No!" Dave shouted. Shaking, he dropped the sailor and staggered back a couple of steps.

'You won! Feed upon him. Take his strength.'

Bringing his fists to his temples, Dave fell to a knee. Ymara's hunger hit him in waves and his body responded. He slowly got to his feet and took a tentative step toward the fallen man.

"Damn it, no! You do not control me!"

Turning in midstride, he ran back to Evan's chamber. He frantically searched the seamen's pockets and pouches until he found the necklace. Kneeling in the carnage, he wiped his forehead with the back of his arm, heedless of the smear of blood it left.

Dave held up the gem, unsure how he could see the balas ruby in the darkness, but, in truth, he didn't care. He placed it around his neck with shaking hands and fumbled with the ends until he had them clasped together.

'Another time, archer. Soon, you will join me.'

The ruby touched his skin, and darkness stole his sight.

Feeling his way across the floor, Dave crawled out of the room and toward the cistern. Relief flooded him when he saw the glow of lamplight coming from the balcony. Regaining his feet, he snatched the lamp from the inlet shaft and retrieved the sack with the Orbuculum.

The jossman lay on the floor. His face and head were a ruined mess, but he still lived. Dave slit the man's throat with his own dirk and wiped the blood on his pants.

"That's for Hector."

Midways up the shaft, Dave doused his light and hunkered down, the sack with the orb beside him. Weariness seemed to seep up from the mud. All he wanted to do was sleep, but he needed a plan. William and Dodz still had Teal. Grabbing the sack, he crawled a few more feet before collapsing. He needed to rest.

'No rest for the weary,' Aislinn's voice whispered in his memory.

"No rest," he echoed. With grim determination, he pushed himself off the floor and climbed a few more feet.

⚬⚬

6:30am

Allyrian woke, hanging limp between two sailors with vice-like grips on her upper arms. One of her eyes had swollen shut and blood trickled from her split lip. It dribbled down her chin and between her exposed breasts, where her shirt had been ripped open. She had a moment to wonder what Mi'dnirr had done to her then someone jerked her head up by a fistful of hair.

A young sun-god in fine clothing stood before her, admiring his handiwork. She could smell his arousal. Evil glimmered in the man's hard blue eyes as he balled his fist and drove it into her gut. The musk in the air grew stronger. Allyrian twisted her hands behind her back, working against her bindings.

Her tormentor caressed her cheek and said, "I love nature. Don't you? I mean being out here all alone. This is *real* freedom."

Count Dodz laughed and said, "But you're not alone, Sir William."

"Tch. Do you plan to stop me? My men won't," replied William.

Allyrian took in the Rhodinan's presence, unsurprised by his betrayal of her and Mistress Consuelo. She would see him pay, but first, this Glaxon knight.

"Stop you?   No," Dodz said.   "After you get the Orbuculum and I the necklace, our deal is complete, and I will leave you to your prize. I only wish you had brought proof of the bounty hunter's death."

William rounded on the count and said, "Do you doubt my word? I put the blade in Hector's heart myself. You don't know how long I've wanted to kill that pompous pissant and his murdering lackey. Hell, I feel like I'm getting everything out of this deal. You're sure all you want is their boat and the necklace Dave was wearing?"

"It is not me, tovarishch, but my employer in Erinskaya who desires proof. He has gone to much trouble to revenge himself on this Damage, Inc."

"Tell your employer that Hector is dead, Aislinn is dead, and soon Dave will be, too."

"As you say," Dodz said with a smile.

"Too bad a bunch of insubstantial ghosts messed things up for you," William sneered. Turning back to Allyrian, a cruel smile stretched over his too perfect face. "But not all that came out of Ruthaer was a waste."

William drew a short knife from his belt, knelt, and cut the cord binding her ankles. He tossed it away, followed by the ripped pants pooled around her feet. As he stood, he ran a hand along the inside of her upper thigh. "Nice," he said.

Quick as a whip, Allyrian headbutted the knight. He staggered back with blood gushing from his already swollen nose. Using the bit of space, Allyrian fell backward and kicked off the knight's chest with her foot. The fall turned into a flip and she landed several feet away from her captors. The bloody cord of her restraint dangled from her right wrist. Deep gashes cut into her left hand where she had worked her way out of it.

William bellowed and launched himself at the tall girl.

Over his shoulder, Allyrian saw Hector de los Santos break from the surrounding trees followed, by a small crew of sailors in blue and white Carolingian uniforms. Shouting as they came, they crashed through the perimeter guard and fell upon William's men with savage determination. The sounds of fighting erupted all around her.

Allyrian leapt toward a tree trunk, pushed off it, and dove at the knight. Twisting at the hip, she channeled her body weight and momentum through her arm to her open palm and struck his jaw. The knight, already disoriented, never saw it coming. His head snapped to the side, and she swore she heard his brain rattle inside his skull. He collapsed to the ground like a sack of flour.

She landed on her feet beside his head. Allyrian drove her heel into his ribcage and bared her teeth in a savage snarl when she heard bones crack. Still seeing red, she lashed out at one of the sailors who had held her and struck him with a knife hand to his throat. Moving on, she kicked the other in the groin. He collapsed to his knees. Allyrian grabbed his head and struck his nose with her knee. It burst like overripe fruit, coating her leg in blood. Tossing him aside, she looked for another victim.

Spying a sailor on his knees, she stalked toward him. Bloodlust consumed her. She wanted them all dead. Allyrian snatched up an abandoned dagger along the way. Cold and calculating, her mind raced through the different weak points inherent with humans. Veins, arteries — what would cause instant death, and what would make them suffer.

The sailor looked up at her. He didn't move; he couldn't. Fear froze his muscles. She raised her dagger.

A strong hand caught her forearm.

"This man has surrendered," a voice growled in her ear.

Allyrian looked over her shoulder into leonine eyes the color of dark whiskey. For a moment, the world shimmered, and then shadows ate her vision.

Teal came to himself on his knees, his raw and bloody wrist gripped by Lord Vaughn, and a blood-stained dagger in his hand. Covered in dirt, blood, and bruises, he barely recognized the girl whose body he inhabited. He opened his hand and let the dagger fall to the ground.

"What happened here?" he asked.

Lord Vaughn's eyes narrowed. "You don't remember?"

"Nay, Milord. The last I recall, Sir William and one called Count Dodz did coerce Dave into leading a small force to retrieve the Orbuculum from its resting place. Upon their departure, Sir William did entertain himself by abusing me." He reached up to gently prod his swollen eye. "He struck me a hard blow and consciousness fled me for a time. Whilst I slept, I dreamt of revenge."

Lord Vaughn silently studied the young woman before him. Finally, he said, "Scavenge yourself something to wear. We need your help finding Dave."

"Yes, Milord," Teal said with a slight bow. He climbed to his feet and staggered across the battlefield.

♂♀♁

7:15am

"Dave is hither!" Teal called out. His voice echoed hollowly from within the concrete pipe. Above him, a dark silhouette blocked the early morning sunlight shining into the cistern inlet.

"Do you need help?" Big Mike asked.

"Nay, I can manage."

Lord Vaughn tromped through the muddy hollow where men in blue and white livery gathered around the inlet. "Is he alive?"

After a bit of shuffling, Dave's head came into view. Big Mike reached down and pressed his fingers to the mud-covered figure's throat. After a silent minute, he turned back to Lord Vaughn. "Barely, Milord."

Big Mike leaned in and hoisted Dave out by the armpits. Even unconscious, the archer gripped a muddy sack. Teal scrambled out of the pipe. He gently pried the archer's fingers loose and handed the sack to the nobleman.

Lord Vaughn glanced inside and nodded. "Good work. Let's get him out of here."

Dave groaned when Big Mike lifted him. Battered and bruised, Teal draped an arm over her shoulder while Mike took the other. Between the two of them, they worked their way up the slippery slope with Lord Vaughn right behind them.

Puddles of blood and gore covered the ground and the dead lay where they had fallen. Sir William knelt under a tree with his hands bound behind his back. Several of his men were arrayed behind him — also with their hands bound — all bearing wounds from the recent fight. Around them, Carolingian sailors scoured the island.

Lord Vaughn approached the young knight, pointed to the sack, and asked, "Sir William, is that what you wanted?"

Sir William stared off into the distance. His mouth clamped shut and his chin jutted out.

"Bah," Lord Vaughn said. "You and your ilk disgust me. You would have started a war. And for what?"

When the knight continued to ignore him, Lord Vaughn turned to a soldier wearing gold chevrons on his collar and said, "Take these men to the *Trinity*. Lock them in the brig."

Giving the nobleman a smart salute, he said, "Yes, Milord," and gathered his men.

"Count Dodz is gone," Hector said, striding out of the woods. "I found a sand circle like he left behind at the Gryphon Inn a few days ago. He could be anywhere now." At the sight of the bounty hunter, Sir William's eyes went wide with surprise and his mouth dropped open, then snapped shut just as quick.

Hector grinned at the captured knight. "The next time you try to murder someone, William, make certain they're truly dead before you leave." He turned his back on Sir William and caught sight of Big Mike and Teal with Dave. Upon seeing Dave's sorry state, Hector rushed toward them.

"I'll take him," Hector said, relieving Big Mike and pulling the archer's arm around his neck.

Big Mike said to Hector, "I want to thank you and your team. Ruthaer wouldn't have survived without your help."

"De nada, Sergeant Hart."

"I am sorry for your loss," Big Mike said, walking with them.

"It's a bittersweet victory," Hector replied, "but I'm glad the town made it."

"And — thanks to Dave — we'll take the Orbuculum away and Ruthaer will be able to put itself back together," added Lord Vaughn with a broad smile.

At the sound of his name, the haggard archer raised his head enough to cast a bleary eye at Teal and then Hector. "You're both alive," he croaked.

"Yeah. Not sure if I can say the same for you."

"Asshole," Dave said with the barest hint of a smile.

"Come on," Lord Vaughn said. "Let's get you all aboard the *Lady Luck* and to Ozera before anything else happens."

CHAPTER 41
HOMECOMING

August 9, 4237 K.E.

5:45am

The rising sun at Brand's back painted Ozera's white cliffs in fire and blood. While the imagery was fitting, his mood called for a storm in place of sunlight dancing over early Autumn leaves. Exhaustion threatened to pull him and Aislinn from the sky. Each beat of his wings sent pain flaring through his back and shoulders, but he would not stop, not until he reached Ozera.

He was so close.

Fragmented bits of nightmare darted through his sleep-deprived mind, distorted bits of information that carried through his and Aislinn's bond before the monstrous clockwork bug had stolen her life and severed their link. Somehow, it wasn't the bug or the phantoms or even the tawny-skinned vampire-woman who evoked terror in Brand's sleep-deprived psyche. It was the image of a dærganfae with the moon at his back and his talon-like fingers clutching Aislinn's head. Dærganfae had killed Aislinn's mentor, Edge Garrett, so Brand could have understood rage at the dark-clad figure, yet that one encounter had frightened Aislinn and, through their bond, him. He wished he knew why.

Leaves and pine needles brushed his belly as he dove past Sunrise Chapel and over their mother's house. He was torn between the need for Phaedrus' help and the need for Emä's comfort. She always knew what to do, but he couldn't thrust the pain of yet another loss upon her. Not while there was a chance, however slim, that Aislinn wasn't gone. He simply *had* to convince Phaedrus to attempt the miracle.

His wings filled the village with rumbling thunder. Brand pulled up in a brief hover over the modest cottage Phaedrus called home. Surrounded by tall mountain firs, the tiny sward and its flower-lined garden was not meant to hold a dragon, even one as young as him. Electricity sparked and danced over his scales, a static charge he'd subconsciously pulled from the atmosphere during the long flight. His body changed and contracted as he dropped toward the short, thick grass between the cottage and the narrow lane, heedless of who might see him.

Brand no longer cared who knew his secret — that he was a shape shifter.

His feet hit the grass harder than he anticipated. Aislinn's added weight threw off his balance, and they tumbled several feet before landing in a jumbled heap. Darkness clawed at the edges of his vision. He struggled to his hands and knees, vaguely aware of distant shouts echoing through the forested village. His only thought was reaching the revered cleric.

A calloused hand settled on his shoulder.

"I'm here, Eidan," said Phaedrus, calling Brand by the name Emä had given him long ago to hide the dragon inside him.

Concern filled the priest's almond-shaped eyes as he took in the scene and helped Brand to his feet. Silver hair and a thin beard brushed the collar of his dark blue robe, in sharp contrast with his tan, angular face. Of both elf and human lineage, yet belonging to neither society, the priest had become an outcast in his youth and forged his own path. It was no wonder Damage, Inc. was drawn to him.

The cleric knelt beside Aislinn and reached a hand to her throat, where the edges of red, fern-like striations emerged from her collar. He pulled aside the fabric enough to see the strange markings spread across her shoulders and seemed to stretch down her chest. "What's happened to Aislinn?"

"Attacked by a giant clockwork bug." Brand pressed his palms to his temples and clenched fistfuls of coppery hair. Anguish twisted his features and made his voice brittle. "I can't hear her. I can't feel her heartbeat. *Please*, Phaedrus. Please save her. Emä..." He stopped, shook his head. "*I* can't live without her."

"I can't promise, but I'll do everything I can." Phaedrus didn't point out the dragon was living, even now, despite his pain. "Go inside and find something to wear. Bring the quilt from my bed for a stretcher."

"But Aislinn —"

"You're tired, Eidan. If the voices I hear are any indication, help will arrive momentarily. We'll carry her the rest of the way for you."

"Yes, Father." Brand staggered through the open door of the cottage and crossed to the bedroom. The sitting room window's open curtains allowed him a view of the crowd gathering around Phaedrus and Aislinn while he plundered the chifforobe for clothes. He made a face when he saw a half-dozen robes, all in the same color blue — a color reserved solely for Phaedrus. He let out a sigh of relief when he found a plain tunic and pants in a side drawer.

"Patrón, what's happening?" A member of one of the original founding families of Ozera, the man used the Espian honorific for their leader. "We saw a dragon, maybe Brand, under attack."

"Fear not, everyone," Phaedrus replied. "Brand wasn't being attacked, but Aislinn is in need of our aid. I've asked Eidan to bring a blanket for a stretcher. Eliezer, run fetch Shayla Yves. She may not be awake yet; she was up most of the night helping Misha Fordham deliver her new daughter. Meet us at the hospital."

"Father Phaedrus!" a new voice shouted. A young healer-in-training raced up the lane to stand panting before the cleric. "A winged horse landed at the hospital. The old blind man riding it brought an elf-girl, near death, and he asked about Brand."

"Go and tell him Brand delivered his charges. See that he and his steed receive breakfast and a place to rest. Tell him I wish to speak with him."

CRBO

6:30am

The hospital was the one place in Ozera which never slept. A matronly woman met Phaedrus and Brand, still in half-elven guise, at the entrance. She directed them and the Ozerans bearing Aislinn on a blanketed stretcher to a vacant room.

They passed an open door, where a team of healers was examining Hummingbird. Brand glimpsed an angry red scar on the girl's exposed shoulder. A thin web of branching lines shot out from the scar's center. It reminded him of ball lightning.

They hardly had Aislinn settled on the bed when one of the healers from Hummingbird's room hurried in. "Phaedrus, thank the Eternal Father you're here! The girl next door isn't responding to anything we've tried. It looks like we may be dealing with a new kind of poison."

"Eidan, wait here with your sister. The rest of you, thank you." Phaedrus hurried out after the healer.

Brand stood beside Aislinn and arranged her blanket. With her eyes closed, she looked asleep. However, there was an unnerving stillness about her, and deep inside him, her voice was missing. His heart shattered.

He wished, once again, things had gone differently between himself and Aislinn back in May. It *should* have gone different. She and he were family, bound together by something stronger than friendship or even blood. He had no memories of a time before they were joined, heart and soul. A Tanjaran seer once called them two halves of a greater whole, and they were. Together, they were stronger, more powerful, but everything they knew about their bond, they'd discovered on their own through accident and happenstance.

Spending his entire life among humans and elves, most of it here in Ozera, he'd never even seen another dragon until a little more than a year ago. The very fact that the one who came here knew Aleuria — the mother he'd never known, whose bones lay in a sea cave near Ruthaer — seemed like an act of fate. The arrival of Aleuria's mate a few short months later was staggering. Brand had never dreamed his father was alive and searching for him all these years.

Brand loved Aislinn's mother, Shayla. She had adopted him without question and had always treated him as her own flesh and blood. However, no matter how much love she gave him, it couldn't fill the hole in his heart, the desire to know who he was and where he'd come from.

He'd expected Aislinn to understand his need to seek out his heritage, and for her to journey with him over the sea to Revakhun Toaglen — the Sacred Isles, homeland of his ancestors. He wanted them to learn his history together. His new-found father had reluctantly agreed to bring Emä with them as well, keeping his family intact.

Yet, Aislinn hesitated. She wanted to know how long they'd be gone, if and when they'd return — questions to which he didn't have answers. He'd felt her reluctance before she ever spoke, but he couldn't imagine her not going with him. When Aislinn said she wanted to think about it, he'd been hurt and made no effort to hide it.

Soul-bound to one another since before his hatching, he and Aislinn had shared thoughts and feelings in an instant his entire life. It was nearly impossible to keep secrets from each other. As a result, they had disagreements from time to time, but they'd never fought like they did the night before she left Ozera.

Brand knew the source of her indecision — a pair of Terrans they called friends. Through their bond, he knew Aislinn's feelings toward Hector and Dave went beyond simple friendship. Even so, he'd pleaded with her to leave them. Finding out about their bond was more important, but she refused to give him an answer about leaving. Aislinn had wanted to talk with Hector and Dave first. The very idea she might choose them over him — over their bond — turned Brand's hurt to angry resentment. They had both said things they didn't really mean. In the end, she fled his cavern through the tunnel to her room in Emä's home.

A yawning void swallowed his heart. The truth was, he'd pushed her away. Worse, he'd refused to come out the next morning and see her on her way to Orleans.

He had tried to make amends. Even though he knew it would mean she would be gone from Ozera and from him longer, he'd relayed Tallinn's request for help. Still, she'd wavered between her commitment to their bond and her devotion to Damage, Inc.

An ember of jealous anger ignited in his mind. Nothing was going to come between them again — not death, and not a pair of Terran men who could neither understand nor love her like he did.

Brand brushed a lock of hair from Aislinn's cheek, then frowned as he noticed one of the red fronds covering her throat curled around and encapsulated two small scars behind her left ear. The scars were new — she hadn't had them when he last saw her — yet, somehow, they seemed familiar. Then it came to him. Dave bore a half-dozen or more similar scars.

He wondered if the bite wound caused the red striations, but the streaks he'd seen emanating from the scar on Hummingbird's shoulder hinted otherwise.

Pulling up the hem of Aislinn's shirt, he discovered the ends of a fractal pinwheel across her belly. Along her sides, the markings met and coiled with others stretching from her back. He pushed the shirt higher until he found the scar's center, an angry red pucker the size of his fist just below her heart. He jerked the fabric back into place, unable to bear the sight.

At one of their few rest stops, Tallinn had related what Hector told him about the clockwork bug in Ruthaer's quarry, and that Hector and Dave had 'patched up' Aislinn and Hummingbird. The two Terrans had only rudimentary healing skills. They could apply a simple bandage or drink a healing potion if they had one handy, but this was something else entirely. Something dangerous, if the healer was right about Hummingbird being poisoned. Dave knew poisons, but Brand had never seen the archer try to cure someone with one, no matter how drastic the situation. If there had ever been a time Dave would have tried something like that, it would have been in the Rhodinan country of Vologda three years ago.

He, Hector, and Dave had barely escaped Vologda's capital, Erinskaya, with the Alashalian ranger, Xandor Tanjara, and his Rhodinan friend, August Sabe, when they were ambushed by a Sha'iry priest and his henchmen. In the ensuing battle, Hector had taken a knife to the ribs. The blade missed his heart, but it punctured his lung. Nothing they tried would make the bleeding stop. The bounty hunter died, despite their efforts.

In an act of desperation, Brand used one of the few magic items he owned —a portal disguised as a gunnysack which led directly to his cave — to carry Hector back to Ozera and help, but there was nothing Aislinn or Phaedrus could do. To everyone's shock twenty-four hours later, Hector was hale and whole, as if he'd never been wounded.

Since that day, they'd come to realize Hector was different. His wounds healed in minutes or hours and rarely left a scar. Hector believed Phaedrus had performed a miracle. Dave attributed the bounty hunter's recovery to troll blood, but whether he thought Hector had been infected during a past battle or had a troll in his family tree, the archer never said. The only thing they knew for certain was magic lived in the bounty hunter's blood.

Suspicion as to exactly what Hector had done struck him like a physical blow. Brand sprinted from Aislinn's room to Hummingbird's. "Phaedrus, may I speak to you a moment?

It's important."   When the two of them were alone in the hallway, Brand said, "I think Hector tried to heal them with his own blood."

"Why would you think that?"

"Two things: the similarity of their scars and the fact that Hummingbird is poisoned. Tallinn said Hector and Dave did something to help Aislinn and Hummingbird after they were attacked. Dave knows poisons, but he wouldn't use one on either of them. However, Hector... Hector is crazy on a normal day. Faced with losing Aislinn and Hummingbird in a single battle, he'd have been desperate. There was only one thing he had that might heal Aislinn and Hummingbird: his blood. You saw him recover from that knife wound after I brought him here from Erinskaya. That wasn't a singular event. It's uncanny the way his body heals itself.

"Their wounds... Those scars..." Brand closed his eyes and took several shuddering breaths. "It's the only thing I can think of that Hector and Dave could have done to close Aislinn and Hummingbird's wounds and stop the bleeding."

Phaedrus contemplated for a moment, then nodded. "I'll tell Brother Giovanus and his healers. It will help them to know her blood is contaminated by more than simple poison." He glanced past Brand, then laid a hand on the dragon-elf's shoulder. "Here comes Eliezer and Sister Inez with your mother."

Shayla descended on Brand. "Eidan, what happened? Where's Aislinn? How badly is she hurt?" With each question, her voice rose. She caught sight of Hummingbird among the healers. Worry transformed into desperate fear, and she turned to Phaedrus. "Where is my daughter?"

"Shayla, we're going to do everything we can," Phaedrus said. "I need you to prepare for the worst but hope and pray for the best. At a time like this, you need to send for friends and family to be with you."

Tears spilled down her cheeks, and she slowly shook her head. "No. Please. I can't lose my baby."

Phaedrus pulled the tiny elf-woman into a gentle hug. "I'll let you and Eidan stay with her while Sister Inez and I gather an ennead, and acolytes ready the sacred henge on Brodgar Tor. You'll have an hour, two at most, before the Sisters of Mercy come to prepare Aislinn." He stepped back but kept his hands on Shayla's shoulders as he held her gaze. "A resurrection ritual is neither quick nor easy, Shayla. It takes time, and the outcome is in the Eternal Father's hands. His mercy and Aislinn's will to live will be the deciding factors, but she has your strength and her father's courage. Have faith in her and the Eternal Father."

CR&O

8:00am

Tallinn made his slow way along the corridor, fingertips brushing the wall on his left. Hushed voices drifted from a few of the rooms he passed, but none were the ones he sought. Eventually, he found himself at an intersection, unable to determine which way to go. Several people, harried healers by the sound of them, brushed past him before a young woman stopped to ask if he needed guidance. As much as it pained him to be unable to find his own way, the ancient lighthouse keeper rested a hand on her shoulder and followed the hospital volunteer to the emergency ward.

The cloying scent of bittersweet medicinal herbs clung to the air. From somewhere nearby, he heard Shayla and Eidan in conversation with two men. It sounded as though they were Eidan's friends. Standing outside the door, Tallinn wanted to go in, to speak to Shayla, but felt certain she would not welcome him, under the circumstances.

"Brother Giovanus, my studies haven't covered anything like this. I don't understand how the poison is causing her body to reject its own blood, and I'm afraid if we neutralize it, we'll kill Hummingbird," a young voice said.

Tallinn turned toward what he guessed was an adjacent room. He leaned against the wall and concentrated on listening.

"That is why I asked Magus Easmond to join us, Novis Efrim," Brother Giovanus replied. "He can place her under a temporalis histēmi spell. It's risky, but I believe it will give us the time we need to perform a purification ritual."

"Are you certain I can't have a single leechful of her blood before we begin?" another voice asked. "I would like to study the anomaly."

"No, Magus Easmond," Brother Giovanus replied. "The child is too weak.

"But —"

"No. We do not have her permission, and there are none here who can give it for her."

"Very well," the mage sighed. "I don't know how long I can hold the spell, Giovanus. Magic and elves are a slippery subject. Be ready to act quickly."

Tallinn heard shuffling, followed by the clink of stones pulled from a cloth bag.

"Amethyst for purity," Novis Efrim recited. "Sapphire for healing, Turquoise for grounding, Bloodstone for detoxification, Cat's Eye for protection, Fire Opal for energy, and Garnet for courage and strength."

"Very good, Efrim," said Brother Giovanus. "Magus Easmond, please begin." The mage began muttering arcane phrases, and the hairs on the back of Tallinn's neck tingled. He could hear the strain in the man's voice as it rose and fell, repeating the phrases a third time. Finally, he said, "Now, Giovanus."

"Let us pray, Efrim." Together, the healers chanted in ancient Korellan. Minutes passed. Their voices rose to a crescendo then stopped. Brother Giovanus said, "Exaudi orationem, Patris Aeterni."

Bright light flared and a hoarse scream split the air. Pain and fear filled the corridor like a wave of suffocating heat. The old man stumbled back, only distantly aware of the cacophony of shouts and running feet around him.

Overwhelming his mind were shadowy images of a battle-torn village, fire, and a monstrous black creature on a cavern wall.

Screams filled the air. Two men — Hector and Dave — charged the creature. Tallinn saw Aislinn, a look of shock and horror on her face, snatched into the air, and a girl cried out in pain. Above Aislinn, a black diamond eye blazed.

Eidan's voice cut through the noise, speaking in Elven. "Se on kunnossa, Hummingbird. Olet turvassa. Olet kotona. You're in Ozera."

The nightmare visions faded, followed by the pain and fear. Tallinn found himself seated on the floor, his quivering legs too weak to hold him. The hall still rang with voices and running feet, but they no longer held the horror of moments before.

"Sir, are you hurt?" a young man asked. "Can you stand?"

"I'll be alright, if you'll help me up. My old bones aren't what they once were," the ranger replied. The young man held Tallinn's elbows in a strong grip and lifted him to his feet. For a moment, the old lighthouse keeper envied the other's youth. "What happened?"

"I don't know. Eidan went into Hummingbird's room to find out. I'm Xandor ap Kynan of Clan Tanjara, scout for the Iron Tower. Eidan said you're a member of the Sea Ranger Corp out of Carolingias?"

"I am. Tried to recruit Aislinn for the Corp years ago, but she chose a different path."

"And yet you lured her back to Ruthaer anyway," Shayla accused. "I told you more than once to leave Aislinn be."

"Ruthaer needed help," Tallinn replied. "You, yourself, told me you approved of her participation with Damage, Inc."

"Because it kept Aislinn and Brand away from Ruthaer!" Shayla shouted.

"Lady Shayla, please," said a new voice. It held the deep timbre of a professional orator. "Let's go back in Aislinn's room where we won't disturb the patients."

"I won't have that man near my daughter, August."

"Emä, why are you angry at Tallinn?" Eidan asked. "It's Hector and Dave who failed to protect her."

"Because he *knew* it wasn't safe for Aislinn or Brand to be anywhere near Ruthaer," Shayla said through gritted teeth, "but he called her there anyway."

"Shayla, it's been twenty-five years," Tallinn protested.

"I made a dying promise to Alaric! That pirate attack wasn't random — they were looking for Brand! We already knew he and Aislinn shared a bond we couldn't understand, and Alaric begged me to take the two of them away from Ruthaer as soon as the dragonling hatched."

"Why didn't you tell us, Emä?" Eidan asked. "All these years, you let us believe you feared and hated Ruthaer because of what happened to Isä."

"I do fear Ruthaer, and with good reason."

"You never told me you promised Alaric," Tallinn said.

"I shouldn't have needed to!" Shayla snapped.   "I thought, by writing to tell you Aislinn had taken up bounty hunting with Damage, Inc., and they worked out of Francesca, you'd give up on luring her back to Ruthaer.

Instead, you found a way to drag her and her friends down there. Now, my daughter is dead!"

"Emä, please, Phaedrus promised —"

"He promised to *try*, Eidan," Shayla said. "Trying is not succeeding."

"Mistress Yves," Brother Giovanus said, "I'm going to need your son and his friends to take you to the Grove Cathedral. Anger and despair are harmful to the atmosphere of healing we're trying to nurture here."

"Will Hummingbird be alright?" Tallinn asked.

"The worst is over, and I feel confident she'll pull through. She's still weak, so I plan to move her into the critical care ward, where someone can be with her day and night. Does she have family we can contact?"

"I don't know anything about her," Tallinn replied, "except she works with Damage, Inc."

"We're her family," said Shayla. "What happened? I heard a mage casting."

"Her body and spirit were out of harmony. Rather than fighting the toxin in her system, her body rejected its own blood as if it was the poison," Brother Giovanus replied. "Master Easmond of Tydway cast a spell to hold her outside the flow of time while we used aura stones. The Eternal Father was merciful, and the toxin is gone. Now, we can start the healing process."

"And the visions?" asked Xandor. "Where did they come from?"

"Hummingbird woke," Giovanus mused, "apparently reliving the moment when she was attacked. I believe what we experienced was an echo, of sorts, amplified by the power still flowing through the aura stones. Eidan's voice, his reassurances, calmed Hummingbird enough to end the onslaught." The priest paused a moment before continuing. "Please, all of you, go to the Grove Cathedral and pray. The Sisters of Mercy are here to make Aislinn ready for her journey to Brodgar Tor."

CRSO

9:00pm

Night blanketed the mountain sky and with it came the smell of rain. At the center of the stone henge on Brodgar Tor, a black cloth flecked with gold, silver, and azure draped the altar beneath Aislinn's still form. Phaedrus stood beside her, his wheel-cross held high as he prayed to the Eternal Father. Eight clerics surrounded the high priest, aligned with the surrounding monoliths. Each stretched their left hand to the shoulder of the person beside them, and their right hand toward Phaedrus, adding the strength of their prayers to his. Rainbow hued light surrounded them in a shimmering dome. The minutes and hours since the ritual began had passed unnoticed. Time held no meaning for them. All their thoughts and prayers bent toward the half-elf, calling her back to the land of the living.

Outside the ring of stones, Shayla and Brand clung to one another, flanked by his friends, with Tallinn a few steps behind. The sun had journeyed across the sky twice while they waited, watched, and prayed. Ozera's residents had gathered amongst grand white oaks on the tor as the second afternoon turned to evening.

Within the ring of standing stones, the light faded, and Phaedrus lowered his cross, placing it back around his neck. The priests surrounding him lowered their hands as one, then took a step back.

The patter of raindrops replaced the silence.

Phaedrus knelt beside Aislinn and bowed his head. Seconds crawled past. Finally, he stood and wrapped the edge of the altar cloth over Aislinn before walking the path to the henge's entrance. In the darkness, voices lifted in a song of benediction.

Offering a sign of peace to Shayla and Brand, Phaedrus said, "Aislinn did not answer our call. She is by the side of the Eternal Father."

Shayla crumpled, and Brand went to his knees beside her. His anguished cry echoed through the grove, piercing hearts, and drawing tears from those closest. Friends and neighbors stepped forward, offering their support.

Phaedrus raised his hands, capturing drops of rain. Addressing the crowd, he said, "Tonight, the sky weeps for Aislinn and her family. Now is a time to grieve. Tomorrow, the sun will herald a new day's dawning and give us the opportunity to celebrate Aislinn's life. Think of her not as she is now, but as she once was and be comforted. She's found peace. If you will, join us in the Grove Cathedral to sit vigil with Shayla and Eidan."

The eight priests laid Aislinn on a wooden bier and followed Phaedrus down the winding path. Behind them, Shayla walked with Brand. Back stiff, she kept her eyes ahead of her, seeing but not seeing.

Lightning flashed, illuminating the mountain peaks. An ash-colored eagle with a tall crown of ragged feathers adorning its head perched atop a high tree. When the sky flickered again, the raptor was gone.

THE END

Author's Note:

From ancient times, cultures around the world have spun myths and fables of other realms, similar to Earth, yet populated by races and creatures possessing powerful magic and strange technology. All a daring hero had to do to reach one of these realms was pass through a magical portal, oft times with rules and dangers of its own. Earth's history and legends give numerous accounts of strange sightings, mysterious disappearances, and bizarre phenomena for which there is no explanation.

In the field of quantum physics, a group of scientists posit the existence of a large, unobservable universe within which our world is but one of many "pockets." This multiverse theory puts forward the concept of an unknowable number of worlds within the expanding space-time continuum, each growing and developing separate from our own, yet emitting energy signatures which affect each other. For some interesting reading on the subject, check out these resources:

https://www.space.com/32728-parallel-universes.html
"This Is Why the Multiverse Must Exits" by Ethan Siegel, Forbes Magazine, March 15, 2019
"Great Books for Non-Physicists Who Want to Understand Quantum Physics" by Chad Orzel. Forbes Magazine, Aug 5, 2015

Gaia, the realm where Phantoms takes place, is one of these alternate realities, replete with magic and alchemy, the divine and the infernal. Its four continents — Parlatheas, Solanacea, Altaira, and Suthose — are home to numerous races and creatures both fair and foul. The sons of Havel (humans, elves, and dwarves), whose cultural regions mirror those of ancient to medieval Earth, vie with the sons of Cayn (orcs, goblins, ogres, trolls, etc.) for dominance. Welcome, and thank you for making the leap from your reality to join us.

Like everyone in your world, the characters you meet here have a past — triumphs, failures, and secrets — which existed before the story begins. As our tales progress, relevant bits of that history and more than a few secrets will be revealed. As you get to know each of the members of

Damage, Inc., we hope you'll come to love them as much as we do, despite (or maybe because of) their many quirks and flaws.

Thank You for Reading!

We hope you've enjoyed your first adventure with Damage, Inc. as much as we enjoyed bringing it to you! No author would be where they are without readers, so please accept a HUGE thank you for taking a chance on our endeavor. Whether you loved it, hated it, or landed somewhere in between, it would be of immense help to us, as well as other readers, if you would take a moment to leave a review on Amazon and/or Goodreads. Even a single sentence will mean a lot.

We love to hear from readers! Feel free to drop us a line at mcdonald.isom@gmail.com Let us know what you loved (or what you hated). If you have questions about the story, we'll do our best to answer them. For more information about cultures, countries, creatures, and races of Gaia, visit the glossary on our website, www.mcdonald-isom.com. You can also find us on Facebook, @McDonald.Isom.author.

There are more adventures yet to come!

Acknowledgements

Phantoms has come a long way since its initial inception as a ghost story in a fantasy setting. It wouldn't be nearly the tale it is today without the wisdom and guidance of our editor, Dana Isaacson. Thank you for taking a chance on a genre outside your comfort zone.

A special thanks also to our Beta Readers: Alan, Allison, Angela, April, Gary, Lacy, Shirley, and Steve. Your comments and questions helped us smooth off the rough edges and fill in the gaps where more info was needed.

About the Authors

Jason McDonald

An engineer by day and world builder by night, Jason is an advocate for using both sides of the brain.

With his stepfather as a guide, Jason traveled the worlds of Edgar Rice Burroughs, Robert E Howard, and JRR Tolkien at an early age. As he grew older, he discovered Dungeons and Dragons and the joys of creating his own campaigns.

During all this, Jason embarked on a career in engineering, graduating from Clemson University, and now owns a successful engineering firm. Still a practicing engineer, he continues to design a wide range of projects. His attention to detail and vivid imagination helps shape the various adventures that challenge his characters.

Stormy McDonald

Born in the midst of a thunderstorm in the darkest hours of a solstice morning, Stormy has been told she has a personality to match: full of sound and fury, and highly unpredictable. She comes from a family of storytellers — traditional, oral storytellers, that is — so it's little wonder that she's driven to weave words as well.

She can't remember a time when she didn't love books — from the feel and smell of the pages, to the information they hold, to the tales that they tell — but storytelling is a labor of love, which doesn't always pay the bills. Over the years, she's worked a ridiculous variety of side jobs to support her writing habit, including waitress, security guard, library minion, salesperson, hairdresser, handyman, engineering drafter, and small business owner.